山东省社科规划项目
国家社会科学基金项目阶段性成果
青岛科技大学资助

A Literary Approach to
the Translation of the *Book of Poetry*

《诗经》翻译探微

李玉良　著

商务印书馆
The Commercial Press

2017年·北京

图书在版编目(CIP)数据

《诗经》翻译探微/李玉良著.—北京:商务印书馆,2017
ISBN 978-7-100-14142-0

Ⅰ.①诗… Ⅱ.①李… Ⅲ.①《诗经》—英语—翻译—研究 Ⅳ.①I207.222②H315.9

中国版本图书馆 CIP 数据核字(2017)第 136371 号

权利保留,侵权必究。

《诗经》翻译探微

李玉良　著

商　务　印　书　馆　出　版
(北京王府井大街36号　邮政编码100710)
商　务　印　书　馆　发　行
北京市白帆印务有限公司印刷
ISBN 978-7-100-14142-0

2017年8月第1版　　　　开本 880×1230 1/32
2017年8月北京第1次印刷　印张 13⅛
定价:48.00元

序

中西会通的尝试

　　随着中国的崛起，中国文化的海外传播开始引起学术界的关注，而中国典籍的外译自然成为一个新的研究领域。以《诗经》翻译研究来说，就国内学术界而言，真正开始研究也不过二十多年，玉良教授是这个领域的重要开拓者，他的《〈诗经〉英译研究》至今仍是典籍外译领域，特别是《诗经》翻译领域的必读之书。在中国翻译界真正从事"中译外"的学者并不多，像许渊冲先生这样的学者更是少见，同样从事"中译外"翻译研究的学者本来就是少数，像玉良教授这样能立足中西文化评判多位译家的更是难得。

　　"外译中"和"中译外"是两种思维方式，这决定了两者呈现出不同的特点："外译中"是一个将抽象概念具象化的过程，将逻辑性思维转换成伦理性思维的过程；"中译外"则是一个将中国传统的伦理思维文本转换成逻辑思维文本的过程。翻译是一种创造性活动，但如何做却是仁者见仁，智者见智。从中国典籍翻译的角度，一些中国学者也是认同这种差别的，因此，在翻译时强调中西思想的不同性，反对归化式的翻译。最著名的例子就是王国维对辜鸿铭

《中庸》英译的批评。王国维认为辜鸿铭的《中庸》翻译有两个根本性的错误，其一是翻译时把中国思想概念统一于西方思想概念之中，其二是"以西洋哲学解释《中庸》"。

《诗经》不同于《中庸》，它有着自己的特点。但无论是翻译哪部中国经典，首先要做到对经典本身的熟悉，对中国上千年的释经历史要熟悉，玉良教授这本书的重要特点就是对《诗经》在中国经学史上的解释历史十分熟悉。文中在评判西方汉学家和中国学者对《诗经》名物翻译出现的问题时，作者指出："以上所分析的翻译问题，皆出自译者对训诂的研判不当。每遇此类问题，译者当详查历代各家训诂，进行综合研判，取其合理者采之，不合理者弃之，方可避免错误。就这首诗的翻译来说，若译者能详研毛、郑、孔、朱、严（粲）、王（念孙）六家训诂，再辅之以《尔雅》《说文》等，即可综合出合理的见解，使译文避免错误。"这段话对于从事"中译外"的学者具有普遍性意义，因为目前从事这个领域研究的学者绝大多数是外语院校的学者，国学修养不足是普遍现象，中国典籍翻译，若本体不精，翻译研究就很难谈上。

同时，对西方语言的熟悉，对汉学历史以及译入语国家历史文化的熟悉，也是对从事中国古代文化典籍翻译者的基本要求，在《〈诗经〉翻译探微》中充分显示出了这一点。尤其是对中国典籍外译所表现出的变异性作者也给予了关注，如玉良教授所说，"因为译诗虽然来自原诗，但其审美价值和艺术价值并不能等同于原诗，其自身必然是独立的艺术个体，具有独立的艺术价值"。

读书以养神，玉良教授这本书读起来使人仿佛畅游中西文化的海洋之中，作者以中西会通之学评判多位译家，游刃有余，没有献媚之词，没有刻薄之语，通达从容，兼取百家之长，铺下中译外研究的坚实之路，是一本不可多得的好书。

是为序。

张西平
2016 年 3 月 24 日

前　　言

自上世纪末以来，我一直在关注并研究《诗经》的英译问题。九年多前，我撰写了《〈诗经〉英译研究》一书，蒙好友修亮相助，得以于齐鲁书社付梓。说起来，有书出版，当是令人高兴的事，但当时我心里却总觉得有种东西难以释怀。而今十年即将过去，这种感觉仍一直耿耿于怀。记得当时开始研究《诗经》翻译，吟咏之间，发现几乎每一篇诗都难以找到一个十分妥帖的英语译文，不是这里有益就是那里有损。虽然心里清楚，翻译诗歌，尤其是翻译《诗经》中的古诗是极难的事，也常常能从方家译文中得到不少感动，但对每篇译诗内心总是有难以抑制的希望。后来，还是因为受到翻译理论的启发，才了解了翻译的真义所在，也理解了翻译的历史与社会文化属性。于是，我试着去探究各译本之后的种种背景，包括对历史的、文化的、经济的、哲学的、文学的、社会的以及个人的因素的层层探索。在这样的努力之下，《〈诗经〉英译研究》划出了一道较明晰的《诗经》翻译实践中西文化视野整合与变异的历史轨迹。而有另一种东西却没能够同时得到深入分析，那就是，每一篇译诗本身的微观元素，尤其是译诗中的文学问题。

自毛亨《毛诗故训传》及郑玄《毛诗故训传笺》以降，直至清末，《诗》一直是经世致用的政教之书，其文学内涵是鲜为人所提及的，只有刘勰是个例外。但刘勰在《宗经》中的呼吁，似乎并没有引起人们太大的重视。《诗经》文学的真面目，还是到了20世纪上半叶才为闻一多、郭沫若先生等人所揭开，其观点也为学界所广泛认可。然而，无论如何，《诗经》是诗，是文学，这是毋庸置疑的。当然，《诗经》并非纯文学，文以载道，"经夫妇，成孝敬，厚人伦，美教化，移风俗"是其精髓所在，所以它是文、道天然合一的典范。那么，《诗经》诸篇什的翻译，其文学性究竟如何？如何用译诗表现原诗的文学性？这些问题，就成了本书最大的关注所在。

然而，要对《诗经》翻译的文学之维进行研究谈何容易。首先是选材的问题。《诗经》凡305篇；虽然其中皆有文学，但毕竟其文学性有高低之分。郭沫若先生等认为，《诗经》最具文学性的部分只有《国风》，《雅》次之，《颂》则长于祝祷，其中鲜有文学。本书并没有受此观念的局限，以《风》为主，《风》《雅》《颂》中皆有选材。其次是观察角度的问题。我认为，对译诗的欣赏是需要从整体出发的，没有整体观念，就无法欣赏译诗意境的高低妙拙，同时，诗的欣赏又离不开对个别词句的品评，所谓诗之新奇与典雅、轻靡与壮丽、显附与远奥、精约与繁缛等，当皆出于词句之间。对译诗的欣赏亦复如此。所以，笔者选择了名物、修辞、韵律、题旨、意象等几个方面作为观察点，以点面结合的方式进行探讨，即在探讨细枝末节的同时，从整体出发，并以最终窥见全篇的艺术性为旨归。

当然，以《诗经》之微言大义，绝非仅止于以上五个方面，也非笔者浅陋之学所能透识。依笔者浅见，探讨《诗经》翻译问题须同时有两方面考虑，首先是译文是否继承了《诗经》的历史文化，即忠实于古训与否，其次是翻译的效果如何，即能否有效传播《诗经》文化。深加考究可以发现，忠实与传播是一对十分辩证的概念，可谓相辅相成又相反相成：一方面，忠实才能深入传播，因为只有翻译忠实了才能传播真义；另一方面，绝对忠实又不利于有效传播，因为翻译忠实了会增加译语读者理解上的困难。因此，评价一篇诗的翻译不能一味地追求忠实性，也不能不顾翻译的忠实性而妄议传播的可能性，而是应该两者兼顾。

需要坦白的是，尽管本书立意如此，但每到译诗的幽微处，囿于功力，往往又难以探及。尽力而已。

最后需要说明的是，本书在译诗文学的探究之外，另有诗歌翻译理论探讨的诉求，聊作对诗歌翻译问题的思考。

恳请方家批评指正。

目　录

第一章　《诗经》名物翻译之文学性问题 1
- 第一节　名物翻译的多样化现象 1
- 第二节　名物翻译多样化对原文的颠覆 10
- 第三节　名物翻译与译诗文化身份重塑及文化传播 24
- 第四节　名物翻译偏离的诗学价值与伦理学解释 26
- 小　结 31

第二章　《诗经》修辞及其翻译 33
- 第一节　兴的修辞手法及其翻译 36
- 第二节　比的修辞手法及其翻译 65
- 第三节　明喻、夸张及其翻译 85
- 第四节　重章叠唱及其翻译 101
- 第五节　叠词及其翻译 109
- 小　结 115

第三章　《诗经》韵律翻译的价值与规律 117
- 第一节　中英诗歌的韵律比较 117
- 第二节　《诗经》的韵律 137
- 第三节　《诗经》的韵律翻译及其效果分析 151
- 第四节　《诗经》韵律翻译之法门——沿袭、变通与无奈 176
- 小　结 194

第四章 《诗经》题旨翻译——诗本义与诗教文化 196

  第一节 诗篇题旨翻译所面临的主要问题 197
  第二节 译诗韵律至上，以义就韵 205
  第三节 无视训诂，臆测文义 216
  第四节 随意反《序》，臆测诗旨 234
  第五节 因《诗经》之名，行创作之实 239
  小 结 245

第五章 《诗经》意象翻译之可能与不可能 247

  第一节 中西意象传统之比较 248
  第二节 中西意象理论之比较 273
  第三节 《诗经》意象功能及其分类 286
  第四节 《诗经》意象翻译——可能与不可能 289
  小 结 337

附 录 339

  附录一、《诗经》名物翻译对照表 339
  附录二、相关《诗经》诗篇的译文 373
  附录三、《诗经》各篇叠词及其出现次数统计 386
  附录四、相关意象所在的诗篇 396

参考文献 405

第一章 《诗经》名物翻译之
　　　　　文学性问题

　　自 19 世纪末理雅各（James Legge）翻译《诗经》以来，已经产生了十种《诗经》英语全译本和数种选译本。在所有译本当中，诗篇中名物的翻译问题，一直颇令人感到困惑。《诗经》中许多名物直接代表了我国古代历史文化状况、先民的社会生活环境和方式等，它们不仅反映了我国先民的物质文化生活，还反映了当时的社会、历史、宗教、伦理乃至政治状况，因此在翻译时不能不认真对待，慎重抉择。这也无形中给译者增加了很大的负担。由于中西之间有历史、文化、语言、地域上的差异，名物翻译无法做到面面俱到，而需做出一定的选择，所以，译文中的名物常有与原文一致者，也有与原文一定程度偏离者。我们应该如何看待这些问题？应该采用怎样的宏观策略和具体方法，才能使名物翻译达到最佳效果呢？

第一节　名物翻译的多样化现象

　　《诗经》诗什中名物之多，其用之大，自古以来就颇受重视。孔子《论语·阳货》云："小子何莫学夫诗？诗，可以兴，可以观，可以群,可以怨。迩之事父,远之事君,多识于鸟兽草木之名。"纳兰成德说:"六经名物之多,无逾于诗者,自天文地理,宫室器用,山川草木,鸟兽虫鱼,靡一不具,学者非多识博闻,则无以通诗人之旨意,而得其比兴之所在。"①《诗经》名物种类繁多,可分为动物、植物、器物、事物四大类。动物又可分为兽类、鸟类、鱼类,植物可分为水生植物和陆生植物,器物可分为生活器物、祭祀器物、宫廷器物、礼乐器物、军用器物、装饰器物等,事物则指自然界中与人的生活密切相关者,如河、沚等。对诗经名物最早关注并进行研究的是东汉时的陆机。其在《毛诗草木鸟兽虫鱼疏》中列举动植物凡133种。清代姚炳《诗识名解》15卷中,动植物名凡255种,其中鸟38种、兽29种、虫27种、鱼19种、草88种、木54种。顾栋高《毛诗类释》中列举动植物名凡273种,其中鸟类43种、兽40种、虫37种、鱼16种、菜38种、谷24种、草17种、花果15种、树木43种。清代多隆阿《毛诗多识》,更是列举名物多达308种,其中不包括如筐、筥、锜、釜、兕觥、佩瑹、裳、布、丝、绨、绤、车等器物,以及洲、沚、坻、岨等自然名物。据笔者调查,《诗经》中的器物,包括生活器物、装饰器物、祭祀器物、宫廷器物、礼乐器物、军用器物等,凡219种,其中《风》中有155种,《雅》中新出38种,《颂》中新出26种。名物在诗篇中功能不一,其主要作用是诗人用来表情达意。若细加分类,则其一,用于起兴之物象。朱熹《诗集传》云:"先言他物以引起所咏之辞也。""他物",即起兴之物象,如"关关雎鸠,在河之洲"中"雎鸠"即"兴"之"他物"。其二,用于比喻之形象,以构成文学

---

① 纳兰成德:《通志堂经解·毛诗名物解·序》。

意象，如"相鼠有皮，人而无仪"中以"鼠"比"人"，以"皮"喻"仪"。其三，生活中所见所用之物，非修辞手法之用，如"氓之蚩蚩，抱布贸丝。匪来贸丝，来即我谋"中的"布"和"丝"，就不是文学之"象"，即非意象之用，而是仅有历史文化认知功能而已。

翻译诗篇，必从文字开始。名物作为诗中所言之事物，译者无法、也不能漠视。以《关雎》的翻译为例。翻译《关雎》，首先是"雎鸠"的翻译问题。"雎鸠"究竟是什么鸟？这是翻译无法回避的问题，也是诗经学一直关注的问题。译者对此不能臆测，而必须调查诗经学研究的观点和成果。从传统经学的解释来看，"关关"是鸟的和鸣。《毛诗传》曰："关关，和声也"；《鲁诗》曰："关关，音声和也"；《玉篇》曰："和鸣也"；《广韵》曰："二鸟和鸣"；朱熹《诗集传》云："雌雄相应之和声也"。今人程俊英《诗经译注》中也说："关关，水鸟相和的叫声。"① 以上观点都表明，"雎鸠"当是一种性情温和、感情专一的鸟。

但是，诗经学所解释的鸟的"和声""和鸣"，与诗篇后文的矛盾是显而易见的。从整体来看，《关雎》当是写"求偶"的诗，所以诗中有"寤寐求之，求之不得，寤寐思服，悠哉悠哉，辗转反侧"的诗句。这在《诗经》其他诗中亦可觅得佐证。如《小雅·伐木》中有"伐木丁丁，鸟鸣嘤嘤。……嘤其鸣矣，求其友声"的诗句。诗中鸟主动发出的"求友"的"嘤嘤"之鸣，与《关雎》"关关"之声一样，均可认为是雄鸟对雌鸟求偶时的"独唱"。《小雅·小弁》说得更清楚："雉之朝雊，尚求其雌。"这是说，雄性野鸡早晨鸣叫求偶，正可作为"关关"之声乃雄雎鸣叫求偶之声的注

---

① 程俊英：《诗经译注》，上海：上海古籍出版社，2004年，第4页。

解。既是"求偶","关关"之鸣声,就不是雄雌鸟之"和鸣",而是情切之鸣;那么,雎鸠就不必是温和的鸟,而完全可以是凶猛的鱼鹰。如果从早期人类社会存在性崇拜的观念这一点来看,人和动物对性的强烈要求应该是一种自然之美,所以《关雎》用鱼鹰这种凶猛的、充满野性的求偶之声起兴,来比喻"君子"如火的爱情并没有不妥,反倒是一种美。当然,鸟兽平时再凶猛,也有情切之时;情切,则必显得缱绻温和。若此,"和鸣"似乎也并不与鱼鹰之"凶猛"相矛盾。

从训诂的角度来看,"雎鸠"也当是鱼鹰。如郭璞注《尔雅·释鸟》云:"雎鸠,雕类,今江东呼之为鹗,好江渚边食鱼。"又如《禽经》曰:"雎鸠鸿,鱼鹰也。"现代高亨《诗经今注》也说,"雎鸠,一种水鸟名,即鱼鹰"[①]。

从性情来看,鱼鹰也与"雎鸠"相吻合。鱼鹰以鱼为食,喜欢单独活动于海边或湖沼,常飞翔于距水十到三十米的上空;双爪呈钩状,锐利,长而有力,爪内侧有成列的刺状角质突起物,外趾能做反转运动,以便抓牢猎物;腿部羽毛紧贴于皮肤,可减少猎捕过程中入水时的阻力,因此擅长猎捕在水中游动的鱼类做食物;发现水中有鱼时,即收缩双翼,俯冲入水中猎捕,然后将猎物携至树上啄食。鱼鹰的这一生活习性,与诗中"关关雎鸠,在河之洲"的诗句,颇相吻合。

对汉儒经学中"关雎"及其"和鸣"之论的反拨,始于20世纪初。闻一多先生在其《神话与诗》(2006)中,从文化人类学的角度,对《诗经》中鱼和食鱼的鸟之间的关系做出了男女求爱隐语

[①] 高亨:《诗经今注》,上海:上海古籍出版社,1980年,第2页。

的解释。孙作云在《诗经恋歌发微》（1957）中，进一步提出《关雎》以鱼鹰求鱼象征男子向女子求爱的观点。在此基础上，赵国华在《生殖崇拜文化论》（1990）中对我国上古时代诗歌及器物图案中的鸟、鱼图形进行考查，认为鸟与鱼有分别象征男女两性的意义，并进一步认为，雎鸠在河洲求鱼，乃是君子执着求爱的象征。

沿着这一阐释思路，刘毓庆（2004：71）在其《关于〈诗经·关雎〉篇的雎鸠喻意问题》一文中提出了这样的质疑：

> 《毛诗传》释雎鸠为王雎，王雎即鱼鹰，郭璞《尔雅》注云："雕类，今江东呼之为鹗，好在江渚山边食鱼。"托名师旷的《禽经》云："王雎，雎鸠，鱼鹰也。"《本草纲目》卷四十九云："鹗，雕类也……能翱翔水上捕鱼食，江表人呼为鱼鹰。"显然雎鸠乃是猛禽类物，何以在汉儒的眼里却变成了具鸳鸯之性的爱情鸟？我们在研究中发现，汉儒以"关关雎鸠"为夫妻和谐象征之说，是缺少根据的。因为在《诗经》的时代，我们没有发现以鸟喻夫妻的证据。日本著名的《诗经》研究专家松本雅明先生就曾说过，就《诗经》来看，在所有的鸟的表现中，以鸟的匹偶象征男女爱情的思维模式是不存在的。不仅在古籍中没有，在春秋前的古器物图案中，也难找到雌雄匹配的鸟纹饰。在良渚文化遗物及金铭图饰中，出现有连体鸟型器物与双鸟纹饰，但那多是为对称而设计的，看不出雌雄相和的意义来。

刘毓庆以考古发现和文化典籍中的鱼鸟关系为旁证，论证了鸟与鱼之间所象征的两性关系。他认为，其实汉儒心里都明白"雎鸠"即

"鱼鹰","关关"乃充满野性的求偶之声。他们之所以"将鱼鹰转换为具有'鸳鸯之性'的鸟,绝不仅仅是因学者的无知而造成的解诗上的错误,而是一次具有文化意义的误读,它反映了民族社会生活及婚姻观的变化与民族追求和谐、温柔的心理趋向"(刘毓庆,2004:79)。这为汉儒《诗经》注释中的矛盾提供了解释,可谓为诗经学中的千年"悬案"找到了一种答案。

从诗篇的内部逻辑、训诂、民俗以及生物学的角度,我们可以进一步得出一致结论:"雎鸠"是性情凶猛的鱼鹰。据此而论,理雅各和阿瑟·韦利(Arthur Waley)将"雎鸠"翻译成"osprey"[①],庞德(Ezra Pound)将其翻译成"fish-hawk",虽一雅一俗,却仍与原文相一致。詹宁斯(William Jennings)和汪榕培将其翻译成"waterfowl"[②],许渊冲将其翻译成"turtledove"[③],皆与原文相悖;高本汉(Bernhard Karlgren)将其译作"ts'ü-kiu bird"[④],则属语焉不详,几近不译。

其次是荇菜。荇菜究竟是什么植物?有什么属性?《毛诗正义》曰:"《释草》云:'苓,接余,其叶苻。'陆机《疏》云:'接余,白茎,叶紫赤色,正员,径寸余,浮在水上,根在水底,与水深浅等,大如钗股,上青下白,鬻其白茎,以苦酒浸之,肥美可案酒'是也。"[⑤] 据今人潘富俊研究,荇菜,今名莕菜。他对莕菜做了颇为详细的描述:

---

① 见附录一。
② 同上。
③ 同上。
④ 同上。
⑤ 孔颖达:《毛诗正义》,李学勤主编《十三经注疏》,北京:北京大学出版社,1999年,第25页。

> 莕菜的形态、习性都和莼菜相似，常见于水泽处，叶片均漂浮在水面上。惟莕菜的基部凹入，而莼菜叶则呈椭圆形，且叶柄盾状着生；莕菜花金黄色，而莼菜花为暗紫色，两者隶属不同科，可以从外形上分。
>
> 莕菜又称"金莲儿"，花开时常"弥覆顷亩"，在阳光下泛光如金，因此得名。叶形与生态习性近于荷花，又称"水荷"。茎和叶均柔软滑嫩，可以供作蔬菜食用；加米煮羹，是江南名菜。（潘富俊，2003：17）

这足以把莕菜和与其酷似的莼菜、水荷区分开来。根据生物学研究，莕菜是多年生浮水草本植物：茎细长、柔软而多分枝，匍匐生长，节上生根，漂浮于水面或生于泥土中；叶互生，卵圆形，基部开裂呈心形，上面绿色具光泽，背面紫色；伞房花序生于叶腋，花冠漏斗状，花鲜黄色，开于水面；果椭圆形，不开裂；种子多数圆形、扁平；喜光线充足的环境，喜肥沃土壤及浅水或不流动的水域。莕菜适应能力极强，耐寒暑，易管理；可做蔬菜煮汤，柔软滑嫩，在上古是美食。

荇菜的译法有四种。理雅各将其译成"duckweed"[①]。duckweed 是浮萍，此植物外形像荇菜，可食用，但实际上并非荇菜。詹宁斯将荇菜译作"waterlily"[②]，意思是睡莲。睡莲外形不像荇菜，也不可食用，但可入药。许渊冲译荇菜为"cress"，意思是水芹，这是生长在池沼边、水沟边或河边的植物，形状与荇菜相差甚大，这种理解与训诂也不相谐。汪榕培将其译作"water grass"，意思笼统，如

[①] 见附录一。
[②] 同上。

果是指一般的水草,则其并无食用价值,诗中女子也没有理由去采了又采。高本汉将荇菜译成"hing waterplant",这种译法也十分含糊,只能表明荇菜是名为"hing"的水生植物而已,无法呈现其确凿形象,更无意象可言。

诗的第四章出现了"琴"和"瑟"两种文化器物。这两种名物与前者的不同之处,是其具有丰富的文化内涵。据古书记载,琴的历史可以追溯到伏羲时,即公元前 2400 年左右,当时的琴为五弦琴,后更为七弦。《古史考》中说:"伏羲作琴、瑟。"(谯周,2003:39)《纲鉴易知录》中说:"伏羲斫桐为琴,绳丝为弦,绠桑为瑟。"(吴乘权,1960:179)也有的书上说琴为神农所做。皇甫谧《帝王世纪·世本·逸周书·古本竹书纪年》说:"神农始作五弦之琴,以具宫商角徵羽之音。历九代至文王,复增其二弦,曰少宫、少商。"(皇甫谧,2010:76)郭沫若《青铜器时代》认为,琴瑟的出现当在春秋。(郭沫若,1957:84)吴钊根据考古成果认为琴的出现在西周。琴是为高贵宾客演奏用的高级乐器,它与瑟常在隆重的社交场合一起用于演奏背景音乐。琴一般置于客人当前,瑟通常置于屏风之后,两者合奏,音声调和;客人围坐于案几,边听音乐边交谈宴乐。(吴钊,1983:47)《诗经·鹿鸣》曰:"我有嘉宾,鼓瑟鼓琴。鼓瑟鼓琴,和乐且湛。"据说,古人发明琴瑟是为了顺畅阴阳之气,使人心地纯洁。因为琴瑟经常配合演奏,后来人们便把琴瑟比作和谐美好的夫妻感情,如"琴瑟之好""琴瑟和鸣""琴瑟相和"等;相反,把夫妻不睦则比作"琴瑟不和""琴瑟不调"。孔颖达《毛诗正义》曰:

知"琴瑟在堂,钟鼓在庭"者,《皋陶谟》云"琴瑟以咏，祖考来格"，乃云"下管鼗鼓"，明琴瑟在上，鼗鼓在下。《大射礼》颂钟在西阶之西，笙钟在东阶之东，是钟鼓在庭也。此诗美后妃能化淑女，共乐其事，既得荇菜以祭宗庙，上下乐作，盛此淑女所共之礼也。乐虽主神，因共荇菜，归美淑女耳。①

孔颖达在此对我国琴瑟文化做了清楚的解释。当然，他解释的不只是《关雎》这篇诗中的琴瑟，而是涉及了古代整个礼乐文化传统。无论《关雎》是否如传统经学所解的那样以"后妃能化淑女"为题旨，其中琴瑟以友"情"、钟鼓以乐"德"的文化传统，当毫无疑问。

但是，译文中琴瑟的翻译却出现了五种情况：（1）理雅各、庞德、许渊冲将其译作"lute"②；（2）阿瑟·韦利将其译作"zithern"③；（3）詹宁斯将其译作"lute"和"harp"④；（4）高本汉将其译作"guitar"和"lute"⑤；（5）汪榕培将琴瑟略去不译。显然，在这五种译法中，无论哪一种，实际上都阉割了原诗中琴瑟的文化特色和寓意。

综观以上名物翻译的偏离现象，可以分析为以下几个方面。其一，语义偏离；其二，地域特色偏离；其三，文学意象偏离；其四，文化寓意偏离。那么，我们应该怎么去理解这些偏离现象呢？

---

① 孔颖达：《毛诗正义》，北京：北京大学出版社，1999年，第27页。
② 见附录一。
③ 同上。
④ 同上。
⑤ 同上。

第二节　名物翻译多样化对原文的颠覆

翻译的多样化是翻译的本质特征之一，它既反映了翻译的无奈，也体现了翻译的再创造性本质。翻译多样化的原因是多方面的，语言的差异、物产的地域性差异、两种文化传统的差异，这些在本质上都是翻译无法逾越的鸿沟。它们留给翻译的空间，也只有采取适当补偿措施。而补偿必然会导致各种尝试，从而表现出翻译结果多样化。《诗经》名物翻译亦复如是。《关雎》中名物虽然为数不多，但它们却规定了一种时代背景、一种文化氛围，也规定了诗篇的基本内容和艺术风格。任何一点改变，都会打破原诗结构的内部和谐，使翻译作品或打上译入语文化的烙印，或换上另一种艺术情调，甚至改变原来的题旨。请看詹宁斯的译文：

> Waterfowl their mates are calling,
> On the islets in the stream.
> Chaste and modest maiden! Fit partner
> For our lord (thyself we deem).
>
> Waterlilies, long or short ones, —
> Seek them left and seek them right.
> 'Twas this chaste and modest maiden
> He hath sought for, morn and night.
>
> Seeking for her, yet not finding,
> Night and morning he would yearn.

Ah, so long, so long! —and restless
On his couch would toss and turn.

Waterlilies, long or short ones, —
Gather, right and left, their flowers.
Now the chaste and modest maiden
Lute and harp shall hail as ours.

Long or short the waterlilies,
Pluck them left and pluck them right.
To the chaste and modest maiden
Bell and drum shall give delight.

孔颖达《毛诗正义》云:"郑以为后妃化感群下,既求得之,又乐助采之。言参差之荇菜求之既得,诸嫔御之等皆乐左右助而采之,既化后妃,莫不和亲,故当共荇菜之时,作此琴瑟之乐,乐此窈窕之淑女。其情性之和,上下相亲,与琴瑟之音宫商相应无异,若与琴瑟为友然,共心同志,故云琴瑟友之。"[①] 这是对诗中的"荇菜""琴""瑟"三种名物最典型、最彻底的文化诠释。而译诗中把最有文化意蕴的三种名物转而代之以无文化意味的"waterlily"(睡莲),以及西洋乐器"lute"(鲁特琴)和"harp"(竖琴)。lute 和 harp 是典型的传统西洋乐器,颇有文化标志性,它们的存在,一下就把诗的文化氛围染上了西方文化色彩。诗中的一切活动都随之转移到了西方某一地方,诗中人物角色也都成了西方人。受此影响,传统经学所谓颂"后妃之德"的题旨不再成立,

---

① 孔颖达:《毛诗正义》,北京:北京大学出版社,1999 年版,第 26-27 页。

原诗艺术结构也随之被打破。"waterlily"出现在译诗中取代"荇菜",其影响也是巨大的。"荇菜"可食,在原诗中可以解释为贵族女子采之以供宗庙祭祀,也可解释为一普通女子采之以为食物,都可通。"荇菜"在原诗中的这种作用,令读者仿佛回到了人们仍信仰巫术和原始宗教的远古时代,仿佛置身于生产力低下时先民以野菜为食的淳朴生活环境,可以感受到诗中悠远的历史和文化旨趣。而"waterlily"在译诗中则绝无这种文化历史意义,至多是一种美丽的花,在前后文中可解释为比喻诗中美貌女子,从而诗的题旨只能被理解为婚恋诗。"bell"的出现,字面上看来与原文一致,其实际作用却与原文迥异。bell在西方,最早是用于教堂宗教礼拜仪式的,这构成了其基本的文化含义,其与"钟"在本篇中的"宗庙祭祀"文化含义颇相类似。但"钟"和"鼓"在中国古代文化中作为高贵乐器仅属于贵族,这种含义则是"bell"所不具备的,这就导致了原文与译文之间一定的文化错位。所以,在译诗中,现代西方读者至多可能把"bell"理解成一种乐器而已。这样,"lute""harp""waterlily""bell"合在一起,实际上已经失去了原文中名物之间在文化历史意义以及文学艺术上的和谐统一性;这也决定了,这首译诗不可能是所谓歌颂"后妃之德"的诗,而只能是一首婚恋诗。

韦利的译文可谓异曲同工:

"Fair, fair," cry the ospreys
On the island in the river.
Lovely is this noble lady,
Fit bride for our lord.

In patches grows the water mallow;
To left and right one must seek it.
Shy was this noble lady;
Day and night he sought her.

Sought her and could not get her;
Day and night he grieved.
Long thoughts, oh, long unhappy thoughts,
Now on his back, now tossing on to his side.

In patches grows the water mallow;
To left and right one must gather it.
Shy is this noble lady;
With great zithern and little we hearten her.

In patches grows the water mallow;
To left and right one must choose it.
Shy is this noble lady;
With bells and drums we will gladden her.①

客观地看，本诗中"zithern"（齐特琴）携带的浓厚西方文化情调，"water mallow"所起到的去原文化历史意味的作用，以及"bell"在中西宗教意味上的巨大差异等，都使译文在总体上无法还原原文的文化历史感和题旨的多解性，而仅能理解为一篇具有西方情调的爱情诗而已。

---

① Arthur Waley. *The Book of Songs*. New York: Grove Press, 1996: 5.

《关雎》中名物翻译的偏离问题并非个例，情况也比较复杂。导致文化器物偏离现象产生的原因也有多重：其一，此有彼无；其二，文学意义相异；其三，文化历史意义相异。其中，后两者导致的偏离现象占多数。由于文化器物的内涵具有民族性和历史性，其在翻译时尤其会出现偏离现象，且偏离常常不在表面，而在内涵。此以《国风·卫风·木瓜》翻译为例：①

> 投我以木瓜，报之以琼琚。匪报也，永以为好也。
> 投我以木桃，报之以琼瑶。匪报也，永以为好也。
> 投我以木李，报之以琼玖。匪报也，永以为好也。

诗中提到的三种玉石属我国古代重要文化器物，其在诗中的作用可见《诗小序》："美齐桓公也。"根据《小序》，这些玉石的意义应是外交信物和礼仪。朱熹《诗集传》对此有别解："疑亦男女相赠答之词，如静女之类。"② 无论是用于外交信用、礼仪还是用于男女赠答，在这两种作用中，玉器的文化内涵无疑是一致的。正因为交好之国或两情相悦之男女看重的同是玉的美好内质，所以玉才有此礼仪、信物之用。

然而，器物文化虽然在物理上的传播和接受比较容易，但随着时间的推移，一旦其含蕴了某种文化观念，其中的文化内涵也同样难以为异文化主体所体验。我国自古以来就有的各种玉器，恰恰就是这样一种器物。

---

① 英译文见附录二。
② 朱熹：《诗集传》，北京：中华书局，1958年，第41页。

研究表明，我国玉器诞生于原始社会新石器时代早期，至今至少已有七八千年历史，是中华民族历史悠久的文化特产之一。从出土的玉器考证，我国是世界上用玉最早，且绵延时间最长的国家。在黄河流域，属于夏文化的后冈第二期文化和二里头文化中，也发现了很多精美玉器，如玉玦、玉刀等。由此可见，在中国历史上最古老的夏朝，玉就有了比较广泛的用途。商朝时，玉器雕刻已达到十分发达的水平。郑州商代遗址和安阳殷墟遗址都出土了大量玉器，其中有礼器、装饰品、艺术品和仿制工具等，同时出土的甲骨刻文上也有"正（征）玉""取玉"的记载。周朝时，玉的使用更加广泛。王公诸侯无不贵用昆仑之玉，"北用禺氏（即月氏）之玉，南贵江汉之珠"①。周穆王曾经专门西巡昆仑，"攻其玉石，取玉版三乘，玉器服物，载玉万只"②。据《周礼》载，当时已有天府、典瑞等专职官员管理玉器："天府，掌祖庙之守藏，与其禁令。凡国之玉镇、大宝器藏焉"；"典瑞，掌玉瑞、玉器之藏，辨其名物，与其用事，设其服饰"。当时，玉被认为是一种神器，在祭祀、仪仗、服饰、交际等各个方面都有广泛使用。《礼记·玉藻》云："天子搢珽，方正于天下也"；又云，"古之君子必佩玉"，"君子于玉比德焉"。《荀子·大略》亦云："聘人以珪，问士以璧，召人以瑗，绝人以玦，反绝以环。"到了汉朝，特别是从张骞通西域以来，昆仑山的玉石大量流入内地，人们对玉喜爱有加，使用也更加广泛，而玉文化传统也一直流传至今。

中国人至今都认为玉石具有神奇力量。无论是道家、儒家，还

---

① 见《管子》。
② 见《穆天子传》。

是佛家，都认为神灵的玉能给予力量和智慧。玉佩中的玉佛、玉观音等题材，都体现了玉器祭礼、避邪、护身等文化元素。玉之所以成为中国传统文化一大特色，是因为其体现了中国古代哲学和宗教以及中国传统文化的特性。

春秋时期，老子创立道家，认为"人法地，地法天，天法道，道法自然"，强调自然界的统一性以及个人与自然合一，寻求宇宙中万物的永生。玉是阴阳二气中阳气之精，其中包含着整个大自然，表现着天地万物的壮美，因而成了道家哲学的宠儿。古代玉器上的夔龙、蟠虺和饕餮花纹以及璧、琮、圭、璋等器形，正是道家思想的艺术体现；而古者陪葬所用之瑱、玲、玉塞和玉衣等，也是取道家之同天共地、与世常存之意。

道家尚自然，儒家则崇尚"礼乐"和"仁义"，重视"伦理道德"。"礼"在甲骨爻辞中作"豊"或作"珡"，从"爵"和"豆"，表示祭祀至上神或宗主神时，要用两块玉盛在一个器皿里去供奉，可见"礼"起源于用玉祭祀神的古俗。因此，古代多用玉做成各种礼器，用于祭祀、仪仗等礼仪场合。儒家所重视的"德"，来自于玉的人格化。《礼记·聘义》中孔子答子贡曰："夫昔者，君子比德于玉焉：温润而泽，仁也；缜密以栗，智也；廉而不刿，义也；垂之如队，礼也；叩之其声清越以长，其终诎然，乐也；瑕不掩瑜，瑜不掩瑕，忠也；孚尹旁达，信也；气如白虹，天也；精神见于山川，地也；圭璋特达，德也；天下莫不贵者，道也。《诗》云：'言念君子，温其如玉。'故君子贵之也。"玉被人格化为品德，在周代就成了国与国之间的外交重器和官阶象征。《周礼·春官·宗伯》载："以玉作六器，以礼天地四方：以苍璧礼天，以黄琮礼地，以青圭礼东方，以赤璋礼南方，以白琥礼西方，以玄璜礼北方。"即明言玉礼器的形制与功用。

不仅如此，时至周代，玉又开始增添了政治意义。朱怡芳（2008：88）认为，玉在西周时政治文化意义已经发轫：

> 佩玉与德性操行仅是萌发于西周。在这个萌发阶段的德行依然服从于政治统治，单件佩及组佩中一定形制、规格、色彩代表宗法体系中不同社会身份之人。以此来观察特定场合下对方的身份、用意，并确定相应的礼束仪式（或者说这种佩带又是局限地应用于一定的礼仪程式）。从符号的意义看，佩玉在西周时期尚属极少数贵族阶层体现权力的物质资本和表征社会关系的符号资本。

《周礼·春官·宗伯》载："以玉作六瑞，以等邦国：王执镇圭，公执桓圭，侯执信圭，伯执躬圭，子执谷璧，男执蒲璧。"而到春秋战国时期，"君子比德于玉""君子无故玉不去身""君子必佩玉"的比德观念进一步发展，"导致原来借以'比德'的'佩玉'从象征美好高贵的德行中抽离出来，有的纯粹作为官位等级的象征而存在，有的因统治阶层的群体变化而成为装饰、文玩之物。由此，玉与君子、比德与操行的意义发生了新的衍化"（朱怡芳，2008：88）。玉器逐渐具有了鲜明的地位等级、政令等特点。

玉文化在我国社会历史中渊源之久、之深，其与道德、宗教、政治、生活关系之密切，构成了中国传统文化的一大特色。而在西方，景象却全然不同。由于玉石文化的历史较短，在民族文化中地位不高，因此英语中玉石的俗名不多，这给翻译造成的障碍不言而喻。即使译文勉强使用了几种玉石名称，玉石原有的明泽温润之德音也已荡然无存。

在西方，玉石文化的发祥地在希腊，约公元前 400 年玉器饰物才开始取代金器饰物。文艺复兴时期，玉器饰物开始盛行，广泛用于衣饰和头饰。① 珠宝文化真正在欧洲盛行是 18 世纪以后的事，而在英美等国的兴盛则要晚得多，其在人们的社会生活中的地位、作用以及社会文化价值，与中国玉石文化相比，更是不可同日而语。请看下图（有改动）：②

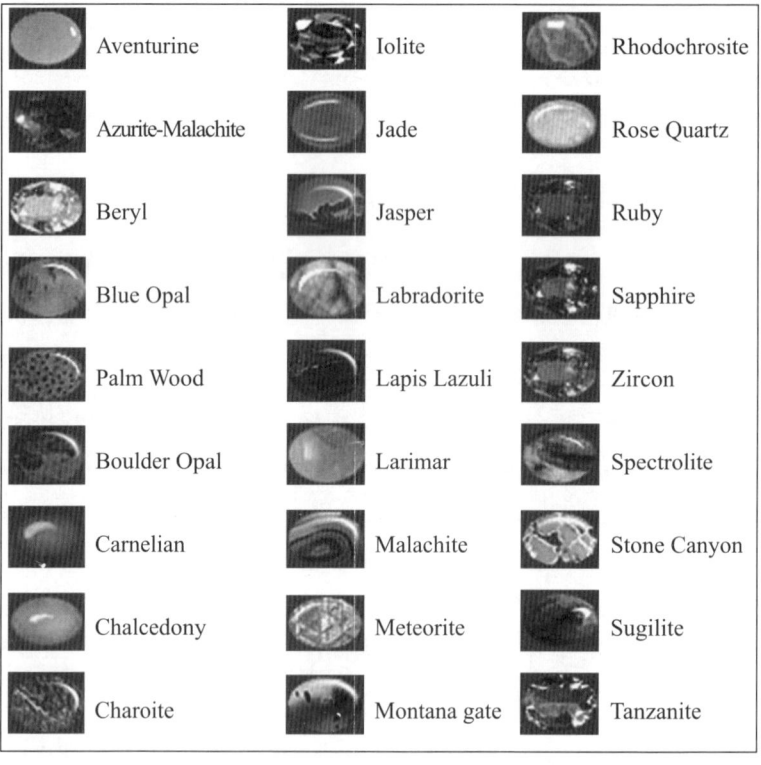

① 见 http://www.jewelrymae.com/gfhistory.html。
② 见 http://www.bernardine.com/gemstones/gemstones.htm。

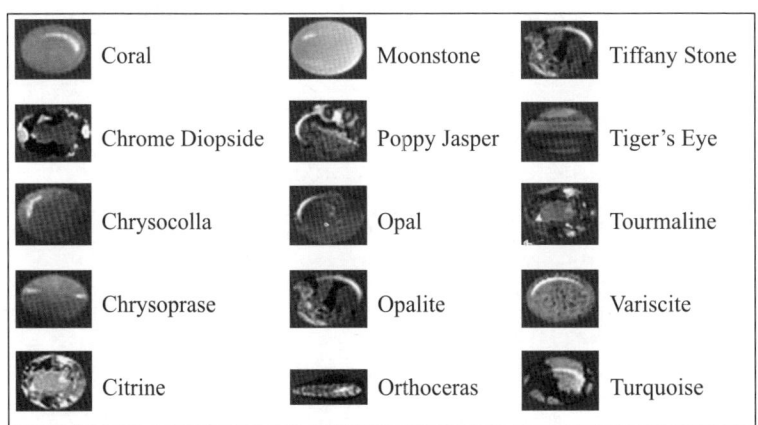

重要的是，西方的珠宝不是以玉石为质料。所以，西方人所爱的并非玉石，而是宝石。宝石仅仅是那些数量稀少的单矿物晶体，色彩瑰丽、坚硬耐久、可琢磨成首饰。钻石、红蓝宝石、祖母绿，是西方人眼中最具价值的宝石。而国人所热爱的玉石，是美观耐久、有工艺价值的稀有矿物集合体。两者从文化内涵到化学构成，都截然有别。

据《圣经》记载，上帝创造伊甸园时就在河里投放了珍珠和红玛瑙；[1] 上帝在创造天国极乐世界时，使用了碧玉、蓝宝石等十二种宝石做这座圣城的十二根基石，并用各种宝石装饰城墙，城墙上刻十二天使和以色列十二支脉的名字；[2] 上帝教摩西为亚伦做圣衣和胸牌时，也用了红玛瑙、红宝石等十二种宝石。[3]

西方神话中认为宝石有神秘魔力。所以，西方的魔幻故事，也

---

[1] 见《圣经·旧约·创世记》。
[2] 见《圣经·新约·启示录》。
[3] 见《圣经·旧约·出埃及记》。

一般有宝石这个角色。例如，欧美魔幻电影中，女巫总是通过一个水晶球来透视未来。在一柄具有神奇力量的宝剑手柄上，也总是镶嵌着火红的宝石。不同月份出生的西方人，也都有自己的诞生石，因为他们都相信诞生石能够给自己带来好运。

宝石在西方也是权力和地位的象征。曾经的英帝国的王冠就是用各类宝石镶嵌，富丽堂皇，昭示着至高无上的权力。

总之，西方的宝石文化属于西方文化系统，其价值主要与饰物相关，其意义主要在于审美、宗教和政治。这与中国玉石文化有一定的相通之处。尽管如此，在西方读者眼中，译诗中的玉石无论如何也无法等同于原文中的玉石。请看理雅各的《木瓜》译文：

> There was presented to me a papaya,
> And I returned for it a beautiful Ju-gem;
> Not as a return for it,
> But that our friendship might be lasting.
> There was presented to me a peach,
> And I returned for it a beautiful Yao-gem;
> Not as a return for it,
> But that our friendship might be lasting.
> There was presented to me a plum,
> And I returned for it a beautiful Jiu-gem;
> Not as a return for it,
> But that our friendship might be lasting.

文中的"Ju-gem""Yao-gem""Jiu-gem"对于英语读者来说，至多

意味着 gem 的不同具体名称而已。那么 gem 又是什么呢？维基百科对 gem 的解释是："一块经过雕琢的石头或矿物。"① 维基百科中 gemstone 的解释有二：（1）珠宝，或一块经过雕琢的、用作饰物的宝石；（2）尤其以完美而备受赞誉的某种东西。②

再看詹宁斯翻译的《木瓜》（Recompenses）译文：

> Some quinces once to me were sent,
> A ruby was my gift again;
> Yet not as gift again;—
> Enduring love was its intent.
>
> Peaches were sent me; I a stone
> Of jasper sent as gift again;
> Nay, not as gift again;—
> Enduring love it meant alone.
>
> Plums I had sent me; and I sent
> A dusky gem for gift again;
> Yet not as gift again;
> But long enduring love it meant.③

显然，无论是理雅各的译文还是詹宁斯的译文，都只能当爱情诗来读，而无法将其理解为《诗小序》中所谓"美齐桓公也"的

---

① 见 http://en.wikipedia.org/wiki/Gem。
② 见 http://en.wikipedia.org/wiki/Gemstone。
③ William Jennings. *The Shi King: The Old "Poetry Classic" of the Chinese*. London and New York: George Routledge and Sons, 1891: 89.

诗篇，因为"琼琚""琼瑶""琼玖"三种器物被译作"gem"和"stone"，都只有饰物的本义，并不具备"美德"的隐喻。其他译诗①也有类似的局限性。如《卫风·芄兰》：

芄兰之支，童子佩觿。
虽则佩觿，能不我知。
容兮遂兮，垂带悸兮。

芄兰之叶，童子佩韘。
虽则佩韘，能不我甲。
容兮遂兮，垂带悸兮。

此诗中有一种植物芄兰和三种文化器物——佩觿、佩韘、垂带。因为历史上英美人在日常生活中从未使用这些器物，所以在翻译这三种器物名称时，就产生了难以逾越的障碍。如韦利的译文：

> The branches of the vine-bean;
> A boy with knot-horn at his belt!
> Even though he carries knot-horn at his belt,
> Why should he not recognize me?
> Oh, so free and easy
> He dangles the gems at his waist!
>
> The branches of the vine-bean;

---

① 见附录二。

A boy with archer's thimble at his belt!

Even though he has thimble at belt,

Why should he not be friends with me?

Oh, so free and easy

He dangles the gems at his waist! ①

理雅各把此三种器物译作"spike"和"archer's thimble",也颇令读者费解。

There are the branches of the sparrow-gourd;—

There is that lad, with the spike at his girdle.

Though he carries a spike at his girdle,

He does not know us.

How easy and conceited is his manner,

With the ends of his girdle hanging down as they do!

There are the leaves of the sparrow-gourd;—

There is that lad with archer's thimble at his girdle.

Though he carries an archer's thimble at his girdle,

He is not superior to us.

How easy and conceited is his manner,

With the ends of his girdle hanging down as they do! ②

---

① Arthur waley. *The Book of Songs*. New York: Grove Press, 1996: 52.
② James Legge. *The Chinese Classics with a Translation, Critical and Exegetical Notes, Prolegomena, and Copious Indexes*. London: Henry Frowde, Oxford University Press Warehouse, Amen Corner, E. C., 1939 年伦敦会香港影印所影印本,Vol. IV-Part I: 103.

与此相类，其他人的译文①，都因为同样的名物翻译问题导致了译文对于原文的偏离。对于这些偏离所造成的颠覆性效果，当作何理解呢？

第三节　名物翻译与译诗文化身份重塑及文化传播

虽然《诗经》中名物数量有限，但是民族特色鲜明的典型文化器物和带有浓厚地域文化色彩的动植物，所释放的文化能量却很大。它们可以表达一种习俗观念，代表一种生活方式，标志一种历史形态，也可以造就一种文化氛围或格调，从而使其所寓居的诗篇，拥有一种文化身份。一个人身穿一身民族服装，就可以标志一种文化身份；同样，一个文化名物用于一首诗，可以使这首译诗读起来有不同文化风味。在詹宁斯、韦利和高本汉的《关雎》译文中，所弹奏的乐器是"lute""harp""zithern""guitar"，那么，诗中人物自然随之成了西洋人，诗中所描述的生活，也成了西洋人的生活。如果这首译诗不标明出处，不标明其翻译属性，那么它获得西方诗歌这样一个文化身份应该是很自然的。西方读者会通过其文化认同感，把它变成一首纯粹的英文诗。即使译者标明了译诗的翻译属性，普通的西方读者也可能产生一种文化错位，误以为中国先民谈情说爱时竟然弹的是西洋乐器，从而在想象中将中国先民的生活方式代之以西方先民的生活方式，用西方古代历史去取代中国古

---

① 见附录二。

代历史。既然诗中人和物已被读者在阅读中西化,那么译诗作为一种艺术形式也会被类推为中国古诗的形式,比如读者会把译文的修辞结构和格律形式想象成原诗的格律形式。而原诗中诸如比兴等艺术手法则不复存在。依此看来,翻译名物,虽然着墨不多,却有牵一发而动全身的效应。如果译诗中名物之间能保持艺术上的和谐统一,则可以构筑译诗的独立文化身份,创造一个具有独立性的艺术个体,这对译入语文学来说,无疑是有建设性的。

同时,名物翻译偏离导致的译诗文化身份的转变,带来了关于译诗文化传播的一个值得探讨的问题。这样经过文化转型的翻译对译入语读者来说会有较大的文化认同感,读起来会比较容易接受,其中的艺术内涵也较容易为读者所欣赏。那么,其文化传播效果如何呢?长期以来的翻译实践证明,这种归化式翻译,其传播和接受速度、广度和深度都会比较大。译诗由于传达了原诗基本内容,也就携带了原诗中的基本文化信息,尤其是原诗欲表达的思想、观念和情感,在一定程度上也会起到文化传播作用。也就是说,能让读者通过译诗了解原诗蕴含的思想文化,从而在很大程度上认识原作面貌,起到钱锺书先生(1985:79)所说的"诱"与"媒"的文化桥梁作用。要使两种文学对话,这是不可或缺的重要一步。但另一方面,同样由于名物翻译带来的译诗文化身份转变,译诗却阻碍了文化传播。因为诗是不可分割的艺术整体,一个名物改变了,也就改变了整首诗和谐如一的结构,虽然其中的思想情感仍然基本上可以传达,但译诗已不是原来完整的艺术有机体。译入语读者即使读了这样的译作,却并不能看到原诗的完整原貌,无法从整体上真正认识原诗的艺术精髓,以及原诗所包含的社会、历史、文化、宗教和生活。从这个意义上说,这种翻译恰恰阻碍了文化的交流与传播。反过来，如果译诗在语义、文化元素上十分对等，甚至注释周全，有人将这种翻译称作深度翻译，则必然会引起阅读的困难，也会大大降低文化交流与传播的速度与广度，可能译诗最终只能成为学术界的研究对象，而永远脱离人民大众这个主流文化群体，从而永远被关在译入语文化的大门之外。所以，要较好地达到文化交流的目的，只有设法把与原文有一定偏离的归化翻译，与尽量忠实的异化翻译结合起来。

第四节　名物翻译偏离的诗学价值与伦理学解释

如上文所述，名物翻译的偏离，可以使译诗的文化身份发生转变，增强译入语读者的文化认同感，更便于译入语读者接受。不仅如此，名物翻译如果与原诗名物有所偏离，并不必然降低译诗本身的艺术价值。因为译诗虽然来自原诗，但其审美价值和艺术价值并不能等同于原诗，其自身必然是独立的艺术个体，具有独立的艺术价值。诗歌翻译，重在情感与诗艺，而不在对个别具体史实和文化信息忠实，所以译文中个别名物的更替或增减，并不能从根本上影响译诗的艺术性。相反，若过分强调名物翻译的忠实性，不仅常常不可行，即使勉强翻译了，也往往令读者费解，从而影响译诗艺术感染力的正常发挥。诗歌翻译在本质上就是用译入语对原诗进行重新创作，译者欲使译诗的艺术性为本民族读者所认识和接受，就不得不顾及本民族文化中的审美心理和文学创作规范。有的译者甚至把民族的或个人的创作理念完全用于译诗过程。庞德的《诗经》翻译就是其实施意象主义诗歌理念的过程。请看其《关雎》译文：

"Hid! Hid!" the fish-hawk saith,
　　by isle in Ho the fish-hawk saith:
　　　"Dark and clear,
　　　Dark and clear,
　　So shall be the prince's fere."

Clear as the stream her modesty;
As neath dark boughs her secrecy,
　　　reed against reed
　　　tall on slight.
As the stream moves left and right,
　　　dark and clear,
　　　dark and clear.
To seek and not find
as a dream in his mind,
　　think how her robe should be,
　　　distantly, to toss and turn,
　　　to toss and turn.

High reed caught in *ts'ai* grass
　　　so deep her secrecy;
Lute sound in lute sound is caught,

27

touching, passing, left and right.

Bang the gong of her delight.

在庞德的笔下,《关雎》已变成一首纯粹的求爱诗。显而易见,诗的主旨是写王子(prince)对心爱的女子的赞美和追求。诗的开头用了比喻,王子被比作"fish-hawk",美丽贞洁的女子被比作幽深清纯的河水。至于"fish-hawk"所追求的是什么,则不得而知。按照事物的逻辑,鱼鹰所追求的应该是水中的鱼而不是河水,但前后文却并没有明显道出鱼的存在。后文接着叙述王子朝思暮想,睡梦中见得女子身披罗绮(robe),默默含羞(secrecy),就禁不住用鲁特琴(lute)和铜锣(gong)演奏乐曲来取悦她。译诗题旨的独立性不言而喻,而原诗"后妃之德"的题旨却无法比附到译诗中去;译诗题解虽然与现代诗经学一致,但译诗艺术上的独立性已赫然存在。译者仅仅突出了"鱼鹰""清清河水""荇草""琴""锣"等意象,并没有竭力一一对应地翻译原诗名物,加之译诗中使用了简洁而意合性强的语言,便重新创造出一首较为典型的现代爱情诗。这首诗的艺术价值显然要高于高本汉在字面上相对比较忠实的译文的艺术性:

Kwan-kwan (cries) the ts'ü-kiu bird,

On the islet of the river;

The beautiful and good girl,

She is a good mate for the lord.

Of varying length is the hing waterplant,

To the left and the right we catch it;

The beautiful and good girl,

Waking and sleeping he (sought her:) wished for her;

He wished for her but did not get her,

Waking and sleeping he thought of her;

Longing, longing,

He tossed and fidgeted.

Of varying length is the hing waterplant,

To the left and the right we gather it;

The beautiful and good girl,

Guitars and lutes (befriend her:) hail her as a friend.

Of varying length is the hing water plant,

To the left and the right we cull it as a vegetable;

The beautiful and good girl,

Bells and drums cheer her.

  其中的原因是,在高氏的译文中,名物翻译拘泥于与原文相统一的标准,但翻译时使用的拼音,又使译诗中名物语义不明,且形象模糊,意象效果也随之暗淡,加之译诗的音韵拖沓散乱,导致整个译诗审美效果大降。

  那么,我们如何看待这种存在明显偏离而却能创造独立艺术价值的翻译呢?众所周知,学术界对于偏离性翻译往往是不赞同,甚至是不屑一顾的。这种观点带有强烈的伦理性质,把在某一方面有所偏离的翻译斥为"不忠"或"叛逆"。然而,如果以原文为评价标准，把适当的偏离贬斥为"不忠"或"叛逆"的不道德行为，那么"忠实"而不可卒读的翻译对艺术本身、译入语读者、文化传播三者来说，是不是道德的呢？回答是否定的。这种贬抑态度显然是短视的，其所本的理念和标准也是片面的。从伦理角度来说，翻译不仅负有忠实于原作的道德义务，而且负有建设本族文学和文化、满足本族语读者审美需要的道德义务。翻译的第一步，是对翻译对象的选择，这个选择本身带有明确的目的性，那就是服务于本民族的文化、艺术、思想、政治的建设和发展。所以，一旦选择了原文文本，那么译者就有义务把这个文本变成服务于本民族文化利益的文本，若违背了这个责任和义务，则是不道德的。所以，对于诗歌译者来说，其所应该做的就是用译入语把原诗重新创造成诗歌，把艺术重新塑造成艺术。相反，如果译者为了盲目追求翻译的"忠实"，而使译文佶屈聱牙，丧失了可读性和艺术性，他就不但辜负了原文的语言艺术，辜负了作者，而且更辜负了本族语读者，辜负了其国家民族，也辜负了艺术本身，遑论翻译道德。所以，以文化传播和艺术发展为最高准则，不盲目拘泥于原文一字一词，才是诗歌翻译及其伦理准则的真谛所在。

基于上文的讨论，名物的翻译应当遵循以下原则：（一）文化一致性原则，（二）文学整体性原则，（三）解释性原则。诗中的名物，从功能上可以分为两类：一是政治、历史、文化功能，二是文学意象功能。所谓名物翻译的文化一致性原则，是指在翻译时应该尽量使名物原有的历史文化功能在译文中得以体现。能够直译的应该予以直译，不能直译的则可采取解释性翻译或加注式翻译。如果翻译侧重的是译文的文学性，那么不能直译的名物，可以用目的语文化中的名物进行替换，但译文须保持自身文化语境的一致性，不能在同一首译诗中一处名物是纯粹中国文化特色，而另一处名物则是纯粹西方文化特色，导致文化语境混乱。这种现象在各个译本中并不鲜见，应该加以避免。所谓文学整体性原则，是指原文中属于被作为意象使用的名物无法翻译成原意象时，可以替换成译入语意象，但一旦原意象被替换，则该译入语名物所构成的意象须与译诗中其他意象保持和谐一致关系，亦即须首先保证译文中的意象组合的整体性和合理性，以及整个译诗的艺术整体性。由于《诗经》名物常蕴涵着丰富的历史文化信息，这些名物若直译过来，常会引起译入语读者理解上的困难，或者会引起译入语读者的文化误读。阐释性原则是，当这些名物不承担文学意象的角色时，译者可以在正文文本中直接采用解释性的翻译方式，把其中所蕴含的历史文化内涵向读者做必要的解释。如果在诗行中直接解释会妨害译诗韵律，那么译者就需要在译文后加一定注释。

小　　结

在《诗经》诗篇当中，名物不仅仅意味着一种动物、植物或器物等，也不只有历史文化意义，而是往往还同时具有文学审美意义，它们一般是可以被当作各种意象来解读和欣赏的。《诗经》作为我国重要的文化典籍，其篇什翻译不仅有传达历史文化内涵的功用，而且也有传达其艺术，服务译入语文学的诉求。为此，名物翻译就面临着翻译策略和方法上的多重选择。然而，《诗经》虽然有历史学、文化学、社会学等意义，但其本质是文学文本而不是文化、历史或政治文本，所以整体翻译策略的采用当以译诗的艺术性为基本准则，并兼顾原诗的历史文化因素。名物翻译亦当遵循这一准则。名物虽小，但有多种意义，在译诗中有营造文化氛围、构建文化身份、决定译诗主题、影响译诗艺术性等多重作用，因此，名物翻译亦当讲求彼此之间和谐统一，并重视其与整篇译诗之间的历史、文化、艺术的整体性的关系。

第二章 《诗经》修辞及其翻译

尽管《诗经》的文学性早已为世人所洞察,但从文学角度对《诗经》进行的研究却迟至宋末才得以初步展开。而对《诗经》的修辞学研究,更是到了当代才真正开始。《诗大序》云:"故诗有六义焉:一曰风,二曰赋,三曰比,四曰兴,五曰雅,六曰颂。"又曰:"颂者,美盛德之形容,以其成功,告于神明者也。"这些论述可以视为古人对《诗经》修辞认识的滥觞。在后来相当长一段历史时期内,《诗经》修辞研究都集中在对赋比兴的研究上。郑玄认为,"赋之言铺也,铺陈善恶,则诗文直陈其事,不譬喻者,皆赋辞也"①。又云:"比,见今之失,不敢斥言,取比类以言之。兴,见今之美,嫌于媚谀,取善事以喻劝之。"② 郑众云:"比者,比方于物。诸言如者,皆比辞也。"又云:"兴者,托事于物则兴者是也。取譬引类,起发己心,诗文诸举草木鸟兽以见意者,皆兴辞也。"③ 刘勰《文心雕龙·比兴》云:"诗文弘奥,包韫六义;毛公述《传》,独标'兴'体。"钟嵘《诗品序》云:"故诗有三义焉:一曰兴,二曰比,三曰赋。文已尽而意有余,兴也;因物喻志,比也;直书其事,寓言写物,赋也。宏斯三义,酌而用之,

---

① 孔颖达:《毛诗正义》,北京:北京大学出版社,1999年,第12页。
② 同上,第11页。
③ 同上,第12页。

干之以风力，润之以丹彩，使味之者无极，闻之者动心，是诗之至也。"在钟嵘这里，三者都已属于文学修辞的范畴，因为赋比兴都要"干之以风力，润之以丹彩"，以实现"味之者无极，闻之者动心""文已尽而意有余"的审美诉求。唐代经学家把对赋比兴三义的理解又往前推进了一步。孔颖达对此进一步解释说："'赋'者，直陈其事，无所避讳，故得失俱言。'比'者，比托于物，不敢正言，似有所畏惧。……'兴'者，兴起志意赞扬之辞，……比之与兴，虽同是附托外物，比显而兴隐。"① 对三者论述得最真切的，当数宋朝的朱熹。朱熹《诗集传》指出："赋者，敷陈其事而直言之者也。"② "比者，以彼物比此物也。"③ "兴者，先言他物以引起所咏之词也。"④ "赋"是陈述、铺陈的意思，"比"相当于现代修辞学的比喻，"兴"是借助其他事物作为诗歌的起始。朱熹在《诗集传》中对赋、比、兴辞都分别做了明确的标记。《诗集传》中标"兴"者，凡256章，其中《国风》中标"兴"者131章，《雅》中标"兴"者121章，《颂》中标"兴"者4章。但是，朱熹并没有把比和兴作为诗学概念进行说明，其区别自然也没有说清楚。在朱熹标"比"的诗章中，有很多在《毛诗传》中标的是"兴"，而且《诗集传》在标"比"的诗章与标"兴"的诗章之间，几乎也无法找出一个明确的区别性客观标准。宋人李仲蒙对三者的解释则深入了许多："叙物以言情谓之赋，情物尽者也；索物以托情谓之比，情附物者也；触物以起情谓之兴，物动

---

① 孔颖达:《毛诗正义》，北京：北京大学出版社，1999年，第11-12页。
② 朱熹:《诗集传》，北京：中华书局，1958年，第3页。
③ 同上，第4页。
④ 同上，第1页。

情者也。"① 这分别从"叙物""索物""触物"的角度,在一定程度上反映了赋比兴的性质。在李氏看来,"作为赋的'叙物'不仅仅是'铺陈其事',还必须与'言情'相结合,就是说作者要把情感表现得淋漓尽致,又要把客观的物象描写得真切生动"(童庆炳,2004:6)。这种解释,就更加符合诗歌创作对"赋"的要求。作为"比"的"索物",即索取和选择物象以寄托感情,也不完全是一个运用比喻手法的问题,作者还须在比喻中表达其真挚感情。作为"兴"的"触物",由外物激发以兴情,反过来又把情感浸透于所描写的物象中。李仲蒙对赋比兴的解说,最终都归结到一个情字上面,直接触及到了审美层次。这就更加符合《诗经》的审美特性,也是其他经学家所没有达到的深度。

  赋比兴固然是《诗经》重要的艺术手法,但是若从现代修辞学观点来看,《诗经》中的修辞手法,远远不止这些。按照陈望道《修辞学发凡》所提出的修辞范畴,修辞有消极修辞和积极修辞两大分野。就积极修辞来说,《诗经》修辞包括音韵、词汇、句法等三个方面。根据王力的《诗经韵读》,《诗经》除了《周颂》的八篇诗完全没有韵律之外,其他每篇诗都有比较整齐的韵律。韵律就是一种重要的声音修辞手段。(关于韵律及其翻译的问题,我们将在下一章单独进行讨论)除此以外,《诗经》的声音修辞还有双声、叠韵、重章叠唱等,这些也都是在《诗经》中复现率很高的修辞手段,对《诗经》的艺术效果有着十分重要的影响。音韵修辞之外,《诗经》则又有词汇层面、句法层面上的修辞。词汇层面上有摹状、比喻、比拟、夸张、借代等;句法层面上有叠句和重

---

① 胡寅:《斐然集(卷十八)·与李叔易书》。

章叠唱等。本章我们专门就《诗经》这三个方面的修辞及其翻译做详细论述。

第一节　兴的修辞手法及其翻译

一、兴——《诗经》最重要的修辞手法

（一）兴的基本性质

兴是《诗经》中最有特色的修辞手法，不仅在诗篇中应用十分广泛，且性质独特。毛亨在《毛诗传》中独标兴体，其重要性不言而喻。因此，我们首先对兴的修辞手法及其翻译进行讨论。

自汉代经学建立以来，关于兴的讨论虽然时而有一些，但都不深入和系统。就连兴的性质、特点、作用、分类等这些基本问题，迄今也都没有得到清楚界定，以致人们在对"兴"的基本判断上还都存在分歧。例如，《周南·卷耳》中"采采卷耳，不盈顷筐"，毛亨《毛诗传》标兴，而朱熹《诗集传》标赋；《秦风·蒹葭》中"蒹葭苍苍，白露为霜"，毛诗标兴，朱熹则标赋；《魏风·伐檀》中"坎坎伐檀兮，置之河之干兮，河水清且涟漪"，毛亨不加标示，朱熹标赋，夏传才认为是兴辞。尤其是，《郑风·野有蔓草》中"野有蔓草，零露漙兮"，毛诗标兴，朱熹则标"赋而兴"，认为是"男女相遇于野田草露之间，故赋其所在以起兴"[①]。这样，朱

[①] 朱熹：《诗集传》，北京：中华书局，1958年，第55页。

熹又别出一格,把赋与兴合为一体。长期以来,朱熹所谓"兴者,先言他物以引起所咏之辞也",是诗经学上认同度较高的关于兴的定义。但是,细做考查就会发现,朱熹对兴的界定仍比较模糊,若以其为标准,在很多地方很难做出判断,也很难理解兴的实际作用。譬如,朱熹在《召南·小星》中每章皆标"兴",并言:"盖众妾进御于君,不敢当夕,见星而往,见星而还,故因所见而起兴。其于义无所取,特取在东在公两字之相应耳。"① 所谓"其于义无所取",是说此兴并没有什么实际意义,仅仅是起兴以引起下文而已,这其实是不准确的。试想,诗人说"嘒彼小星,三五在东。肃肃宵征,夙夜在公。寔命不同!",其用意究竟如何?诚然,诗的头两句似乎确实与后文没有直接逻辑关系,但其与后文所发生的"宵征"之事,在时间上却是一致的。这说明,头两句起码有向读者表明时间的作用,也就是说,这两句兴辞有渲染时间环境的作用。此外,作者为什么选用"小星"起兴,而不选择月亮或者其他明星呢?作者在此也完全可以把小星说成明星。之所以说"小星",关键是作者看重这里"小"的含义,意欲以此表明诗中主人公的态度,即主人公皆以自我为"小",为"从",所处的地位是卑微的、从属的,所以才有"寔命不同"的慨叹。由此可见,兴之义在起,其所兴者,必是缘于其与后文"所咏之辞"之间的某种关联性。如果不存在关联,从发生学观点来看,兴就不会发生。原因很简单,兴即起或启,其本质在于一种联想的产生,若与所启之事没有任何关系,那么兴从何来?而且,兴什么呢?

所以,兴中的关联性毋庸置疑。第一种关联可以是意义上的,

---

① 朱熹:《诗集传》,北京:中华书局,1958年,第12页。

如兴与所咏之事的相似性。夏传才先生将此称为兴的比喻作用。例如《周南·关雎》每章开头的兴辞中就有四种相似性存在:(1)雎鸠之间的同声相求与文王和太姒之间的恩爱;(2)采荇菜的动作与求淑女的感情;(3)采荇菜与寄情于淑女;(4)采荇菜与以钟鼓愉悦淑女。这些相似关系,就是这组兴辞存在的前提。

《诗经》中的兴大多建立在这种相似性的基础上,有的一读便知,有的却并不容易被识别出来。例如《周南·麟之趾》中的兴就很容易辨别:

麟之趾。振振公子……
麟之定。振振公姓……
麟之角。振振公族……

这些兴辞建立在麟的"趾""定""角"与"公子""公姓""公族"的美德之间的相似性上,诗人欲以此祝愿公子王孙拥有麟一样的美德。相比之下,《召南·野有死麕》中的兴就不那么容易理解:

野有死麕,白茅包之。
有女怀春,吉士诱之。
林有朴樕,野有死鹿。
白茅纯束,有女如玉。

若读者稍有不慎,就会将这组兴辞误认为是一种对事件过程的铺陈。其实,这组兴辞的相似性存在于一、二句和三、四句之间,以及五、六句和七、八句之间。这里要说的是,如果有人发现田野里有死鹿，则会拿白茅将之包起来带回家享用。同理，如果有美貌女子长大成人，则会有英俊的小伙子去追求她。林中会有朴樕，田野中会有死鹿。同理，是白茅就会洁白；是女子，长大后就会美丽如玉。所以，这四句诗说的并不纯粹是少年发现死鹿用白茅包起来然后献给美貌女子以表示爱情的过程，而是还有不同事物之间的比喻以及过程描述。朱熹在其《诗集传》中将此诗标兴，大概就是做此种理解。《毛诗传》对此则没做任何标识。

再如《鄘风·柏舟》的兴辞也很晦涩：

> 泛彼柏舟，在彼中河。
> 髧彼两髦，实维我仪。
> 之死矢靡它。母也天只！不谅人只！
>
> 泛彼柏舟，在彼河侧。
> 髧彼两髦，实维我特。
> 之死矢靡慝。母也天只！不谅人只！

乍看开头的兴辞"泛彼柏舟，在彼中河"，似乎与后文"髧彼两髦，实维我仪。之死矢靡它。母也天只！不谅人只！"没有什么逻辑关系。实际上，这首诗写的是"卫世子共伯早死，其妻共姜守义，父母欲夺而嫁之，故共姜作此以自誓"[①]。舟必在河的正中航行，与诗人至死不另嫁他人，为夫守义这两者之间有"正"的共性。

第二种关联是事物之间生态上的关联性，也就是事物存在与发

---

① 朱熹：《诗集传》，北京：中华书局，1958年，第28页。

展运动过程中自然产生的关联。如《秦风·黄鸟》：

> 交交黄鸟，止于棘。
> 谁从穆公？子车奄息。……
>
> 交交黄鸟，止于桑。
> 谁从穆公？子车仲行。……
>
> 交交黄鸟，止于楚。
> 谁从穆公？子车𫘧虎。……

其中"兴"与"事"的关系就更加隐晦。夏传才（1985：94）先生评论说："黄莺的飞翔和停落，与上下文意义没有什么联系，只是发端起情。"但若仔细品味，其实不然。

这首诗是对穆公用活人殉葬，尤其是用人民爱戴的武将奄息、仲行、𫘧虎殉葬这一残暴行为的讽刺。诗人的怜悯和悲愤之情跃然纸上。三章中开头两句是兴辞，其与后文的关联可能存在于两个方面：一是黄鸟栖止于棘、桑、楚等树上这一动作过程与奄息、仲行、𫘧虎等因殉葬而死于穆公之墓穴之间有相似性。这两者中都有"止"的意思。值得注意的是，"交交"寓意比较深。"交交"指黄鸟的欢叫声，可以看作是对生龙活虎的奄息等三公在世时谈笑风姿的比喻。欢叫的黄鸟在林中栖息，犹如谈笑风生的三公葬身于穆公之穴。另一种关联可能是，黄鸟常在墓地的荆楚等树上栖息，诗人用"交交黄鸟，止于棘"的情景，来唤起读者关于坟墓和死亡的联想。无论从以上哪一种可能来看，这三章头两句的兴，不能被说成是与后文的意义无关。如果作者所用的真是后一种关联，那么兴辞与所咏之辞之间的关联，就由较为浅层的相似性转为事物之间更深层的生态上的相关性。

第三种关联是基于事物之间的对照与联想。例如,《魏风·伐檀》,据夏传才(1985: 99)先生分析,其中的兴辞是因为"有一些现实生活中的形象触动了诗人,使诗人产生了由此及彼的联想"。究其根本,这种联想是因为兴辞与所咏事物之间有一定对照作用,从而激发了诗人的感情。《伐檀》中的兴,在于诗人把劳动者整日"坎坎伐檀兮,置之河之干兮"之辛劳和贫困与"君子"整日"不稼不穑,胡取禾三百廛兮?不狩不猎,胡瞻尔庭有县貆兮?"之不劳而食和悠闲富足进行对照,在经过对照而产生巨大心理反差之后,诗情便喷涌而出:

> 坎坎伐檀兮,置之河之干兮,河水清且涟猗。
> 不稼不穑,胡取禾三百廛兮?
> 不狩不猎,胡瞻尔庭有县貆兮?
> 彼君子兮,不素餐兮!
>
> 坎坎伐辐兮,置之河之侧兮,河水清且直猗。
> 不稼不穑,胡取禾三百亿兮?
> 不狩不猎,胡瞻尔庭有县特兮?
> 彼君子兮,不素食兮!
>
> 坎坎伐轮兮,置之河之漘兮,河水清且沦猗。
> 不稼不穑,胡取禾三百囷兮?
> 不狩不猎,胡瞻尔庭有县鹑兮?
> 彼君子兮,不素飧兮!

应当指出的是,这种对照并不等于上文所讲的相似性或比喻。对照的两个事物之间不一定相似，恰恰相反，两者之间可以是相反的关系。《诗经》中这样的兴辞并非一二。如《鄘风·相鼠》中"相鼠有皮，人而无仪"，以鼠虽可恶而犹"有皮"兴人"无仪"，其中"有"与"无"是相反关系。当然这里还有一层关联是，"皮"和"礼仪"之间有两者皆作为外表的相似性。再如《鄘风·鹑之奔奔》："鹑之奔奔，鹊之彊彊。人之无良，我以为兄。鹊之彊彊，鹑之奔奔。人之无良，我以为君。"郑《笺》云："奔奔、彊彊，言其居有常匹，飞则相随之貌。刺宣姜与顽非匹耦。"① 这里诗人是以鹑、鹊等飞禽的常匹之德兴公子顽与其母宣姜淫乱之丧德之行，言顽竟至不如禽兽，其中所含的辛辣讽刺之意是较为明显的。这也是一组比较典型的反义兴辞。

兴辞与所咏之辞之间还有一种关联，即历史关联。在这种关联中，兴辞的作用是诗人触物生情而产生联想。例如《王风·黍离》：

  彼黍离离，彼稷之苗。行迈靡靡，中心摇摇。……
  彼黍离离，彼稷之穗。行迈靡靡，中心如醉。……
  彼黍离离，彼稷之实。行迈靡靡，中心如噎。……

本诗三章，每章开头两句都是兴辞，与后文既没有相似性关联，也没有生态上的本然性关联，或对照性关联。夏传才（1985：97）先生认为，这里的兴辞"只是诗人见到遍地黍稷，触发了自己的情思，借以发端起情"。笔者认为，这种解释颇为牵强。这里的问题

---

① 孔颖达：《毛诗正义》，北京：北京大学出版社，1999年，第193页。

是,"遍地黍稷"何以触发诗人的情思?何必以"黍稷"而非他物触发情思?《诗小序》之说颇通:"闵宗周也。周大夫行役至于宗周,过故宗庙宫室,尽为禾黍。闵周室之颠覆,彷徨不忍去,而作是诗也。"《诗集传》也持此说:"周既东迁,大夫行役至于宗周,过故宗庙宫室,尽为禾黍。闵周室之颠覆,彷徨不忍去,故赋其所见黍之离离,与稷之苗,以兴行之靡靡,心之摇摇。既叹时人莫识己意,又伤所以致此者,果何人哉。追怨之深也。"[①] 余冠英《诗经选》(1982)所谓"从诗的本身体味,只见出这是一个流浪人诉忧之辞"一说,则缺乏考证,只是把经学注疏中所言的历史事实化实为虚而已,似不足信。试想,"知我者谓我心忧,不知我者谓我何求"这样的诗句中的优雅与含蕴,岂是一般流浪之人可以企及?因此,兴辞中的历史蕴含,才是此兴辞的本体。

兴辞的历史关联性的实现有一个前提,那就是兴辞本身必须是一个关于历史事件的隐喻。隐喻使兴辞变成委婉之辞,并在语义上完成与后文所咏之辞的对接。对这一类兴辞,读者若没有对诗人所暗指之事的了解,往往会感到很难理解。再如《邶风·北风》:

  北风其凉,雨雪其雱。
  惠而好我,携手同行。
  其虚其邪?既亟只且!

  北风其喈,雨雪其霏。
  惠而好我,携手同归。

[①] 朱熹:《诗集传》,北京:中华书局,1958年,第42页。

> 其虚其邪？既亟只且！
>
> 莫赤匪狐，莫黑匪乌。
> 惠而好我，携手同车。
> 其虚其邪？既亟只且！

仅在字面上，前两章的兴辞"北风其凉，雨雪其雱"和"北风其喈，雨雪其霏"可以看作是环境描写。但这样一来，就阻断了兴与后文合理的逻辑关联性。根据郑《笺》，"寒凉之风，病害万物。兴者，喻君政教酷暴，使民散乱"①。若如此理解，则后文"惠而好我，携手同行"与"惠而好我，携手同归"在逻辑上就有了前提或归因。其实，前两章的兴辞之隐喻意义，在第三章的兴辞出现以后，已被另一个隐喻所佐证。这里"狐"与"乌"均被用来比喻昏君和佞臣。郑《笺》云："赤则狐也，黑则乌也，犹今君臣相承，为恶如一。"②孔颖达《毛诗正义》又云："由狐赤乌黑，其类相似，人莫能别其同异，以兴今君臣为恶如一，似狐、乌相类，人以莫能别其同异。"③这样，三章中的兴辞就在喻意上统一起来，并被合理地织入了全诗的逻辑。因此，没有历史关联及隐喻的实现，这种兴辞的意思和作用，是很难解释得通的。

（二）兴的种类、结构、位置

在清楚了兴的性质与作用以后，如果要准确判别诗篇中的兴辞，我们有必要厘清几个问题，即兴辞种类、兴辞结构以及兴在诗

---

① 孔颖达：《毛诗正义》，北京：北京大学出版社，1999年，第171页。
② 同上，第172页。
③ 同上，第173页。

篇中的位置。

从形态上来看，兴可以分为静态兴与动态兴两种。所谓静态兴，即兴辞所指的是一个特定的事物或事物的形貌、状态。诗人由这一事物发端，由此及彼，抒发自己的胸臆。如《周南·关雎》中的"关关雎鸠""参差荇菜"，《周南·麟之趾》中的"麟之趾""麟之定""麟之角"等，都是典型的事物型兴辞。诗人由在沙洲上"关关"鸣叫的雎鸠，联想到琴瑟和合的夫妻；由麟的身体部位，联想到贵族之品德。摹态型兴辞一般是描绘性的，常常涉及事物的形貌或状态。如《周南·桃夭》中"桃之夭夭，灼灼其华"这个兴的主体是桃树和桃花，摹态词是"夭夭"和"灼灼"，"夭夭"即茂盛，"灼灼"即明媚。诗人用茂盛而明媚的桃花来起兴，赞美成年女子的美貌与令德，十分和谐优美。又如《唐风·杕杜》中"有杕之杜，其叶湑湑"这两个诗句共同描写了高大孤立的杜树，树冠丰满，树叶茂密。其所引起的下文是"独行踽踽，岂无他人？不如我同父"。杕杜与独行之人相比，湑湑与踽踽相应，两两之间构成一层明显的比拟关系。

动态的兴则是描绘一个动作过程，常常由两个诗句来完成，在句法上有时表现为主谓结构，有时表现为动宾结构。朱熹有时把这种兴辞标作"赋而兴"。如"参差荇菜，左右采之"这两句合起来的意思，就是淑女时左时右地采摘荇菜。诗人用这个动作过程来兴君子寤寐以求其所歆慕的淑女。再如《小雅·鹿鸣》："呦呦鹿鸣，食野之苹"这个兴，就是欢鸣的鹿在旷野食草的动作情景，由此引发出"我有嘉宾，鼓瑟吹笙"。这种兴辞含有赋的成分，因为其中同时含有叙述的部分，但从整体功能上来看，其仍然属于兴辞。

从兴在诗篇中的语境意义来看,兴可分比喻性和非比喻性两种类型。

总的来看,大多数兴辞与所引起的咏辞之间比喻关系不明显。虽然也起到比喻的作用,但其中并没有比喻词提示,这类兴辞是隐喻性的。隐喻性兴辞可以进一步分成两类,一类是所喻之事物在后文中出现。如雎鸠以兴君子淑女,两者都出现在诗篇中。有的时候,两种相比的事物之间的相似性不那么容易辨别,却也可以看得清楚。例如《小雅·谷风》:

> 习习谷风,维风及雨。
> 将恐将惧,维予与女。
> 将安将乐,女转弃予!
>
> 习习谷风,维风及颓。
> 将恐将惧,置予于怀。
> 将安将乐,弃予如遗!
>
> 习习谷风,维山崔嵬。
> 无草不死,无木不萎。
> 忘我大德,思我小怨。

诗的三章中每章头两句都是兴辞,其后四个诗句整体上都与前面的兴辞构成比喻关系。两者之间的共性在于"转变",兴辞中说风转变成雨。诗的核心部分是诗人在借此以怨诉患难时你我为友,互相依靠,安乐时你我为敌,以怨报德,相离相弃。这种比喻关系不是在两件具体事物之间发生,而是在两个事件过程之间发生。

另一类是所喻之物并不直接出现，如"彼黍离离，彼稷之苗"以兴周臣之哀叹，其所比喻的"衰亡的周室"并没有在诗文中出现，所以这种比喻关系十分隐晦。从修辞学观点来看，这颇像借代，但又不是借代，因为借代是两个相关事物之间虽无共性，却有不可分割的关系。比如曹操诗句"何以解忧？唯有杜康"，杜康是酒也是酒的品名，名实不可分，所以可以用杜康来代替酒。但黍稷和周室之间却并没有这种关系。所以，这种兴辞就比较晦涩难懂。

从兴辞与所咏之辞的关系来说，比喻性兴辞更宜说成比。而所谓兴辞，应该主要是从诗人的创作过程来说的。所以，兴辞尽管有比喻意义，但其本质则是在过程上起兴。也正是因为这一点，兴才必须在全诗的开头，或者是在一章的开头。从这个观点来讲，非比喻性的兴才是真正意义上的兴，其仅仅引发一种联想，与所咏之辞没有什么语义逻辑上的必然关系，而诗人只是在创作过程中偶然触物，从而产生了某种联想。譬如《草虫》中以"喓喓草虫，趯趯阜螽"兴"未见君子，忧心忡忡"，就是诗人以诗中主人公的口气写成的诗。诗中女子与丈夫长期离别，于田间劳作之时看见跳跃的蚱蜢，便蓦然想到时令已是秋天，大半年时间已过，不由得想起年初离别服役的丈夫，思念之情油然而生。这两句兴辞的引发作用，在后文中越发清楚：

> 喓喓草虫，趯趯阜螽。
> 未见君子，忧心忡忡。
> 亦既见止，亦既觏止，我心则降。
>
> 陟彼南山，言采其蕨。
> 未见君子，忧心惙惙。

亦既见止，亦既觏止，我心则说。

陟彼南山，言采其薇。
未见君子，我心伤悲。
亦既见止，亦既觏止，我心则夷。

朱熹《诗集传》云："南国被文王之化，诸侯大夫行役在外，其妻独居，感时物之变，而思其君子如此。"① 这是符合诗篇本文逻辑的。而《毛诗传》在此也标兴，郑《笺》则解释说："草虫鸣，阜螽跃而从之，异种同类，犹男女嘉时以礼相求呼。"② 为了消除郑玄所谓"嘉时"的错误，孔颖达又在《正义》中说："嘉时者，谓嘉善之时，郑为仲春之月也。以此善时相求呼，不为草虫而记时也。"③ 这种解释矛盾重重，不仅在事实上相互矛盾，而且与后文的"忡忡""惙惙""伤悲"等语辞也无法在逻辑上取得一致。既然是"嘉时以礼相求"，何来伤悲一说！

从现代语法角度说，兴辞结构可以是名词短语、主谓结构、动宾结构，也可以是两三个句子。例如，"麟之趾"是一个名词短语，它被用来比喻后文的"振振公子"。"扬之水，不流束楚"是一个主谓结构，"扬之水"可以看作是主位，"不流束楚"则是述位。"参差荇菜，左右流之"是动宾结构，前句的"荇菜"是宾语成分，是后句动作"流"所涉及的对象。《采芑》中"薄言采芑，于彼新田，于此菑亩"，是三个句子，第一句言事，第二句和第三句分别交代事情发生的两种地方。朱熹《诗集传》说，"军行采芑而食，故赋

---

① 朱熹：《诗集传》，北京：中华书局，1958年，第9页。
② 孔颖达：《毛诗正义》，北京：北京大学出版社，1999年，第69页。
③ 同上。

其事以起兴曰，薄言采芑，则于彼新田，于此菑亩矣"。这种兴辞，常常是以赋的形式来实现的，故朱熹称其为赋而兴。《诗经》中大多数兴辞都属于这一种。

因为兴是诗人首先言及的人或事物，也就是其首先有所感触的事物，所以无论是从诗的发生学角度还是从诗的叙事结构角度来看，兴都是位于全诗或者其中一章的开头，用以引发有关其他事物的吟咏之辞。如果全诗是重章叠唱的形式，那么兴辞则可以在每章的开头。譬如《关雎》《葛覃》《樛木》《鹊巢》《摽有梅》《鹿鸣》等，每章都是以相似的兴辞开头的。

二、兴的英译

兴辞究竟有什么性质，历史上的经学家并没有解决这个问题。自汉至清，经学家们各抒己见，主观性都较大，并未形成理性的、一致的意见。后学虽然倾向于朱熹的观点，但朱氏之论显然未能解决一个最基本的问题，即兴和比的区别究竟在哪里。朱熹在《诗经》中明确标"兴"256处，但其与《毛诗传》所标的"兴"存在许多相互矛盾之处；朱熹所标"比"处，很多正是毛氏所标"兴"处。据笔者调查，《诗集传》中每章标"比也"的诗篇共有22篇，其中有19篇《毛诗传》标的是"兴也"，另有《硕鼠》《伐檀》《木瓜》三篇未标"兴"或"比"。从朱熹本人的论述来看，他认为兴兼比。这就很难把兴和比从内涵上分清楚。所以，朱熹标比与兴的诗篇，实际在类别上是相当混淆的。譬如，若把朱熹标"比也"的《卫风·有狐》与标"兴也"的《邶风·燕燕》两篇诗相对比，委实看不出为什么前者标"比"而后者标"兴"。在此，我们不妨把《有狐》和《燕燕》做一比较。先看《有狐》：

> 有狐绥绥，在彼淇梁。心之忧矣，之子无裳！
> 有狐绥绥，在彼淇厉。心之忧矣，之子无带！
> 有狐绥绥，在彼淇侧。心之忧矣，之子无服！

朱熹说："绥绥，独行求匹之貌。……国乱民散，丧其妃偶，有寡妇见鳏夫而欲嫁之，故托言有狐独行，而忧其无裳也。"[①] 看来，朱熹标比的原因在于寡妇"托言"，即把丧偶的鳏夫比作"有狐"。故标"比也"。再看《燕燕》：

> 燕燕于飞，差池其羽。
> 之子于归，远送于野。
> 瞻望弗及，泣涕如雨！
>
> 燕燕于飞，颉之颃之。
> 之子于归，远于将之。
> 瞻望弗及，伫立以泣！
>
> 燕燕于飞，下上其音。
> 之子于归，远送于南。
> 瞻望弗及，实劳我心。
>
> 仲氏任只，其心塞渊。
> 终温且惠，淑慎其身。
> "先君之思"，以勖寡人！

---

① 朱熹：《诗集传》，北京：中华书局，1958年，第40-41页。

朱熹说:"戴妫大归于陈,而庄姜送之,作此诗也。"①看来,庄姜送戴妫回陈时,看见上下翻飞的"燕燕",正是戴妫颠沛远行之状,触景生情,于是在诗中把戴妫比作了飞燕。后文中的"之子"就是这个比喻中的本体戴妫,正如《有狐》中"之子"是比喻中的本体"鳏夫"一样。这样一来,按《有狐》的判断标准,《燕燕》应该标"比也"才是合理的,而朱熹将三章皆标"兴"。类似的诗篇,如《邶风·终风》《邶风·凯风》《王风·兔爰》等朱熹皆标"比",而《毛诗传》皆标"兴"。

其实,无论是从毛亨所标的"兴",还是从朱熹所标的"兴"来看,兴都具有由此及彼的功能,即兴皆兼比,上文的分析也都证明了这一点。所以,兴的判断标准不是其中有没有比,而应当是孔颖达所说的"比显而兴隐"。所以,我们在此讨论兴的翻译时,仍以《毛诗传》中兴的观念为标准,承认兴皆兼比,但比喻或比拟关系比较隐晦的才是兴,兴与"所咏之辞"之间的关系是隐喻的,甚至是借代的,其与喻体之间的关联性一般是微妙的,有的是历史关联,有的甚至是通过想象而获得的临时性关联。这样才有利于把问题说清楚。

我们讨论兴的翻译,首先是兴辞能否翻译的问题,其次是兴辞翻译的价值问题,其三是兴辞的翻译方法,以及为什么不同译本中兴辞的翻译方法各异。

关于第一个问题,答案似乎很简单,但实际上并非如此。如果要回答这个问题,恐怕第一要考察语言因素,第二要考虑翻译

---

① 朱熹:《诗集传》,北京:中华书局,1958年,第16页。

的意图，即翻译是本着什么态度和为了怎样的目的。纯粹从语言的角度考虑，兴辞的翻译大部分是可行的，这已经为众多译本的翻译实践所证明。但是，由于兴辞本身的隐晦性特点，其可译性受到多方面的限制，譬如，由于兴辞与所比喻之事物之间的关联性比较隐晦，其逻辑关系不容易理解，仅依靠文本内语境进行翻译，对习惯于逻辑思维的西方读者来说，译文往往就会显得前言不搭后语。因此，如何解决兴辞与所咏之辞之间的逻辑断裂问题，大概是兴辞翻译需要解决的首要问题。有些译文，从兴辞本身的翻译来看，很贴切也很有情调，但从整体上看，与后文在逻辑上不协调。例如：

> 防有鹊巢，邛有旨苕。
> 谁侜予美？心焉忉忉！
> 中唐有甓，邛有旨鹝。
> 谁侜予美？心焉惕惕。

韦利将其译作：

> On the dike there is a magpie's nest,
> On the bank grows the sweet vetch.
> Who has lied to my lovely one,
> And made my heart so sore?
>
> The middle-path has patterned tiles,
> On the bank grows the rainbow plant.

Who has lied to my lovely one,

And made my heart so sad? ①

可以看出，译诗的训诂依据是朱熹的《诗集传》。但"邛"的翻译有训诂上的错误。《毛诗传》训曰："邛，丘也。"②朱熹《诗集传》："邛，丘。"③ 这些且不讨论，只看各章开头两句的兴辞。兴辞本身的意思对读者理解来说没有问题，但若读到第三句，疑问则会产生，因为在逻辑上开头两句和第三、四两句是没有什么关系的，这对不了解"忧谗贼也。宣公多信谗，君子忧惧焉"这一历史背景的西方读者来说，费解是必然的。

詹宁斯的译文感情更加充沛，但仍没有摆脱这一缺陷：

The dyke retains the magpie's nest,

　The brae the bright wild-pea.

But oh! What anguish fills my breast!

　Who lured my Love from me?

Fair tiles adorn the temple-path,

　Bright ribbon-plants the brae.

But oh! My heart! What pain it hath!

　Who lured my Love away? ④

---

① Arthur Waley. *The Book of Songs*. New York: Grove Press, 1996: 110.
② 孔颖达:《毛诗正义》，北京：北京大学出版社，1999年，第450页。
③ 朱熹:《诗集传》，北京：中华书局，1958年，第83页。
④ William Jennings. *The Shi King: The Old "Poetry Classic" of the Chinese*. London and New York: George Routledge and Sons: 1891: 150.

为了照顾韵律，译者把行的顺序做了调整，这无可厚非。但是，即便如此，就整个译文来说，篇章连贯性仍然薄弱。每章第三句与开头两句缺乏上下文逻辑依据，因此显得突兀。句中"anguish"是从何而来呢？读者必然对此感到疑惑。

汪榕培的译文似乎运力于在前后文中使用逻辑，以便于读者理解，但却在无意中消解了兴辞的存在：

> A magpie nest is on a dyke!
> Waterweeds grow on a height!
> Who is imposing on my wife?
> I'm so puzzled by life.
>
> The tiles are laid upon the ground!
> The wild weeds overspread the mound!
> Who is imposing on my wife?
> I'm so annoyed by life. ①

郑《笺》曰："防之有鹊巢，邛之有美苕，处势自然。"②《毛诗正义》曰："《释宫》又云：'瓴甋谓之甓。'李巡曰：'瓴甋一名甓。'郭璞曰'甗砖也。今江东呼为瓴甓。'"③ 由此可见，汪译不符合经学训诂，而是信从了后人臆说，这样，每章头两句也就不再是原来的兴辞了。起"兴"者应该是诗人眼前所见之事物，而不是一两句谎

---

① 汪榕培、任秀桦（译注）：《诗经》（中英文版），大连：辽宁教育出版社，1995 年，第 565 页。
② 孔颖达：《毛诗正义》，北京：北京大学出版社，1999 年，第 450 页。
③ 同上，第 451 页。

言。汪榕培把兴辞当谎言来理解和翻译,看起来似乎第一章全章上下逻辑贯通,但一、二两句随之失去了兴辞的基本特征。兴辞的特点是"隐",所以它反对在字面上有显性逻辑贯穿其中。而第二章中两句兴辞不仅意思翻译错了,译文本身也仍然没有逻辑可循,所以也就无法在译文中充当兴辞。

许渊冲的译文,其训诂依据也是现代诗经学,因此译文中有一定的逻辑线索,但同样也因逻辑而抹杀了"兴"的存在:

> By riverside magpies appear;
> On hillock water grasses grow.
> Believe none who deceives, my dear,
> Or my heart will be full of woe.
>
> How can the court be paved with tiles
> Or hillock spread with water grass?
> Believe, my dear, none who beguiles,
> Or I'll worry for you, alas! ①

译文第一章的逻辑在第三句中似乎显现出来,因为"deceive"一词暗示出了前两句是谎言。但是,"By riverside magpies appear"又是常见的自然现象,并不违背常理。这里译者在寻求逻辑的过程中不知不觉犯了另一个逻辑错误。但此处最值得关注的是,译文因为使用了逻辑,致使原有的兴辞不复存在了。第二章的问题有如第一章,此不赘述。

---

① 许渊冲(译):《诗经》,北京:中国对外翻译出版公司,2009年,第145页。

至此我们发现，《诗经》兴辞的逻辑是隐性的，并不易被读者捕捉到，如果按原文的修辞习惯来翻译，那么英美读者会因上下文缺乏逻辑线索而感到费解。但是，如果在译文中强行使用逻辑，即把逻辑表面化，那么反过来又会使兴辞由隐变显，从而使兴辞不再成其为兴辞，实际上是消解了兴辞的存在。这颇令人进退两难。

　　兴辞与所咏之辞之间逻辑上的隐蔽性已被证明是兴辞翻译的一大障碍。另一大障碍，则是中西诗学观念上的差异。兴辞在中国诗学中是"六义"之一，其在诗艺中艺术价值非同一般，一直为人们所重视，对后世诗学影响深远。而在西方诗学中，这一观念基本是空缺的。在英语诗中可能有景物描写，但其功能毕竟与兴辞有很大不同。在《诗经》译者中，确实有不识庐山真面目，把兴辞仅当作景物描写去翻译的。譬如，阿连璧（C. F. R. Allen）这样翻译《防有鹊巢》：

　　　　'Tis spring. The flowers and blossoms now
　　　　　　With brightest robes the hills invest.
　　　　The magpies flit from bough to bough
　　　　　　To build their nest.

　　　　Where coloured tiles the path inlay,
　　　　　　The merry sunbeams glance and shine.
　　　　And all men's hearts are blithe and gay;
　　　　　　All, all but mine.

　　　　By base deceit a maiden fair

Has from my loving arms been torn;

And I am left in blank despair

To pine forlorn. ①

译诗开头两句描写的完全是一幅春天的风景画：春天，朵朵鲜花给丛山披上鲜艳的外衣，喜鹊从一根树枝上跳到另一根树枝上筑巢，彩色的瓦铺在路上，明媚的阳光在那里欢快地照耀。后文写的是，在这样一个美丽的春天一个男子害单相思的心理感受。且不说译诗主题如何，可以肯定的是，原来的兴辞手法已踪影全无。值得注意的是，在阿连璧译本中，大部分兴辞都被译者这样武断地改写了。以《国风·陈风》中的《东门之池》《东门之杨》《墓门》《防有鹊巢》《月出》《泽陂》六篇诗兴辞为例，阿连璧在译文中，把原来的兴辞统统变成了景物描写。如《东门之池》的兴辞，被变成了一个地点：

Near the east moat wide and deep,

Where hemp and rush are set to steep,

Lives a modest beauteous maiden,

With such store of learning laden,

　That it is in vain to try

Or by speech or song to task her,

For to anything you ask her

　Prompt and quick comes her reply. ②

---

① Clement F. R. Allen. *The Shih Ching*. London: Kegan Paul, Trench, Trubner & Co., Ltd., 1891: 177.

② 同上，第 175 页。

《东门之杨》的兴辞成了这个样子:

By the east gate the willows are growing;
　　Their leaves are so thick and green
That a man may stand 'neath their branches,
　　And scarcely fear to be seen.①

原来的杨树变成了柳树,因为树叶茂密,所以人站在下面,别人看不见。在这样的场景下,译文又说:

So I said, "I will go in the gloaming
　　To meet there a lovely maid,
With never an eye to spy us
　　Concealed in the dusky shade."②
　　　…

这完全是译者自己的想象,哪里还有什么"兴"的意味可言。

这里不妨把阿连璧翻译的以下几篇诗的兴辞部分的译文也列出来,其真伪读者自有明辨:

(1)《墓门》:

Before the tombs the thorns grow rank and foul,

---

① Clement F. R. Allen. *The Shih Ching*. London: Kegan Paul, Trench, Trubner & Co., Ltd., 1891: 175.
② 同上。

No man may pass unless he hews a road.
And on the plum trees growing near the owl
　　　　Has chosen her abode. ①

...

（2）《泽陂》：

The iris, lotus, orchis, light
With shining flowers the marshy lea.
A maiden stately, tall and bright,
I love, though she is cold to me. ②

...

（3）《月出》：

The moon's clear lamp is shining bright.
Her beams illuminate the night.
　My words are feeble to express
Your beauty, charms, or sprightliness.
Have Mercy. Tranquillize my heart,
Remove love's fetters, heal love's smart. ③

---

① Clement F. R. Allen. *The Shih Ching*. London: Kegan Paul, Trench, Trubner & Co., Ltd., 1891: 176.
② 同上，第 179 页。
③ 同上，第 178 页。

这种把兴辞随便进行改写的做法反映出译者很有可能缺乏对《诗经》兴辞的审美知识，所以在做翻译处理时，都一味从逻辑上入手，把兴辞变成了场景描写。也有可能是译者本人并不认同和接受《诗经》兴辞的修辞艺术及其价值。这在阿连璧译本前言中可以寻得部分证据。这一现象也在一定程度上说明，西方读者可能不认同兴辞的审美价值，所以他们就通过改写使其在译文中成为西方读者能够接受的东西。然而，这样改写出来的译文，遮蔽了原来的诗歌艺术，剥夺了读者学习和欣赏原作艺术的权利，虽然可以暂时满足急功近利的心态，但从长远来看，这实际上限制了本民族文化的发展，实乃得不偿失之举，并非文学翻译之正道。

庞德试图以其意象主义诗学理念翻译《诗经》，结果兴辞多半被改写了，成了意象主义的牺牲品，甚至成了必须在译文中被抛弃的东西。例如《小雅·杕杜》前两章：

> 有杕之杜，有睆其实。
> 王事靡盬，继嗣我日。
> 日月阳止，女心伤止，征夫遑止！
>
> 有杕之杜，其叶萋萋。
> 王事靡盬，我心伤悲。
> 卉木萋止，女心悲止，征夫归止！

庞德的译文完全没有原诗的面目：

> There's fine fruit on
> the lone pear-tree

and no rest for the king's armee.
One day, then another day,
Sun and moon wearin' away,
October now, let a torn heart grieve,
Will they ever get their winter leave?

Lonely pear-tree full of leaves,
Government work, no reprieves,
Heart can break here in the shade,
Will they ever come back from that raid?①

原文第一章的兴辞,是诗人看到桃树上果实浑圆,联想到果树尚能得息生子,而王室事务繁多,没完没了,丈夫犹无闲暇以得子嗣。在庞德的译文中"有杕之杜""有睆其实""王事靡盬"三句话被强行拉到一起,不知其意欲何为。第二章"有杕之杜,其叶萋萋"被当作主人公身边的实物,从译诗第三句"Heart can break here in the shade"可以看出,这两句兴辞已经失去了起兴的功能和意味。

《蓼莪》兴辞部分的译文读来非常怪异,有点让人哭笑不得。

蓼蓼者莪,匪莪伊蒿。
哀哀父母,生我劬劳。

蓼蓼者莪,匪莪伊蔚。
哀哀父母,生我劳瘁。

---

① Ezra Pound. *Poems and Translations*, New York: The Library of America, 2003: 848.

Waving ling? Not ling but weed,
You two begat me, by labour to need.

Weed or plant that gives no grain,
you two begat me in toil and pain.①

开头四句兴辞,《毛诗传》、郑《笺》解释得都过于政教化,在文脉上不通。朱熹的解释是,孝子以无用的蒿草自比,言无力奉养父母的悔愧罪己之情。这是十分合理的。而庞德仅靠上下文进行臆断,这样得来的译文,必然令人费解。

不过兴辞并不是绝对不可翻译的。出路之一,是要巧妙地利用中西诗歌艺术中的类比因素,利用事物之间的隐喻关系,这样,在有的情况下,可以较好地把兴辞翻译出来。例如《小雅·青蝇》:

营营青蝇,止于樊。
岂弟君子,无信谗言。

营营青蝇,止于棘。
谗人罔极,交乱四国。

营营青蝇,止于榛。
谗人罔极,构我二人。

Flies, blue flies on a fence rail,
Should a prince swallow lies wholesale?

---

① Ezra Pound. *Poems and Translations*, New York: The Library of America, 2003: 880.

Flies, blue flies on a jujube tree,
Slander brings states to misery.

Flies, blue flies on a hazel bough
even we two in slanderers' row
  B'zz, B'zz, hear them now. ①

  庞德借中西文化中共有的对苍蝇的憎恶感,在译文中塑造了苍蝇的意象,把苍蝇描绘成和谗言一样有害而可憎的东西,从手法到诗意,都颇符合原诗情致。

  综合以上分析,我们发现,《诗经》中的兴辞既然是一种比喻,那么翻译时须忌用逻辑来表现其含义;同时,由于兴辞具有隐性的特点,所以也不能把它们翻译成明喻或者其他有明显比喻特征的语言形式,否则,兴辞就会失去它原来的性质和特点。鉴于这种情况,从诗歌艺术传播的角度出发,对这类兴辞的翻译最有效的出路就是求助于文后的注释。理雅各的译文体例或许能给我们一些启发。例如《防有鹊巢》,理雅各在译文中先较为直接地把兴辞翻译出来:

On the embankment are magpies' nests;
On the height grows the beautiful pea.
Who has been imposing on the object of my admiration?
—My heart is full of sorrow.

The middle path of the temple is covered with its tiles;

---

① Ezra Pound. *Poems and Translations*. New York: The Library of America, 2003: 898.

> On the height is the beautiful medallion plant.
> Who has been imposing on the object of my admiration?
> —My heart is full of trouble. ①

接着又在后面加注说：

> Allusive. A lady laments the alienation of her lover by means of evil tongues. The Preface says we have here 'sorrow on account of slanderous villains,' and goes on to refer the piece to the time of duke Seuen（宣公; B. C. 691-647), who believed slanderers, filling the good men about his court with grief and apprehension. Much more likely is the view of Choo, that the piece speaks of the separation between lovers effected by evil tongues. He does not give his opinion as to the speaker, whether we are to suppose the words to be those of the gentleman or of the lady. In this I have ventured to supplement his interpretation. ②

在译本中对诗的题旨进行注释，在一定程度上可以帮助读者理解兴辞。但仅对诗篇题旨进行注释是不够的，有时还需要对兴辞的背景知识进行专门注释。理雅各的译本正是这样做的。这样一来，译文就颇能让一个严肃的读者顺利完成对《诗经》兴辞全貌的认知和理解。

---

① James Legge. *Chinese Classics with a Translation, Critical and Exegetical Notes, Prolegomena, and Copious Indexes*. London: Henry Frowde, Oxford University Press Warehouse, Amen Corner, E. C., 1939年伦敦会香港影印所影印本，Vol. IV-Part I: 211.

② 同上。

第二节　比的修辞手法及其翻译

与"兴"一样,"比"也是《诗经》中重要的修辞手段。《诗经》中"比"的运用也十分普遍。历史上"比"有几种含义。郑玄《笺》云:"比者,比方于物。诸言如者,皆比辞也。"① 他把句中有"如"字的,都看作比,主要指相当于明喻的"比"。《毛诗正义》云:"比,见今之失,不敢斥言,取比类以言之。"② 既然是"不敢斥言,取比类以言之",那么这里所说的比就是比较隐晦的,可能是言喻体而不言本体,以讽刺时弊。这里刘焯所见到的,主要是相当于隐喻的"比"。另外,钟嵘《诗品》说:"因物喻志,比也。"朱熹《诗集传》云:"比者,以彼物比此物也。"③ 李仲蒙说:"索物以托情谓之比,情附物者也。"④ 这些立义都比较模糊,因此所包含的种类自然也就比较多。明喻、隐喻、借代、比拟等比喻手法皆在其中。当然,朱熹眼里的比,不仅是在词或句的层面,还有篇章层面上的比,也就是通篇比。《诗集传》中通篇标比的诗有22篇。综合历史上各种观点,再从现代修辞学观点来看,《诗经》中的比就相当于明喻、隐喻、借喻、比拟。以下我们按朱熹对"比"的划分标准,分别进行分析。

首先来看通篇比。夏传才(1985:73)认为纯乎比体的诗只有

---

① 孔颖达:《毛诗正义》,北京:北京大学出版社,1999年,第12页。
② 同上,第11页。
③ 朱熹:《诗集传》,北京:中华书局,1958年,第4页。
④ 胡寅:《斐然集(卷十八)·与李叔易书》。

《硕鼠》《鸱鸮》《蠡斯》《鹤鸣》四篇，他称这类诗为比体诗。根据朱熹《诗集传》，《诗经》中通篇用比的诗共有22篇，分别是：《邶风·绿衣》，三章皆比；《邶风·终风》，四章皆比；《邶风·北风》，三章皆比；《卫风·木瓜》，三章皆比；《卫风·有狐》，三章皆比；《王风·兔爰》，三章皆比；《齐风·甫田》，三章皆比；《齐风·敝笱》，三章皆比；《魏风·伐檀》，三章皆比；《魏风·硕鼠》，三章皆比；《唐风·扬之水》，三章皆比；《唐风·鸨羽》，三章皆比；《唐风·有杕之杜》，三章皆比；《唐风·采苓》，三章皆比；《曹风·蜉蝣》，三章皆比；《曹风·下泉》，四章皆比；《豳风·鸱鸮》，四章皆比；《豳风·伐柯》，两章皆比；《小雅·彤弓之什·鹤鸣》，两章皆比；《小雅·祈父之什·黄鸟》，三章皆比；《小雅·都人士之什·白华》，八章皆比，是整个《诗经》中最长的一篇通篇比诗；最后一篇通篇比诗是《小雅·都人士之什·绵蛮》，三章皆称比。

通篇用比的诗，其最大特点是全诗每一章都用比的手法展开。从内容上看，通篇比一般是隐喻，有的以物比物，有的以物比人，有的以人比物。明显的比是比拟者和被比拟者都出现，两者之间有一定相似关系。例如《汉广》第三章：

南有乔木，不可休息。
汉有游女，不可求思。
汉之广矣，不可泳思。
江之永矣，不可方思。

诗的开头两句述说南国有乔木太高，树冠离地太远，无法在下乘凉。后两句述说汉河两侧有交游的女子，虽然身材窈窕娇好，男子却无法追求。这里的比在游女和乔木之间展开，属于以人比物，相当于现代修辞学的比拟。后面四句"汉之广矣，不可泳思。江之永矣，不可方思"则是以汉江之广、之长而"不可泳""不可方"比拟汉水畔上的游女之不可追求。

有的诗确是诗人"见今之失，不敢斥言，取比类以言之"。由于比喻的本体在诗中不出现，不易读出其中的隐喻关系。例如《邶风·北风》：

> 北风其凉，雨雪其雱。
> 惠而好我，携手同行。
> 其虚其邪？既亟只且！
>
> 北风其喈，雨雪其霏。
> 惠而好我，携手同归。
> 其虚其邪？既亟只且！
>
> 莫赤匪狐，莫黑匪乌。
> 惠而好我，携手同车。
> 其虚其邪？既亟只且！

诗中"北风""雨雪""狐""乌"等语辞都是"言北风雨雪，以比国家危乱将至，而气象愁惨也。故欲与其相好之人去而避之"[①]。《毛诗传》云："卫国并为威虐，百姓不亲，莫不相携持而去焉。"[②] 毛亨

---

① 朱熹：《诗集传》，北京：中华书局，1958年，第26页。
② 孔颖达：《毛诗正义》，北京：北京大学出版社，1999年，第171页。

将本诗每章头两行都标为兴辞。郑《笺》云："喻君政教酷暴，使民散乱。"① 这里的比喻关系，委实十分隐晦。

詹宁斯在翻译这首诗时没有对原诗的比做任何调整。后文的"虚"字和"邪"字，《毛诗传》训作"虚，虚也"②。郑《笺》云："邪读如徐。言今在位之人，其故威仪虚徐宽仁者，今皆以为急刻之行矣，所以当去，以此也。"③ 孔颖达《毛诗正义》进一步解释说："我所以去之者，非直为君之酷虐，而在位之臣，虽先日其宽虚，其舒徐，威仪谦退者，今莫不尽为急刻之行，故己所以去之。"④ 按孔颖达的解释，诗的末尾两句是交代原因的，从篇章连贯的角度看，这比较牵强。《诗集传》训为："虚，宽貌。邪，一作徐，缓也。"⑤ 又云："故欲与其相好之人去而避之。且曰是尚可以宽徐乎？彼其祸乱之迫已甚，而去不可不速矣。"⑥ 按朱熹的解释，末两句的主语仍然是前文的"惠而好我"者，与孔氏的解释相比，上下文连贯性较好。程俊英《诗经译注》将其解释为假借："虚：舒的假借字。邪：徐的假借字。其虚其邪，即舒舒徐徐，缓慢犹豫不决的样子。"⑦ 这与朱熹的训诂颇相似。既然理雅各的译文训诂所依据的是《诗集传》，从这个角度看，译文相当忠实：

    Cold blows the north wind;

---

① 孔颖达：《毛诗正义》，北京：北京大学出版社，1999年，第171页。
② 同上，第172页。
③ 同上。
④ 同上。
⑤ 朱熹：《诗集传》，北京：中华书局，1958年，第26页。
⑥ 同上。
⑦ 程俊英：《诗经译注》，上海：上海古籍出版社，2004年，第63页。

Thick falls the snow.

Ye who love and regard me,

Let us join hands and go together.

Is it a time for delay?

The urgency is extreme!

The north wind whistles;

The snow falls and drifts about.

Ye who love and regard me,

Let us join hands, and go away for ever.

Is it a time for delay?

The urgency is extreme!

Nothing red is seen but foxes,

Nothing black but crows.

Ye who love and regard me,

Let us join hands, and go together in our carriages.

Is it a time for delay?

The urgency is extreme! [1]

但是，译文忠实并不意味着容易理解，实际情况往往正好相反。因为本诗的比是对一个历史事件的隐喻，所以对缺乏相应历史知识的

---

[1] James Legge. *Chinese Classics with a Translation, Critical and Exegetical Notes, Prolegomena, and Copious Indexes*. London: Henry Frowde, Oxford University Press Warehouse, Amen Corner, E. C., 1939 年伦敦会香港影印所影印本, Vol. IV-Part I: 67-68.

英美读者来讲,这个比就不可理解。理雅各看到了这一点,所以在文后加上了题解:"Metaphorical. Some one of Wei presses his friends to leave the country with him at once, in consequence of the prevailing oppression and misery",题解之后紧接着又加注:"The first two lines in all the stanzas are a metaphorical description of the miserable condition of the State."。题解和注释的作用是有效地补充译诗中隐藏的逻辑线索。叶维廉(1992:90-100)说,西方诗学有知性传统,诗人对于事物之间的关系的感悟总受到其知性的介入,而无法保持事物的自然状态。看来字里行间的逻辑线索,也是西方读者解诗的命脉。詹宁斯的译文,在处理方法上与理雅各如出一辙:

> Cold north winds are blowing,
>   Heavy falls the snow.
> Friend, thy hand, if thou art friendly!
>   Forth together let us go.
> Long, too long, we loiter here:
> Times are too severe.
>
> How the north wind whistles,
>   Driving snow and sleet!
> Friend, thy hand, if thou art friendly!
>   Let us, thou and I, retreat.
> Long, too long, we loiter here:
> Times are too severe.
>
> Nothing red, but foxes!

Nothing black, but crows!
Friend, thy hand, if thou art friendly!
Come with me—my wagon goes.
Long, too long, we loiter here:
Times are too severe. ①

这篇译诗不仅在语义上相当忠实于原作，而且在风格上也如此。译诗韵律整齐，感情丰沛。但是，若从译文本身的连贯性来看，这个译文在逻辑上仍无法讲通。詹宁斯意识到了这个问题，所以在文后分别为首章和末章的比分别加注为："The opening lines are merely symbolical of the oppressed felt by the people. ""The fox and the crow were regarded as ill omens. "。这样一来，诗中比的喻意被显示出来，在逻辑上就自然充当了后文的原因，整篇诗一下就变得语义通畅可解了。

许渊冲也用注释的方法，使译文获得了较好的效果：

The cold north wind does blow
And thick does fall the snow.
To all my friends I say:
"Hand in hand let us go!
There's no time for delay;
We must hasten our way. "

---

① William Jennings. *The Shi King: The Old "Poetry Classic" of the Chinese*. London and New York: George Routledge and Sons, 1891: 68.

The sharp north wind does blow
And heavy falls the snow.
To all my friends I say
"Hand in hand let's all go!
There's no time for delay;
We must hasten our way."

Red-handed foxes glow;
Their hearts are black as crow.
To all my friends I say
"In my cart let us go!
There's no time for delay;
We must hasten our way."①

译者在译文后加了这样的注释:"The hard-pressed people left the State of Wei in consequence of the prevailing oppression and misery. The first two lines in all the stanzas are a metaphorical description of the miserable condition of the State. Foxes and crows were both creatures of evil omen."。这个注释,综合了理雅各和詹宁斯两个译本的优点,在诗旨、比辞、比喻义三方面进行了有效的注解。

译者如果不识"比"的面目,而将其误当作景物描写,那么这首诗就会文脉不通,很难理解。譬如汪榕培将其译作:

Cold blows the northern wind;

---

① 许渊冲(译):《诗经》,北京:中国对外翻译出版公司,2009年,第40页。

Thick falls the rain and snow.
My family dear, my kin,
Let's take the way and go.
Can't you make up your mind?
It's no time to be slow!

Hard blows the northern wind;
Fast falls the rain and snow.
My family dear, my kin,
In haste now we must go.
Can't you make up your mind?
It's no time to be slow!

Dressed in red is the fox,
Dressed in black the cow.①
My family dear, my kin,
The cart must take us now.
Can't you make up your mind?
It's no time to be slow! ②

译者在文后加注："This poem describes the running away of the common people from their homeland in the northern wind and heavy snow because of the tyranny."。这抹杀了本诗中比的修辞手法，从而译文

---

① cow 疑是拼写错误，从上下文看当为 crow。
② 汪榕培、任秀桦（译注）:《诗经》（中英文版），大连：辽宁教育出版社，1995 年，第 167、169 页。

失去了原来的比喻意义。另外，译诗各章第五行与诗经学训诂不相符，是误译。

韦利的译文也是用直译手法处理了头两句的比，意思比较忠实，但他并不清楚头两句的喻意，或者是不认可经学的传疏，所以后文竟成了一对男女谈情说爱的对话场面。译者自以为这样翻译意思是清楚的，殊不知，其中的隐喻实际上已经阻断了译文的内部逻辑。

Cold blows the northern wind,
Thick falls the snow.
Be kind to me, love me,
Take my hand and go with me.
Yet she lingers, yet she havers!
There is no time to lose.

The north wind whistles,
Whirls the falling snow.
Be kind to me, love me,
Take my hand and go home with me.
Yet she lingers, yet she havers!
There is no time to lose.

Nothing is redder than the fox,
Nothing blacker than the crow.
Be kind to me, love me,
Take my hand and ride with me.

Yet she lingers, yet she havers!
There is no time to lose.①

译文每章头两行与后文的逻辑断层是明显存在的。细心的读者会发出疑问，为什么诗人要在寒风凛冽的日子向一个女子求爱呢？末章里的"fox"和"crow"又有什么作用呢？

在《诗集传》标比的诗篇中，喻意比较隐晦的比辞占多数，其隐晦程度似乎并不亚于其所标的兴辞，大概这也正是《毛诗传》将这些"比"标为"兴"的原因。如《齐风·敝笱》：

敝笱在梁，其鱼鲂鳏。
齐子归止，其从如云。

敝笱在梁，其鱼鲂鱮。
齐子归止，其从如雨。

敝笱在梁，其鱼唯唯。
齐子归止，其从如水。

其中每章开头两句都是比喻。"敝笱在梁，其鱼鲂鳏（其鱼唯唯）"是诗人"以敝笱不能制大鱼"，比喻"鲁庄公不能防闲文姜，故归齐而从之者众也"②。"敝笱在梁"意为破败的渔网废弃在水坝上，比喻鲁国纲纪败坏，淫乱之风盛行；"其鱼鲂鳏"以大鱼都自由自在不为渔网所逮，喻齐襄公与文姜淫乱，从者众多。所喻之事隐在言外。

---

① Arthur Waley. *The Book of Songs*. New York: Grove Press, 1996: 35-36.
② 朱熹：《诗集传》，北京：中华书局，1958 年，第 61 页。

这篇诗理雅各翻译得也相当忠实，但译文却留下了问题：

Worn out is the basket at the dam,
And the fishes are the bream and the *kwan*.
The daughter of Ts'e has returned,
With a cloud of attendants.

Worn out is the basket at the dam,
And the fishes are the bream and the tench.
The daughter of Ts'e has returned,
With a shower of attendants.

Worn out is the basket at the dam,
And the fishes go in and out freely.
The daughter of Ts'e has returned,
With a stream of attendants.①

译文的问题就是每章开头两句与后文究竟有什么关系。译者虽然在文后对题旨进行了加注，却忽视了开头的比辞的比喻意义隐晦而难懂。译文注释是："Metaphorical. The bold licentious freedom of Wan Keang in returning to Ts'e. The preface says, further, that the piece was directed against Duke Hwan of Loo, unable in his weakness to impose any restraint on his wife."。这个注释的不足在于仅靠 metaphorical 一词，

---

① James Legge. *Chinese Classics with a Translation, Critical and Exegetical Notes, Prolegomena, and Copious Indexes*. London: Henry Frowde, Oxford University Press Warehouse, Amen Corner, E. C., 1939 年伦敦会香港影印所影印本，Vol. IV-Part I: 159.

没法让译入语读者了解诗的比喻在哪里，以及比喻义是什么。

詹宁斯就照顾到了译文读者的这一弱点：

> Rent is the fish-trap at the weir,
>   Where bream and sturgeon crowd.
> Ts'i's daughter seeks her former home, —
>   Her escort like a cloud.
>
> No more the fish-trap at the weir
>   Can roach or bream retain.
> Ts'i's child comes back, —and onward sweeps
>   Her escort like the rain.
>
> It fails—the fish-trap at the weir:
> In—out—the fishes gleam.
> Ts'i's child comes back, —and onward flows
>   Her escort like a stream. ①

因为文后注释解释了题旨和"比"的比喻义，这等于帮助读者超越了文化障碍。注释是："After the murder of her husband (see on ode 6), the lady continues her unlawful visits to Ts'i, unrestrained by her son, Duke Chwang. His power over her was no better than that of a broken fish-trap over the fish."。从以上译例来看，当"比"的喻意较隐晦时，针对"比"的喻意在文后专门作注，还是翻译过程中十分重要的一环。

---

① William Jennings. *The Shi King—The Old "Poetry Classic" of the Chinese*. London and New York: George Routledge and Sons, 1891: 117.

《诗经》中有的比喻是本体和喻体都出现,乍看似乎是人与物相比,实则是两事相比。如《齐风·甫田》:

> 无田甫田,维莠骄骄。无思远人,劳心忉忉。
> 无田甫田,维莠桀桀。无思远人,劳心怛怛。
> 婉兮娈兮,总角丱兮。未几见兮,突而弁兮。

这首诗中诗人并非拿"甫田"与"远人"相比,而是把种田太多则生莠草与思念远方之人则空生忧愁之心两事相比,也是隐喻的典型例子。

有的"比"是以物比人,使物具有生命和人的特征。这实际上就是现代修辞学的比拟手法。例如《邶风·终风》前三章:

> 终风且暴,顾我则笑。
> 谑浪笑敖,中心是悼!
>
> 终风且霾,惠然肯来。
> 莫往莫来,悠悠我思!
>
> 终风且曀,不日有曀。
> 寤言不寐,愿言则嚏。

《诗集传》云:"庄公之为人,狂荡暴疾,庄姜盖不忍斥言之,故但以终风且暴为比。"① 在这篇诗中,诗人把庄公比作终风。诗中终风有性格,有行动,有情感,能言笑,完全具有人的特征,属于比拟

---

① 朱熹:《诗集传》,北京:中华书局,1958年,第18页。

的修辞手法。

《小雅·祈父之什·黄鸟》是较为典型的比拟：

> 黄鸟黄鸟，无集于榖，无啄我粟。
> 此邦之人，不我肯榖。
> 言旋言归，复我邦族。
>
> 黄鸟黄鸟，无集于桑，无啄我粱。
> 此邦之人，不可与明。
> 言旋言归，复我诸兄。
>
> 黄鸟黄鸟，无集于栩，无啄我黍。
> 此邦之人，不可与处。
> 言旋言归，复我诸父。

诗人以"黄鸟"比当地恶邻，"黄鸟"是喻体，"此邦之人"是本体。由于这个比喻是把人比作物，所以也可以看作是比拟。这一比拟手法，用"黄鸟"以及"集"和"啄"三个意象，形象地描绘了"此邦之人"的自私、无情、贪婪与数量之众，十分生动。

以上三篇诗，因为比的喻体和本体都出现在了上下文中，即使按照原样来翻译，也不会产生读者理解上的问题。请看理雅各《甫田》译文：

> Do not try to cultivate fields too large;—
> The weeds will only grow luxuriantly.
> Do not think of winning people far away;—
> Your toiling heart will be grieved,

> Do not try to cultivate fields too large;—
> The weeds will only grow proudly,
> Do not think of winning people far away;—
> Your toiling heart will be distressed.
>
> How young and tender
> Is the child with his two tufts of hair!
> When you see him after not a long time,
> Lo! he is wearing the cap! [①]

译者没有为章首的比专门做注释,但译文中的两组比的寓意并不难识别,整章的逻辑畅通,意思也是清楚的。

再看詹宁斯的译文:

> Broad fields plant not,
> Where thrive most the weeds;
> Man's years want not,
> To heartaches it leads.
> Broad fields plant not,
> Or weeds will prevail;
> Man's years want not,

---

① James Legge. *Chinese Classics with a Translation, Critical and Exegetical Notes, Prolegomena, and Copious Indexes*. London: Henry Frowde, Oxford University Press Warehouse, Amen Corner, E. C., 1939 年伦敦会香港影印所影印本, Vol. IV-Part I: 157-158.

For grief 'twill entail.

    Sweet, ay, and pretty,
The twin tufts of hair!
    Soon, ah the pity,
The cap will be there! ①

译者也没有为章首的比加注释，而只在题旨注释之外又为"cap"加了一项有关古代士冠礼的注释："There was a ceremony of capping when the youth arrived at maturity."。这样，整篇诗的意思就十分清楚。

韦利的译文没有加任何注释，译文本身也一样清楚明白：

Do not till too big a field,
Or weeds will ramp it.
Do not love a distant man,
Or heart's pain will chafe you.

Do not till too big a field,
Or weeds will top it.
Do not love a distant man,
Or heart's pain will fret you.

    So pretty, so lovable,

---

① William Jennings. *The Shi King: The Old "Poetry Classic" of the Chinese*. London and New York: George Routledge and Sons, 1891: 116.

With his side-locks looped!
A little while, and I saw him
In the tall cap of a man.

就第一、二章内容来讲，每章的头两行和末两行，由于句式相同，其间的比喻关系，即使是英美读者，也不难读得出来。

我们再看詹宁斯《黄鸟》的译文：

Yellow birds, yellow birds!
　　Do not crowd the tree-tops;
　　Come not pecking our crops. ——
From the folk of this land
　　We no welcoming win;
Up, let us return
　　To our country and kin.

Yellow birds, yellow birds!
　　——Not the mulberry-trees.
　　Come not pecking our maize. ——
With the folk of this land
　　Understanding is vain;
Up, let us return
　　To our brethren again.

Yellow birds, yellow birds!
　　——Nor the thicket of thorn.

> Come not pecking our corn.
>
> With the folk of this land
>
> We can never remain;
>
> Up, let us return
>
> To our fathers again. ①

译者没有在文后为本诗的比加注释，但是读者仍可以看出诗人以鸟之侵人比人之害人的用意。这种比喻对英美读者来说，既是陌生的，又是可理解的，符合比喻的性质，也符合文学语言"陌生化"的特性。

所以，就以上分析可以看出，如果比辞所包含的本体和喻体，一旦在译诗中同时出现，两者之间的相似性，即比的喻意所在就不难发现。有时，比的喻意会在上下文中得以显现。例如，《卫风·木瓜》就是通过第三行"匪报也"，把"木瓜""木桃""木李""琼琚""琼瑶""琼玖"的"友好"的比喻义显现出来。理雅各和詹宁斯分别按不同的诗经学观点翻译了这篇诗，两个译文本身的意思清楚，韵味十足。理雅各按《毛诗传》的政教解释翻译如下：

> There was presented to me a papaya,
>
> And I returned for it a beautiful *keu*-gem;
>
> Not as a return for it,
>
> But that our friendship might be lasting.

---

① William Jennings. *The Shi King: The Old "Poetry Classic" of the Chinese*. London and New York: George Routledge and Sons, 1891: 205.

There was presented to me a peach,
And I returned for it a beautiful *yaou*-gem;
Not as a return for it,
But that our friendship might be lasting.

There was presented to me a plum,
And I returned for it a beautiful *këw*-stone;
Not as a return for it,
But that our friendship might be lasting. ①

詹宁斯明显将此诗当作婚恋诗,其译文是:

Some quinces once to me were sent,
A ruby was my gift again;
Yet not as gift again;—
Enduring love was its intent.

Peaches were sent me; I a stone
Of jasper sent as gift again;
Nay, not as gift again;—
Enduring love it meant alone.

Plums I had sent me; and I sent

---

① James Legge. *Chinese Classics with a Translation, Critical and Exegetical Notes, Prolegomena, and Copious Indexes*. London: Henry Frowde, Oxford University Press Warehouse, Amen Corner, E. C., 1939 年伦敦会香港影印所影印本, Vol. IV-Part I: 107-108.

> A dusky gem for gift again;
> Yet not as gift again;
> But long enduring love it meant.①

在这样的情况下，译者往往不需要进行任何修辞上的调整，只要如法炮制，便可在译文中意味俱获。

如果拿比辞和兴辞的翻译做比较，我们可以发现，由于两者之间有较多共同之处，所以在翻译上遇到的问题有许多是相同或相似的，而在解决方法上也很类似。

第三节 明喻、夸张及其翻译

一、明喻及其翻译

明喻在《诗经》中的应用十分广泛，其比喻词是"如"字。据考查，"如"字在《诗经》四个部分中的应用情况分别是——《国风》61见，《小雅》64见，《大雅》47见，《颂》6见，共178见，使用率较高。明喻有时在一篇诗中连续使用，这可谓《诗经》的一大特色。例如《小雅·天保》："天保定尔，以莫不兴。如山如阜，如冈如陵。如川之方至，以莫不增。""如月之恒，如日之

---

① William Jennings. *The Shi King: The Old "Poetry Classic" of the Chinese*. London and New York: George Routledge and Sons, 1891: 89.

升。如南山之寿，不骞不崩。如松柏之茂，无不尔或承。"又如《卫风·硕人》："手如柔荑，肤如凝脂，领如蝤蛴，齿如瓠犀。"明喻虽然不是《诗经》中使用率最高的修辞手法，却也是重要的修辞方式之一。

由于明喻在中西文学作品中都是常用的修辞手法，比喻意义在上下文中容易理解，所以翻译时比较容易处理，译者一般采用直接翻译的方法。例如《卫风·硕人》中"手如柔荑，肤如凝脂。领如蝤蛴，齿如瓠犀。螓首蛾眉，巧笑倩兮，美目盼兮"，理雅各的译文是由四个完整的句子和两个省略句组成，使用六个"like"把喻体和本体联结起来，意思清楚，形象鲜明：

> Her fingers were like the blades of the young white-grass;
> Her skin was like congealed ointment;
> Her neck was like the tree-grub;
> Her teeth were like melon seeds;
> Her forehead cicada-like; her eyebrows like [the antennae of] the silkworm moth;
> What dimples, as she artfully smiled!
> How lovely her eyes, with the black and white so well defined! [1]

詹宁斯没有使用完整的句子翻译诗行，只用四个介词 as 直接把喻体和本体联结起来，外加两个名词短语，诗行在语言形式上与原文

---

[1] James Legge. *Chinese Classics with a Translation, Critical and Exegetical Notes, Prolegomena, and Copious Indexes*. London: Henry Frowde, Oxford University Press Warehouse, Amen Corner, E. C., 1939 年伦敦会香港影印所影印本，Vol. IV-Part I: 95.

十分相像，意思简洁明快，流畅可读：

> Fingers, as softest buds that grow!
> Skin, as unguent, firm and white!
>   Neek, as the tree-worm's breed!
>   Teeth, as the gourd's white seed!
> Mantis' front, and the silk-moth brow!
> Dimples playing in witching smile;
> Beautiful eyes, so dark, so bright! [①]

许渊冲的译文使用的是完整的句子，其中有的是部分倒装句，有的句子是省略句，同样以"like"联结喻体和本体：

> Like lard congealed her skin is tender,
> Her fingers like soft blades of reed;
> Like larva white her neck is slender,
> Her teeth like rows of melon-seed,
> Her forehead like a dragonfly's,
> Her arched brows curved like a bow.
> Ah! dark on white her speaking eyes,
> Her cheeks with smiles and dimples glow, [②]

---

① William Jennings. *The Shi King: The Old "Poetry Classic" of the Chinese*. London and New York: George Routledge and Sons, 1891: 83.
② 许渊冲（译）：《诗经》，北京：中国对外翻译出版公司，2009年，第57-58页。

韦利的译文使用省略句，喻体和本体用介词"as"和"like"联结：

> Hands white as rush-down,
> Skin like lard,
> Neck long and white as the tree-grub,
> Teeth like melon seeds,
> Lovely head, beautiful brows.
> Oh, the sweet smile dimpling,
> The lovely eyes so black and white. [①]

二、夸张及其翻译

夸张是《诗经》中熟练使用的修辞手法之一。夸张的对象有具体事物，有抽象概念。例如，作者用夸张时间长度的方式表达思念之情，竟成千古绝唱：

> 彼采葛兮，一日不见，如三月兮。
> 彼采萧兮，一日不见，如三秋兮。
> 彼采艾兮，一日不见，如三岁兮。

夸张的手法可以用亦步亦趋的方法来翻译，如韦利的译文：

> Oh, he is plucking cloth-creeper,

---

① Arthur Waley. *The Book of Songs*. New York: Grove Press, 1996: 48.

For a single day I have not seen him;

It seems like three months!

Oh, he is plucking southernwood,

For a single day I have not seen him;

It seems like three autumns!

Oh, he is plucking mugwort,

For a single day I have not seen him;

It seems like three years! ①

许渊冲使用了韵律，也能自然地把夸张手法翻译出来：

To gather vine goes she.

I miss her whom I do not see,

One day seems longer than months three.

To gather reed goes she.

I miss her whom I do not see,

One day seems long as seasons three.

To gather herbs goes she.

I miss her whom I do not see,

One day seems longer than years three. ②

---

① Arthur waley. *The Book of Songs*. London: George Allen & Unwin Ltd, 1969: 61-62.
② 许渊冲（译）:《诗经》，北京：中国对外翻译出版公司，2009年，第74页。

《诗经》中的祝祷辞多用夸张修辞法，共有 14 见。例如《豳风·七月》最后一章：

> 二之日凿冰冲冲，三之日纳于凌阴。
> 四之日其蚤，献羔祭韭。
> 九月肃霜，十月涤场。
> 朋酒斯飨，曰杀羔羊。
> 跻彼公堂，称彼兕觥，万寿无疆！

"万寿无疆"有时说成"万寿无期"，如《小雅·南山有台》：

> 南山有台，北山有莱。
> 乐只君子，邦家之基。
> 乐只君子，万寿无期。
>
> 南山有桑，北山有杨。
> 乐只君子，邦家之光。
> 乐只君子，万寿无疆。

有时也说成"万寿攸酢"，如《小雅·北山之什·楚茨》第三章：

> 执爨踖踖，为俎孔硕，或燔或炙。
> 君妇莫莫，为豆孔庶，为宾为客。
> 献酬交错，礼仪卒度，笑语卒获。
> 神保是格，报以介福，万寿攸酢！

有时还说成"寿考万年",如《小雅·信南山》第三、六章:

> 疆场翼翼,黍稷彧彧。
> 曾孙之穑,以为酒食。
> 畀我尸宾,寿考万年。

夸张的祝祷辞还有另外的表达方式,如《大雅·既醉》:

> 既醉以酒,既饱以德。
> 君子万年,介尔景福。
> 既醉以酒,尔肴既将。
> 君子万年,介尔昭明。
> ……
> 其类维何?室家之壸。
> 君子万年,永锡祚胤。
> 其胤维何?天被尔禄。
> 君子万年,景命有仆。
> ……

又如《大雅·江汉》第五、六章:

> 釐尔圭瓒,秬鬯一卣。
> 告于文人,锡山土田。
> 于周受命,自召祖命。
> 虎拜稽首,天子万年!

> 虎拜稽首，对扬王休。
> 作召公考。天子万寿！
> 明明天子，令闻不已。
> 矢其文德，洽此四国。

"君子万年""天子万年""天子万寿"直接把祝祷的对象说了出来。

《诗经》中常用百、万、亿，乃至万亿、亿亿等这样的数量单位极言事物数量之巨。其第一例出自《秦风·黄鸟》：

> 交交黄鸟，止于棘。谁从穆公？子车奄息。
> 维此奄息，百夫之特。临其穴，惴惴其慄。
> 彼苍者天，歼我良人！如可赎兮，人百其身！
>
> 交交黄鸟，止于桑。谁从穆公？子车仲行。
> 维此仲行，百夫之防。临其穴，惴惴其慄。
> 彼苍者天，歼我良人！如可赎兮，人百其身！
>
> 交交黄鸟，止于楚。谁从穆公？子车鍼虎。
> 维此鍼虎，百夫之御。临其穴，惴惴其慄。
> 彼苍者天，歼我良人！如可赎兮，人百其身！

诗中的"百"字，并非表示确切的数量，而是用来夸大所要表达的意义。"百夫之特"是说其英俊程度百里挑一，"百夫之防""百夫之御"是指鍼虎等三人勇猛过人，"人百其身"意思是人们宁愿失去自己的生命一百次，来换取鍼虎等三人的生命。又如《小雅·北山之什·楚茨》第四章中，诗人使用了"万"和"亿"这样大的数字：

> 我孔熯矣，式礼莫愆。工祝致告，徂赉孝孙。
> 苾芬孝祀，神嗜饮食。卜尔百福，如几如式。
> 既齐既稷，既匡既敕。永锡尔极，时万时亿。

而《周颂·丰年》则更进一步，竟至用了"万亿"和"秭"，即亿亿这样的极端数字：

> 丰年多黍多稌。亦有高廪，万亿及秭。
> 为酒为醴，烝畀祖妣，以洽百礼，降福孔皆。

《毛诗传》曰："数万至万曰亿，数亿至亿曰秭。"[①] 诗中使用的数字夸张，其程度之巨在后世诗歌中都不多见。理雅各翻译时没用相同的数量单位，只是用一串数字单位，以表达"多"之意：

> Abundant is the year, with much millet and much rice;
> And we have our high granaries,
> With myriads, and hundreds of thousands, and millions (of
>   measures in them);
> For spirits and sweet spirits,
> To present to our ancestors, male and female,

---

① 孔颖达：《毛诗正义》，北京：北京大学出版社，1999 年，第 1326 页。

And to supply all our ceremonies.

The blessings sent down on us are of every kind.

詹宁斯在译文中只用了一个简单的"million",似乎觉得语气不足,于是又在文后做了注释。译文如下:

Exuberant is the year!

Of millet and rice what store!

And the corn-lofts high are filled

With million loads and more,

For brewing sweet drinks and strong,

For offerings to our sires

And granddames gone before,

And for all each rite requires.

Ay blessings without end

Of every sort descend. ①

注释为: The numerals are strictly "10, 000, — 100, 000, —to millions."。

韦利在译文中用"myriads"和"millions"来夸张数量之多:

Abundant is the year, with much millet, much rice;

But we have tall granaries,

To hold myriads, many myriads and millions of grain.

---

① William Jennings. *The Shi King: The Old "Poetry Classic" of the Chinese*. London and New York: George Routledge and Sons, 1891: 353.

> We make wine, make sweet liquor,
> We offer it to ancestor, to ancestress,
> We use it to fulfill all the rites,
> To bring down blessings upon each and all. ①

有时诗中的夸张手法形式更加多样化，诗人不仅用数字，还用夸张的比喻来进行描绘，令人印象深刻。如《小雅·甫田》第四章：

> 曾孙之稼，如茨如梁。
> 曾孙之庾，如坻如京。
> 乃求千斯仓，乃求万斯箱。
> 黍稷稻粱，农夫之庆。
> 报以介福，万寿无疆！

方玉润《诗经原始》曰："《甫田》，王者祈年因以省耕也。……至末章极言稼穑之盛，乃后日成效，因'农夫克敏'一言推而言之耳。"②诗人祈求上天保佑后代收获的稼禾堆积得比屋顶高，比桥面宽。"如茨如梁"，孔颖达《毛诗正义》解释为："墨子称茅茨不剪，谓以茅覆屋，故笺以茨为屋盖。传言茨积，非训茨为积也，言其积聚高大如屋茨耳。"又："梁谓水上横桥。桥有广狭，得容车渡，则高广者也，故以比禾积。"③朱熹《诗集传》云："梁，车梁，言其穹

---

① Arthur Waley. *The Book of Songs.* New York: Grove Press, 1996: 297.
② 方玉润:《诗经原始》，北京：中华书局，1986 年，第 436-437 页。
③ 孔颖达:《毛诗正义》，北京：北京大学出版社，1999 年，第 845 页。

隆也。"① 又祈求"庚"能"如坻如京"。关于"京",孔颖达引《释丘》云:"'绝高为之京。'是'京,高丘'也。"② 即祈求"庚"堆积得如水中之沙洲一样多,如陆上之山岗一样高。后文又以"千斯仓""万斯箱"言收获之丰。语言之夸张,用心之虔诚,令人感动。

理雅各在译文中同样使用了明喻和不确定数字进行夸张:

The crops of the distant descendant,

Look [thick] as thatch , and [swelling] like a carriage cover.

The stacks of the distant descendant,

Will stand like islands and mounds.

He will seek for thousands of granaries;

He will seek for myriads of carts.

The millets , the paddy, and the maize,

Will awake the joy of the husbandmen;

[And they will say], 'May he be rewarded with great happiness. '

With myriads of years, life without end!

韦利的夸张方式也与原文十分相似:

The Descendant's crops

Are thick as thatch, tall as a shaft;

The Descendant's stacks

---

① 朱熹:《诗集传》,北京:中华书局,1958 年,第 157 页。
② 孔颖达:《毛诗正义》,北京:北京大学出版社,1999 年,第 845 页。

Are high as cliffs, high as hills.
We shall need thousands of carts,
Shall need thousands of barns,
For millet, rice, and spiked millet;
The laborers are in luck.
"Heaven reward you with mighty blessings!
Long life to you, age unending!" ①

由以上举例看来，作为修辞手法，以数字进行夸张的方式，在英汉两种语言中都是可以行得通的。而有的以数字进行夸张的方式，在译文中并不一定有采用的必要。理雅各和韦利等翻译的祝祷辞"万寿无疆"就是如此。这是因为，这句祝祷辞的意思主要在于长寿，而不在于"万"这一数字本身。

《诗经》还用夸张手法来缩小具体事物的形态，如《卫风·河广》：

谁谓河广？一苇杭之。谁谓宋远？跂予望之。
谁谓河广？曾不容刀。谁谓宋远？曾不崇朝。

"一苇杭之""曾不容刀"两个词句，通过缩小河的宽度和长度，形象地刻画了诗人的思乡之情，获得了生动的艺术效果。

这种反向的夸张，其意义并不难理解，似乎对任何民族的人都不能形成挑战，所以翻译的时候就比较省力，译文读起来也有滋有味。例如詹宁斯的译文：

---

① Arthur Waley. *The Book of Songs*. New York: Grove Press, 1996: 200.

> Who saith the Ho is wide?
> 　　A single rush will span it.
> Who saith that Sung is far?
> 　　On tiptoe I can scan it.
> Who saith the Ho is wide?
> 　　—E'en narrow boats impeding!
> Who saith that Sung is far?
> 　　—Not a morning walk exceeding! ①

诗人极言河之长、之广的语气和含义在译文当中也清晰可见。译文使用"narrow boats"翻译"刀"字,十分准确。由于英语中没有直接对应的词汇,故而用"narrow boats"直接将原来的意思译出,也大致保持了原文的夸张效果。

理雅各的译文读起来更加忠实,只是没有用韵而已:

> Who says that the Ho is wide?
> With [a bundle of] reeds I can cross it.
> Who says that Sung is distant?
> On tiptoe I can see it.
> Who says that the Ho is wide?
> It will not admit a little boat.
> Who says that Sung is distant?
> I would not take a whole morning to reach it.

---

① William Jennings. *The Shi King: The Old "Poetry Classic" of the Chinese*. London and New York: George Routledge and Sons, 1891: 87–88.

诗中逆向夸张之极端,大概在于使用"无"的概念。在这一点上,《郑风·叔于田》中的夸张手法,已经达到了很高的艺术境界:

叔于田,巷无居人。岂无居人?不如叔也,洵美且仁。
叔于狩,巷无饮酒。岂无饮酒?不如叔也,洵美且好。
叔适野,巷无服马。岂无服马?不如叔也,洵美且武。

诗人不从正面直言"叔"对于爱他的女子来说是多么的英俊、豪放和英武,而用"巷无居人""巷无饮酒""巷无服马"三个诗句,来从反面来描绘"叔"无人可比。这种手法对后世文学影响也很大。

詹宁斯的译文与原文稍有不同,但夸张的手法却保留得相当完整:

When Shuh goes to the meet,
There's ne'er a man left in the street.
　　Nay, scarce may that be true, ——
　　Yet none there is like Shuh,
In grace and manliness complete.

When Shuh goes to the chase,
No feasting is there in the place.
　　Nay, scarce may that be true, ——
　　Yet none there is like Shuh,
For right good-fellowship and grace.

When Shuh goes to the plains,

No horsemen are there in the lanes.
Nay, scarce may that be true, —
Yet never one like Shuh,
For grace and dash indeed remains. [①]

不知是为了韵律的缘故，还是因为不了解"田"的涵义，译文中詹宁斯三改措辞，诗义稍有受损。

如果不了解诗中的夸张手法，翻译效果就会彻底遭到破坏。理雅各1876年的译文似乎在努力追求字句上的忠实，同时在韵律上也颇下了番功夫，采用双行韵加抱韵的韵式，译诗中可见得一丝浪漫的诗意：

Shuh has gone hunting;
And in the streets there are no inhabitants.
And there indeed no inhabitants?
[But] they are not like Shuh,
Who is truly admirable and kind.

Shuh has gone to the grand chase;
And in the streets there are none feasting.
And there indeed none feasting?
[But] they are not like Shuh,
Who is truly admirable and good.

---

① William Jennings. *The Shi King: The Old "Poetry Classic" of the Chinese*. London and New York: George Routledge and Sons, 1891: 100.

Shuh has gone into the country;

And in the streets there are none driving about.

Are there indeed none driving about?

[But] they are not like Shuh,

Who is truly admirable and martial.

但是，译者由于不懂诗中的夸张手法，所以未从细节上译出诗人的真意。从译诗来看，叔一旦去狩猎，真的就引得万人空巷，无人再留下饮酒宴乐，也无人再在街上骑马穿行。译者根本没有意识到"叔"在诗人心中至高无上的地位，以及诗人对"叔"的仰慕和怀恋之情。如此经营，译诗被掏成空壳，变得干瘪无味了。

第四节　重章叠唱及其翻译

在《诗经》众多修辞手法中，重章叠唱是比较特殊和应用相对较多的一种。陈望道《修辞学发凡》并没有把重章叠唱列入修辞手法的行列。但是，按照陈望道的修辞学理论，重章叠唱却是作者为了"说得使人明白"和"说得使人感动"而对"形音的利用"，属于典型的积极修辞的范畴。

重章叠唱从形式上看，其特点是每章的行数和内容基本相同，只是在个别行中换用个别同义词，譬如《芣苢》《采葛》《芃兰》等。用重章叠唱手法写成的诗篇在《诗经》中共130篇，占诗篇总数的43%。《国风》中重章叠唱的使用率最高，共104篇。其中，

《周南》中有 6 篇，《召南》9 篇，《邶风》5 篇，《鄘风》6 篇，《卫风》6 篇，《王风》9 篇，《郑风》18 篇，《齐风》6 篇，《魏风》6 篇，《唐风》11 篇，《秦风》7 篇，《陈风》5 篇，《桧风》3 篇，《曹风》3 篇，《豳风》4 篇。《小雅》中重章叠唱的使用率则较低，共 20 篇；《大雅》中数量较少，仅 4 篇。《颂》中更少，仅 2 篇。以上是全篇都用重章叠唱的诗。诗中含部分重章叠唱的诗也占有很高比例，如《关雎》《卷耳》《都人士》等。

重章叠唱虽然讲求各章在形式上相同，内容上相近，但却并非简单地为重复而重复，而是为获取一种一唱三叠，使诗的情感螺旋式上升的艺术效果。据诗经学研究，《诗经》中大部分诗篇最初就是用来吟唱的民歌，歌唱时需要一唱三叠，给人以回肠荡气之感，以深化情感表达。从这个角度来看，重章叠唱当是《诗经》必不可少的重要修辞手法。

从翻译的可能性上来说，重章叠唱还是比较容易翻译的。至于是不是要在译文中翻译这种修辞形式，那就要看译者是否把诗篇当文学作品来翻译，是否承认这种艺术手法的价值。从译本本身来看，詹宁斯和理雅各是重视这一修辞手法的艺术价值的，因此他们把每一篇重章叠唱的诗，都以与原文相同的形式翻译成英文。据我们考查，詹宁斯译本和理雅各译本中重章叠唱诗篇的数量和原文是吻合的。在这一点上，詹宁斯和理雅各都在译文中很好地传达了原文的修辞特色，这对丰富英文诗歌的语言艺术形式无疑是有益的。如果说理雅各是一味地追求忠实，战战兢兢于经典之神圣，詹宁斯则大概是有师人长技的意愿。例如，他翻译的《陈风·月出》（Lover's Chain）读来颇有一唱三叹之情趣：

月出皎兮，佼人僚兮。
舒窈纠兮，劳心悄兮！

月出皓兮，佼人㑣兮。
舒忧受兮，劳心慅兮！

月出照兮，佼人燎兮。
舒夭绍兮，劳心惨兮！

  O moon that climb'st effulgent!
    O ladylove most sweet!
  Would that my ardour found thee more indulgent!
    Poor heart, how dost thou vainly beat!

  O moon that climb'st in splendour!
    O ladylove most fair!
  Couldst thou relief to my fond yearning render!
    Poor heart, what chafing must thou bear!

  O moon that climb'st serenely!
    O ladylove most bright!
  Couldst thou relax the chain I feel so keenly!
    Poor heart, how sorry is thy plight! [①]

  理雅各的无韵体译文也用三章复制了原文形式，不仅准确反映

---

① William Jenning. *The Shi King: The Old "Poetry Classic" of the Chinese*. London and New York: George Routledge and Sons, 1891: 151.

了原诗主题，而且在内容细节上也要比詹宁斯的译文忠实得多。唯一的不足，是译诗中没有用韵。

> The moon comes forth in her brightness;
> How lovely is that beautiful lady!
> O to have my deep longings for her relieved!
> How anxious is my toiled heart!
>
> The moon comes forth in her splendour;
> How attractive is that beautiful lady!
> O to have my anxieties about her relieved!
> How agitated is my toiled heart!
>
> The moon comes forth and shines;
> How brilliant is that beautiful lady!
> O to have the chains of my mind relaxed!
> How miserable is my toiled heart!

我国的两位译者，许渊冲和汪榕培，也做到了在译文中如法炮制重章叠唱的修辞形式。但我们相信，他们和詹宁斯的出发点并不相同。作为中国译者，他们更多的是欣赏祖国的文化，因此愿以白璧相送。例如许渊冲的译文：

> The moon shines bright;
> My love's snow-white.
> She looks so cute.

Can I be mute?

The bright moon gleams;
My dear love beams.
Her face so fair,
Can I not care?

The bright moon turns;
With love she burns.
Her hands so fine,
Can I not pine？①

在语义细节上，译文与原文有很大不同。原文中的"僚""舒窈""纠""劳心""悄""悗""舒忧""受""慅""燎""舒夭""绍"等在译文中都没有充分得到修辞艺术上的体现。虽然译文大致描绘出一幅单相思的生活画面，但相较于原文，其只是一幅素描而已。这说明，若要在译文中获得重章叠唱的修辞效果，译者还需要深入到语义细节中去耐心经营，而不仅是机械地把重章的形式复制下来。

虽然从语言的角度来说重章叠唱是可译的，但译者却不一定去翻译它。庞德就把这种修辞形式彻底抛弃了：

The erudite moon is up, less fair than she
who hath tied silk cords about

---

① 许渊冲（译）:《诗经》，北京：中国对外翻译出版公司，2009 年，第 145-146 页。

　　　　　　　　　　a heart in agony,
She at such ease
　　　so all my work is vain.

My heart is tinder, and steel plucks at my pain
so all my work is vain,
　　　she at such ease
　　　as is the enquiring moon.

A glittering moon comes out
less bright than she the moon's colleague
that is so fair,
　　　of yet such transient grace,
at ease, undurable, so all my work is vain
　　　torn with this pain. ①

当然，庞德所抛弃的还有原文的质地，译文中只剩下了原文所蕴含的诗人的单相思。在这里，我们是无法简单地用对与错，抑或用忠实与背叛来评价庞德的译文。语言上可译而译者不去翻译的东西，不能说是译者所犯的错误，而是他的选择。艺术上的选择是自由的。从译文的内容来看，译者全文所用的意象只有月亮，月亮被译者赋予了人的某种知性和情感，表达了诗人对恋人的相思之情。译者之所以如此，有一种可能是他并没有认识到《诗经》

---

① Ezra Pound: *Poems and Translations*. New York: The Library of America, 2003: 828.

中重章叠唱这一修辞手法及其艺术价值,而更大的可能则是译者借原诗的启发而进行新的诗歌创作——意象主义的诗歌创作。笔者在《庞德〈诗经〉翻译中译古喻今的"现实"原则与意象主义诗学》一文中说:"意象主义原则使他的翻译更具有意象派诗歌的艺术魅力,且对进一步发展和完善其意象主义诗学有重要意义。"(李玉良,2009:94)把庞德的《诗经》翻译说成是意象主义诗歌创作理念的进一步实践和发扬,是符合事实的。当然,从美国诗歌自身发展的角度来看,这种做法无可厚非;但从文化传播的角度来看,这样翻译《诗经》,传播效率是很低的,甚至会误导读者,阻碍其对中国古典文化的认知,不宜提倡。这种做法,也为普遍性翻译规范所不允许。庞德《诗经》译本在美国一直不太受欢迎,大概就是由于这个缘故。

与庞德在翻译中借题发挥,发展英语诗歌艺术的动机相比,阿连璧译的《月出》则又表现出另一种心态,一种文化傲慢和极端的文化保守主义心态。[1]阿连璧在其1891年英译本的前言中说:"在当代中国人看来,理雅各的译文与原文十分对应,很是完美,但作为英语诗歌,就无甚价值可言了。"[2]他在译本的前言中表达了如下主张:

> 对中国人来说,四行一章的四言诗,是一种简单率真的表达方式。而在英语诗中,使用这样的结构则至多是一种特殊

---

[1] 译文见第59页。
[2] Clement F. R. Allen: *The Shih Ching*. London: Kegan Paul, Trench, Trubner & Co., Ltd., 1891: xx.

技法。英语诗需要的是史文朋（Swinburne）先生那样的诗艺，向诗中注入音乐性一类的东西。若略降一格，就是必须改变诗的结构，并用另一种形式对原文进行重写。这就是我一直所遵循的方法。我尽最大的努力把诗译得富有韵律而且使之与诗歌主题和谐一致。如果一首诗是由一句话重复几次组成的，句中变化很小，我就把它压缩成一章。[①]

据考查，阿连璧的确是把所有重章叠唱形式都按照英诗的审美标准改写了（李玉良，2007: 123-140），可见阿氏所言不虚。这样，虽然译诗仍反映了原诗的爱情主题，从音韵到意象再到境界创造都有一定的艺术性，但诗中原有的重章叠唱的独特审美价值所剩无几。从文化交流与传播的角度来说，这样的译文不利于文学的共生与发展。这种过度强调译入语文学规范，并把这种规范强加到翻译作品头上，是对文学多样性的漠视和无知；把文学置入某种形而上学的樊篱，强行令其服从某种固定模式，抹杀原文化本色，这在本质上已经不是一种文学行为，而是一种文化操纵行为，乃至文化政治行为。这种文化自负心理并非罕见，在其驱使下，翻译虽然也或多或少能吸收异域文化的某些长处，但从长远来看，其文化保守性和狭隘性必然会掣肘两种文化艺术之间的交流，阻碍自身文化的正常发展。上世纪后半叶以来，英国国势持续式微，岂非导源于此！

---

① Clement F. R. Allen: *The Shih Ching*. London: Kegan Paul, Trench, Trubner & Co., Ltd., 1891: xx.

第五节　叠词及其翻译

在《诗经》的众多修辞手法当中，还有一种十分独特而重要的修辞手法——叠词。谓其独特，是因为它在我国其他诗歌中应用并不广泛；谓其重要，是因为它在《诗经》中十分普遍。陈望道（2001: 52）在《修辞学发凡》中说：

> 积极修辞却经常崇重所谓音乐的、绘画的要素，对于语辞的声音、形体本身，也有强烈的爱好。走到极端，甚至为了声音的统一或变化，形体的整齐或调匀，破坏了文法的完整，同时带累了意义的明晰。……但在不改动主意的范围内，为了声音或形体的妥适而有种种的经营，却是一种常见的现象，也是一种不必讳言的事实。不必说讲求格律的诗和词，不免有这类经营；就是不讲求格律的散文，有时也不免有这类经营的痕迹。

《诗经》中的叠词，正应了陈先生的这一判断。这种以音乐要素来进行的声音修辞，竟然在古老的《诗经》中就已经大行其道，这不能不为我们所重视和研究。同样，其翻译问题也不能不成为我们关注的对象。

据我们统计，《诗经》中使用叠词的诗篇共有173篇，包括重复出现的叠词在内，共581见，平均每篇诗就有1.91个叠词；若除去重复出现的叠词（语义不同者除外，如"采采卷耳"和"蒹葭采采"),共计 375 种,平均每篇诗里就有 1.23 种新的叠词出现。其中,《国风》66 篇,180 见,合 144 种:《周南》9 篇,32 见,合 19 种;《召南》3 篇,7 见,合 7 种;《邶风》9 篇,16 见,合 14 种;《鄘风》4 篇,11 见,合 6 种;《卫风》6 篇,17 见,合 15 种;《王风》6 篇,23 见,合 11 种;《郑风》5 篇,15 见,合 9 种;《齐风》4 篇,15 见,合 15 种;《魏风》2 篇,4 见,合 2 种;《唐风》3 篇,11 见,合 7 种;《秦风》6 篇,14 见,合 10 种;《陈风》3 篇,7 见,合 7 种;《桧风》2 篇,6 见,合 4 种;《曹风》1 篇,1 见,合 1 种;《豳风》3 篇,12 见,合 9 种。《小雅》57 篇,204 见,合 138 种;《大雅》26 篇,121 见,合 66 种。《颂》21 篇,76 见,合 27 种。①

叠词数量庞大,种类也较多。从词性上分,可主要分为动词和形容词两大类,比如"采采卷耳"中的"采采"是动词,"桃之夭夭"中的"夭夭"是形容词。动词中有的叠词是拟声词,比如"关关雎鸠""大车槛槛""大车啍啍";有的是摹状词,这类动词是用来描写动作形态的,比如"驷介麃麃"。形容词则可以分为摹状形容词、写景形容词、写人形容词等三类。比如,"绿竹猗猗""彼黍离离""鹑之奔奔"是状物形容词,"申伯番番""忧心炳炳"是摹人形容词。

就效果而论,叠词的修辞作用主要有两个方面。其一,叠词可以增强读者听觉上的音乐感;其二,叠词可以给读者以视觉形象,增强诗的形象性和生动性。譬如,《螽斯》是《诗经》中叠词使用率最高的一篇诗,诗中共使用了"诜诜""振振""薨薨""绳绳""揖揖""蛰蛰"等六组叠词,占诗篇总词数的 30.8%。叠词

---

① 《诗经》各篇中的叠词,详见附录三。

的使用，增强了诗的节奏感，使诗篇读起来充满音乐性，尤适于歌唱。而这些叠词还在诗中创造了不同的意象："诜诜"是数量意象，两字叠用，给人以数量众多，成群结队，场面宏大的印象；"绳绳""蛰蛰"则给人以绵延不绝的意象，十分形象逼真，使读者仿佛眼有所见，心有所感。所以，叠词的艺术性和审美价值，不言而喻。

叠词虽然美而独特，翻译却难以曲尽其妙。形容词性叠词尤其如此。例如，擅长音韵翻译的詹宁斯，也只能把《螽斯》翻译到这种程度：

> How do the locusts crowd—
> 　A fluttering throng!
> May thy descendants be
> 　Thus vast, thus strong!
>
> How do the locusts' wings
> 　In motion sound!
> May thy descendants show,
> 　Like them, no bound!
>
> How do the locusts all
> 　Together cluster!
> May thy descendants too
> 　In such wise muster! [①]

[①] William Jennings. *The Shi King: The Old "Poetry Classic" of the Chinese*. London and New York: George Routledge and Sons, 1891: 39.

诗中的"诜诜""振振""薨薨""绳绳""揖揖""蛰蛰"等叠词的声音连缀效果,没有一处被翻译出来。可见,译者只能止于叠词词意的翻译而已。

与形容词性叠词相比,动词性叠词的翻译方法常有所不同,在不少情况下,多少能见得一点原文叠词的韵味。例如,詹宁斯翻译的《芣苢》:

> To gather, to gather the plantain,
>   To gather it in, we go;
> To gather, to gather the plantain,
>   See now we begin, yoho!
>
> We gather, we gather the plantain,
>   Ho this is the way 'tis clipped!
> We gather, we gather the plantain,
>   And so are the seeds all stripped!
>
> We've gathered, we've gathered the plantain,
>   Ho now in our skirts 'tis placed;
> We've gathered, we've gathered the plantain,
>   Now bundled, see, round each waist! [①]

理雅各的翻译因为使用了类似叠词手法,也同样充满了生活气息:

[①] William Jennings. *The Shi King: The Old "Poetry Classic" of the Chinese*. London and New York: George Routledge and Sons, 1891: 41.

We gather and gather the plantains;

Now we may gather them.

We gather and gather the plantains;

Now we have got them.

We gather and gather the plantains;

Now we pluck the ears.

We gather and gather the plantains;

Now we rub out the seeds.

We gather and gather the plantains;

Now we place the seeds in our skirts.

We gather and gather the plantains;

Now we tuck our skirts under our girdles. [①]

理雅各翻译《卷耳》,第一行的"采采",也使用了叠词的手法:

采采卷耳,不盈顷筐。

嗟我怀人,置彼周行。

陟彼崔嵬,我马虺隤。

I was gathering and gathering the mouse-ear,

[①] James Legge. *Chinese Classics with a Translation, Critical and Exegetical Notes, Prolegomena, and Copious Indexes*. London: Henry Frowde, Oxford University Press Warehouse, Amen Corner, E. C., 1939 年伦敦会香港影印所影印本, Vol. IV-Part I: 14-15.

But could not fill my shallow basket.
With a sigh for the man of my heart,
I placed it there on the highway. ①

拟声叠词常常在译文中得以展现。例如《关雎》中的"关关",理雅各翻译成"kwan-kwan",韦利翻译成"fair, fair",庞德翻译成"hid, hid"。再看理雅各翻译的《周南·兔罝》第一章:

Carefully adjusted are the rabbit nets;
Clang clang go the blows on the pegs.
That stalwart, martial man
Might be shield and wall to his prince. ②

但是,这种把各种词重叠的言语方式,在英语诗歌中毕竟不是常态。而汉语的叠词,其意思多能用一个英文单词单独表达,譬如,"营营"(《青蝇》)可以用 buzz 来表达,"槛槛""哼哼"(《大车》)可以用 rumble 来表达。所以一般来说,由于叠词的修辞手法有违英语拼音文字的特性,所以它不可能成为英语诗歌的修辞方式。这就决定了《诗经》中叠词的修辞手法在翻译时基本上无法得以重现。即使可为,也仅是偶然而已。

---

① James Legge. *Chinese Classics with a Translation, Critical and Exegetical Notes, Prolegomena, and Copious Indexes*. London: Henry Frowde, Oxford University Press Warehouse, Amen Corner, E. C., 1939 年伦敦会香港影印所影印本, Vol. IV-Part I: 8.
② 同上。

小　　结

　　从学理上讲，修辞是任何一种语言都必须使用的手法，广义修辞如此，狭义修辞也如此。就狭义修辞来说，修辞是一种语言艺术，其本质诉求是求新和求美。譬如，比喻作为修辞，其生命力在于其创新性，陈旧的比喻是不能为读者带来多少审美价值的。由此可以推断，修辞的翻译有一种内在动力，那就是，如果在译文中引进原文的修辞方式，常常可以为译入语语言文学带来新的生机和活力，因为对读者来说，它们代表着一种新的表达方式和思维方式。修辞作为艺术，也是所有文学文本的特性。因此，对修辞的翻译，也有中外文学文本的修辞艺术共性做基础。然而，尽管如此，要对修辞手法进行翻译，毕竟还有许多障碍。障碍之一是语言上的差异性。在很多情况下，语言上的差异性导致个别修辞手法不可译。譬如，叠词作为《诗经》中经常使用的修辞手法，其在声音重叠和文字重叠的形式方面，在英语中就是无法翻译的；如果要翻译，就只能把重心放到叠词的意义上，而放弃形式上的一致性。障碍之二则是审美习惯上的差异。尽管在每一种语言的文学文本中都有修辞手法，但毕竟其种类有别，两种语言中共同的修辞手法，其可译性更强，因为译文读者在审美习惯上对它是接受的；而两种语言中不同的修辞手法，在翻译时则可能会受到拒斥。如果译者考虑译文读者的审美习惯，并顺从这一习惯，他在翻译过程中就会对原文的修辞手法采取忽略态度，要么在译文中略掉修辞形式，只取其含意，要么在译文中对原来的修辞手法进行修改或替换。譬如《诗经》中的重章叠唱，在英语读者的审美观念中就是一种不受欢迎的修辞方式，所以阿连璧、克拉默宾（Cranmer-byng）、庞德等译者就在各自的译文中将其进行剪裁或整合。所以，修辞的可译性，可以说是建立在语言和文化两者的共性基础之上，并且受到译者翻译态度和翻译目的的直接制约，因而从本质上来说，它是相对的。

第三章 《诗经》韵律翻译的价值与规律

诗歌的翻译在世界范围内开始得很早。佛经中有诗歌，即佛经中的偈语；《圣经》中也有诗歌，那就是赞美诗；而佛经与《圣经》翻译都在两千多年前就开始了。《诗经》与前两者有所不同，但就诗歌翻译来说，其所遇到的问题却是类似的。人们所关心的问题一直是，诗歌翻译中形式和内容的关系是什么？诗的韵律应该如何对待？《诗经》的韵律如果要翻译，应该以什么为标准？翻译时应该采取什么方法和策略？不同的译者对这些问题有不同的看法。本章我们将从文学的基本观点出发，以审美价值为根本依据，通过英汉两种诗歌的对比，从古音韵的角度出发对《诗经》韵律翻译的价值与规律进行讨论。

第一节 中英诗歌的韵律比较

翻译建立在相同性或相似性的基础之上。贺麟（1990）说，翻译之所以可能，是因为"人同此心，心同此理"。人的"心"同，说明其感觉和认知能力也是相同的，所以关于客观世界和人类社会的知识，可以通过翻译来相互交流；另一方面，人心相同，也是指人类所拥有的情感是相同的，即儒家所谓喜、怒、哀、惧、爱、恶、欲。所以，不同民族的语言所表达出的感情，是可以通过翻译得以沟通的。诗歌作为承载和传达思想感情的文学形式，其翻译也需要建立在这一共性基础之上，而且诗歌翻译还需要另一个共性基础，即两种语言文化中诗歌韵律的相似性，以及两个语言文化群体对于韵律在审美情趣上的相似性。基于这种基本认识，我们在讨论《诗经》韵律翻译之前，首先对中英诗歌的韵律进行对比分析。

韵律是中英文诗歌的共同属性之一。英文诗歌的押韵格式主要分为普通诗歌韵式和定型诗歌韵式两大类。普通诗韵式，主要分为三类：双行韵式、隔行交互韵式和抱韵式。定型诗歌韵式也主要有三类：十四行诗体、斯宾塞诗体、回旋诗体。

双行韵式是英语诗歌最基本、最常见的押韵格式。双行诗节又分开放双行诗节和完整双行诗节。开放双行诗节是跨行的双行诗体。例如拜伦（Byron）的《哭吧》（Oh! Weep for Those）：

> Oh! Weep for those that wept by Babel's stream,
> Whose shrines are desolate, whose land a dream:
> Weep for the harp of Judah's broken shell;
> Mourn—where their God hath dwelt the godless dwell!
>
> And where shall Israel lave her bleeding feet?
> And when shall Zion's songs again seem sweet?
> And Judah's melody once more rejoice
> The hearts that leap'd before its heavenly voice?

Tribes of the wandering foot and weary breast,
How shall ye flee away and be at rest!
The wild-dove hath her nest, the fox his cave,
Mankind their country—Israel but the grave!

这些诗行的特点是：首先，每两行押韵；其次，第一行是完整句，第二行要表达的意思跨入下面数行才结束。整首诗的押韵格式就成了 aabbccdd…。

完整双行诗节不仅要求两行诗押韵相同，而且要把意思表达完整。如蒲柏（Alexander Pope）的《温莎森林》（Windsor Forest）的前 20 行：

Thy forests, Windsor! and thy green retreats,
At once the Monarch's and the Muse's seats,
Invite my lays. Be present, sylvan Maids!
Unlock your springs, and open all your shades.
Granville commands; your aid, O Muses, bring!
What Muse for Granville can refuse to sing?

The groves of Eden, vanish'd now so long,
Live in description, and look green in song:
These, were my breast inspired with equal flame,
Like them in beauty, should be like in fame.
Here hills and vales, the woodland and the plain,
Here earth and water seem to strive again;
Not chaos-like, together crush'd and bruised,

> But, as the world, harmoniously confused;
> Where order in variety we see,
> And where, though all things differ, all agree.
> Here waving groves a chequer'd scene display,
> And part admit, and part exclude the day;
> As some coy nymph her lover's warm address
> Nor quite indulges, nor can quite repress.

这段诗是抑扬格五韵步，每两行押韵，每两行的韵不同，其押韵格式为 aabbccddeeff...。

在双行上加一行并与之押韵所形成的诗节叫三行同韵诗节。丁尼生（Alfred Tennyson）的《鹰》（The Eagle）可谓著例：

> He clasps the crag with crooked hands;
> Close to the sun in lonely lands,
> Ring'd with the azure world, he stands.
>
> The wrinkled sea beneath him crawls;
> He watches from his mountain walls,
> And like a thunderbolt he falls.

贝茜·史密斯（Bessie Smith）的"Empty Bed Blues"是用这种韵式写成的一首较长的诗，全诗共 33 行，分为 11 节。请看其前 4 节：

> I woke up this morning with an awful aching head,
> I woke up this morning with an awful aching head,

My new man had left me just a room and an empty bed.

Bought me a coffee grinder, got the best one I could find,
Bought me a coffee grinder, got the best one I could find,
So he could grind me coffee, cause he had a brand new grind.

He's a deep-sea diver with a stroke that can't go wrong.
He's a deep-sea diver with a stroke that can't go wrong.
He can touch the bottom, and his wind holds our so long.

He knows how to thrill me, and he thrills me night and day,
He knows how to thrill me, and he thrills me night and day,
He's got a new way of loving, almost takes my breath away.

如果是三个以上的诗行押同一个韵，就叫作单韵（monorhyme）。例如弗罗斯特（Robert Frost）的《蔷薇科》（The Rose Family）就是一首诗只押一个韵的典型例子：

The rose is a rose,
And was always a rose.
But the theory now goes
That the apple's a rose,
And the pear is, and so's
The plum, I suppose.
What will next prove a rose.
You, of course, are a rose—
But were always a rose.

在我国诗歌中，双行押韵一向就有。自《诗经》开始，在一首诗中，两行同韵的现象就不少见。例如《诗经·卷耳》中就有"陟彼崔嵬，我马虺隤"和"陟彼高冈，我马玄黄"这样的双行押韵的例子。在汉乐府诗《孔雀东南飞》开头一节，就有六对双行押韵的诗行：

> 孔雀东南飞，五里一徘徊。
> 十三能织素，十四学裁衣，
> 十五弹箜篌，十六诵诗书。
> 十七为君妇，心中常苦悲。
> 君既为府吏，守节情不移，
> 贱妾留空房，相见常日稀。
> 鸡鸣入机织，夜夜不得息。
> 三日断五匹，大人故嫌迟。
> 非为织作迟，君家妇难为！
> 妾不堪驱使，徒留无所施，
> 便可白公姥，及时相遣归。

在后代兴起的绝句与律诗中，首行入韵的诗，首联读起来就颇似英语的双行诗。但是，双行押韵的诗歌在我国诗歌传统中只能算作偶然现象，而一直不是我国诗歌的典型韵式。完全用双行韵式写成的汉语诗歌，真可谓凤毛麟角。岑参的《轮台歌奉送封大夫出师西征》虽然不是百分之百地像英文双行体诗，可也算得上是典型一例：

轮台城头夜吹角，轮台城北旄头落。
羽书昨夜过渠黎，单于已在金山西。
戍楼西望烟尘黑，汉兵屯在轮台北。
上将拥旄西出征，平明吹笛大军行。
四边伐鼓雪海涌，三军大呼阴山动。
虏塞兵气连云屯，战场白骨缠草根。
剑河风急雪片阔，沙口石冻马蹄脱。
亚相勤王甘苦辛，誓将报主静边尘。
古来青史谁不见，今见功名胜古人。

有趣的是，《诗经》中有大量的诗篇嵌有双行韵式，双行韵式在诗篇中的浮现率仅次于偶句韵和单韵韵式。比较完整的双行韵诗篇当属《齐风·卢令》，这是《诗经》中唯一通篇使用双行韵写成的诗，其韵式是 aabbcc，酷似英诗的双行韵，但与英诗的不同之处是，每组双行韵属于不同的诗章：

卢令令（lyen），其人美且仁（njien）。
卢重环（hoan），其人美且鬈（giuan）。
卢重锊（muə），其人美且偲（tsə）。

至于三行同韵，虽然其并非我国诗歌的常见韵式，但在《诗经》中也已经使用过。例如《豳风·九罭》：

九罭之鱼鳟鲂（biuang）。
我觏之子，

衮衣绣裳（zjiang）。

鸿飞遵渚（tjia），
公归无所（shia），
于女信处（thjia）。

鸿飞遵陆（liuk），
公归不复（biuk），
于女信宿（siuk）！

是以有衮衣（iəi）兮，
无以我公归（kiuəi）兮，
无使我心悲（pəi）兮！

整首诗每行都押同一个韵，在我国诗歌中是几乎没有的。有一种押通韵的诗，仅是偶数行从头至尾押同一个韵。在《诗经》里可以找到一章内押一个韵的例子。如《国风·出其东门》：

出其东门（muən），有女如云（hiuən）。
虽则如云（hiuən），匪我思存（dzuən）。
缟衣綦巾（kiən），聊乐我员（hyuən）。
出其闉阇（ta），有女如荼（da）。
虽则如荼（da），匪我思且（tzia）。
缟衣茹藘（lia），聊可与娱（ngiua）。

根据王力《诗经入韵字音表》，这篇诗的第一章押文部韵，第二章押鱼部韵，每章押一个单韵。

单韵诗数量不多，宋词里也很少能找到自始至终一韵到底的词，只是偶尔见得一两首而已。如周密的《四字令·眉消睡黄》：

眉消睡黄。春凝泪妆。
玉屏水暖微香。听蜂儿打窗。
筝尘半妆。绡痕半方。
愁心欲诉垂杨。乃红飞正忙。

无名氏写的《长相思》，读起来更加活泼：

去年秋，今年秋，湖上人家乐复忧。西湖依旧流。
吴循州，贾循州，十五年前一转头。人生放下休。

虽然韵律没有律诗那么整齐和严格，但也算得上是一种单韵了。

在英语诗歌中，比双行韵式使用率稍低的，是隔行韵式。隔行韵又称交叉韵，其格式为abab。这种韵式一般用于四行诗节，其基本特征就是单数行和双数行分别押韵。如罗伯特·彭斯（Robert Burns）的《麦田有好埂》（Corn Rigs Are Bonie）第一诗节：

It was upon a Lammas night,
When corn rigs are bonie,
Beneath the moon's unclouded light,
I held awa ato Annie:
The time flew by, wi' tentless head,
Till, 'tween the late and early;

> Wi' sma' persuasion she agreed,
> To see me thro' the barley.

这种押韵格式来自双行诗节的押韵格式，是双行诗节的变体。隔行韵本身也同样存在变体，形成另外一种格式，即单数行可以不押韵。例如，弗罗斯特（Froster）的《取水》（Going for Water）第一、二节：

> The well was dry beside the door,
> And so we went with pail and can
> Across the fields behind the house
> To seek the brook if still it ran;
>
> Not loth to have excuse to go,
> Because the autumn eve was fair
> (though chill), because the fields were ours,
> And by the brook our woods were there.

读着这样的英文诗，令人不禁联想到我国绝句和律诗的韵式。因为这一韵式正好与我国自《诗经》以来的传统韵律相吻合，尤其与隋唐以来兴起并流行的绝句和律诗的韵律相一致。所以，有了英语诗歌这一典型韵式，就比较容易把汉语诗歌的内容和形式一同翻译给西方读者，并为西方读者所喜闻乐见。

英语诗歌中第三种常见的韵式是抱韵，其典型韵式为abba，即每节第一诗行与第四诗行押韵，第二诗行和第三诗行押韵。例如，济慈（John Keats）《咏大海》（On the sea）的一、二两节：

It keeps eternal whisperings around
　　Desolate shores, and with its mighty swell
　　Gluts twice ten thousand caverns, till the spell
Of Hecate leaves them their old shadowy sound.

Of 'tis in such gentle temper found
　　That scarcely will the very smallest shell
　　Be moved for days from where it sometime fell,
When last the winds of heaven were unbound.

　　抱韵也可以用于三行诗节，格式为 aba。这样的诗行叫抱韵三行诗节。例如，毕晓普（Elizabeth Bishop）的《一门艺术》（One Art）的第一、第二诗节：

The art of losing isn't hard to master;
so many things seem filled with the intent
to be lost that their loss is no disaster,

Lose something every day. Accept the fluster
of lost door keys, the hour badly spent.
The art of losing isn't hard to master.

　　第四种常见韵式当属链韵式又名连锁韵，是英语诗歌中较为复杂的押韵格式，主要用于四行诗节或三行诗节。其特征是一个诗节中的某一行诗用于链接下一个诗节中某一行诗的韵。雪莱（Percy Bysshe Shelley）的《西风颂》（Ode to the West Wind）便是用链韵写成的，其第四段如下：

If I were a dead leaf thou mightiest bear;
If I were a swift cloud to fly with thee;
A wave to pant beneath thy power, and share

The impulse of thy strength, only less free
Than thou, O Uncontrollable! If even
I were as in my boyhood, and could be

The comrade of thy wanderings over Heaven,
As then, when to outstrip thy skiey speed
Scarce seem'd a vision; I would ne'er have striven

As thus with thee in prayer in my sore need.
O! life me as a wave, a leaf, a cloud!
I fall upon the thorns of life! I bleed!

A heavy weight of hours has chained and bowed
One too like thee: tameless, and swift, and proud.

前四个诗节的押韵格式为 aba bcb cdc ded，每个诗节单独来看都是抱韵，而且每个诗节的中间诗行成为链接诗行，它与下一诗节的首尾两诗行押尾韵，这样，所有诗行就被链接起来。

除了以上四种基本韵式外，还有复合韵式。以上四种基本押韵格式都与二行、三行和四行诗节联系在一起。有时，一个诗节会有五个或五个以上诗行，甚至有多达十个诗行，这时就会出现两种或两种以上的押韵格式的组合。例如，华兹华斯（William

Wordsworth)的《我独自漫游,犹如一朵云》(I Wandered Lonely as a Cloud)就很典型:

I wondered lonely as a cloud
That floats on high o'er vales and hills,
When all at once I saw a crowd,
A host, of golden daffodils;
Beside the lake, beneath the trees,
Fluttering and dancing in the breeze.

Continuous as the stars that shine
And twinkle on the Milky Way,
They stretched in never-ending line
Along the margin of a bay:
Ten thousand saw I at a glance,
Tossing their heads in sprightly dance.

The waves beside them danced, but they
Outdid the sparking waves in glee: —
A Poet could not but be gay
In such a jocund company:
I gazed—and gazed—but little thought
What wealth the show to me had brought.

For oft, when on my couch I lie
In vacant or in pensive mood,
They flash upon that inward eye

> Which is the bliss of solitude,
> And then my heart with pleasure fills,
> And dances with the daffodils.

每个诗节中的押韵格式为ababcc，而各节之间又互不相同。这是隔行押韵的变体形式，也可以说前四行是隔韵式，后两行是双行韵式，所以是隔韵式和双行韵式的复合韵式。

  复合韵式写成的诗节，很多达到了八九行。拜伦（Byron）的《唐璜与海蒂》（Don Juan and Haidee）整篇都是用八行复合韵式写成的。例如第一节：

> As they drew night the land, which now was seen
>   Unequal in its aspect here and there,
> They felt the freshness of its growing green,
>   That waved in forest-tops, and smooth'd the air,
> And fell upon their gazed eyes like a screen
>   from glistening waves, and skies so hot and bare—
> Lovely seem'd any object that should sweep
> Away the vast, salt, dread, eternal deep.

这一节的复合韵式为abababcc。前四行是隔行韵式，最后两行诗双行韵式。

  九行诗节以斯宾塞诗节（Spenserian stanza）为典型代表，这是斯宾塞（Edmund Spenser）在长诗《仙后》（Faerie Queen）中创造的一种诗节。以下是《仙后》第一章的第一诗节：

Gentle Knight was pricking on the plaine,

Ycladd in mightie armes and silver shielde,

Wherein old dints of deepe wounds did remaine,

The cruell markes of many a bloudy fielde;

Yet armes till that time did he never wield:

His angry steede did chide his foming bitt,

As much disdayning to the curbe to yield:

Full jolly knight he seemd, and faire did sitt,

As one for knightly giusts and fierce encounters fitt.

这种诗节的押韵格式是 ababbcbcc，是在隔行韵和链接韵基础上发展起来的。斯宾塞的这种九行诗节押韵格式后来被逐渐固定下来，后人称其为斯宾塞诗节。

但是，也有很多九行诗节的韵式比较随便，如菲利普·拉金（Philip Larkin）的《上教堂》（Church Going）就是这样的一首诗。全诗共七节，其每节的复合韵式都不相同。开头两节如下：

Once I am sure there's nothing going on

I step inside, letting the door thud shut.

Another church: matting, seats, and stone,

And little books; sprawlings of flowers, cut

For Sunday, brownish now; some brass and stuff

Up at the holy end; the small neat organ;

And a tense, musty, unignorable silence,

Brewed God knows how long. Hatless, I take off

My cycle-clips in a awkward reverence,

Move forward, run my hand around the font.
From where I stand, the roof looks almost new—
Cleaned or restored? Someone would know: I don't.
Mounting the lectern, I peruse a few
Hectoring large-scale verses, and pronounce
"Here endeth" much more loudly than I'd meant.
The echoes snigger briefly. Back at the door
I sign the book, donate an Irish sixpence,
Reflect the place was not worth stopping for.

这首诗每个诗节都用 ababcdece 韵式，前四行是规范的隔行押韵，最后五行是隔行韵式的变体，或隔两行押韵，或隔一行押韵。这种组合是比较自由的。这种自由韵式颇像我国《诗经》里的诗，大部分韵式都比较自由，经常一章中韵式有几次转换。例如，《豳风·七月》第二节：

七月流火（xuəi），
九月授衣（iəi）。
春日载阳（jiang），
有鸣仓庚（keang）。
女执懿筐（khiuang），
遵彼微行（heang），
爰求柔桑（sang）。

春日迟迟（diei），
采蘩祁祁（giei）。
女心伤悲（pəi），
殆及公子同归（kiuəi）。

该诗韵式是 aabbbbbccaa，即一、二两句押双行韵，三至七句押单韵，最后两句又押双行韵。

十行诗节没有固定的押韵格式，但大多数是从基本押韵格式上变化而来。例如济慈《夜莺颂》（Ode to a Nightingale）的第四诗节：

>   Away! Away! For I will fly to thee,
>   Not charioted by Bacchus and his pards,
>   But on the viewless wings of Poesy,
>   Though the dull brain perplexes and retards:
>   Already with thee! Tender is the night,
>   And haply the Queen—Moon is on her throne,
>   Cluster'd around by all her starry Fays;
>   But here there is no light,
>   Save what from heaven is with the breezes blown
>   Through verdurous glooms and winding mossy ways.

这个诗节的韵式是 ababcdecde，前四行押隔行韵，后六行也押隔行韵，但隔的是两行而非一行。

在我国诗歌中，唐诗只有律诗和绝句，分别有八行和四行诗句。八行以上且韵式有些规律的诗，《诗经》《楚辞》和古诗十九首及汉乐府诗中反倒不少，如《诗经·雅》中的诗篇，大多都是长诗。唐以后则有宋词和元曲，词牌或曲牌不同，词的行数和韵式各不相同，其韵式在数量上远远超过了英语诗歌。有些宋词行数则超过了十行，且在意思上有跨行现象，如苏轼《定风波》：

> 莫听穿林打叶声，
> 何妨吟啸且徐行。
> 竹杖芒鞋轻胜马，
> 谁怕？
> 一蓑烟雨任平生。
>
> 料峭春风吹酒醒，
> 微冷，
> 山头斜照却相迎。
> 回首向来萧瑟处，
> 归去，
> 也无风雨也无晴。

《一剪梅》的词是十二行。如李清照《一剪梅》：

> 红藕香残玉簟秋，
> 轻解罗裳，
> 独上兰舟。
> 云中谁寄锦书来？
> 雁字回时，
> 月满西楼。

花自飘零水自流,
一种相思,
两处闲愁。
此情无计可消除,
才下眉头,
却上心头。

宋词的韵式比唐诗灵活许多,但其基本韵式仍是双行或隔行押韵的变体。有不少词行数较多,韵式也更加复杂。如周邦彦的《夜飞鹊》长达23行:

河桥送人处,
良夜何其?
斜月远堕余辉。
铜盘烛泪已流尽,
霏霏凉露沾衣。
相将散离会,
探风前津鼓,
树杪参旗。
花骢会意,
纵扬鞭,
亦自行迟。

迢递路回清野,
人语渐无闻,
空带愁归。

何意重经前地，

遗钿不见，

斜径都迷。

兔葵燕麦，

向残阳，

影与人齐。

但徘徊班草，

欷歔酹酒，

极望天西。

这首词的押韵更加灵活，其韵脚皆是相似韵，包括"其""辉""衣""会""旗""意""迟""归""地""迷""齐""西"等。其中"辉"韵与其他诸字的韵相差最大，整体上该词的韵式也是隔行韵式的变体。

通过以上比较可见，中西诗歌的基本韵律格式都是隔行押韵和双行押韵，并在此基础上衍生出诸多变体。从韵式的总数上来看，英语诗歌不过十数种，而汉语诗歌，若说唐诗仅有偶数行押韵的典型格式，那么，仅是宋词，其不同的词牌名就有800多个，元曲则分为15宫调，共447支曲牌。词牌名、曲牌名不同，韵式就有别。所以，诗、词、曲、赋各种诗歌加到一起，其韵式则逾千种。然而，尽管不同诗体整体韵式千差万别，这些不同诗体中所用的基本韵式却是相同的，不外乎隔行押韵和双行押韵。所以，从音韵的角度和读者接受的角度来看，中西诗歌之间是可以翻译的。

当然，随着诗歌的不断向前发展，无韵诗早已经产生，所以诗歌翻译并没有必要一律以有韵诗译有韵诗，有韵诗完全可以翻译成无韵诗，关键是要看译者的价值取向如何。

第二节 《诗经》的韵律

在我国诗经学历史上，研究《诗经》音韵的学者并不多。宋朝朱熹曾经对《诗经》的韵律进行研究，并创叶韵说，结果证明是错误的。明朝经学家陈第，第一个反对叶韵说。陈第写过一部《毛诗古音考》，是关于《诗经》韵律的第一部研究论著。深入而全面的《诗经》韵律研究，当属王力先生的《诗经韵读》。王力先生认为，朱熹的叶韵说有四种错误，其"理论的错误是缺乏历史观造成的"（王力，1980：3）。夏传才在《诗经语言艺术》一书中也用了三章的内容来探讨《诗经》的韵律问题。他认为，《诗经》所用的都是自然韵律，即所有诗篇的韵律，都是随着感情起伏而自然呈现出来的，没有丝毫斧凿的痕迹。

那么，《诗经》的韵律究竟是怎样的呢？由于《诗经》的历史久远，今天，我们仅从字面上已经无法看到其音韵的本来面貌，要真正认识其韵律，必须借助考古的方法和审音的方法，从古音韵角度去判断，而不能根据字的当代读音去判断诗篇的韵律。根据王力先生的研究，《诗经》305篇诗中，除了《周颂》八篇全章无韵外，其他297篇全部是有韵诗，只是部分诗篇，如《豳风》中的《鸱鸮》、《大雅》中的《常武》《召旻》、《周颂》中的《烈文》《我将》《臣工》《维天之命》《访落》《有客》《小毖》《载芟》《良耜》等诗篇中的部分诗句无韵而已。按照王力先生的划分方法，《诗经》的韵律有11种：偶句韵、首句入韵、句句用韵、交韵、抱韵、疏韵、遥韵、叠韵、回环、尾声、无韵。其实，这11种韵律并不是就一篇诗整体而言的，而是就诗的局部而言存在这11种韵律形式。而就整篇诗而论，比较纯粹的偶句韵诗有 93 篇，其中包括首行入韵的偶句韵诗 18 篇。全诗通押单韵的共 16 篇。其他诗篇则主要是由偶句韵、单韵、双行韵、交韵、抱韵、疏韵、遥韵、尾声等这些基本韵式复合而成。而在复合韵式的诗篇中，浮现率最高的四种韵式依次分别是偶句韵、单韵、双行韵、交韵、抱韵。下面就其中几种主要韵式分别进行论述。

（一）偶句韵

偶句韵是《诗经》中最常见的韵式，其对中国诗歌韵律的影响也是最大的。隋唐以后的律诗和绝句，采用的基本都是偶句押韵的韵式。例如《邶风·柏舟》第一章：

> 耿耿不寐，如有隐忧（iu）。
> 微我无酒，以敖以游（jiu）。

（二）首句入韵

在《诗经》中，首句入韵的诗篇相当普遍，这种韵式后来成为唐诗中律诗和绝句的重要押韵格式。例如《郑风·风雨》：

> 风雨凄凄（tsyei），
> 鸡鸣喈喈（kei）。
> 既见君子，
> 云胡不夷（jiei）！
>
> 风雨潇潇（syu），
> 鸡鸣胶胶（keu）。
> 既见君子，

云胡不瘳（thiu）！

风雨如晦（xuə），
鸡鸣不已（jiə）。
既见君子，
云胡不喜（xiə）！

此诗共三章，每章四句。第一章的韵脚为 ei，第二章的韵脚为 u，第三章的韵脚为 ə，三章的首句都分别入韵，韵律十分整齐。

再如《小雅·正月》共十三章，基本上每章一个韵脚（只有第十二章中间有换韵现象）。如第一章：

正月繁霜（shiang），我心忧伤（sjiang）。
民之讹言，亦孔之将（tziang）。
念我独兮，忧心京京（kyang）。
哀我小心，瘋忧以痒（jiang）。

本章八句，韵脚为 ang，首句"霜"字即已入韵，偶数行皆押 ang 韵。

（三）句句用韵和单韵

《诗经》许多诗篇每句都用韵。这样可以出现两种情况：一是同一章内形成交韵，即单数行和双数行分别押不同的韵，形成章内交韵；二是同一章内都押一个单韵。例如，《邶风·终风》第一章押章内交韵：

终风且暴（bôk），顾我则笑（siô）。
谑浪笑敖（ngô），中心是悼（dôk）！

又如《召南·野有死麕》第二章押章内单韵：

> 林有朴樕（sok），野有死鹿（lok）。
> 白茅纯束（sjiok），有女如玉（ngiok）。

此章四句，首行即入韵，韵脚均为 ok 韵，均属屋部。

（四）交韵

在每句都用韵的诗篇中，如果诗行的韵脚押的不是单韵，那就是交韵。交韵有三种情形，一种是纯交韵，即一章有四句、六句或八句，章内单数行与偶数行分别押韵。例如《召南·野有死麕》首章：

> 野有死麕（kyuən），白茅包（peu）之。
> 有女怀春（thjiuən），吉士诱（jiu）之。

此章四句，单数行押 uən 韵，属文部；偶数行押 eu 韵，其中 eu 与"诱"协音，同属幽部。

《诗经》中使用最为典型的纯粹交韵的韵例是《周南·兔罝》：

> 肃肃兔罝（tzia），椓之丁丁（teng）。
> 赳赳武夫（piua），公侯干城（zjieng）。
>
> 肃肃兔罝（tzia），施于中逵（giu）。
> 赳赳武夫（piua），公侯好仇（giu）。
>
> 肃肃兔罝（tzia），施于中林（liəm）。
> 赳赳武夫（piua），公侯腹心（siəm）。

全诗共三章，交韵的韵式如下：第一章，雨部—耕部—鱼部—耕部；第二章，鱼部—幽部—鱼部—幽部；第三章，鱼部—侵部—鱼部—侵部。其中，"罝"与"夫"协音，属鱼部；"丁"（teng）与"城"协音，属耕部；"逵"与"仇"协音，属幽部；"林"与"心"协音，属侵部。这样，就形成了整齐的纯交韵韵式。

第二种是复交韵，一般是一章中两个以上的交韵重叠在一起而成。例如《邶风·谷风》首章：

习习谷风（piuən），以阴以雨（hiua）。
黾勉同心（siəm），不宜有怒（na）。
采葑采菲（phiuəi），无以下体（thyei）。
德音莫违（hiuəi），及尔同死（siei）。

本章韵式为：侵部—鱼部—侵部—鱼部—微部—脂部—微部—脂部。其中，"风"与"心"协音，同属侵部；"雨"与"怒"协音，同属鱼部；"菲"与"违"协音，同属微部；"体"与"死"协音，同属脂部。

第三种是不完全交韵。这种情形是指一个诗章只有一部是交韵的。例如《王风·黍离》：

彼黍离离（liai），彼稷之苗（miô）。
行迈靡靡（miai），中心摇摇（jiô）。
知我者谓我心忧（iu），不知我者谓我何求（giu）。
悠悠苍天（thyen），此何人（njien）哉！

彼黍离离（liai），彼稷之穗（ziuet）。

行迈靡靡（miai），中心如醉（tziuət）。

知我者谓我心忧（iu），不知我者谓我何求（giu）。

悠悠苍天（thyen），此何人（njien）哉！

彼黍离离（liai），彼稷之实（djiet）。

行迈靡靡（miai），中心如噎（yet）。

知我者谓我心忧（iu），不知我者谓我何求（giu）。

悠悠苍天（thyen），此何人（njien）哉！

全诗共三章，每章只有开头四句是交韵，且韵式各有所不同。第一章，歌部—宵部—歌部—宵部；第二、三章，歌部—质部—歌部—质部。其中"离"与"靡"协音，同属歌部。

（五）双行韵

《诗经》中双行韵的浮现率是相当高的，但是通篇使用双行韵的诗却是凤毛麟角，《齐风·卢令》可谓是绝无仅有：

卢令令（lyen），其人美且仁（njien）。

卢重环（hoan），其人美且鬈（giuan）。

卢重鋂（muə），其人美且偲（tsə）。

《国风》中使用双行韵的诗篇似乎并不太多，越是到了《小雅》之后，双行韵式浮现率越是趋高。《小雅》中有 17 篇诗使用双行韵，《大雅》中有 13 篇诗使用双行韵，《颂》中有 12 篇使用双行韵。从而双行韵成为《诗经》比较常用的韵律形式之一。例如《小雅·车辖》第一章：

间关车之牽（heat）兮，
思娈季女逝（zjiat）兮。
匪饥匪渴（khat），
德音来括（kuat），
虽无好友（hiuə），
式燕且喜（xiə）。

（六）抱韵

在《诗经》中，抱韵的例子并不多，但却是一种重要的韵式，表明抱韵在我国的诗歌中也有着古老的历史渊源。抱韵可以细分为两种表现形式：一个是纯抱韵，即一章中一、四句押一种韵，二、三句押另一种韵，两韵相异；另一个是准抱韵，即六句押两韵，或者是第二句起韵，到第五句押韵。例如，《周颂·思文》以下四句就是纯抱韵：

思文后稷（tziək），
克配彼天（thyen）。
立我烝民（mien），
莫匪尔极（giək）。

一、四句押职部韵，二、三句押真部韵。再如，《大雅·大明》中的以下四句：

有命自天（thyen），
命此文王（hiuang），

于周于京（kyang）。
缵女维莘（shen），

一、四句押真部韵，二、三句押阳部韵。

《诗经》中部分用纯抱韵的例子很少，而整篇诗都用纯抱韵的例子就完全寻不得了。

《大雅·抑》中的这一章是准抱韵的典型例子：

如彼泉流，无沦胥以亡（miuang）。
夙兴夜寐（muət），
洒扫廷内（nuət），
维民之章（tjiang）。

本章从第二句起阳部韵，与第五句的章字押阳部韵。"寐"和"内"押物部韵。

（七）疏韵

《诗经》最常见的是隔句用韵，其次是句句用韵。也有许多诗篇是隔两句才用韵，这种韵式称作疏韵。疏韵可以分为两种形式：一种是第三句才开始用韵，叫作"三句起韵"；另一种是章内疏韵。例如《大雅·卷阿》第七、八章：

凤皇于飞，
翙翙其羽，
亦集爰止（tjiə）。
蔼蔼王多吉士（dzhiə），

维君子使（shiə），
媚于天子（tziə）。

凤皇于飞，
翙翙其羽，
亦傅于天（thyen）。
蔼蔼王多吉人（njien），
维君子命（myen），
媚于庶人（njien）。

第七章自第三句起之部韵，自第四句至第六句押韵。第八章自第三句起真部韵，自第四句至第六句均押韵。再如《大雅·桑柔》最后一章：

民之未戾，
职盗为寇。
凉曰不可（khai），
覆背善詈（liai）。
虽曰匪予，
既作尔歌（kai）。

本章自第三句起歌部韵，此后至第六句押歌部韵。又如《大雅·烝民》第六章：

人亦有言，
德輶如毛，

民鲜克举（kia）之。
我仪图（da）之，
维仲山甫举（kia）之，
爱莫助（dzhia）之。
衮职有阙，
维仲山甫补（pua）之。

本章自第三句起鱼部韵，第四、五、六、八句皆押鱼部韵。

章内疏韵是隔句入韵，或首句即入韵，中间两句不押韵，而在后面的末句押韵。例如《大雅·韩奕》第二章：

四牡奕奕，
孔修且张（tiang）。
韩侯入觐，
以其介圭，
入觐于王（hiuang）。

第二句用阳部韵，隔两句后，第五句押阳部韵。

（八）遥韵

《诗经》中有不少重章叠唱现象，所以有一种韵是在两章之间遥相呼应的，王力先生将其称作遥韵。遥韵的基本模式是在不同诗章的同一个位置上押韵，可以是在章末尾，也可以是在章开头。例如《周南·麟之趾》，每一章内部头两句分别押之部和耕部韵，每章末尾韵脚押真部韵。

麟之趾（tjiə）。
振振公子（tziə），
于嗟麟（lien）兮！

麟之定（dyeng）。
振振公姓（sieng），
于嗟麟（lien）兮！

麟之角（keok）。
振振公族（dzok），
于嗟麟（lien）兮！

再如《王风·君子阳阳》两章，章内头三句分别押阳部和幽部韵，每章末押鱼部韵：

君子阳阳（jiang），
左执簧（huang），
右招我由房（biuang），
其乐只且（tzia）！

君子陶陶（du），
左执翿（du），
右招我由敖（ngô），
其乐只且（tzia）！

（九）叠韵

《诗经》不少诗篇有章内诗句重复或部分重复的现象，由重复而产生的押韵称为叠韵。例如《王风·葛藟》：

绵绵葛藟，在河之浒（xa）。
终远兄弟，谓他人父（biua）。
谓他人父（biua），亦莫我顾（ka）！

绵绵葛藟，在河之涘（zhiə）。
终远兄弟，谓他人母（mə）。
谓他人母（mə），亦莫我有（hiuə）！

绵绵葛藟，在河之漘（djiuən）。
终远兄弟，谓他人昆（kuən）。
谓他人昆（kuən），亦莫我闻（miuən）！

三章中"谓他人父""谓他人母""谓他人昆"分别进行重复，分别押鱼部、之部和文部韵，从而形成叠韵。

诗句重复，如果句中的字不完全相同，也可以形成叠韵。例如《秦风·黄鸟》：

交交黄鸟，
止于棘（kiək）。
谁从穆公？
子车奄息（siək）。
维此奄息（siək），
百夫之特（dek）。
……

交交黄鸟,

止于桑(sang)。

谁从穆公?

子车仲行(hang)。

维此仲行(hang),

百夫之防(biuang)。

……

交交黄鸟,

止于楚(tshia)。

谁从穆公?

子车铖虎(xa)。

维此铖虎(xa),

百夫之御(ngia)。

……

三组诗行中"奄息""仲行""铖虎"分别在相邻诗句中重复,分别押职部、阳部和鱼部韵,从而形成叠韵。

(十)回环

回环是指在不同诗章中相同的字句反复出现。回环是《诗经》的特色,也是一种音韵美。这种回环往往与韵律发生关系。例如《召南·甘棠》:

蔽芾甘棠,勿翦勿伐(biuat),召伯所茇(buat)。

蔽芾甘棠,勿翦勿败(beat),召伯所憩(khiat)。

蔽芾甘棠,勿翦勿拜(peat),召伯所说(sjiuat)。

（十一）尾声

《诗经》的尾声就是诗篇的副歌，相同诗句反复出现在诗篇末尾。尾声的主要特点是，其组成必须是两句以上，并在尾声中自己押韵。尾声只能出现在诗章末尾。例如《周南·汉广》：

南有乔木，不可休（xiu）息。
汉有游女，不可求（giu）思。
汉之广（kuang）矣，
不可泳（hyuang）思。
江之永矣（hyuang），
不可方（piuang）思。

翘翘错薪，言刈其楚（tshia）。
之子于归，言秣其马（mea）。
汉之广（kuang）矣，
不可泳（hyuang）思。
江之永（hyuang）矣，
不可方（piuang）思。

翘翘错薪，言刈其蒌（lio）。
之子于归，言秣其驹（kio）。
汉之广（kuang）矣，
不可泳（hyuang）思。
江之永（hyuang）矣，
不可方（piuang）思。

《汉广》三章，每章八句，后四句就是尾声部分，用以起到反复咏叹，加深情感的作用。

从古音韵角度来分析，《诗经》中出现的韵式主要有以上十一种。严格地说，如果要在译文中完全呈现《诗经》原貌，那么《诗经》的韵律当在译文中较为完整地反映出来。而要反映出《诗经》韵律，就要以《诗经》的古代读音所形成的韵律为根据，而不能以现代读音所形成的韵律为根据，因为依现代音韵的观点来看，很多地方是不押韵的。但是，在实际翻译中，《诗经》古韵律无法得到完整的再现，而再现《诗经》古韵律也没有必要。但这并非说《诗经》韵律不重要，因为韵律毕竟是《诗经》文学审美价值的一种体现，其在翻译中应该得到重视，并以适当方式得到体现。那么译者应当做的是，从历史角度，也就是从《诗经》古音韵角度，弄清楚每篇诗的韵式，然后力图在译文中再现原来的韵式，或者也可以采用另一种适合英文译诗本身的韵式进行翻译。《诗经》韵律翻译的原则和方式不外乎此：首先，《诗经》翻译应当讲求韵律；其次，从文化传播角度来说，译者应当尽量贴近原来的韵律进行翻译，但这会使翻译十分困难；最后，从译入语文化自身发展角度来说，译者可以结合诗篇内容，采用译诗本身所能允许的英语诗歌韵律来翻译，这是一种归化式翻译，是诗歌韵律翻译的主要方式。

第三节 《诗经》的韵律翻译及其效果分析

《诗经》翻译实践证明，《诗经》的韵律是可以在译文中体现出来的。体现原诗韵律，不是要用与原文韵律完全相同的音韵，而是在译文中使用同样的韵式结构来翻译。由于《诗经》中九种韵式结构都没有超出诗歌常用的隔行押韵、双行押韵、偶数行押韵、抱韵、单韵这五种基本韵式，而这五种韵式又正好是英语诗歌的基本韵式，这一相同点，就为《诗经》韵律的翻译奠定了基础。所以，《诗经》虽然古老，但其韵律是可以认识，也是可以翻译的。但就翻译方式而言，应该是以原诗的韵律为基本根据，力争在译诗中使用原诗韵式；在不得已的情况下，可以把五种基本韵式中的某些韵式相互结合起来翻译。至于《诗经》韵律的独到之处，比如叠韵、遥韵、回环、尾声等，翻译时在细节上很难做到面面俱到，译者则只好退而求其次，设法在译诗语篇中其他位置上进行适当补充，某些音韵元素甚至可以舍弃。因为韵律毕竟不是诗歌审美价值的全部，翻译应该以诗篇的内容为核心，不能以音害义。下面我们分别讨论韵律翻译方法及其效果问题。

一、以交叉韵翻译偶行韵或章内换韵

如果原诗是偶行韵式，那么在译诗中采用隔行韵式，是颇行得通的翻译方法。因为这种韵式在两种语言诗歌文学中都普遍使用，若用同样的韵式来翻译十分自然可读，所以中外译者都普遍采用这种翻译方法。在实践中，《诗经》的偶行韵式比较容易判断，所以中外译者的翻译效果往往也比较好。例如《王风·大车》。先看原诗韵式：

  大车槛槛（heam），
  毳衣如菼（tham）。

岂不尔思？

畏子不敢（kam）。

大车啍啍（thən），

毳衣如璊（muən）。

岂不尔思？

畏子不奔（pən）。

穀则异室（sjiet），

死则同穴（hyuet）。

谓予不信，

有如皦日（njiet）！

整篇诗的韵式是比较工整的偶行押韵的韵式。全诗三章。第一章押谈部韵，第二章押文部韵，第三章押质部韵。

译文也是偶行押韵：

His grand carriage—hark, how it is rumbling!
　The furred robes, green-emblazoned, are there!
Are my thoughts, then, to thee never turning?
　But I fear him, and nothing must dare.

Slowly, pond'rously moves his grand carriage,
　His furred robes as with garnets bedight.
Are my thoughts, then, to thee never turning?
　Fear of him makes me halt in my flight.

  Though in life we have separate dwellings,
   Yet in deathin one grave may we lie.
  Call me faithless, yet still am I faithful,
   While the sun yonder shines in the sky!①

  译诗偶行分别押偶行末尾 there/dare、bedight/flight、lie/sky 这三组韵，韵式工整，意思也没受到影响，与原诗韵律十分妥帖。
  在《周南》十一篇诗中，基本上属于偶行押韵的就有十篇之多，只有《葛覃》是押遥韵。使用偶行押韵的韵式来翻译这些诗，都取得了比较好的韵律效果，既保持了原诗韵式原貌，又易于为译诗读者所接受。

二、以抱韵翻译《诗经》的抱韵及遥韵

  英语中的抱韵主要使用在每节四句的诗歌中，但英语诗歌中采用四行抱韵的诗，数量并不多。这大概与抱韵诗难写有一定关系，同时，这也说明抱韵在英语诗歌中不是最受欢迎的韵式。《诗经》很多诗是章四句，对于这样的诗篇，抱韵却很少能派得上用场。但有些诗篇，其韵律使用的正是三行抱韵，用抱韵来翻译却颇能显示长处。例如《王风·采葛》的韵式就是典型的抱韵：

   彼采葛（kat）兮，
   一日不见，如三月（ngiuat）兮。

---

 ① William Jennings. *The Shi King: The Old "Poetry Classic" of the Chinese*. London and New York: George Routledge and Sons, 1891: 96-97.

彼采萧（syu）兮，
一日不见，如三秋（tsiu）兮。
彼采艾（ngat）兮，
一日不见，如三岁（siuat）兮。

根据古韵表（王力，1980：131），"葛""月""艾""岁"都属于月部，"萧""秋"都属于幽部，"见"属于元部。每章首尾两句押韵。詹宁斯采用同样的韵式结构，译文韵味丰赡：

> Ha, there he crops the creepers, see!
> 　One only day, with him away,
> Is aye three months to me!
>
> Ha, there he crops the fragrant grass!
> 　Be he away one only day,
> Three autumns seem to pass!
>
> Ha, there the mugwort now he clears!
> 　One only day, with him away,
> Is aye to me three years! ①

尽管翻译时抱韵不容易在一篇诗中自始至终单独运用，却可以在必要时与其他韵式结合着使用。上文谈到的《葛覃》是遥韵韵

---

① William Jennings. *The Shi King: The Old "Poetry Classic" of the Chinese*. London and New York: George Routledge and Sons, 1891: 96.

式,詹宁斯用双行韵加抱韵的复合韵式,即用 aabccb 韵式来翻译,且各章的复合韵式有所不同,从效果上看,整首诗韵式颇为整齐,也基本上反映出了原诗遥韵的味道——

>   Rarely my creepers grow
>   Into the vale they flow:
>   O, 'tis a leafy sea!
>   Golden orioles, taking flight,
>   Now on the bosky trees alight,
>   Chirruping all with glee.
>   Rarely my creepers grow!
>   Into the vale they flow;
>   Thick are their leafy beds.
>   These will I cut, prepare, and boil,
>   Lawn, coarse and fine, that ne'er will soil,
>   Weaving out of their threads.
>
>   Then let the matron know, —
>   Know I must homewards go;
>   So be my wardrobe clean;
>   So be my robes rinsed free from spot.
>   Which then be sullied, and which be not?
>   —Parents must aye be seen. [1]

---

[1] William Jennings. *The Shi King: The Old "Poetry Classic" of the Chinese*. London and New York: George Routledge and Sons, 1891: 36–37.

《麟之趾》和《驺虞》都是比较典型的遥韵韵式，即在诗的不同章节同一位置上押韵。詹宁斯翻译的《驺虞》，其用韵值得借鉴：

Out there where the reeds grow rank and tall,
One round he shoots, five wild boars fall.
Hail the Tsow Yu!

And there where the grass is waving high,
One round he shoots, five wild hogs die.
Hail the Tsow Yu! [①]

《诗经》的遥韵韵式与英语诗歌的抱韵有些相似。两者的差别在于抱韵是在一个诗节之内押韵，且中间的诗行必须同韵，而遥韵是在不同的诗章之内押韵，尤其是中间的诗行不一定同韵。如果译者用抱韵来翻译遥韵，也会取得英语读者所熟悉的抱韵效果。

抱韵在翻译时也可以用得很灵活。譬如詹宁斯在翻译《九罭》时，就用抱韵翻译了原诗的偶行韵和单韵。原诗如下：

九罭之鱼鳟鲂（biuang）。
我觏之子，
衮衣绣裳（zjiang）。

鸿飞遵渚（tjia），

---

① William Jennings. *The Shi King: The Old "Poetry Classic" of the Chinese.* London and New York: George Routledge and Sons, 1891: 53.

公归无所（shia），
于女信处（thjia）。

鸿飞遵陆（liuk），
公归不复（biuk），
于女信宿（siuk）！

是以有衮衣（iəi）兮，
无以我公归（kiuəi）兮，
无使我心悲（pəi）兮！

《九罭》全诗共四章，首章押偶行阳部韵，第二章押鱼部单韵，第三章押觉部单韵，第四章押微部单韵。詹宁斯把韵式做了改写，自始至终使用了三行抱韵。

> We have netted the fish, —the rudd, the bream!
> We have met with our chief in the dragon-robe
>   And the skirts that with broideries gleam.
>
> There the wild-geese wing o'er the isles their way!
> And the Duke returns? Hath he here no room?
>   Must our guest but a brief time stay?
>
> Ha, the wild geese fly o'er the upland plain!
> So the Duke must leave, to return no more!
>   Could our guest but two nights remain?
>
> O for *this* was the dragon-robe worn!

>   Yet O suffer our Duke not thus to go,
>   　Nor allow us his loss to mourn! ①

译诗的韵式是 aba cdc efe ghg。詹宁斯把原诗头两行并作一行翻译，译诗比原诗少了一行，但韵式却比原诗更加整齐。

三、以单韵韵式翻译三句诗章及单韵诗章

《诗经》一部分诗篇的结构是每章三句，第二句起韵，第三句押韵。从现有英语译本来看，这种韵式处理起来可以有三种方法：一种是如法炮制；另一种是使用单韵韵式，即每一章内句尾都押同一个韵；第三种是使用抱韵韵式，即每章一、三行押韵。就效果而论，使用单韵或者抱韵式来翻译，会令读者更乐于接受。例如《召南·甘棠》：

>   蔽芾甘棠，
>   勿翦勿伐（biuat），
>   召伯所茇（buat）。
>
>   蔽芾甘棠，
>   勿翦勿败（beat），
>   召伯所憩（khiat）。
>
>   蔽芾甘棠，

---

① William Jennings. *The Shi King: The Old "Poetry Classic" of the Chinese*. London and New York: George Routledge and Sons, 1891: 169.

勿翦勿拜（peat），

召伯所说（sjiuat）。

詹宁斯在译诗中使用单韵韵式，读起来自然流畅：

O pear-tree, with thy leafy shade!
Ne'er be thou cut, ne'er be thou laid;—
Once under thee Shâu's chieftain stayed.

O pear-tree, with thy leafy crest,
Ne'er may they cut thee, ne'er molest;—
Shâu's chief beneath thee once found rest.

O pear-tree, with thy leafy shroud,
Ne'er be those branches cut, nor bowed,
That shelter to Shâu's chief allowed. ①

汪榕培的译文直接模仿原文的韵式，读起来也别有风味：

The birch-leaf pear is lush!
Don't cut or trim the pear;
Earl Shao once lived near there.

The birch-leaf pear is lush!

---

① William Jennings. *The Shi King: The Old "Poetry Classic" of the Chinese*. London and New York: George Routledge and Sons, 1891: 47.

Don't cut or break the pear;
Earl Shao once stayed near there.

The birch-leaf pear is lush!
Don't cut or ruin the pear;
Earl Shao once stopped near there. ①

这种韵式虽然在英语诗中没有直接对应韵式，但英语读者对此并不陌生，因为每一章可以看作有个双行韵。如果从译诗整体来看，其中还有两个抱韵。所以，从读者接受角度来看，这种韵式在效果上仅次于单韵韵律。《诗经》中章三句的篇什数量不少，詹宁斯常用单韵来翻译，如《十亩之间》，译者拿捏得也十分妥当。请先看原文韵律：

十亩之间（kean）兮，
桑者闲闲（hean）兮。
行与子还（hoan）兮！

十亩之外（nguat）兮，
桑者泄泄（jiat）兮。
行与子逝（zjiat）兮！

第一章三句押原部韵，第二章三句押韵部韵。詹宁斯的译文如下：

---

① 汪榕培、任秀桦（译注）：《诗经》（中英文版），大连：辽宁教育出版社，1995 年，第 63 页。

Mid his acres ten, contented, free, —

O the mulberry-planter's life for me!

There fain would I, friend, retire with thee.

By his acres ten, without one care, —

O the mulberry-planter's life to share!

There fain would I, friend, with thee repair.①

再看詹宁斯翻译的《桧风·素冠》。请先看原诗韵式：

庶见素冠（kuan）兮，
棘人栾栾（luan）兮，
劳心慱慱（duan）兮！

庶见素衣（iəi）兮，
我心伤悲（pəi）兮！
聊与子同归（kiuəi）兮。

庶见素韠（piet）兮，
我心蕴结（kyet）兮！
聊与子如一（iet）兮。

第一章押元部韵，第二章押微部韵，第三章押质部韵。詹氏译文如下：

---

① William Jennings. *The Shi King: The Old "Poetry Classic" of the Chinese*. London and New York: George Routledge and Sons, 1891: 124.

O for a sight of the bonnet white,

And the rigorous wearer, spare and slight!

Sore were my heart at the moving sight!

O for a sight of the plain white dress!

How my heart would feel for the fatherless!

Fain would I homeward with him press.

O that I saw the white apron worn!

How my heart would cling to the youth forlorn,

Ay, and as *one* with him would mourn! ①

译文与原文的韵式惟妙惟肖，原诗每章换韵，译诗也每章换韵，颇为流畅自然。

单韵诗在英语诗歌中数量并不多，但在《诗经》中却有不少，而个别诗章中出现单韵的情况就更多见。两种诗歌文化在韵式上的偶合，给《诗经》翻译中的用韵提供了很多方便。詹宁斯在译文中运用单韵十分出色，例如他在翻译《商颂·长发》这篇长诗的前六章时使用了单韵，这表明译者不仅对原诗单韵韵式的判断十分准确，而且善于利用中西诗歌韵律上的相似性，表现了其高超的诗歌翻译艺术。《长发》原文前六章是单韵，最后一章是双行韵。其韵式为：第一章，阳部；第二章，月部；第三章，微脂合部；第四章，幽部；第五章，东部；第六章，月部；最后一章分别押盍部、

---

① William Jennings. *The Shi King: The Old "Poetry Classic" of the Chinese*. London and New York: George Routledge and Sons, 1891: 154.

之部、阳部的双行韵。韵式总貌如下：

濬哲维商（sjiang），长发其祥（ziang）。
洪水芒芒（mang），禹敷下土方（piuang）。
外大国是疆（kiang），幅陨既长（diang）。
有娀方将（tziang），帝立子生商（sjiang）。

玄王桓拨（puat），受小国是达（dat），受大国是达（dat）。
率履不越（hiuat），遂视既发（piuat）。
相土烈烈（liat），海外有截（dziat）。

帝命不违（hiuəi），至于汤齐（dzyei）。
汤降不迟（diei），圣敬日跻（tzyei）。
昭假迟迟（diei），上帝是祇（tjiei），帝命式于九围（hiuəi）。

受小球大球（giu），为下国缀旒（liu），何天之休（xiu）。
不竞不絿（giu），不刚不柔（njiu），
敷政优优（iu），百禄是遒（dziu）。

受小共大共（kiong），为下国骏厖（meong），何天之龙（liong）。
敷奏其勇（jiong），不震不动（dong），
不戁不竦（song），百禄是总（tzong）。

武王载旆（bat），有虔秉钺（hiuat），
如火烈烈（liat），则莫我敢曷（hat）。
苞有三蘖（ngiat），莫遂莫达（dat）。
九有有截（dziat），韦顾既伐（biuat），昆吾夏桀（giat）。

昔在中叶（jiap），有震且业（ngiap）。

允也天子（tziə），降于卿士（dzhiə）。
实维阿衡（heang），实左右商王（hiuang）。

请看詹宁斯译文的前两章：

In Shang was wisdom most profound,
And long with blessing it was crowned.
When the Great Flood increased around
Yü led its waters through the lowland ground.
To each great border State he placed a bound,
Till far the frontier-lines extended round.
Then, when the State of Sung became renowned,
Did God raise up a son, the House of Shang to found.

The dusky monarch made success his aim:
Had he a small State, greater it became;
Had he a great one, still it was the same.
The course he followed was devoid of blame;
At his mere glance quick men's response thus came.
Siang-t'u, a Chief of glorious fame,
Could foes beyond the seas subdue and tame. [①]

用单韵韵式翻译单韵韵式，不但真实反映了原诗韵律状况，而且也

---

① William Jennings. *The Shi King: The Old "Poetry Classic" of the Chinese*. London and New York: George Routledge and Sons, 1891: 379-380.

可以为西方读者所乐于接受。

《小雅·车攻》也是《诗经》中少有的比较整齐的一篇单韵诗（只有一章不押韵）：

> 我车既攻（kong），我马既同（dong），
> 四牡庞庞（beong），驾言徂东（tong）。
>
> 田车既好（xu），四牡孔阜（biu），
> 东有甫草（tsu），驾言行狩（sjiu）。
>
> 之子于苗（miô），选徒嚣嚣（xiô），
> 建旐设旄（mô），薄狩于敖（ngô）。
>
> 驾彼四牡，四牡奕奕（jyak）。
> 赤芾金舄（syak），会同有绎（jyak）。
>
> 决拾既佽（tsiei），弓矢既调（dyu）。
> 射夫既同（dong），助我举柴（dzhe）。
>
> 四黄既驾（keai），两骖不猗（iai），
> 不失其驰（diai），舍矢如破（phai）。
>
> 萧萧马鸣（mieng），悠悠旆旌（tzieng），
> 徒御不惊（kieng），大庖不盈（jieng）。
>
> 之子于征（tjieng），有闻无声（sjieng），
> 允矣君子，展也大成（zjieng）。

令人印象深刻的是，詹宁斯的译文也亦步亦趋，除两章外，每一章也都使用了单韵韵式：

Our cars are stoutly made and manned,
In equal drafts the horses stand
In teams of four, superb and grand: —
Then Eastward ho! there lies the land.

Trim are the hunting-cars, and sound,
Right sturdy teams for each are found.
Fine covers in the East abound: —
Away! there lies our hunting-ground.

The masters of the chase appear,
Tell off their men, give orders clear,
The banners fix, the "oxtails" rear: —
At Ngâu, (quotha), we'll have the deer.

Ho now the teams are on the way,
Four after four in long array!
Gilt shoes, red aprons, —what display!
The pageant of an audience-day!

Gantlet and thumb-ring we attach,
And to the bows the arrows match;
Each bowman has the same despatch;
Each adds to our great pile his batch.

The teams of bays are now inspanned;
The off-steeds well are kept in hand,
Nor e'er their rapid pace relax.
Each shaft goes hurtling like an axe!

《诗经》翻译探微

> And now what noise of neighing steeds,
> As the long bannered train recedes!
> Runners and drivers made so scare,
> So yields the Larder each a share.
>
> And they who led the chase to-day
> Great praise have won, without display.
> Ay, lordly men indeed are they;—
> Of skill consummate, sooth to say! [1]

译诗忽略了原诗中不押韵的一章,几乎全部使用了单韵韵式,把轰轰烈烈的狩猎场面描绘得威武雄壮,获得了辉煌壮阔的音乐效果。

四、双行韵韵式在翻译中的应用

我国《诗经》以后的诗歌里尽管押双行韵的为数不多,但在《诗经》中,含有双行韵式的诗章却不鲜见。这些诗章,使用双行韵式来翻译,在音韵效果上,可以说是琴瑟调和。在詹宁斯的译本中,双行韵的使用率仅次于交韵和偶行韵,收到了很好的音韵效果。例如《豳风·东山》,译者从头至尾都使用了双行韵式。请看原文和译文第一章:

> 我徂东山(shean),
> 慆慆不归(kiuəi)。

---

[1] William Jennings. *The Shi King: The Old "Poetry Classic" of the Chinese*. London and New York: George Routledge and Sons, 1891: 197-198.

我来自东（tong），
零雨其濛（mong）。
我东曰归（kiuəi），
我心西悲（pəi）。
制彼裳衣（iəi），
勿士行枚（muəi）。
蜎蜎者蠋（zjiok），
烝在桑野（jya）。
敦彼独宿（siuk），
亦在车下（hea）。

To the hills in the East we marched away,
And ne'er came home for many a day;
When we did come back from the East again,
Then down came the dripping, drizzling rain.
In the East when we talked of our return,
O then for the West our hearts would burn.
"Make ready the gear we then shall wear;—
No marching there, no gagging there!"
Like caterpillars that creep and crawl
In mulberry grounds, there were we all,
And each in his lonely shelter slept,
Ay, under the wagons, too, we crept. [1]

---

[1] William Jennings. *The Shi King: The Old "Poetry Classic" of the Chinese*. London and New York: George Routledge and Sons, 1891: 166-167.

从原文来看，其基本韵式并不是双行韵，而是每章首行"我徂东山"押遥韵，双行韵在诗章中时而出现。译者抓住原诗中多有双行押韵这一特点，通篇使用双行韵式来翻译这篇诗，读来颇富美感。押遥韵的观念在英语诗学中是没有的，本篇诗中押遥韵的诗行又相隔太远，不容易被译文读者感受到，所以译者不采用原诗韵式，而是改用双行韵式，诚为明智之举。

如果原文是押双行韵，那么用双行韵式来翻译，无疑是一举两得，既能传达原文韵律，也符合译文读者的审美习惯。如果原文不是双行韵，而是偶行韵，那么译文在不便使用偶行韵的情况下，改用双行韵来翻译，也是一种很好的途径。实际上，在英语诗歌中，通篇押偶行韵的并不多见，英美人更习惯复合韵式，即在诗中把几种基本韵式结合起来使用。例如《大雅·崧高》，原诗虽然并不是双行韵式，詹宁斯用双行韵式来翻译，读起来就很美。因为原诗和译诗都比较长，这里只录译诗中的三章：

  Where mountains huge and high
   Their peaks rear to the sky,
A god descended from the height,
And Fu and Shin first saw the light.
  And Shin and Fu are now
   The buttresses of Chow.
Of every State are they the shield;
On every hand great power they wield.

   Shin's chief was so robust,
   The king could re-intrust

> A seat in Sié into his hand,
> Whence he should guide that southern land
>   Shau's earl by royal decree
>   Fixed where this seat should be;
> And thus that southern State had birth
> Where still Shin's line uphold his worth.
>
> The king gave Shin command:
>   "Guide thou that southern land,
> And use its people in such way
> As thine own merit to display."
>   He bade Shau's earl assign
>   Shin's lands, their bounds define.
> He bade again Shin's chamberlain
> Take thither his domestic train. ①

  英雄双行体在译诗中的使用，大概与原诗的主题有着密切的关系。在英国文学史上，杰弗里·乔叟首先在《坎特伯雷故事集》中使用了双行体。由于《坎特伯雷故事集》是长篇叙事诗，以此为起点，这个韵式就几乎成了以后的叙事诗传统。比如莎士比亚也常使用双行体韵式。后经约翰·德莱顿进一步创造与亚历山大·蒲柏等诗人的发展，遂成为英国十八世纪英雄史诗的惯用韵式。无论是从《毛诗传》还是从郑《笺》来看，《大雅·崧高》都是赞美诗，在题

---

① William Jennings. *The Shi King: The Old "Poetry Classic" of the Chinese*. London and New York: George Routledge and Sons, 1891: 327.

材上颇似英国的英雄史诗，所以译者选用了这个韵式来翻译，颇具匠心。

五、复合韵式翻译功能最强

由于英汉两种语言之间差异巨大，两种文化中诗歌的节奏与韵律微观上有形形色色的差别，尤其是《诗经》韵律千变万化，翻译时要做到通篇用一种韵式常常是十分困难的。因此，唯一的出路，也是行之有效的出路，就是用复合韵式来翻译。由于复合韵式是英美诗歌中常用的韵律形式，加之复合韵式可以在必要时转换变通，这一声韵结构自然就成为诗篇翻译功能最强大、效果最佳的途径。

在《诗经》翻译中，采用复合韵式的译文占了较大的比例。从效果上看，这些译诗也十分悦人。例如《郑风·野有蔓草》，原文音韵流转，余音绕梁：

野有蔓草，零露漙（duan）兮。
有美一人，清扬婉（iuan）兮。
邂逅相遇，适我愿（ngiuan）兮。

野有蔓草，零露瀼瀼（njiang）。
有美一人，婉如清扬（jiang）。
邂逅相遇，与子偕臧（tzang）。

詹宁斯使用复合韵式来翻译，译文读来也细腻幽婉，荡气回肠：

  Where creeping plants grow on the wild
    And heavy dews declined,
  There was a fair one all alone,
    Bright-eyed, good-looking, kind.
  Chance brought us to each other's side,
    And all my wish was gratified.

  Where creeping plants grew on the wild,
    And thick the dew-drops stood,
  There was the fair one all alone,
    Kind, as the looks were good.
  Chance let us meet each other there,
    Our mutual happiness to share.①

  原诗两章，章六句，均押偶行韵。第一章押元部韵，第二章押阳部韵。译文用偶行韵和双行韵的复合韵式，第一节韵式为 abcbdd，第二节韵式为 aefegg。

  复合韵式可以有多种。例如《小雅·杕杜》就不同于上一首诗，用的是交韵加三句单韵的复合韵式。

    有杕之杜（da），
    有睆其实（djiet）。
    王事靡盬（ka），

---

  ① William Jennings. *The Shi King: The Old "Poetry Classic" of the Chinese*. London and New York: George Routledge and Sons, 1891: 110.

《诗经》翻译探微

继嗣我日（njiet）。
日月阳（jiang）止，
女心伤（sjiang）止，
征夫遑（huang）止。

有杕之杜（da），
其叶萋萋（tsyei）。
王事靡盬（ka），
我心伤悲（pəi）。
卉木萋（tsyei）止，
女心悲（pəi）止，
征夫归止（kiuəi）！

陟彼北山，言采其杞（khiə）。
王事靡盬，忧我父母（mə）。
檀车幝幝（sjian），
四牡痯痯（kuan），
征夫不远（hiuan）！
匪载匪来（lə），
忧心孔疚（kiuə）。
期逝不至（tjiet），
而多为恤（siuet）。
卜筮偕（kei）止，
会言近止，征夫迩（njiei）止！

请看詹宁斯的译文：

Alone the russet pear-tree grows,
　　With fruit upon it fair to see.
Kings' service knows not speedy close;
　　Day in, day out, 'tis long to me.
　　　　The year is fast receding, O;
　　　　My woman's heart is bleeding, O;
　　　　My soldier rest is needing, O.

Alone the russet pear-tree grows
　　And now is full of leaves (again).
King's service knows not speedy close;
　　My heart still battles with its pain:—
　　　　While trees and plants are springing, O,
　　　　My woman's heart 'tis wringing, O;
　　　　Then speed my brave's home-bringing, O.

Up yonder northern hills I'll climb,
　　The fruit to pluck from medlar-trees.
Kings' service takes no count of time;
　　The old folks' hearts are ill at ease.
　　　　Their teams are tired and flagging, sure;
　　　　Their sandal-cars are dragging, sure;
　　　　Not far my brave is lagging, sure.

But no, they come not yet away!
　　And o, my heart misgives me sore.
The time is past, and still they stay;

175

> I grow despondent more and more.
> But shell and straw now cheer me, O!
> Both tell me he is near me, O!
> My brave will soon be near me, O! ①

如果说章末双行韵的复合韵式最适合章六句的诗篇的翻译，那么章末用三句单韵，则最适合章七句的诗篇的翻译。在前四句使用交韵或者偶行押韵之后，最后三句中若再用一次交韵，那么最后一句只能再押上句尾韵，这样就会形成 ababab 或 ababcdd 的韵式。这两种韵式使人联想起斯宾塞诗体 ababbcbcc 的韵式，虽然并非典型复合韵式，倒也不会使人觉得陌生，也可以作为译文韵式的一种选择。

第四节 《诗经》韵律翻译之法门——沿袭、变通与无奈

《诗经》翻译用不用韵？怎样用韵？这大概是每个《诗经》译者都要思考的问题。就诗歌理论与翻译实践两方面来说，多数译者都是主张用韵的，因为韵律本身是诗歌审美价值的一部分。许渊冲认为，翻译诗歌"要在传达原文'意美'的前提下，尽可能传达原文的'音美'；还要在传达原文'意美'和'音美'的前提下，尽可能传达原文的'形美'；努力做到三美齐备"（许渊冲，1983）。

---

① William Jennings. *The Shi King: The Old "Poetry Classic" of the Chinese.* London and New York: George Routledge and Sons, 1891: 184-185.

我国老一辈诗歌翻译家如徐志摩、戴望舒、何其芳、卞之琳、飞白、屠岸、孙大雨、穆旦、李文俊、曹葆华等，他们翻译的诗歌都是用韵的，其韵律之美，不亚于创作。《诗经》翻译用韵，当然也是再现其艺术美不可或缺的手段。那么，究竟如何在译诗中用韵呢？从诗歌的性质和特点、韵律的性质，以及英汉两种诗歌的文化共性来看，《诗经》翻译的用韵不外乎两种方式：一是沿袭原诗的韵律，二是根据译入语民族的审美情趣，对原诗的韵律进行变通。但是，无论是哪一种用韵方式，都有可行和不可行之处，即有的韵律形式可以在译诗中模仿，有的则会因各种限制而不能模仿。就押韵方面来说，《诗经》的隔行韵、交叉韵、偶行韵、双行韵、连续韵、抱韵、遥韵、尾声，在本质上来讲是可以翻译的，也就是说，韵式具有可译性。但这并不意味着原韵式在语义相同的条件下，在与原诗同样的位置上可以翻译。恰恰相反，因为两种语言在语音、词汇、句法方面的差异，原诗的韵律，往往不是在译诗的同一局部位置上反映出来，而是在整个诗篇中才能做到韵律大致相等。译诗即使能用和原诗同样的韵式结构，其韵也不一定是由相同的声母和韵母组成的，也就是说，韵律的翻译大多不能直接体现在具体音素上，而是只能体现在韵律结构上，如原诗是 abab 韵式，译诗则多是 cdcd 韵式，即 a 和 c、b 和 d 分别是不同的两种音节结构。除此以外，《诗经》中还有双声和叠韵。双声指的是相邻的两个字的声母相同，叠韵是指相邻的两个字的韵母相同。双声类似于英语诗歌中的押头韵，但英语诗歌的头韵则是指同一行中有两个以上开头辅音相同的单词前后相呼应。叠韵在英语诗歌中找不到对应的韵律形式。那么，这两种韵式在局部更是几乎不能翻译的，多数情况下只能在整篇诗中得以体现。从韵律的节奏方面来说，《诗经》用的是顿，两字一顿，或者三字一顿，而英语的节奏靠音步来体现，这在本质上就是完全不能翻译的了。

既然韵律有可译处和不可译处，那么，不可译处就只能变通。变通也有两法：其一，在意思不变的前提下，根据译诗内在的韵律流向确定译诗的韵律结构，譬如可以在英语诗歌惯用的韵式中选择一种韵式，或者将几种基本韵式复合在一起共同体现原诗的韵律；其二，只专注于意思的精确性而忽略原诗的韵律，忽略意味着不用韵，无韵虽为没有韵律，但没有韵律也是自古就有的一种韵式，所以无韵即为一种韵式，《诗经》中绝对不用韵的诗就有六篇，所以这一手法在把《诗经》作为"经"来翻译的时候，并不失为一种有效的韵律策略。下面分开来论述。

一、偶行韵、交韵、双行韵、叠韵、遥韵、尾声常可沿袭

综观《诗经》的每篇诗，一篇中各章之间韵律都相互一致的为数并不多，只有一部分短篇韵律比较规则统一，比如《桃夭》《鹊巢》。而所谓规则统一，也仅是在韵式的意义上说的，就具体的韵脚来说，前后还是总有些变化的。《雅》中的长篇，其韵律就更是复杂多变，规则统一的韵律只能在某些诗章之间，甚至只能在某一诗章内部才能见到。所以，在翻译过程中要从整体上完全沿袭原诗的韵律，实际上是非常困难的，仅是一些篇幅较短的诗，才有可能在翻译时沿袭原来的韵式。如《关雎》《桃夭》《樛木》《螽斯》等偶行押韵且韵律相对比较整齐的诗，其韵式在翻译时相对来说都比较容易模仿。而有些诗虽然篇幅短，若其韵式在诗中仍变化较多，翻译时就得做特别处理。例如，詹宁斯翻译的《葛覃》，韵式就比

较特殊，在整体上既没有借用英诗的韵式，也没有沿用原来的韵式，而是用双行韵与抱韵的复合韵式。有的诗篇，韵式十分整齐，译者翻译时却不一定模仿，而是另起炉灶。例如《卫风·木瓜》的韵式是一个双行韵加一个两行尾声：

> 投我以木瓜（koa），
> 报之以琼琚（kia）。
> 匪报（pu）也，
> 永以为好（xu）也。
>
> 投我以木桃（dô），
> 报之以琼瑶（jiô）。
> 匪报（pu）也，
> 永以为好（xu）也。
>
> 投我以木李（liə），
> 报之以琼玖（kiuə）。
> 匪报（pu）也，
> 永以为好（xu）也。

詹宁斯在其译文中用的却是典型的抱韵：

> Some quinces once to me were sent,
> A ruby was my gift again;
> Yet not as gift again;—
> Enduring love was its intent.

> Peaches were sent me; I a stone
> Of jasper sent as gift again;
> Nay, not as gift again;—
> Enduring love it ment alone.
>
> Plums I had sent me; and I sent
> A dusky gem for gift again;
> Yet not as gift again;
> But long enduring love it meant.

为了形成抱韵格式，作者在第二章和第三章的前两行都使用了跨行的手法。大概这与译者不愿意重复每章的末尾两句不无关系。译者还是顺从了读者的审美眼光。

原诗的韵式或许总能够模仿，或许更适宜于重构，但无论如何，译者都不能刻意，以免以韵害义。如《葛覃》最后一章的韵式是前四行交叉韵加后两行双行韵：

> 言告师氏，
> 言告言归（kuəi）。
> 薄污我私，
> 薄浣我衣（iəi）。
> 害浣害否（piuə），
> 归宁父母（mə）。

许渊冲的译文试图用 aabbcc 的双行韵式来翻译：

I tell Mother-in-law

Soon I will homeward go.

I'll wash my undershirt

And rinse my outerskirt.

My dress cleaned, I'll appear

Before my parents dear.[①]

但"师氏"并非"Mother-in-law","私""衣"也非"underskirt"和"outerskirt"。该译文总体上不如詹宁斯译文在语义上来得忠实，而韵律虽有所不同却又感情充沛、自然悦耳：

Then let the matron know, —

Know I must homewards go;

 So be my wardrobe clean;

So be my robes rinsed free from spot.

Which then be sullied, and which be not?

 —Parents must aye be seen.

  经考查发现，《诗经》的偶行韵、交韵是比较容易模仿的。这与英诗也常用这些韵式不无关系。偶行韵和交韵如果押的是通韵，则翻译时一般易于采取中间换韵的办法。例如《小雅·正月》是押偶行韵的一篇长诗，每章一韵。韵律如此整齐的长诗在《诗经》中并不多见。詹宁斯翻译时自始至终也采用了偶行韵，但章内没押通

---

① 许渊冲（译）：《诗经》，北京：中国对外翻译出版公司，2009年，第4页。

韵,而是中间换了一次韵。限于篇幅,仅看开头两章:

正月繁霜(shiang),我心忧伤(sjiang)。
民之讹言,亦孔之将(tziang)。
念我独兮,忧心京京(kyang)。
哀我小心,癙忧以痒(jiang)。

父母生我,胡俾我愈(jio)?
不自我先,不自我后(ho)。
好言自口(kho),
莠言自口(kho)。
忧心愈愈(jio),
是以有侮(mio)。

Hard frost 'neath a summer moon!
 With its sorrow my heart is sore.
The scandal the people spread
 Is increasing more and more.
Methinks how I stand alone,
 And the trouble grows hard to bear;
Ah me for my anxious thought!
 Smothered grief will my health impair.

Ye parents, who gave me life,
 Why thus was I born for pain?
Not thus was it ere my time,
 Not thus will it be again.

Words, now both of praise and blame,
　　From the lips (not the heart) proceed;
And though deeper my sorrow grows,
　　Contempt is my (only) meed. ①

交韵也常在译文中被模仿。例如《鄘风·鹑之奔奔》首章用的是偶行韵，末章用的是交韵。

鹑之奔奔，
鹊之彊彊（kiang 阳部）。
人之无良（liang 阳部），
我以为兄（xyuang 阳部）。

鹊之彊彊（kiang 阳部），
鹑之奔奔（pən 文部）。
人之无良（liang 阳部），
我以为君（kiuən 文部）。

许渊冲在译文中则全部用了交韵：

The quails together fly;
The magpies sort in pairs.
She takes an unkind guy
For brother unawares.

---

① William Jennings. *The Shi King: The Old "Poetry Classic" of the Chinese*. London and New York: George Routledge and Sons, 1891: 212-213.

>   Together magpies sort in pairs;
>   The quails together fly.
>   For master unawares
>   She takes an unkind guy.①

为了构建交韵韵式，译者使用了跨行翻译手法。但遗憾的是，译者为了完成这一韵律而改变了原文的意思。每章的后两句，原文本意是抒发不得已的悲叹之情，而译文却因为用了"unawares"，将诗句变作陈述一种"没有意识到"的失误。

交韵虽然在中英诗歌中都有，但英语诗歌对此种韵律仿佛并不十分青睐，所以使用这种韵律翻译出来的英语诗歌数量不多。在翻译交韵诗篇的时候，英国译者往往将其转成偶行韵或者其他韵式。例如詹宁斯翻译《鹑之奔奔》用的就是偶行韵：

>   Quails consort and fly with quails,
>   Jays will only join with jays;—
>   I must own as elder brother
>   One who takes to wanton ways.
>
>   Jay will only have his jay,
>   Quail goes with his consort quail;—
>   One who takes to wanton courses
>   I must as "my lady" hail.②

---

① 许渊冲（译）:《诗经》，北京：中国对外翻译出版公司，2009年，第48-49页。
② William Jennings. *The Shi King: The Old "Poetry Classic" of the Chinese*. London and New York: George Routledge and Sons, 1891: 76.

遥韵是《诗经》的特色韵律，隔章同一位置押韵。虽然英文诗歌传统中没有这种韵律形式，翻译时却常常被较逼真地复制出来。例如《郑风·狡童》二章，章四句，每章一、三两句互押遥韵，同时每章之内又押偶行韵：

> 彼狡童兮，
> 不与我言（ngian）兮。
> 维子之故，
> 使我不能餐（tsan）兮！（元部）
>
> 彼狡童兮，
> 不与我食（djiək）兮。
> 维子之故，
> 使我不能息（siək）兮！（职部）

> O the artful boy!
> Now so dumb to me whene'er we meet,
>   And for his sole sake
> I must be unable now to eat!
>
> O the artful boy!
> Now no more to be table-guest,
>   And for his sole sake
> I must be unable now to rest! [①]

[①] William Jennings. *The Shi King: The Old "Poetry Classic" of the Chinese*. London and New York: George Routledge and Sons, 1891: 106.

不过，尽管译文中呈现了遥韵，但笔者还是倾向于认为译者仅是在译文中用偶行韵，遥韵是其下意识所为。虽然英语诗学并不认同这种韵式，但由于两句相隔较远，译者并不认为这种重复会破坏审美效果。另外如《褰裳》《东门之墠》《野有蔓草》，也都这样被詹宁斯呈现出来。再如《齐风·甫田》前两章的译文：

> 无田甫田（dyen），
> 维莠骄骄（kiô）。
> 无思远人（njien），
> 劳心忉忉（tô）。
>
> 无田甫田（dyen），
> 维莠桀桀（giat）。
> 无思远人（njien），
> 劳心怛怛（tat）。

> Broad fields plant not,
> Where thrive most the weeds;
> 　Man's years want not,
> To heartaches it leads.
>
> Broad fields plant not,
> Or weeds will prevail;
> 　Man's years want not,
> For grief 'twill entail. [1]

---

[1] William Jennings. *The Shi King: The Old "Poetry Classic" of the Chinese*. London and New York: George Routledge and Sons, 1891: 116.

对于《诗经》的遥韵,理雅各、詹宁斯、许渊冲、汪榕培四位译者的处理方法基本上是一样的。

二、抱韵、疏韵等韵式多数情况下需要重构

与偶行韵、交韵和遥韵相比,抱韵和疏韵不那么容易模仿。每遇到这样的韵式,译者往往就改用其他韵式。例如《大雅·大明》第六章前四行有一个抱韵:

> 有命自天(thyen),
> 命此文王(hiuang),
> 于周于京(kyang)。
> 缵女维莘(shen),
> 长子维行(heang),
> 笃生武王(hiuang)。
> 保右命尔,燮伐大商(sjiang)。

许渊冲译文用的是交韵式:

> At Heaven's call
> Wen again wed in capital
> Xin nobly-bred.
> She bore a son
> Who should take down,
> When victory's won,
> The royal crown.[①]

[①] 许渊冲(译):《诗经》,北京:中国对外翻译出版公司,2009年,第310-311页。

詹宁斯用的是偶行韵式：

> 'T was an ordinance of Heaven,
> Thus ordained that our King Wăn
> To Chow's capital be given. ——
> Jen's successor was from San:
> She, San's eldest, was that bride:
> Blessed, at length, to bear King Wu,
> Your Preserver, Helper, Guide, ——
> Who, as such, great Shang o'erthrew. ①

疏韵不好判别，更不易在译文中复制。例如《大雅·韩奕》第二章：

> 四牡奕奕，
> 孔修且张（tiang）。
> 韩侯入觐，
> 以其介圭，
> 入觐于王（hiuang）。

第二句起阳部韵，隔两句后，第五句押阳部韵。翻译时，译者就很难在做周到的叙述的同时，再照顾到局部的特色韵律。詹宁斯在这里用的是偶行韵，译文第五行没有与前文押韵，而是换了另一组偶行韵。

---

① William Jennings. *The Shi King: The Old "Poetry Classic" of the Chinese*. London and New York: George Routledge and Sons, 1891: 280-281.

Thence, with his team accoutred proudly,
—Full tall and stately all the four, —
Han's Prince to Court came, craving audience,
And his great sceptre forward bore,
Advancing to the royal presence.
The King then gave the Prince of Han
The dragon-flag, all gaily mounted,
A checkered screen, an ornate span, ①

而许渊冲用的是双行韵,也没有保持前五行的疏韵结构:

His cab was drawn by four steeds
Long and large, running high speeds.
The marquis at court did stand,
His mace of rank in hand.
He bowed to Heaven's Son,
Who showed him his gifts one by one. ②

三、译诗的节奏当顺应英文诗句本身的需要

韵律并不仅限于尾韵,节奏也是构成韵律的要素之一。如果说尾韵不好处理,那么节奏就更是《诗经》翻译的一大难点。可以

---

① William Jennings. *The Shi King: The Old "Poetry Classic" of the Chinese.* London and New York: George Routledge and Sons, 1891: 332.
② 许渊冲(译):《诗经》,北京:中国对外翻译出版公司,2009年,第377—378页。

说，分属意音文字系统和拼音文字系统的汉语和英语之间的巨大差别，使节奏成为《诗经》翻译无法追求与原文和译文之间对等的语音因素。《诗经》的诗句多为四言和五言，每行只有两顿，如果用英语的音步来翻译，那就只能用两个抑扬格或扬抑格；如果要再进一步保持对节奏的忠实，那只好用两音步，而两音步的诗在英文诗歌中少之又少，读起来不免有一种不适感。例如，许渊冲翻译的许多诗篇诗行比较短，其中体现出译者对原文节奏效果的追求，但译文读起来往往节奏过于急促，而意思也难以表达得充分。《齐风·猗嗟》就是一例：

> 猗嗟昌（thjiang）兮！
> 颀而长（diang）兮。
> 抑若扬（jiang）兮，
> 美目扬（jiang）兮。
> 巧趋跄（tsiang）兮，
> 射则臧（tzang）兮！

> 猗嗟名（mieng）兮！
> 美目清（tsieng）兮，
> 仪既成（zjieng）兮。
> 终日射侯，不出正（tjieng）兮。
> 展我甥（sheng）兮！

> 猗嗟娈（liuan）兮！
> 清扬婉（iuan）兮。
> 舞则选（siuan）兮，
> 射则贯（kuan）兮。

四矢反（piuan）兮，

以御乱（luan）兮！

许渊冲的译文如下：

Fairest of all,

He's grand and tall,

His forehead high

With sparkling eye;

He's fleet of foot

And skilled to shoot.

His fame is high

With crystal eye;

In brave array

He shoots all day;

Each shot a hit,

No son's so fit.

He's fair and bright

With keenest sight;

He dances well;

Each shot will tell;

Four shots right go;

He'll quell the foe. ①

----

① 许渊冲（译）：《诗经》，北京：中国对外翻译出版公司，2009年，第106页。

译文每行只有四个音节，与原文每行的音节数相同，基本上属于抑扬格两音步的节奏。若论音节数，译文和原文完全一致；论音步数，译文与原文四字两顿的顿数也一致。译者的努力着实不易。但是，以效果而论，译诗节奏则略显急促短暂，并不自然。虽然理论上英文诗每行的音步数可以是从单音步到八音步不等，但整首诗完全用两音步写成的可谓寥若晨星；而如果每行字数太少，则会限制语义得到自然和充分的表达，难免给人以穿凿之感。若将许先生译文与原文两相比较，原文对动作、情状和姿态的描述惟妙惟肖，十分细腻，而译文则略显笼统粗糙，如"巧趋""臧""名""仪""候""正""甥""选""贯""反"等字义在译文中都没有得到适当的表达。这些问题都与译者刻意追求韵律有直接关系。相比之下，詹宁斯的译文在这两方面就自然和谐得多：

  What pity! and a man so fine!
  Erect and tall, straight as a line!
  What graces in his looks combine!
  What fire is in those glancing eyen!
  In every movement how divine!
  And as an archer doth he shine.

  What pity! praised by every one!
  Brighter than those fine eyes be none!
  Perfectly all his acts are done.
  Before the disc, till sinks the sun,

Never a shot but centre won!
Ay, none mistakes Our Sister's Son!

What pity! and so winsome he!
What countenance more fair to see?
Who'll dance a dance so gracefully?
Who'll shoot a shaft so sure as he?
Where enters one, there follow three!
Born queller, sure, of anarchy! ①

译文用四音步抑扬格，韵律、情感和诗意表达得都比较自然。

通过以上讨论，我们可以做如下结论。首先，韵律是中英诗歌所认同的审美价值之一，其在译文中的再现可谓天经地义。译诗韵律虽然难成，但这并不能成为否定韵律翻译的托词。好的译者总是能够赋予其翻译作品合适的韵律，并使译诗韵律达到与诗意琴瑟调和的境界。在这一点上，詹宁斯和理雅各的《诗经》翻译可谓著例。当然，追求音韵之美，是仅就《诗经》翻译的文学之维而论的，若《诗经》翻译以义理为旨归，则另当别论。其次，再现原诗的韵律，并不意味着译诗的韵律必定和原诗的完全一致。这当然并非说一致了就一定不好，而是一致了不一定好。这可以从中西诗学之间的差异中得到诠释。我们的诗歌中所使用的韵律，不一定是西方读者所熟悉和认可的，比如《诗经》中的尾声、叠韵、回环等，这些重复手法在英语诗歌传统中是没有的。所以，如果在翻译时将

---

① William Jennings. *The Shi King: The Old "Poetry Classic" of the Chinese.* London and New York: George Routledge and Sons, 1891: 118-119.

其照搬过去，在译诗的审美价值上就会产生相反的效果。而"颠倒衣裳"和"颠倒裳衣"这样的回环，在英文中则是不可复制的，遑论原文和译文的韵律一致。第三，把《诗经》作为文学来翻译时，担负着两个任务：一是为英语文学输入新鲜血液，丰富英语诗歌文学；二是文学交流，让译文读者通过翻译，了解《诗经》的本来面貌。与前者相应的基本翻译策略是兼容并蓄，融合变通，即归化翻译；而与后者相应的则是原、译文之间的忠实与一致，即异化翻译。这两者之间在本质上是矛盾的。凡是翻译的发生，往往丰富和发展译入语文化是其第一任务，所以，《诗经》翻译若以其文学本质为重，译诗则当遵循归化与异化适度结合的原则——求归化而不宜使译文失去原来的民族特色，谋异化而不宜违背译文语言本身的规律，也不能超出当代读者的诗学观念所能认同的范围。第四，诗歌的灵魂在于诗意与境界，而韵律、修辞等则皆为追求诗意与境界的手段，所以从根本上说，译文的韵律须顺从诗意表达的需要。这要求译诗有自己相对独立的韵律。因此，归根结底，就诗歌翻译而论，译诗的韵律往往要从译诗本身的需要出发来进行重构，无须受任何其他准则的约束。换言之，如果原诗韵律并无特殊审美价值需传达，则译诗主要遵循译入语文化中的审美价值规律即可。

小　　结

韵律是诗歌的重要属性之一，即使是现代无韵诗，其内在的韵律也是存在的。仅就《诗经》翻译来说，韵律更是一个无法舍弃的因素。在现有的十个全译本中，有八个是有韵律诉求的，理雅各的首译本因为没有韵律，在1876年又进行了重译，从而又有了理雅各韵体《诗经》版本。韦利译本的部分诗篇没有韵律，有的则也有韵律。但翻译中对韵律的追求是十分困难的，译者所能做到的至多是再现原诗的韵式，要在译文中求得更微观层次上的一致性，一般是不可能的。然而，韵律尽管重要，翻译时也须知难而止。我们不必执着于追求原诗与译诗在韵律上绝对一致，而是要更多地着眼于译诗自身的音韵之美，着眼于译诗的韵律与译诗的意境的和谐统一。好的译诗并不意味着其韵式与原诗韵式丝毫不差，而是其韵式与译诗的内在韵律要吻合得天衣无缝。历史上的《诗经》翻译实践，已经很好地证明了这一点。在这样的观念之下，译诗韵律问题并不会构成译诗的梗阻，译者可以通过灵活变通，创造性地重塑译诗韵律之美。所以，在了解中英诗歌艺术的同异的基础上，在立足于诗的本事与意境的同时充分发挥译者的主观能动性，大概就是诗歌韵律翻译的活的根本法门。

第四章 《诗经》题旨翻译——
诗本义与诗教文化

　　历经三千年沧桑，《诗经》中几乎每一篇诗都染上了些许神秘色彩。自汉初至唐，毛、郑、孔三家相继用政教思维去解读《诗经》的每一篇诗，在诗篇题旨问题上或以诗证史，或以史附诗，在以诗为"经"进行政教风化这一点上，代相承传，因成一统；宋朱熹作《诗集传》，主张破《序》立旨，尽管常另立新说，但仍未悖政教传统；至清末，方玉润作《诗经原始》，疑诗反序之意更甚，然而政教传统仍不失为《诗经》之根本。二十世纪初以来，《诗经》学界开始把诗篇本文完全置于文化人类学和文学视野之下。闻一多、郑振铎、刘大杰等学者将《诗经》主题按内容重新分类，今人洪湛侯（2002：657-684）又据其综合为祭祀诗、婚姻诗、颂祷诗等十大类；郭沫若则大力发明《诗经》文学。《诗经》从此正式步入文学时代。《诗经》研究的文学转向，在满足了新时代对《诗经》的政治及审美诉求的同时，也给《诗经》文化传统带来了危机，《诗经》从此不再是统治阶级用以施政言教的经书，而是摇身一变，一夜之间成了以审美为终极诉求的文学诗集，数千年的《诗经》政教文化传统就此断裂。这种状况，自然给19世纪以来的《诗经》翻译带来了很大困难，也为我国今后的文化翻译传播战略带来了巨大课题：关于《诗经》，我们究竟应该翻译什么？是翻译《诗经》文化，还是只翻译《诗经》文学？这是一个值得深入思考的问题。

第一节　诗篇题旨翻译所面临的主要问题

综观《诗经》两千多年的传承史，自东周时期开始，《诗经》就被君臣卿士用于外交及朝政中的聘问应对，汉初被立为"经"，汉以降直至清末，一直是统治阶级用以"经夫妇，成孝敬，厚人伦，美教化，移风俗"的经世治国之经典。《诗大序》云："诗者，志之所之也，在心为志，发言为诗。……情发于声，声成文谓之音。治世之音，安以乐，其政和。乱世之音，怨以怒，其政乖。亡国之音，哀以思，其民困。故正得失，动天地，感鬼神，莫近于诗。先王以是经夫妇，成孝敬，厚人伦，美教化，移风俗。"由此可见，《诗经》之精髓集中体现在三点：一者"志"，二者"情"，三者"教"。三者之间的关系是，情以言志，志以施教，更进一步说，"志"和"教"的关系是"志"以寓"教"。

显然，《诗经》的这一典籍性质，使我们无法将其作为一般意义上的文学诗集来翻译。若翻译仅致力于出其情，则有轻薄《诗经》之虞，若仅运斤于达其志，则有隔靴搔痒之不足。那么，我们究竟应该翻译什么？

根据现代哲学阐释学"效果历史"的理论，以及接受美学的"作品"理论，无论《诗经》本文及其"本义"如何，《诗经》在我国历史上被传承的，主要是作为典籍的《诗经》，是在经学家们的传、笺、疏、注中得以实现的、作为政治教化工具的《诗经》。政教的《诗经》，既是数千年中《诗经》作品的实现，也是《诗经》文化价值的实现。如果罔顾这一点，我们在理解《诗经》的意义和价值时，就会犯本末倒置的错误，翻译《诗经》就会去本就末，就会仅翻译"诗歌"，而恰恰丢失这些"诗歌"的特殊之处，即丢失其所代表的中华民族的历史和文化。因此，翻译《诗经》，就是要翻译其中的"情""志"与"政教"，其核心任务就是在表现诗篇情志的同时，保全《诗经》的历史文化蕴含，概言之，就是翻译《诗经》文化。

什么是《诗经》文化？具体而言，《诗经》文化就是《诗经》的接受史，是《诗经》在其传承过程中对中国社会和历史所产生的深刻影响，是《诗经》所塑造的中华民族精神传统。《诗经》在传承过程中主要发挥了两个社会作用：其一，作为经书的"经夫妇，成孝敬，厚人伦，美教化，移风俗"的政教作用。朱熹《诗集传序》云："人事浃于下，天道备于上，而无一理之不具也。……修身及家，平均天下之道，其亦不待他求而得之于此矣。"① 自商末周初至20世纪初新文化运动以前两千多年的时间里，《诗经》始终处在中国文化之尊的地位，是统治阶级经世治国的重要政治工具。在历代封建王朝统治时期，《诗经》虽然本身具有文学性，但其审美价值却一直未被重视。司马迁说："夫上古明王举乐者，非以娱心自乐，快意恣欲，将欲为治也。"② 举《乐》之古明王欲为治，举《诗经》之帝王卿士，亦复如此。如果将这一时期的《诗经》称

---

① 朱熹：《诗集传》，北京：中华书局，1958年，第2页。
② 《史记·乐书》。

第四章 《诗经》题旨翻译——诗本义与诗教文化

为文学，那么它也只是政治和教化的一种形式，更准确地说，它是政教文学，即以政教为最终目的的文学，而非以审美为最终目的的文学。刘勰《文心雕龙·原道》说，"道沿圣以垂文，圣因文而明道"。《诗经》乃载道之文，如此而已。其二，作为文学诗集的审美作用。20世纪初新文化运动以来，随着马克思主义意识形态和新文化在我国的兴起，《诗经》的地位由经书降为诗集，其政教内涵一度为学界所否认和抛弃，人们开始仅从文学的角度去解读和接受《诗经》。从此，《诗经》的性质似乎发生了彻底的改变，从古代的"因圣明道""将欲为治"，变成了怡情快意的文学诗集。

然而，人们虽然欲将《诗经》纯文学化，其深远的历史文化内涵却并没有因此而泯灭。近年来，《诗经》学界兴起了一股关于《诗经》文化诗学研究的热潮，《诗经》作为历史文化经典的原貌正在逐步恢复。这使《诗经》始终无法与普通的文学诗集相类。因此，纵观《诗经》长期以来所发挥的社会作用，客观地说，其文化本质就是经世治国的政教文学。从文本角度来看，《诗经》政教文学表现于以篇什为核心的整个《诗经》文本系统，包括被称为《诗经》之门户的《诗序》、诗篇本文及其传、笺、注、疏。这个文本系统，共同构成了以文学为载体、以政教为目的的《诗经》文化系统。

至此，《诗经》翻译的对象已经十分清楚。既然《诗经》是政教文学，那么就要既翻译其情志，又翻译其政教，而重中之重则是保全其政教文化蕴含。概言之，《诗经》翻译的对象，就是整个《诗经》文化系统。

要翻译《诗经》文化系统，就不能局限于《诗经》篇什的语言学及文学意义，而要在移译篇什本文的同时，传达整个《诗经》文化系统所阐发的社会寓意。这意味着，我们不仅要翻译《诗经》的篇什本文，还要翻译《诗序》。

但是，《诗序》在历史上一直是备受争议的问题，对其翻译有必要进行深入探讨。鉴于《诗序》本身的复杂性，在此有必要先对其进行一番简要的讨论。

因为历史的原因，《诗经》篇什的主题问题十分复杂，自东汉郑玄以来两千余年，在《诗经》学史上一直是一个重大课题。问题的指向是《诗序》的所出与真伪。关于《诗序》的作者，自东汉始即成为《诗经》学"第一争诟之端"①。此后，经学界先后出现了四十余家不同的观点。撮其要者则是：子夏、毛公说（郑玄、沈重），子夏说（王素），卫宏说（范晔、陆机、朱熹、叶梦得、姚际恒、崔述、魏源、顾颉刚等），汉儒说（韩愈、郭绍虞），大、小毛公说（苏辙、朱自清），村野妄人说（郑樵）、孔子、国史说（程颐），"诗人自作"说（王安石），刘歆、卫宏说（康有为），汉代"毛诗家"说（胡念贻）等。（洪湛侯，2002：157-161）学者们争论的焦点是《诗序》的真伪问题，包括《诗序》所言是否真的概括反映了诗篇的本义，所附史实是否准确无误，所宣美刺教义是否是诗人的本意等。郑樵《诗辨妄》一书对《诗序》进行了专门考证，发现其存在多处错误，仅《诗辨妄》顾颉刚辑本中就达59则（洪湛侯，2002：330），分为附会史传、虚构史实、妄定时代、随文生训、杂入后世词语、据诗文妄释篇名等类。朱熹从最初疑序以致最终破序，其在《朱子语类·诗传遗说》卷二引中说："熹向作诗解文字，初用《小序》，至解不行处，亦曲为

---

① 参见《四库全书总目》。

之说；后来觉得不安，第二次解者，虽存小序，间为辨破，然终是不见诗人本意，然后方知尽去《小序》，便可自通，于是尽涤荡旧说，诗意方活。"（转引自洪湛侯，2002：331）闻一多、郑振铎，以及今人高亨、程俊英等更是从疑序之风，另辟现代诗经学，且较前贤更进一步——彻底把《诗经》解释成文学。尽管如此，相较之下，历史上《诗序》的尊奉者仍居多，疑《诗序》之集大成者朱熹也不例外。与此同时，范处义、吕祖谦、严粲、陈傅良等尊《序》派之申说也多理据兼备，不无道理。这两种观点长时间交锋，也给了我们许多思考。其一，疑序者的目的是什么？其疑序之论是否成立？其二，《诗序》究竟有无合理之处？其价值究竟在哪里？首先，应该承认，对《诗序》的质疑和辩论，反映出了历代《诗经》学家对篇旨问题的终极关怀，有学术研究上的积极意义。但是，我们也应该考察疑序者的动机及其历史背景，这有利于我们对《诗序》进行客观的认识和评价。从《诗经》学史来看，第一个疑序者是唐代著名文学家韩愈。众所周知，韩愈领导了中唐时期的古文运动，在诗歌创作方面，他针对大历以来浮荡绮靡的诗风，自觉继承和发扬李白、杜甫在诗歌创作上的业绩，力图恢复盛唐诗歌气象。韩愈力图革新诗歌的情结，使他不能满足于经学家对于《诗经》所做的政教解释，而是力图发明《诗经》中的文学新意，这当属自然之事。唐宋八大家之一的欧阳修是我国卓越的文学家和史学家，是北宋诗文革新运动的领袖。欧阳修的诗歌创作在艺术上主要受韩愈影响较深。作为一代鸿儒，他对《诗序》的怀疑当出于与韩愈同样的原因。郑樵是宋代史学家和目录学家，他对《诗序》的批评是基于其对史实的忠实态度，其《诗辨妄》确实指出了《诗序》中的一些错误。朱熹对《诗序》的批评则主要是源于其对理学的诉求，他意欲以《诗》说理，而并非真正从中发现了文学。五四新文化运动之后今人的批评，则主要是出于摆脱儒教、革新思想的时代需要，其背后既有人类思想发展的内在动力，也有新时期意识形态革命的强烈动机。在这种精神的指引下，否定《诗经》中的传统"政教""礼教"而将其脱胎换骨成属于人民大众的民间文学，是符合时代精神发展要求的。值得注意的是，历代经学家对《诗序》的批评确实有许多虚妄含糊之词。例如，朱熹《诗集传·卷耳》云："此亦后妃所自作，可以见其贞静专一之至矣。岂当文王朝会征伐之时，羑里拘幽之日而作欤？然不可考矣。"又方玉润《诗经原始·葛覃》："……盖此亦采之民间，与《关雎》同为房中乐，前咏初婚，此赋归宁耳。"①如此之类，皆属疑而未考之论。疑《序》者欲以一方之唏嘘含糊之词强加于另一方，置另一方于不义，这自然不合乎客观逻辑。况且，疑序者所论也常常不能自圆其说，更不必说缺乏确凿证据。例如，《葛生》小序曰："《葛生》，刺晋献公也。好攻战，则国人多丧矣。"杨简在其《慈湖诗传》中反驳《葛生》小序说："夫本诗妇思其夫也。卫宏不知夫妇之道正大，故外推其说以及于君焉。既失诗人之情，又失先圣之旨。"（洪湛侯，2002：347）杨简既确言《诗序》为卫宏所作，说明其妄信《后汉书·儒林传》关于《诗序》作者的一家之言，据此可推知其此番辨说也必属虚妄之辞。况且，即使《葛生》真的是"夫本诗夫思其妇也"，何以肯定作者不能用寡女思夫来讽刺当时当政之昏君？相反，观诗篇之首句"葛生蒙楚，蔹蔓于野"可知，诗人以诗言"刺"是完全可能

---

① 方玉润：《诗经原始》，北京：中华书局，1986年，第76页。

的，如若仅是女子观葛而生发思夫之念，则诗篇怎么有必要描绘"敛蔓于野"这样一种荒草丛生的凄凉漫漫之状？可见作者所悼者并非一人，而完全可能是泛指在战乱中大批死亡的士兵。文学善于举偶喻常，尤惯以暗喻为能事，岂能把一女子悼念亡夫看作是生活现实中的真实个例？某些反《序》论者之虚妄，由此可窥一斑。冯浩菲批评反序者说："《诗》之《小序》不是'全不可信'，也不是'胡说'。亦可见其当年的评论有失公允，过于偏激。朱子之说犹如此不可靠，其他追随者多欠用功，实乃吠声之辈，赶潮流、瞎起哄而已。"（冯浩菲，2003：172）而最重要的是，《诗序》本身的真伪与《诗序》的文化塑造作用完全是两码事。也就是说，无论在何种意义上对或错，《诗序》毕竟还是《诗序》，其是历代解经的必由门户，是历代帝王鸿儒将之与《诗经》一起用以施政言教、经世治国的《诗序》，是《诗经》文化不可或缺的有机组成部分。

至此，我们已经可以回答以下两个问题：一是《诗序》需不需要翻译？二是《诗序》在翻译中究竟应该如何对待？

从文化传承与发展的观点来看，文化典籍的传承过程所划定的轨迹决定着一个民族文化发展的道路，这个轨迹并不是典籍的真伪决定的，而是典籍的传承方式决定的。换成现代学术话语来说，就是由典籍在传承过程中被运用或解读的方式决定的。世世代代，人们对典籍的解读不断释放着文化蕴藏，从而构成了一个民族的文化传统。中华民族的文化传统是由典籍的经、传、注、疏、解、释所构成的一条生生不息的河流。人们在这条河流中汲取营养，涤濯灵魂，对他们来说，河流中的每一滴水对其生命都是不可或缺的因子，但却鲜有人问及河流的源头。试想，有几人曾去证明中华民族最古老神话的真伪？而从学术和文化的角度来说，神话又有多少证明的可能和必要。然而，中华文明却离不开这些古老神话的滋养，因为它们毕竟是中华文化之根。由此观之，既然翻译的功能是文化交流而非标新立异，那么对于翻译来说，经学家们对《诗序》的种种聚颂褒贬，并不能改变《诗经》作为"经"为数千年中华文化传统所划定的轨迹。《诗序》真伪，以及其作者何人，早已无足轻重，而最重要的是《诗序》在我国历史中究竟是以何种形态对我国文化的发展施加影响。以这样的科学态度，我们就能够确定一条《诗经》篇旨的衍变路线，并在变动不居中寻求和把握其确定性，从而走出历代诗经学所造成的迷雾，确立我们的翻译方针。

从《诗序》研究真伪杂糅的现实情况出发，我们对《诗序》的翻译可以立足于这样的基本原则，即正确的要照样翻译，错误的也要翻译，但要做必要的说明。对于受到质疑但尚无定论者，翻译时要有适当说明，但不能盲从质疑者的观点。具体来说，就是把《诗序》与《诗经》及其传、笺、注、疏、解、释等分成《诗经》的三种发展形态来翻译，即按底本将其分成汉唐底本、宋清底本、现代底本。汉唐底本即阮元《十三经注疏》校勘的《毛诗正义》，宋清底本即朱熹的《诗集传》，现代底本为高亨的《诗经今注》、陈子展的《诗经直解》或程俊英的《诗经译注》。这样我们可以得到至少三大类译本。我们也可以将三个阶段的解读放在一个译本里处理，即每篇译诗都配一个题解，题解的内容包括《诗序》，在有争议处附加朱熹题解和现代诗经学题解。用这种方式，把《诗经》在中华文化史中所发挥的不同作用描绘出来。大概也唯有采用这样的策略，才能把《诗经》文化全面介绍给西方。

第二节　译诗韵律至上，以义就韵

如上文所言，由于历代中外译者对《诗序》的理解程度及所持的态度不同，造成了违《序》译诗的普遍现象。其表现主要分为四个方面：（一）有的译者对诗旨妄加臆测，从而导致译文旨义与原文相悖；（二）有的译者忽视历代经学家的训诂成果，望文生义，造成了译文的细节性错误，影响了原文本义的传达；（三）有的译者过于接受现代《诗经》学的影响，视《诗经》仅为文学，随意损益诗文内容，致使译诗旨义整体上不伦不类；（四）有的译者在翻译中借翻译《诗经》之名行创作之实，生产出近乎伪英文《诗经》。以上现象都不同程度地误导了西方读者，对《诗经》文化的传播造成了一定的危害。在此，我们专门就以上四种现象进行讨论。

在诸译本中，重视译诗韵律的译本至少有四个：一是理雅各的有韵本，二是詹宁斯译本，三是许渊冲译本，四是汪榕培译本。四者均以韵律为译诗之要，从中追求审美价值。那么，其效果如何呢？

为了以诗译诗，增加诗的韵味，理雅各于1876年将其1872年的《诗经》无韵体首译本修订成韵体译本。与1872年版译文相较，1876年版本中的很多篇什诗行变得冗长臃肿，诗味虽略有所增强，文义却受到了较大影响。例如《东门之池》的译文：

> To steep your hemp, you seek the moat,
> 　　Where lies the pool, th' east gate beyond.
> I seek that lady, good and fair,

Who can to me in song respond.

To steep your grass-cloth plants, you seek
　　The pool that near the east gate lies.
I seek that lady, good and fair,
　　Who can with me hold converse wise.

Out by the east gate, to the moat
　　To steep your rope rush, you repair.
Her pleasant converse to enjoy,
　　I seek that lady, good and fair.^①

从译诗内容本身来看，诗中有两个人，一是"you"，一是"I"。诗人把两个人所做的事情进行了对照：前者为了沤麻等事而四处寻找池塘，后者则为了寻觅异性知己而四处奔波。然而，若细加分析，沤麻和觅偶这两者之间，本身可谓风马牛不相及，并无什么可比性，译者将两者硬拉到一起，颇显穿凿痕迹。如果译者是考虑将寻找池塘和寻找知音的过程相对比，虽然在"寻找"过程上有些相似性，但这两种"寻找"之间的意义和价值也无法相类。这样的类比只能是让人读来感到一片惑然。我们再来看原文：

　　　东门之池，可以沤麻。
　　　彼美淑姬，可与晤歌。
　　　东门之池，可以沤纻。

---

① James Legge. *The Book of Poetry*. Shanghai: The Chinese Book Company, 1931: 153-154.

> 彼美淑姬，可与晤语。
> 东门之池，可以沤菅。
> 彼美淑姬，可与晤言。

关于诗的每章首句，《毛诗传》均解释为"兴也"①。意思是说，作者看到"东门之池"有"沤麻""沤纻""沤菅"之用，就联想到了"彼美淑姬"有与我"晤歌""晤语""晤言"之益，故讴歌之。而译者没有抓住其中的精神，致使译文貌合神离。而这种效果的由来，不能不说与译者追求译诗的隔行押韵有关。译者为了凑足韵律，分别在第二、六、十行设"beyond""lies""repair"三个单词，从而凑成 /ɔnd/、/aiz/、/pɛə/ 三种韵。如此经营，译文的本义与原文的相比就改变了许多。译文第一章说："为了沤麻你找到了城门外护城河旁边的池塘。我找到了善良美丽的姑娘，她能与我对歌"；第二章说："你找到池塘沤麻，我则找到了善良美丽的姑娘进行有智慧的交谈"；第三章又说："为了沤麻，你来到护城河，而我则找到善良美丽的姑娘快乐地聊天"；如此等等。《诗小序》的解释则是："《东门之池》，刺时也。疾其君之淫昏，而思贤女以配君子也。"反复咀嚼译诗，却仍不见此意。而理雅各在译诗前所加题解"The Tung Men Chih Ch'ih; allusive. The praise of some virtuous and intelligent lady"，也属独出心裁。这样一来，译诗在整体上仍不能摆脱隔靴搔痒之缺陷。

受现代《诗经》学的影响，许渊冲对《诗经》的文学性十分重视。按其翻译理论，《诗经》翻译当是音、形、义三美兼备。可是，

---

① 孔颖达：《毛诗正义》，北京：北京大学出版社，1999年，第445页。

观其各篇译文，音与形两者，尤其是音韵，似乎占了上风，即每首译诗讲求押韵，每个诗行力求短小，这是其译本的突出特点。然而遗憾的是，对译诗的音和形的追求却直接影响了诗义的准确性。请看许先生《蒹葭》的翻译：

蒹葭苍苍，白露为霜。
所谓伊人，在水一方。
溯洄从之，道阻且长。
溯游从之，宛在水中央。

蒹葭凄凄，白露未晞。
所谓伊人，在水之湄。
溯洄从之，道阻且跻。
溯游从之，宛在水中坻。

蒹葭采采，白露未已，
所谓伊人，在水之涘。
溯洄从之，道阻且右。
溯游从之，宛在水中沚。

Where Is She?

Green, green the reed;
Frost and dew gleam.
Where's she I need?
Beyond the stream.

Upstream I go;

The way's so long.

And downstream, lo!

She is there among.

White, white the reed,

Dew not yet dried.

Where's she I need?

On the other side.

Upstream I go;

Hard is the way.

And downstream, lo!

She is far away.

Bright, bright the reed,

With frost dews blend.

Where's she I need?

At river's end.

Upstream I go;

The way does wind

And downstream, lo!

She is far behind. ①

译诗的韵式比较复杂，通篇的韵式结构有三个类型，即ababcdcd、aeaecfcf、agagchch，均属隔行押韵，韵律较为整饬。但是，译者

---

① 许渊冲（译）：《诗经》，北京：中国对外翻译出版公司，2009年，第133-134页。

为赢得韵律而付出的代价也十分明显。首先,每章首句有凑韵的痕迹。根据《毛诗传》,原文"苍苍""萋萋""采采"并无表示芦苇颜色之义。《毛诗传》曰:"苍苍,盛也。"[①]"萋萋,犹苍苍也。""采采,犹萋萋也。"[②]三者可以互释,可见都是芦苇生长茂盛之义。而译文则将其分别译成绿色、白色和亮色。其次,各章中"所谓伊人"一句都被译作"Where is she I need?"这样一个问句。其中"she"后的定语"I need"完全是冗余之词。既然本句是一个问句,"寻求"之义自在其中,何必复赘之以限定词语?而根据经学解释,"伊人"本义当为贤德之士,并非男女恋爱的一方。第三,"水"在原诗中的意象是莽莽苍苍,无边无际,所以诗人以"在水一方"喻难寻求之义。而译诗中的"stream"仅是一条山涧小溪,怎可与原诗的"水"意象相比。第四,第一章末句"She is there among"与"宛在水中央"无法对应,前者是确定的在河水中之义,而后者则是茫然不知在何处之义。第五,"在水之湄",《毛诗传》曰:"湄,水隒也。"[③]《毛诗正义》援引《释水》云:"水草交为湄"[④],意思是水草相交之处,亦即水边之义。此句译文则是"On the other side",意思相差甚远。第六,"道阻且跻",《毛诗传》云:"跻,升也"[⑤]。郑玄《笺》云:"升者,言其难至,如升阪。"[⑥]译文则是"Hard is the way",回译回来其实可以是"路面很硬"的意思,其误自不待

---

① 孔颖达:《毛诗正义》,北京:北京大学出版社,1999年,第422页。
② 同上,第424页。
③ 同上。
④ 同上。
⑤ 同上。
⑥ 同上。

言。第七,"宛在水中坻"。《毛诗传》曰:"坻,小渚也。"① 渚,小洲之义。译文则是"She is far away",意思是她在远方。第八,末章中的"白露未已"。《毛诗传》曰:"未已,犹未止也。"② 亦即上章中的"未晞"。可见不能译成"With frost dews blend"(露和霜混合到一起)。最后,本章中"在水之涘"及"宛在水中沚"。《毛诗传》云:"涘,厓也。""小渚曰沚也。"③ 所以其义亦非"At river's end"(在河的尽头)和"She is far behind"(她远在身后)之谓。这样,整个一篇译诗在内容上几乎就与原诗没有多少相同之处了。

请再看汪榕培翻译的一首《桃夭》:

The Beautiful Peach

The peach tree stands wayside,
　　With blossoms glowing pink.
I wish the pretty bride
　　Affluence in food and drink.

The peach tree stands wayside,
　　With fruits hanging rife.
I wish the pretty bride
　　Abundant wealth in life.

The peach tree stands wayside,

---

① 孔颖达:《毛诗正义》,北京:北京大学出版社,1999年,第424页。
② 同上。
③ 同上。

With leaves thick and dense.
I wish the pretty bride,
　　A pleasant home e'er since. ①

译者为译诗加题旨为:"In this poem, the beautiful peach blossom is compared to the pretty bride and her happy marriage."。若将这首英文诗反译成汉语,大致应该是这样:

　　桃立路边,英华粉然。
　　吾祝丽子,无忧饮餐。

　　桃立路边,其实颤颤。
　　吾祝丽子,财富满满。

　　桃立路边,其叶蓁蓁。
　　吾祝丽子,家乐殷殷。

我们再看原文:

　　桃之夭夭,灼灼其华。
　　之子于归,宜其室家。

　　桃之夭夭,有蕡其实。
　　之子于归,宜其家室。

---

① 汪榕培、任秀桦(译注):《诗经》(中英文版),大连:辽宁教育出版社,1995年,第23、25页。

第四章 《诗经》题旨翻译——诗本义与诗教文化

> 桃之夭夭,其叶蓁蓁。
> 之子于归,宜其家人。

《诗小序》云:"桃夭,后妃之所致也。不妒忌,则男女以正,婚姻以时,国无鳏民也。"[①] 将译文及其题解与原文及《诗小序》两相比较,可见译文有三处与原文不合。原文旨在歌颂周民被文王之化,男女以正,婚姻以时,国无鳏民;译文仅以"桃树的花繁叶茂来比喻新娘的美貌,并祝福她婚姻美满"[②],其言外之旨浅薄。此其一。原文以桃夭起兴,言男女婚姻当值年盛之时;而译文中不见此种意思。此其二。女大当嫁,其用在于"宜其室家"。《左传》云:"女有家,男有室"。宜其室家,即和合夫妇,繁衍后代,如桃之结实,并使家族繁荣壮大,如桃叶之蓁蓁。译文显然也无此义,而仅有祝愿女子富足快乐之义而已。此其三。此三点核心意思若不译出,那么就等于这首诗所有民俗文化蕴含整个都没有翻译。另外,从内容细节上看,原文并没有桃"树立于路边(stands wayside)""饮餐充足(abundance in food and drink)""一生富有(abundant wealth in life)"等义,译者似乎发现在此不便直译,而欲翻译原文的引申意义。但这里的引申并不准确,还不如尽量直译,把想象的事留给英文读者。如果不这样受韵律的拘束,这些诗行的意思,就可以翻译得更加贴切。

为了满足韵律的需要,翻译必然不得不增损或改换词语,这种增损看似无大碍,实际上并非如此。如汪榕培译《草虫》:

[①] 孔颖达:《毛诗正义》,北京:北京大学出版社,1999年,第45页。
[②] 汪榕培、任秀桦(译注):《诗经》(中英文版),大连:辽宁教育出版社,1995年,第24页。

喓喓草虫，趯趯阜螽。
未见君子，忧心忡忡。
亦既见止，亦既觏止，我心则降。

陟彼南山，言采其蕨。
未见君子，忧心惙惙。
亦既见止，亦既觏止，我心则说。

陟彼南山，言采其薇。
未见君子，我心伤悲。
亦既见止，亦既觏止，我心则夷。

The Grasshopper

The grasshopper chirr in the mead;
The locusts hop in the weed.
My dear one is not there;
I'm full of worry and care.
As soon as I see my dear,
As soon as I meet my dear,
All worries will disappear.

Atop the southern hill,
I pick the fern at will.
My dear one is not there;
I'm full of worry and care.
As soon as I see my dear,
As soon as I meet my dear,

All sorrows will disappear.

Atop the southern hill
I pick the herb at will.
My dear one is not there;
I'm full of woe and care.
As soon as I see my dear,
As soon as I meet my dear,
All woes will disappear. [1]

这首译诗改动原文的地方多达19处，除了后两章的首句外，几乎句句都有。"in the mead"和"in the weed"属为押双行韵而增加，实际上是武断的，草虫岂止生活在杂草中？"at will"显然是为了呼应前行的"hill"，而原文的"言采其蕨"与"言采其薇"哪有随意（at will）之意？若真的是随意采摘山菜，哪会有什么忧愁可言？"care"是为"there"而增益，但"care"的单数形式并不具有忧患的意思，复数才有此意，如"earthly cares"。这实际上造成了意思上的错误。"my dear"是为后文的"disappear"而改写的，或者从译者思维过程上来说后者是为前者而改写的，但无论如何，"my dear"是不适当的，因为这种称呼直接违背了中国古代道德礼仪中的男女之礼，透出狎亲而无敬，但原文的"君子"则是"亲而有敬"。最后，"All woes will disappear"并不是"我心则降""我心则说""我心则夷"等意思，因为痛苦消失了并不等于内心安静、

---

[1] 汪榕培、任秀桦（译注）:《诗经》（中英文版），大连：辽宁教育出版社，1995年，第55、57页。

高兴或平静。另外，译文在表达的角度和方式上也已经改变，前者间接写心中的感觉，而后者则是直接写。

　　上述问题的根源，并非是译者不懂原文的意思，而是一味追求韵律造成的结果。译者不惜采取随意损益或改写的手法，以歪曲原诗本义为代价来凑齐韵律，实属下策，当为典籍翻译界所戒。一首诗的价值，即便是只讲审美价值，也非止于韵律。今天，无论是中国还是西方，早就已经进入现代诗时代，无韵诗已经广为人们所接受。所以我们的《诗经》翻译何必对韵律锱铢必较，更何况《诗经》本身就不是每篇都韵律整齐。译诗若有现代无韵诗那样的自然节奏，读来朗朗上口，于韵亦无不可。诗者，贵在诗味，诗味的获得需要多方面要素的有机结合，如语言的艺术性、诗意的深刻性等，对诗的审美诉求，中西方是一致的。所以，诗的审美价值完全可以在其他诸多方面得到补偿。至于《诗经》翻译，韵律更不应该取代意与境而成为首要的关注之所在。

第三节　无视训诂，臆测文义

　　《诗经》是先秦典籍，其中含有大量古语、古代民俗和典故，对现代读者来说，阅读起来比较困难，一般需要借助传、笺、注、疏的训诂。对于《诗经》翻译来说，训诂的问题就更加突出，需要译者仔细研读传、笺、注、疏的原著，确切了解每个字的古义与寓意，不能妄加猜测。遗憾的是，在现有的诸译本中，忽视训诂，妄测文义的现象比较普遍，对译本质量造成了很大危害。例

第四章 《诗经》题旨翻译——诗本义与诗教文化

如《汉广》：

南有乔木，不可休息。
汉有游女，不可求思。
汉之广矣，不可泳思。
江之永矣，不可方思。

翘翘错薪，言刈其楚。
之子于归，言秣其马。
汉之广矣，不可泳思。
江之永矣，不可方思。

翘翘错薪，言刈其蒌。
之子于归，言秣其驹。
汉之广矣，不可泳思。
江之永矣，不可方思。

詹宁斯的译文如下：

THE UNAPPROACHABLE MAIDENS

In the South are stately poplars,
   Vainly there we rest for shade;
By the Han maids wander freely,
   Vainly there love's quest is made.
      O the Han's great breadth (divides us)!

> Baffling to the diver's craft.
> O the Kiang's great length (divides us)!
> Baffling to the toiling raft.
>
> Some are piling high their firewood;
> O to cut away each thorn!
> Others leaving to be married;
> O to give their steeds their corn!
> But the breadth of Han (divides us),
> Baffling to the diver's craft,
> And the length of Kiang (divides us),
> Baffling to the toiling raft.
>
> Some are piling high their grass-loads;
> O to cut the fragrant weed!
> Others leaving to be married;
> O their two-year-olds to feed!
> But the breadth of Han, &c. ①

译诗中至少有四处原文被曲解：一是"南有乔木"，二是"翘翘错薪"，三是"言刈其楚""言刈其蒌"，四是"言秣其马""言秣其驹"。下面我们具体来分析。

首先，关于"南有乔木"。《毛诗传》云："南方之木，美乔上

---

① William Jennings. *The Shi King: The Old "Poetry Classic" of the Chinese.* London and New York: George Routledge and Sons, 1891: 41-42.

竦也。"①所以不是"stately poplars",stately 是庄严之义,poplar 则是白杨树。

其次,关于"翘翘错薪"。《毛诗传》曰:"翘翘,薪貌。错,杂也。"②又《毛诗正义》曰:"翘翘,高貌。"③译文"Some are piling high their firewood"的意思是"有些(姑娘)把柴堆得高高的",与原文相左。

第三,关于"言刈其楚"。《毛诗正义》云:"薪,木称,故《月令》云'收秩薪柴',注云:'大者可析谓之薪。'下章蒌草亦云薪者,因此通其文。楚亦木名,故《学记》注以楚为荆,《王风》《郑风》并云'不流束楚',皆是也。言楚在'杂薪之中尤翘翘',言尤明杂薪亦翘翘也。"④根据以上解释,把此句与上句相联系,意思是说诸木相杂,都长得高,荆木也在其中,尤高,故砍荆为用。而译文"O to cut away each thorn!"的意思则是,"错薪"全是荆木,全部砍掉。"言刈其蒌"之义与"言刈其楚"相同,只是"楚"易为"蒌",即蒌蒿,译文却成了"O to cut the fragrant weed"。原文的"翘"字,在这里衍变成了芳(fragrant)字。

最后,关于"言秣其马""言秣其驹"。原文"翘翘错薪,言刈其楚;之子于归,言秣其马"的意思十分清楚,即诗人咏叹汉水游女难以追求,要求则求最贞洁者,若有贞女愿嫁,宁愿给她喂马喂驹;这两句的译文"O to give their steeds their corn!"和"O their two-year-olds to feed!"中的"their"却指代不明,而原文中"秣"

---

① 孔颖达:《毛诗正义》,北京:北京大学出版社,1999年,第53页。
② 同上,第54页。
③ 同上,第55页。
④ 同上。

马、"秣"驹者则明显是出嫁的女子。

再看詹宁斯译的《采蘋》：

> She goes to gather water-wort,
> Beside the streams south of the hills;
> She goes to gather water-grass
> Along the swollen roadside rills;
>
> Goes now to store her gathered herbs
> In basket round, in basket square;
> Goes now to seethe and simmer them
> In tripod and in cauldron there;
>
> Pours out libations of them all
> Beneath the light within the Hall. —
> And who is she—so occupied?
> —who, but (our lord's) young pious bride? [①]

原诗是用一问一答的形式写成的，叙述了周代女子勤劳的美德和采蘋、采藻以奉祭祀的原始宗教风俗。译诗明显没有翻译原文的七个"予以"，而全部代之以陈述句，原诗的表达形式在此面目全非。"南涧"义为南方之山涧，译文则变成"Beside the streams south of the hills"（山南溪流旁边）。另外，"蘋"非"water-wrot"，"藻"亦非"water-grass"。问题最大的是最后一章四句，译文里已经找

---

① William Jennings. *The Shi King: The Old "Poetry Classic" of the Chinese*. London and New York: George Routledge and Sons, 1891: 46-47.

不到一点原文的影子。我们不妨把译文最后一节回译如下：

> 把她们的酒奠下来祭神
> 就在堂内的灯光下
> 如此忙碌——她是谁？
> 除了是我公虔诚的新娘之外，还能是谁？

本章译文中，"牖"（窗）、"尸"（主持）、"齐"（斋）、"季女"（少女）等字的古义全部被篡改。这些文字之误，貌似寥寥数语，微不足道，实际上却使译文遮掩了我国古代采蘋祭祖、少女为"尸"主持祭祀仪式的原始宗教文化的原貌。

庞德的《诗经》译本中，很少能见到忠实翻译的诗篇，偶尔有之，也往往难以见到译者对文字训诂的研究和重视，相反，重要的古字义，如《敝笱》中的"笱""鲂""鳏""鲇""从"等，其意思或被篡改或被略去，最终使译文落得不伦不类。例如《敝笱》的翻译：

> 敝笱在梁，其鱼鲂鳏。
> 齐子归止，其从如云。
> 敝笱在梁，其鱼鲂鲇。
> 齐子归止，其从如雨。
> 敝笱在梁，其鱼唯唯。
> 齐子归止，其从如水。

The wicker of the weir is broke,

> loose fish are out again
> as the Lady of Ts'i comes home
> with a cloud in her train.
>
> The wicker of the weir is broke
> as ex-Miss Ts'i comes home again,
> luce and perch be broken out
> as many as drops of rain.
>
> The wicker of the weir is broke
> and these fish make a very great clatter.
> The Lady of Ts'i comes home with a train,
> all of them loose as water. ①

《诗小序》云:"《敝笱》,刺文姜也。齐人恶鲁桓公微弱,不能防闲文姜,使至淫乱,为二国患焉。"文姜是齐襄公之妹,嫁鲁桓公后仍与其兄齐襄公私通;齐人恶鲁桓公懦弱,不能制止文姜淫乱,故作诗讽刺。诗以被遗弃在渔梁上的破渔具比喻桓公之软弱无能,以鲂鳏等逍遥自在的游鱼比喻文姜淫荡无度,诗义鲜明。

在很多情况下,诗中的文字在不同经学家的训诂中早就有分歧,这使得后世的译者往往感到无所适从,稍有不慎,就会犯错误。如《齐风·著》:

> 俟我于著乎而,

---

① Ezra Pound. *The Classic Anthology Defined by Confucius*. London: Faber and Faber Ltd., 1954: 49.

充耳以素乎而,

尚之以琼华乎而!

俟我于庭乎而,

充耳以青乎而,

尚之以琼莹乎而!

俟我于堂乎而,

充耳以黄乎而,

尚之以琼英乎而!

我们先来看汪榕培和理雅各的译文:

汪译:

He waits for me within the hall;

His pendants hang on silken strings.

How his ruby shines and swings!

He waits for me within the yard;

His pendants hang on azure strings.

How his ruby gleams and swings!

He waits for me within the court;

His pendants hang on gilded strings.

How his ruby glows and swings! [1]

---

[1] 汪榕培、任秀桦(译注):《诗经》(中英文版),大连:辽宁教育出版社,1995年,第391页。

理译：

He was waiting for me between the door and screen.
The strings of his ear-stoppers were of white silk,
And there were appended to them beautiful *hwa*-stones.

He was waiting for me in the open court.
The strings of his ear-stoppers were of green silk,
And there were appended to them beautiful *yung*-stones.

He was waiting for me in the hall.
The strings of his ear-stoppers were of yellow silk,
And there were appended to them beautiful *ying*-gems.①

这篇诗的翻译问题，主要出在"著""充耳""素""青""黄""尚""琼华""琼莹""琼英"等名物训诂上。其中，历代经学家的解释分歧最大的是"充耳"。《毛诗传》将"充耳"解释为象牙做的用来塞耳避听的"瑱"："素，象瑱。"②所谓"充耳以素"，毛亨以为，在这个上下文中"素"即充耳。郑玄不把"素"当充耳解，而是将其解释为悬瑱用的白色丝线："待我于著，谓从君子而出至于著，君子揖之时也，我视君子则以素为充耳。谓所以县瑱

---

① James Legge. *Chinese Classics with a Translation, Critical and Exegetical Notes, Prolegomena, and Copious Indexes*. London: Henry Frowde, Oxford University Press Warehouse, Amen Corner, E. C., 1939 年伦敦会香港影印所影印本，Vol. IV-Part I: 152-153.

② 孔颖达：《毛诗正义》，北京大学出版社，1999 年，第 332 页。

者，或名为纮，织之，人君五色，臣则三色而已。此言素者，目所先见而云。"① 东汉王肃同意《毛诗传》训诂，反对郑玄对"素"的解释："王后织玄纮。天子之玄纮，一玄而已，何云具五色乎？"② 西晋经学家孙毓不同意王肃"以美石饰象瑱"之说："即如王肃之言，以美石饰象瑱，象骨贱于美石，谓之饰象，何也？下传以青为青玉，黄为黄玉，又当以石饰玉乎？"③ 他也反对郑《笺》对"素""青""黄"三字的解释："案礼之名充耳，是塞耳，即所谓瑱悬当耳，故谓之塞耳。悬之者，别谓之纮，不得谓之充耳，犹瑱不得名之为纮也。故曰玉之瑱兮。"④ 他又联系后文"尚之以琼华乎而"说："言充耳者，固当谓瑱为充耳，非谓纮也。但经言充耳以素，素丝悬之，非即以素为充耳也。既言充耳以素，未言充耳之体，又言饰之以琼华，正谓以琼华作充耳。……以经之文势，既言'充耳以素'，即云饰之以琼华，明以琼华为充耳，悬之以素丝，故易传以素丝为纮，琼华为瑱也。"⑤ 这是唐以前经学史上有代表性的三种观点，孔颖达对此未置可否。朱熹《诗集传》："充耳，以纩悬瑱，所谓纮也。尚，加也。琼华，美石似玉者，即所以为瑱也。"⑥ 今人明确把充耳解释为丝线加瑱而构成的整体。程俊英《诗经译注》："充耳：是古代男子的一种装饰品，它挂在冠的两旁，正好垂在耳边。充耳挂在冠上的丝线，叫做'纮'，是杂色的。丝线上挂着一个棉球，叫做'纩'，棉球下挂着玉，叫做'瑱'。所以，充耳包

---

① 孔颖达：《毛诗正义》，北京：北京大学出版社，1999年，第332页。
② 同上，第334页。
③ 同上。
④ 同上。
⑤ 同上。
⑥ 朱熹：《诗集传》，北京：中华书局，1958年，第59页。

含着纮、纩、瑱三部分。这里指的是纮，即丝线。素：白。"① 袁愈荌《诗经全译》："[充耳]古代挂在冠冕两旁的饰物，以玉制成，下垂到耳。[充耳以素]严粲《诗缉》：'见其充耳以素丝为纮也。其纮之末加以美石如琼之华，谓瑱也。'"② 高亨《诗经今注》曰：

"充，塞也。素，白色。古代富贵者，男子帽的左右各系一条丝绳，绳的下端有穗，垂到胸部。丝绳用白、青、黄三色的三股丝编成，在当耳的地方，丝绳打成一个圆结，左右各一，正好塞着两耳，即所谓充耳。充耳以素，以青，以黄，乃是分别描写三色的三股丝的圆结……男子充耳的圆结上各穿上一块圆玉，叫做瑱。尚之以琼华、琼莹、琼英，都是描写玉瑱。"③

对比古今诸家注释，从诗篇上下文来看，《毛诗传》之失在于孤立了"素"字在文中的意义。郑《笺》所注"素"字，符合上下文的意思，但失之于对"尚"字的解释。若把"尚"解释为"饰"，则后文"尚之以琼华"则不可通，因为素丝、青丝、黄丝皆贱，玉石则贵，以贵饰贱，于理不通。若把"尚"解作"加"，则郑《笺》可通。孙毓与朱熹的解释符合此意，所以与上下文契合。今人的解释以高亨最为详细合理，其关键是把充耳看作丝线与瑱的整体。其他诗篇如《淇澳》之"有匪君子，充耳琇莹，会弁如星"，《都人士》之"彼都人士，充耳琇实"，都可以证明这一点。从上下文来

---

① 程俊英：《诗经译注》，上海：上海古籍出版社，2004年，第145页。
② 袁愈荌：《诗经全译》，贵阳：贵州人民出版社，1981年，第133-134页。
③ 高亨：《诗经今注》，上海：上海古籍出版社，1980年，第130-131页。

看,"充耳以素乎而"与"尚之以琼华乎而",以及后两章的末两句,都应读作相连的一句话,即"充耳以素,尚之以琼华(琼莹、琼英)",意思为:充耳用素丝(青丝、黄丝)加上琼华(琼莹、琼英)制成。诗人为什么只反复咏叹充耳?这可能与男子冠冕上的充耳色杂而美,较引人注意有关。

从译文来看,汪榕培将充耳之瑱译作"pendant"有歧义,这很容易让西方读者联想到西方首饰上的垂饰,如耳环上的钻石缀、项链上的钻石或玉石缀等;理雅各将其译作"ear-stopper",道出了充耳的功能,颇能体现民族文化特色。关于丝线的颜色,汪译中的"silken""azure""gilded"显然无法与"素""青""黄"三种丝线颜色相提并论。理译中把"青"译作"green"也是一个明显的错误。"著"指的是"门屏之间",汪译作"within the hall",也错了。而每章的末句,汪译皆译作诗人赞叹玉石的话语,与原文不相符。究其主要原因,似乎是译者在对"尚"字的理解上出了问题。至于"琼华""琼莹""琼英"都用"ruby"(红玉)来翻译,也是笼统的,与原文不相符,对于介绍中国古老婚俗文化中的亲迎习俗来说,译文似乎起不到作用。

相比之下,詹宁斯的译文较有所本,但失之于过分依赖郑《笺》的训诂:

> At the gate awaits me now, screened from sight, hi-ho!
> One with tassels o'er his ears all of white, hi-ho!
> And adorned with coloured gems, gleaming bright, hi-ho!
>
> Now he waits me in the court, past the screen, hi-ho!
> And the tassels o'er his ears are of green, hi-ho!

And his jewels have a lustre rarely seen, hi-ho!

In the hall he waits me last (now more bold), hi-ho!
And the tassels o'er his ears are of gold, hi-ho!
And his jewels—they are brilliant to behold, hi-ho! ①

不难看出,"著"没有译出,"充耳"被译作"tassel"不准确,充耳是瑱,而不是缨。把"尚"译作"adorn"也不准确,以致后文的"gem"成了装饰,上下文自相矛盾。译者对"尚"的理解还导致了后两章末句语焉不详,所谓的"jewels"位置究竟在哪里,也没说清楚。

以上所分析的翻译问题,皆出自译者对训诂的研判不当。每遇此类问题,译者当详查历代各家训诂,进行综合研判,取其合理者采之,不合理者弃之,方可避免错误。就这首诗的翻译来说,若译者能详研毛、郑、孔、朱、严(粲)、王(念孙)六家训诂,再辅之以《尔雅》《说文》等,即可综合出合理的见解,使译文避免错误。

《诗经》是典籍,译者在关注其文学价值的同时,当致力于还原其历史和上古民俗文化价值,对诗篇中所蕴含的我国先民的价值观、审美习惯、宗教情感等忠实地进行传达。但有一种翻译却是故意违背训诂,原因是为了使译文符合当今读者的审美诉求。例如《硕人》:

---

① William Jennings. *The Shi King: The Old "Poetry Classic" of the Chinese*. London and New York: George Routledge and Sons, 1891: 113–114.

第四章 《诗经》题旨翻译——诗本义与诗教文化

……

手如柔荑，肤如凝脂。

领如蝤蛴，齿如瓠犀。

螓首蛾眉，巧笑倩兮，美目盼兮。

……

汪榕培将其译作：

Her hands are small, her fingers slim;

Her skin is smooth as cream.

Her swan-like neck is long and slim;

Her teeth like pearls do gleam.

A broad forehead and arching brow

Complement her dimpled cheeks

And make her black eyes glow[①].

译诗中"柔荑""蝤蛴"都不见了，"瓠犀"成了"pearl"（珍珠），"蛾眉"成了"arching brow"（弯眉）。译者的判断可能是，翻译《诗经》关键在于"传神达意"（汪榕培，1994），译文中若用"柔荑""蝤蛴""瓠犀""蛾眉"来比喻美人的"手""领""齿""眉"，就会让西方读者觉得不可思议，从而使译诗失去美感。然而，原文

---

① 汪榕培、任秀桦（译注）：《诗经》（中英文版），大连：辽宁教育出版社，1995年，第231、233页。

古韵没有了，遑论传神。况且，西方读者岂不能判断古今审美观有别？这种担心，似属多余。

对训诂视而不见，肆意篡改字义者，当属英国译者阿连璧，其《诗经》译本的每篇译诗变异程度之巨令人咋舌，个中动机，无疑也是为了迎合英国读者的诗学观念和审美诉求。请看阿连璧翻译的《鹊巢》：

> The dove, that weak and timid bird,
> Scant wit hath she her nest to build;
> Unlike the pie, whose house well lined
> Within, and strong with labour skilled,
> Might seem a palace. Yet the dove
> Will to herself appropriate
> The magpie's nest, and snug therein
> Dwell in contentment with her mate.
>
> My sweet, thou art the tender dove!
> Hath fate's decree then nought more fair
> For thee than in these barren fields
> A peasant's hut and life to share?
> My lands are wide, my halls are high,
> And steeds and cars obey my call;
> My dove, within my magpie nest,
> Thou shalt be mistress of them all. [①]

---

① C. F. R. Allen. *The Book of Chinese Poetry*. London: Kegan Paul, Trench, Trubner & Co., Ltd., 1891: 22.

第四章 《诗经》题旨翻译——诗本义与诗教文化

原文则是：

> 维鹊有巢，维鸠居之。
> 之子于归，百两御之。
>
> 维鹊有巢，维鸠方之。
> 之子于归，百两将之。
>
> 维鹊有巢，维鸠盈之。
> 之子于归，百两成之。

在这首诗中，个别字的训诂问题，如"鹊""鸠""御""方""将""盈""成"等，都已经无从谈起；译文在整体上也已非《诗经》之谓。这样的翻译，大概已至无视原文训诂之极端，其价值也只剩下译文作为英语诗歌自身的那一点点韵味，而与中国《诗经》文化没有半点关系。

重视经学家的注疏，懂得训诂的重要性，是翻译好《诗经》的第一法门。与此同时，翻译时也不可拘泥于个别经学注疏的训诂，而应该广参众家，以考证最深、最可信者为依据。例如，《静女》中"彤管"的翻译问题就十分复杂，大概是《诗经》翻译训诂的一个典型例子：

> 静女其娈，
> 贻我彤管。
> 彤管有炜，
> 说怿女美。

詹宁斯的译文一看便知是毛、郑训诂的产物：

The modest maid—how winsome was she then,
The day she gave me her vermilion pen!
Vermilion pen was never yet so bright, —
The maid's own loveliness is my delight.①

其实，关于"彤管"，历史上至少有四种训诂：（一）彤管是古代宫廷女史手中的笔管。持此说者为毛亨和郑玄。《毛诗传》曰："古者后夫人必有女史彤管之法，史不记过，其罪杀之。"②郑《笺》曰："彤管，笔赤管也。"③《正义》曰："彤，赤也。管，笔管。"④（二）一种像笛的乐器。高亨《诗经今注》说："彤，红色。管，乐器。"⑤在此诗附录中又说：

> "彤管，欧阳修《毛诗本义》：'古者铖笔皆有管，乐器亦有管，不知此彤管是何物也。'按：彤管当是乐器，就是红色的乐管。《诗经》里的管字，都是指乐管。《周颂·有瞽》：'箫管备举。'《商颂·那》：'嘒嘒管声。'又《周颂·执竞》：'磬筦将将。'《汉书·礼乐志》、《说文》都引筦作管。所以说此诗的彤管当是乐器。"⑥

---

① William Jennings. *The Shi King: The Old "Poetry Classic" of the Chinese*. London and New York: George Routledge and Sons, 1891: 69.
② 孔颖达：《毛诗正义》，北京：北京大学出版社，1999年，第174页。
③ 同上。
④ 同上。
⑤ 高亨：《诗经今注》，上海：上海古籍出版社，1980年，第59-60页。
⑥ 同上。

第四章 《诗经》题旨翻译——诗本义与诗教文化

(三)与下文荑属同一物。余冠英《诗经选》:"'彤管'是涂红的管子,未详何物,或许就是管笛的管。一说,彤管是红色管状的初生之草。郭璞《游仙诗》:'陵冈掇丹荑',丹荑就是彤管。依此说,此章的彤管和下章的荑同指一物。"① 袁愈荌《诗经全译》:"[彤管]一说涂红的管子;一说和荑应是一物。一说彤管为红管草,即红色管状的初生植物。一说红管的笔。"② (四)不置可否。朱熹《诗集传》:"彤管,未详何物,盖相赠以结殷勤之意耳。"程俊英《诗经译注》:"彤管,有人说是赤管的笔,有人说是一种像笛的乐器,有人说是红管草,都可通。"③ 汪榕培的翻译就是以当代诗经学训诂为依据的:

> The maiden chaste, demure,
> Gives me a flute all red.
> The flute with notes so pure
> Puts dances in my head.

不过,这样来翻译《静女》之彤管,似乎与原诗的本义没有关系。"炜"与乐符(notes),"说怿女美"与舞蹈(dances),又有什么关系呢?依笔者之见,这样翻译并不能摆脱臆测之嫌,更没有翻译两千年来的《诗经》文化,尚需另加注解方可让读者了解几千年来中华民族所理解的《诗经》。若如詹宁斯所译,尚古义,从毛郑,虽

---

① 余冠英:《诗经选》,北京:人民出版社,1982年,第48页。
② 袁愈荌:《诗经全译》,贵阳:贵州人民出版社,1981年,第62页。
③ 程俊英:《诗经译注》,上海:上海古籍出版社,2004年,第64页。

不一定准确，但也无人能证明其不准确，而译诗也并不见得不美，且道出了传统《诗经》文化的真实面貌。

第四节　随意反《序》，臆测诗旨

　　无论是读《诗经》，还是翻译《诗经》，一个无法绕过的问题就是诗篇的题旨。其实，读《诗经》并不同于翻译《诗经》。读《诗经》可以有两种读法：一则欣赏诗篇的美，把诗篇当作唐诗宋词一样的诗歌来读。这种读法，可以尽情享受诗篇中的人文情怀、艺术之美，而可无视其中的道德礼乐等政教内容；也可以把自己完全融入诗篇之情境，自由发挥自己的想象力在诗中尽情畅游，充分实现英伽登所谓文学欣赏过程中的"具体化"。这种阅读的最大特点是自由，自由地想象，自由地欣赏，完全从文本本身出发，而不必受传统经学或现代诗经学的约束。二则借读诗反观历史，领略诗篇中的道德礼乐、民俗文化，追寻中华民族的文化传统。这种读法无法脱离传统经学的帮助。要翻译《诗经》，需要首先理解其中内涵，这种解读颇像后者。因为翻译不同于自由地阅读和欣赏，而是要服务于一定的目的。最根本的目的之一，就是传达中国古代历史文化，让世界了解中华民族数千年来的人文传统。那么如上文所论，如果我们要翻译《诗经》文化，诗篇题旨的确定就需要一个根据，这个根据就是《毛诗传》留给我们的《诗序》。虽然《诗序》在历史上聚讼颇多，但其言之成理者却在绝大多数。翻译时总想别出心裁是不可取的。然而，以往的译本当中却充斥着疑序现象，值

得文化翻译界注意,例如《采蘩》:

> 于以采蘩?于沼于沚。
> 于以用之?公侯之事。
>
> 于以采蘩?于涧之中。
> 于以用之?公侯之宫。
>
> 被之僮僮,夙夜在公。
> 被之祁祁,薄言还归。

《诗小序》云:"《采蘩》,夫人不失职也。夫人可以奉祭祀,则不失职矣。"按《诗小序》的解释,《采蘩》一诗颇能讲得通,因为这种解释符合当时的社会思想状况,以及商周王室按时节祭祀天地或宗庙的礼俗。但现代诗经学研究以还原诗篇中的历史为名,其对诗篇题旨的探讨常以标新立异、获得突破为旨归。例如程俊英说,《采蘩》"是一首描写蚕妇为公侯养蚕的诗"[①]。这种探讨颇具代表性。作为诗经学研究,这是无可厚非的,但并不足以成为翻译的依据。请看汪榕培的译文:

Wormwood Leaves

Where to pick wormwood leaves?
In the pond or in the ford.

---

① 程俊英:《诗经译注》,上海:上海古籍出版社,2004年,第19页。

> Where to use wormwood leaves?
>
> > To feed silkworms for the lord.
>
> Where to pick wormwood leaves?
>
> > In the stream in the valleys.
>
> Where to use wormwood leaves?
>
> > To feed silkworms in the palace.
>
> Apply a thin layer of leaves;
>
> > I'm busy night and day.
>
> Apply a thick layer of leaves;
>
> > I'll go home right away.

译文下的注解说："In this poem, a girl is described to be collecting wormwood leaves and feeding the silkworms."。[①] 很明显，译诗题旨就是根据程氏"养蚕"说。但是，程说与历史虽然可能有一定程度的相符，却并无实质性考据；而毛传同样可能与历史事实相符。商、周人曾经养蚕只是一种可能，但周人当时有祭祀天地与宗庙的风俗却是经过科学研究证明的事实，两者相比，难道我们宁信后人揣测，而妄疑古人之言？这种翻译例子颇多，请再看《小雅·鸳鸯》的译文：

> 鸳鸯于飞，毕之罗之。
> 君子万年，福禄宜之。

[①] 汪榕培、任秀桦（译注）：《诗经》（中英文版），大连：辽宁教育出版社，1995年，第51、53页。

鸳鸯在梁，戢其左翼。
君子万年，宜其遐福。

乘马在厩，摧之秣之。
君子万年，福禄艾之。

乘马在厩，秣之摧之。
君子万年，福禄绥之。

许渊冲译本对该诗的题解为："The love-birds flying in pairs alluded to the newly-wed and the four horses were used to draw the carriage of the bride."。[①]（比翼双飞的鸳鸯指一对新婚夫妇，四匹马用来拉新娘乘坐的车子。）在此题解的指导下，译文就变成如下的样子：

Flying love-birds need rest
When large and small nets spread.
May you live long and blest,
Wealthy and happily wed!

On the dam love-birds stay,
In left wing hid the head.
May you live safe for aye,
Duly and happily wed!

Four horses in the stable

---

① 许渊冲（译）：《诗经》，北京：中国对外翻译出版公司，2009年，第277页。

With grain and forage fed.

May you live long and stable,

For you're happily wed.

Four horses in the stable

With forage and grain fed.

May you live comfortable,

For you're happily wed.①

而《诗小序》曰:"《鸳鸯》,刺幽王也。思古明王交于万物有道,自奉养有节焉。"郑《笺》曰:"交于万物有道,谓顺其性,取之以时,不暴夭也。"② 朱熹的解释则是:"此诸侯所以答《桑扈》也。鸳鸯于飞,则毕之罗之矣。君子万年,则福禄宜之矣。亦颂祷之辞也。"③

据考查,汪榕培译本的篇什题解一般比较模糊。由于译者持《诗经》为古代民间文学的观点,所以题解与《诗序》相异者居多数。许渊冲译本的篇什题解亦多以现代诗经学观点为根据,与《诗序》相异者达147篇。依此来看,这两个译本在很多情况下是自说自话,并没有忠实地通过翻译传达数千年的传统《诗经》文化。

---

① 许渊冲(译):《诗经》,北京:中国对外翻译出版公司,2009年,第277-278页。
② 孔颖达:《毛诗正义》,北京:北京大学出版社,1999年,第864页。
③ 朱熹:《诗集传》,北京:中华书局,1958年,第160页。

第五节　因《诗经》之名，行创作之实

《诗经》翻译实践中有一种相当普遍的现象，即在翻译时进行创作。从理论上讲，创作是翻译过程中不可避免的规律性元素，其动因是两种语言文化之间存在的差异。从文化翻译的功能和目的来看，从他文化到母文化的顺译，其性质是文化上的归化。因为译者从选择翻译对象到制定翻译策略，再到处理文本细节，整个翻译过程都贯穿着对异文化的审视、批判和借鉴。译者的审视和批判是因为译者所在的文化给予他的价值观与异文化价值观体系可能相同，也可能不同，而在更多的情况下则是不同。就当前的世界文化格局来看，世界上按宗教、文化传统的差别，分成了若干不同的价值观体系，比如儒家文化价值观体系、基督教文化价值观体系、伊斯兰教文化价值观体系等。译者受所在价值观体系的熏染，自然而然地形成对陌生文化的一种注视和价值判断，这会首先对翻译对象的选择发生直接作用，进而对翻译策略的制定产生影响。如果译者断定其所审视的翻译对象整体上有利于母语文化的发展和完善，他才能最终决定选择这个翻译对象。然后，在对翻译对象进行具体翻译处理的时候，则会对文本内容进行新一轮的进一步审视和判断，并对具体的字句采取一定的翻译措施。译者自觉和不自觉地所做的这一切，都是出于一个目的，那就是借鉴别的民族文化来发展和完善本民族文化。从表面上看这是一种文化交流，但这种交流实质上并非理想化的平等交流，而始终是以译者文化利益为中心的。这可以很好地解释为什么向内译介别国的作品译者总是倾向于采用归化翻译模式。而对外译介本民族的作品，总是倾向于采用异化翻译模式，

因为译者总是以对外介绍本民族文化为目的。这种介绍可以有两种更深层的目的，一是影响乃至演变目的语文化，这实际上是一种文化霸权和文化侵略，二是让目的语文化读者充分了解自己民族的优秀文化，实现优秀文化资源共享和共同发展的目的。我国目前所开展的儒家经典外译工程，性质上就属于后者。

在《诗经》翻译史上，外国译者翻译《诗经》多数采取的是归化策略，所以译文中总免不了有改写、增损原诗内容的现象。但除此之外，还有采取极端归化策略的译者，如阿连璧和庞德。阿连璧翻译《诗经》，采用的是以《诗经》去适应英语诗歌的基本策略，所以改写、增损现象在其译本中俯拾即是，而且幅度很大。庞德翻译《诗经》，其目的则是通过《诗经》改革美国诗歌艺术形式，完善其于20世纪初所提出的意象主义诗学。（李玉良，2007：210-246）但这种策略客观上歪曲了《诗经》的原貌，给西方读者造成了错觉，所以对《诗经》的传播造成了影响。例如阿连璧译《小雅·鹿鸣》：

呦呦鹿鸣，食野之苹。
我有嘉宾，鼓瑟吹笙。
吹笙鼓簧，承筐是将。
人之好我，示我周行。

呦呦鹿鸣，食野之蒿。
我有嘉宾，德音孔昭。
视民不恌，君子是则是效。
我有旨酒，嘉宾式燕以敖。

呦呦鹿鸣，食野之芩。

第四章 《诗经》题旨翻译——诗本义与诗教文化

我有嘉宾,鼓瑟鼓琴。
鼓瑟鼓琴,和乐且湛。
我有旨酒,以燕乐嘉宾之心。

As we sit down to feast, from the meadow hard by,
Hark! the stags as they browse, call a musical cry.
We have music as well. Let no organ be mute;
Let us gladden our hearts with the sound of the lute.

Now hand round the dainties to each honoured guest;
The friends who love me, and the friends I love best.
They are models and patterns to all, for they show
The respect we should feel for the humble and low.

Bid the music, and the lutes great and small
Be struck till their sweet notes resound through the hall.
And pour out the wine,—it is plentiful here.
Thus all the day long we'll enjoy the good cheer. [①]

与原诗相比,译诗行数整整少了一半。内容上,译文所剩下的只有宴乐的场面,宴乐的场所也被改为草坪。原诗修辞手法、文学意象、叙事方式、文中细节内容几乎完全被改写。译诗整体上的艺术性与原诗也无法相提并论。

---

① C. F. R. Allen. *The Book of Chinese Poetry*. London: King Paul Trench, Trubner & Co., Ltd., 1891: 211.

又如庞德翻译的《东方未明》：

东方未明，颠倒衣裳。
颠之倒之，自公召之。

东方未晞，颠倒裳衣。
倒之颠之，自公令之。
折柳樊圃，狂夫瞿瞿。
不能辰夜，不夙则莫。

Still dark,

mistaking a kilt for a coat

upside down:

        "To the Duke, sir, since..."

It was not yet light,

mistaking a coat for a kilt,

down for up,

        and to audience!

Break thru the close garden fence

with staring eyes, a fool tries.

Milord's lost all sense of tense

night, day, audience,

day, night,

and no time ever right. [1]

---

[1] Ezra Pound. *The Classic Anthology Defined by Coufucius*. London: Faber and Faber Ltd., 1954: 47.

整首诗的译文,仅从意思上看就有出入。最为明显的是第三章,原文中是诗人批评时的官员无能,而译文则变成指责前文中的"颠倒衣裳"、忙于准备上朝面君的官员。译诗中译者插入了人物对话,这种叙事方式,也与原文大相径庭。再看其翻译的《东方之日》:

> 东方之日兮,彼姝者子,在我室兮。
> 在我室兮,履我即兮。
>
> 东方之月兮,彼姝者子,在我闼兮。
> 在我闼兮,履我发兮。

> Sun's in the East,
> her loveliness
> Comes here
> To undress.
>
> Twixt door and screen
> at moon-rise
> I hear
> Her departing sighs. [①]

译诗读起来就是一首描写同居乃至姘居者伤离别的诗,这在诗意上与经学传统相似。《东方之日》小序曰:"刺衰也。君臣失道,男女

[①] Ezra Pound. *The Classic Anthology Defined by Coufucius*. London: Faber and Faber Ltd., 1954: 47.

淫奔，不能以礼化也。"但是，在诗句的语义层次和诗意的表现方式上，译诗完全不同于原诗。

当然，在我国译者的译本当中，也有随意创作的影子。例如《载驱》：

> 载驱薄薄，簟茀朱鞹。
> 鲁道有荡，齐子发夕。
>
> 四骊济济，垂辔濔濔。
> 鲁道有荡，齐子岂弟。
>
> 汶水汤汤，行人彭彭。
> 鲁道有荡，齐子翱翔。
>
> 汶水滔滔，行人儦儦。
> 鲁道有荡，齐子游敖。

许渊冲的译文为：

> The duke's cab drives ahead
> With screens of leather red;
> The duchess starts her way
> Before the break of day.
>
> The duke's steeds run amain;
> Soft looks their hanging rein.
> The duchess speeds her way
> At the break of the day.

The river flows along;

Travellers come in throng.

Duke and duchess meet by day

And make merry all the way.

The river's overflowed

With travellers in crowd.

Duke and duchess all day

Make merry all the way.①

译诗中第三、七、十一、十二、十五、十六等行都被大幅度改写，译诗中主人公的行为过程和原诗相差较大。不过，细节上的改写，似乎并不能直接地完全改变诗的主题，所以译诗尚能与原诗在主题上保持联系。

小　　结

题旨是诗歌的首脑。译诗的首要任务是保持原诗的题旨。译诗失去或改变原来的题旨，就几近于创作了。在《诗经》翻译实践中，这的确是个难题。因为历史的原因，《诗经》中的许多诗篇题旨已经无法考证，甚至在经学中就已经成为见仁见智的悬案。但这

---

① 许渊冲（译）：《诗经》，北京：中国对外翻译出版公司，2009 年，第 104-105 页。

并不能成为译者随便在译诗中改变题旨的理由，因为经学研究历经数千年，它已经成为《诗经》文化传统的本体。我们翻译《诗经》，并不是仅仅在于翻译《诗经》中的个别诗篇，而在于翻译整个《诗经》传统。这就要求我们在翻译过程中，严格继承经学传统的合理成分，从中寻求正确的训诂依据，使翻译不致成为臆测或苟且之举。《诗经》的经学研究虽然政教至上，但并不否认诗篇的文学性，孔子所谓"乐而不淫，哀而不伤"，既是对《诗经》创作原则的客观评价，也是对其文学性的清醒认识。刘勰《文心雕龙》中对《诗经》的文学地位的高度评价，也充分证明了前人对《诗经》文学本质的认识。我们不能以经学的不足，来否定经学的千载之功，更不能以其来当作随意翻译《诗经》的借口。《诗经》既然是载道的文学，那么在翻译过程中遇到困难时，所能变通的就仅是诗的言说方式，而不是诗中的"道"。因为天地之大道不仅仅属于个别文化，也属于整个人类。

第五章 《诗经》意象翻译之可能与不可能

根据当代诗经学研究,意象在《诗经》中应用十分广泛,其审美作用也多种多样,如有的意象用于"兴",有的用于"比",有的用于象征,有的用于衬托。意象的使用使诗篇意境更富有韵味,艺术性更加丰富多彩,也使《诗经》成为万世流芳的文学经典。

《诗经》意象究竟能不能翻译?亦即意象究竟能不能跨越文化和语言,并为另一文化和语言的读者所理解和欣赏?如果能,那么应该怎样翻译?这是《诗经》翻译研究的一个重要课题。

从语言、历史文化、文学传统的综合角度来看,意象的可译性取决于三个重要前提:(一)两种语言文化须有相同,至少是相似的意象传统。这并不意味着两种语言文化中的具体意象在种类和数量上相等,而是说两种语言文化在历史上都有运用意象表达的传统;(二)两种语言文化须有相同,至少是相似的意象理论。这是指两种语言文化的意象理论中要有相同或相似点,至少是关于意象概念、意象分类、意象功能、意象构成等相似的理论观念;(三)意象之寓意或象征能够为异文化读者所理解。从接受美学的角度来看,意象不是摆在纸面上的物象;意象不属于文本,只属于读者。以上三个要素缺一不可,否则,意象的翻译将受到影响。其中最后一条,是三者当中最基本的要素。如果意象连最基本的可理解性都不具备，那么象中之意便无迹可寻，其可译性也无从谈起。以下我们就四个方面进行论述。

第一节　中西意象传统之比较

　　意象在我国诗歌中的运用，最早可以追溯到《诗经》。《诗经》中每一篇诗几乎都离不开意象的经营。例如，作为四始之首的《关雎》就使用了关关、雎鸠、河、洲、荇菜、琴、瑟、钟、鼓等九种意象。诗人用这些意象或"兴"，或"比"，或"赋"。按现代意象理论来讲，这些意象的作用是象征、比喻和营造气氛。其中"关关"是和悦的求偶之鸣，"琴""瑟""钟""鼓"是乐器之鸣，这两者渲染出温馨欢乐的氛围。"雎鸠"突出夫妻恩爱和合的形象，"荇菜"象征女子的婀娜多姿，"河""洲"寓意求偶者的笃切之情。这些意象使整篇诗形象生动，字里行间充满生命活力，弥漫着生活气息。根据现代诗经学研究，《诗经》所有诗篇共采用258种动植物意象，数百种自然意象，近百种文化名物意象，以抒情言志，风化美刺，开启了我国优秀的诗歌意象传统。

　　《楚辞》中意象也十分丰富，多为楚地方物，在楚地文化中有其特殊的文化内涵。如香草、美人、湘夫人等意象都与楚地出产和神话传说有关。屈原以香草、美人自比来表现自己人格高洁，并寄寓了深刻的哀怨与悲愤之情。如《少司命》：

　　　　秋兰兮麋芜，罗生兮堂下。绿叶兮素华，芳菲菲兮袭予。

夫人自有兮美子,荪何以兮愁苦?秋兰兮青青,绿叶兮紫茎。满堂兮美人,忽独与余兮目成。入不言兮出不辞,乘回风兮载云旗。悲莫悲兮生别离,乐莫乐兮新相知。荷衣兮蕙带,儵而来兮忽而逝。夕宿兮帝郊,君谁须兮云之际?与女游兮九河,冲风至兮水扬波。与女沐兮咸池,晞女发兮阳之阿。望美人兮未来,临风恍兮浩歌。孔盖兮翠旌,登九天兮抚彗星。竦长剑兮拥幼艾,荪独宜兮为民正。

王夫之《楚辞通释》说:"大司命统司人之生死。而少司命则司人子嗣之有无。以其所司者婴稚,故曰少。"诗中少司命"竦长剑兮拥幼艾",一手举着长剑,一手拥抱着婴儿,既威武又慈爱,是一位人类守护神的形象。中间部分描写人神恋爱之情,从另一方面表现这位女神的温柔与多情,从而使少司命的形象更加丰满动人。"悲莫悲兮生别离,乐莫乐兮新相知"两句,概括了人们的相思离别之情,具有浓郁的民歌风味,脍炙人口,常为后人所引用。诗中所用意象有三种:麋芜是楚地一种香草,七八月间开白花,香气浓郁,诗中借以喻指娇好纯洁的初生小儿;荪是另一种香草,诗中隐喻少司命;彗星俗称扫帚星,古人认为是灾星,"抚彗星"即隐喻扫除污秽之意。

汉乐府诗忠实地继承了《诗经》的淳朴风格,也发扬了《诗经》立象以抒情达意的传统。著名的《江南》[①]一诗中,诗人将莲、叶、鱼和没有明言的湖泊等意象组合到一起,描绘了一个万类竞自由的和谐世界,创造出欢乐温馨、自然美好的意境。相比

[①] 《江南》原文:江南可采莲,莲叶何田田。鱼戏莲叶间,鱼戏莲叶东,鱼戏莲叶西,鱼戏莲叶南,鱼戏莲叶北。

之下，《孔雀东南飞》之末的"两家求合葬，合葬华山傍。东西植松柏，左右种梧桐，枝枝相覆盖，叶叶相交通。中有双飞鸟，自名为鸳鸯，仰头相向鸣，夜夜达五更"，更是用"松柏""梧桐""枝""叶""双飞鸟""鸳鸯"等意象，赞美超越生死的高尚爱情。《长歌行》中"青青园中葵，朝露待日晞。阳春布德泽，万物生光辉"是生命之华发的象征；"百川东到海，何时复西归"则是时间一去不复返的象征。

南朝梁代萧统所辑《古诗十九首》，标志着我国诗歌正式摆脱了《诗经》四言诗体的局限性，开创了五言诗、七言诗的先河。意象在《古诗十九首》中的使用更加广泛，每一首诗都有至少一个意象。《冉冉孤生竹》是意象最多的一首，多达七个，用以表达一个女子对婚姻的企盼之情：

> 冉冉孤生竹，结根泰山阿。
> 与君为新婚，兔丝附女萝。
> 兔丝生有时，夫妇会有宜。
> 千里远结婚，悠悠隔山陂。
> 思君令人老，轩车来何迟。
> 伤彼蕙兰花，含英扬光辉。
> 过时而不采，将随秋草萎。
> 君亮执高节，贱妾亦何为。

竹"冉冉""孤生"，是女子自喻其孑孑孤立，柔弱而无依靠。"泰山"之阿，可以避风，这是女子以山喻男方可以依靠。《文选》李善注曰："结根于山阿，喻妇人托身于君子也。"兔丝（即"菟丝"）

和女萝是两种蔓生植物，其茎蔓互相牵缠，比喻两个生命结合与相互依赖。《文选》五臣注："兔丝女萝并草，有蔓而密，言结婚情如此。""兔丝"是女子自喻，"女萝"比喻男方。"兔丝生有时，夫妇会有宜"仍是以"兔丝"自喻，既然兔丝之生有一定时间，则夫妇之会亦当及时。言外之意是不要错过了自己的青春时光。"伤彼蕙兰花，含英扬光辉。过时而不采，将随秋草萎"这四句又用比，蕙和兰是两种香草，女子用以自比。"含英"是指花朵初开，喻年华正茂。意为如要采花，当趁此时，过时不采，蕙兰亦将随秋草而凋萎，隐喻女子盼望男方早日来迎娶，不要错过了好时光。

　　意象的发展，在唐诗、宋词、元曲里可谓达到了前所未有的高度。杜甫《春望》是典型一例：

　　　　国破山河在，城春草木深。
　　　　感时花溅泪，恨别鸟惊心。
　　　　烽火连三月，家书抵万金。
　　　　白头搔更短，浑欲不胜簪。

诗的头四句，诗人睹物伤情，用移情手法表达战乱之苦和亡国之悲。诗人用山河破碎、荒草遍野、烽火连天、百花溅泪、飞鸟惊心、白发如雪等意象，刻画出国破城荒的凄凉景象和人心悲苦之状。

　　与唐诗相比，宋词中意象的使用有过之而无不及。如李清照《如梦令》：

　　　　昨夜雨疏风骤，
　　　　浓睡不消残酒。
　　　　试问卷帘人，

却道海棠依旧。
知否？知否？
应是绿肥红瘦。

雨、风意象象征着毁灭的力量，把美艳的海棠吹打得凋零不堪，而风雨后凋零的海棠，正是诗人因思念煎熬而愁苦憔悴的写照。

元朝马致远的《天净沙·秋思》则标志着我国诗歌意象艺术的另一座高峰：

枯藤老树昏鸦，
小桥流水人家，
古道西风瘦马。
夕阳西下，
断肠人在天涯。

诗中连续并置十一个单独意象：枯藤、老树、昏鸦、小桥、流水、人家、古道、西风、瘦马、夕阳、天涯。这些意象组合到一起，描绘出旅人愁途怀乡的悲苦情状。其最大特点是中间没有任何解说或关联词语，仅将单独意象连缀，便勾勒出一幅天然逼真的艺术画面。意境之高远，尽在不言之中。意象的这种使用手法，在唐诗和宋词中似乎还不多见，相似的一首是温庭筠的《商山早行》：

晨起动征铎，客行悲故乡。
鸡声茅店月，人迹板桥霜。
槲叶落山路，枳花明驿墙。
因思杜陵梦，凫雁满回塘。

第五章 《诗经》意象翻译之可能与不可能

在现代诗中，意象作为一种艺术手法似乎悄然发生了转变，那就是传统的日、月、竹、菊、莲、英、云、鸟等美好意象被从来不堪入诗的另一类意象所取代，这在穆旦等人的现代诗中表现得尤为突出，标志着意象艺术的新发展。例如穆旦《还原作用》[①]一诗中就使用了"猪""天鹅""跳蚤""耗子""丝""蜘蛛""花园""荒原"等意象，表达了一个青年人想在社会上通过努力获得成功而不得的"悲痛的呼喊"和"变形的枉然"。作者说，这首诗表现旧社会中"青年人如陷入泥坑的猪（而又自认为天鹅）必须忍住厌恶之感来谋生活，处处忍耐，把自己的理想都磨完了，由幻想是花园变为一片荒原"[②]。《出发》[③]中野兽意象隐喻人类依靠现代文明变成杀人机器，表达了对人类兽性的愤怒和对文明堕落的嘲讽。这些意象的特点是丑陋和奇特，不落传统的窠臼。

意象作为文学艺术表现手法在西方诗歌中应用已历史悠久。在英语诗歌史上，意象使用可以看作以莎士比亚诗歌为滥觞，十八世纪浪漫主义诗歌中意象获得长足发展，至二十世纪初美国意象主义诗歌形成意象理论自觉。华兹华斯所创造的云（cloud）[④]意象、济慈的夜莺（nightingale）[⑤]意象、布莱克的老虎（tiger）[⑥]意象、彭斯的红玫瑰（red rose）[⑦]意象、庞德《地铁车站》的花瓣（petal）意象、威廉·卡洛斯·威廉姆斯的手推车（wheelbarrow）意象、T. S.

---

① 见附录四。
② 查良铮:《致郭保卫的信》（四），《蛇的诱惑》，曹元勇编，珠海出版社，1997年，第228页。
③ 见附录四。
④ 同上。
⑤ 同上。
⑥ 同上。
⑦ 同上。

艾略特的荒原（wasteland）意象等，早以其独特的内涵植根于英语诗歌传统，成为英语诗歌意象系统中的有机组成部分。

英国浪漫主义诗人华兹华斯认为，古罗马诗人维吉尔的诗中就已经使用了十分鲜明的意象。华兹华斯在其《抒情歌谣集》(1815)序言中提到维吉尔《牧歌》中的"悬挂"意象：

> 今后我见不到你，绿油油的，悬挂在
> 长满树木的岩前，离开那岩石很远很远。
> ——在半山腰上
> 悬挂着一个采茴香的人。

这是牧羊人想到他要和他的田庄告别时对他的羊群说的话。诗中所展现的是羊群在山上吃草，山农在岩壁上采茴香的意象。诗人所展现的只是远景中物体居高临下"悬挂"的姿态美，除此之外，似乎再没有其他"隐意"。

华兹华斯还举了维吉尔《决心和独立》的例子：

> ……
> 好像是一块大石头，有时候
> 高卧在黄山的峰顶上，
> 人人都会惊讶，只要发现
> 它怎样到了这里，打从何处而来，
> 它仿佛是具备了五官，
> 象一支海兽从海里爬上来，躺在岩石或沙滩上休息，晒着
> 　　太阳。
> 这个人正是这样；半死半活，

似睡非睡，真是老态龙钟。
……
老人站住不动，象一片白云，
听不见咆哮的大风，
一要移动，就整个移动起来。
……

华兹华斯评论说：

在这些意象中，想象力的赋予的能力、抽出的能力和修改的能力，不论直接地或间接地发生作用，三者都是联合在一起的。大石头被赋予了某种生命力，很像是海兽；海兽被抽去一些重要的特征，跟大石头相似。这样处理间接的意象是为了使原来的意象（即石头的意象）跟老人的形状和处境更相象。因为老人已经失去了这么多生命和行动的标记，所以他已经接近上面两个对象相联接之点。说了这些以后，就不必再谈白云这个意象了。①

这其中所谓的三个"意象"，其意义也是在外形上的相似，而没有牵涉更深的寓意，而且它们不具有我国传统意象所重的"隐"的性质。其实，这些"意象"在本质上相当于中国诗歌中的明喻，只能算作艺术创作中使用的一种艺术形象。

在英语诗歌中，意象的出现可以追溯到文艺复兴时期的诗歌。

---

① 华兹华斯：《〈抒情歌谣集〉一八一五年版序言》，《西方文艺理论名著选编》（中卷），伍蠡甫、胡经之主编，北京：北京大学出版社，2001年，第61-62页。

如莎士比亚《爱的徒劳》中的"Spring":

> When daisies pied and violets blue,
>   And lady-smocks all silver-white,
> And cuckoo-buds of yellow hue,
>   Do paint the meadows with delight,
> The cuckoo then, on every tree,
>   Mocks married men, for thus sings he—
>   "Cuckoo;
> Cuckoo, cuckoo" —O, word of fear,
> Unpleasing to a married ear!
>
> When shepherds pipe on oaten straws,
>   And merry larks are ploughmen's clocks,
> When turtles tread, and rooks, and daws,
>   And maidens bleach their summer smocks,
> The cuckoo then, on every tree,
>   Mocks married men; for thus sings he—
>   "Cuckoo;
> Cuckoo, cuckoo" —O, word of fear,
> Unpleasing to a married ear!

诗中"lady-smocks""cuckoo-buds""turtles""rooks""daws"分别是花意象和鸟意象,花意象渲染了春天万物复苏、生机盎然的气氛,这是一个布谷鸟鸣情求偶、交媾繁殖的时节。与华兹华斯诗中象征春天到来的鸟鸣声不同,莎士比亚这首诗中布谷鸟的叫声,则象征着对遭到妻子背叛的男人的嘲讽。

再如《安东尼与克里奥佩特拉》(Antony and Cleopatra):

> Cleopatra: I dreamed there was an emperor Antony:
> O, such another sleep, that I might see
> But such another man.
> Dolabella: If it might please ye, —
> Cleopatra: His face was as the heav'ns, and therein stuck
> A sun and moon, which kept their course and lighted
> The little O, th' earth.
> Dolabella: Most sovereign creature, —
> Cleopatra: His legs bestrid the ocean; his reared arm
> Creasted the world; his voice was propertied
> As all the tuned spheres, and that to friends; But when he
> wants to quail and shake the orb,
> He was as rattling thunder. For his bounty,
> There was no winter in't, an autumn 'twas
> That grew the more by reaping; his delights
> Were dolphin-like, they showed his back above
> The element they lived in; in his livery
> Walked crowns and crownets; realms and islands were
> As plates dropp'd from his pocket.
> Dolabella: Cleopatra, —
> Cleopatra: Think you there was, or might be, such a man

>   As this I dreamed of?
>   Dolabella: Gentle madam, no.

罗伯特·沃伦（Robert Penn Warren）[①]认为，莎士比亚在这段描写中违背逻辑常规，使用天宇、太阳、月亮、地球、海洋、岛屿、霹雳等形象塑造了一个"上帝般的巨人"的高大意象。但克里奥佩特拉正是借这个意象，抒发了其波涛汹涌的感情，表达了她对安东尼的无限崇敬和怀念。这个意象除"隐"性稍弱以外，与我国诗学中的组合意象十分近似。

与莎士比亚同时代的抒情诗人托马斯·坎品（Thomas Campion, 1567-1620），其爱情诗也擅长使用意象来抒发感情。其"Corinna"中的弦（strings）、"When Thou Must Home to Shades of Underground"[②]中的地狱等形象，都具有鲜明的西方传统文化特色，给人以深刻的印象。而"Follow Fair Sun, Unhappy Shadow"里的太阳和影子则是

[①] Robert Penn Warren. *Understanding Poetry.* Beijing : Foreign Language Teaching and Research Press, 2004: 228.

[②] When thou must home to shades of underground,
　　And there arrived, a new admirèd guest,
　　The beauteous spirits do engirt thee round,
　　White Iope, blithe Helen, and the rest,
　　To hear the stories of thy finished love
　　From that smooth tongue whose music hell can move,
　　Then wilt thou speak of banqueting delights,
　　Of masques and revels which sweet youth did make,
　　Of tourneys and great challenges of knights,
　　And all these triumphs for thy beauty's sake.
　　When thou hast told these honors done to thee,
　　Then tell, Oh tell, how thou didst murther me.

一组隐喻意象。太阳形象喻指美丽女子，影子形象喻指痴情男子，太阳寓意美丽和高贵，影子寓意丑陋和卑微。

> Follow thy fair sun, unhappy shadow,
>
> Though thou be black as night,
>
> And she made all of light,
>
> Yet follow thy fair sun, unhappy shadow.
>
> Follow her whose light thy light depriveth,
>
> Though here thou liv'st disgraced,
>
> And she in heaven is placed,
>
> Yet follow her whose light the world reviveth.
>
> Follow those pure beams whose beauty burneth,
>
> That so have scorchèd thee,
>
> As thou still black must be,
>
> Till her kind beams thy black to brightness turneth.
>
> Follow her while yet the glory shineth:
>
> There comes a luckless night,
>
> That will dim all her light;
>
> And this the black unhappy shade divineth.
>
> Follow still since so thy fates ordainèd;
>
> The sun must have his shade,
>
> Till both at once do fade,
>
> The sun still proud, the shadow still disdainèd.

十七世纪，玄学派诗人执诗坛之牛耳。以约翰·多恩（John Donn, 1572-1631）为代表的玄学派诗人虽然在诗中极尽推理之能事，但在玄学派诗歌中，我们仍能找到其善于使用意象的代表作。与莎士比亚意象相比，约翰·多恩的诗中使用的意象要"隐"得多，基本上具备了内外意交融、隐显相结合的品格。例如，"A Lecture upon the Shadow"：

> Stand still, and I will read to thee
> A lecture, Love, in love's philosophy.
>   These three hours that we have spent,
>   Walking here, two shadowes went
> Along with us, which we our selves produc'd.
> But, now the Sunne is just above our head,
>   We doe those shadowes tread:
>   And to brave clearnesse all things are reduc'd.
> So whilst our infant loves did grow,
> Disguises did, and shadowes, flow
> From us and our cares; but now 'tis not so.
> That love hath not attain'd the high'st degree,
> Which is still diligent lest others see.
>
> Except our loves at this noone stay,
> We shall new shadowes make the other way.
>   As the first were made to blinde
>   Others; these which come behinde
> Will worke upon our selves, and blind our eyes.

> If our loves faint, and westerwardly decline,
>　　To me thou, falsely, thine
> 　　And I to thee mine actions shall disguise.
> The morning shadowes weare away,
> But these grow longer all the day;
> But oh, love's day is short, if love decay.
> Love is a growing, or full constant light,
> And his first minute, after noone, is night.

此诗中的意象有多个，包括"morning""noone""after noone""light""night""shadow"等。这些意象都具有隐的性质，而且象中有意。"shadow"是一个总意象，"morning"寓意开始，"noone"寓意高潮，"after noone"寓意衰败，"light"寓意希望，"night"寓意绝望和幻灭。"shadow"的寓意十分隐晦，综观全文，"shadow"似乎是指与爱情的至真相对立的虚伪。爱情初萌时，两个恋人之间即存在虚伪，就像上午时跟随在身边的影子；爱情到达巅峰时期，虚伪似乎完全消失，但只是如正午时我们把自己的影子踩在脚下隐藏着而已；巅峰过后，爱情又开始有了更大的虚伪，正如下午时我们身边的影子更长。爱情与虚伪如影随形。所以诗人说，真爱过后的"下午"（after noone），每一分钟都是黑夜般的绝望和幻灭。

再如安德鲁·马维尔（Andrew Marvell，1621-1678）的"To His Coy Mistress"：

> Had we but world enough, and time,
> 　　This coyness, Lady, were no crime

We would sit down and think which way
To walk and pass our long love's day.
Thou by the Indian Ganges' side
Shouldst rubies find: I by the tide
Of Humber would complain. I would
Love you ten years before the Flood,
And you should, if you please, refuse
Till the conversion of the Jews.
My vegetable love should grow
Vaster than empires, and more slow;
An hundred years should go to praise
Thine eyes and on thy forehead gaze;
Two hundred to adore each breast,
But thirty thousand to the rest;
An age at least to every part,
And the last age should show your heart.
For, Lady, you deserve this state,
Nor would I love at lower rate.

  But at my back I always hear
Time's wingèd chariot hurrying near;
And yonder all before us lie
Deserts of vast eternity.
Thy beauty shall no more be found,
Nor, in thy marble vault, shall sound
My echoing song: then worms shall try

That long preserved virginity,

And your quaint honour turn to dust,

And into ashes all my lust:

The grave's a fine and private place,

But none, I think, do there embrace.

    Now therefore, while the youthful hue

Sits on thy skin like morning dew,

And while thy willing soul transpires

At every pore with instant fires,

Now let us sport us while we may,

And now, like amorous birds of prey,

Rather at once our time devour

Than languish in his slow-chapt power

Let us roll all our strength and all

Our sweetness up into one ball,

And tear our pleasures with rough strife

Through the iron gates of life:

Thus, though we cannot make our sun

Stand still, yet we will make him run.

这首玄学诗写的是真爱难觅、相爱当及时的主题。虽然整首诗呈现的是严密的逻辑推理，诗人却仍在其中使用了形象思维，是一首颇具特色的抒情诗。整首诗以逻辑推理的方式劝告两心相悦的人恋爱要及时，勿羞怯矜持。诗的开头，诗人似乎说他愿意花千百万年时间去爱心上人，等候她的允诺，与她执手相伴。不过这些都建立在一个假设之上："如果我们的世界够大，时间够多"。事实上，人生的空间和时间都十分有限。对此诗人虽未明言，且语气温和诚恳，但至此我们已清楚诗人的弦外之音：若前提不成立，后面的推论自然也就被推翻。诗人在运用逻辑推理的同时，连珠似地抛出青春如朝露、灵魂散发火焰、猛禽大口吞噬、甜蜜滚成圆球冲破生命栅栏等意象，说服其心仪的人接受求爱，勿辜负青春年华。

到十八世纪，英国浪漫主义诗歌开始萌芽。英国浪漫主义诗歌有两位先驱，一位是罗伯特·彭斯，一位是威廉·布莱克。如果说彭斯的诗歌现实主义成分多一些，那么，布莱克则是浪漫主义诗歌的真正开创者。在彭斯的诗里，我们可以发现不少物象，比如玫瑰、虱子、狗等，作者用这些形象去赞美或讽喻社会现实。它们或者无甚寓意，或者寓意比较浅显，还不是真正意义上的意象。布莱克诗歌中的形象却常常是比喻或象征性的，内涵十分丰富，具备十足的意象性，经常让读者难以确定其所指。例如"The Blossom"：

> Merry, merry sparrow,
>
> Under leaves so green,
>
> A happy blossom
>
> Sees you, swift as arrow,
>
> Seek your cradle narrow
>
> Near my bosom.
>
> Pretty, pretty robin,
>
> Under leaves so green,
>
> A happy blossom
>
> Hears you sobbing, sobbing,

Pretty, pretty robin

Near my bosom.

诗中的花朵指什么？麻雀和知更鸟又是什么？诗中花朵已经不是现实中的花朵，而是一个有情有义、时刻关注着鸟的行踪、感受鸟的声音的灵魂。这个灵魂让我们联想到一个窈窕柔美、含情脉脉的姑娘；而那个来回穿梭的麻雀和喈喈啼鸣的知更鸟，则是一个活泼可爱的少年。整个诗篇让人感受到少男少女之间纯真的爱情，恰像一朵鲜花，羞涩袅娜，含苞待放。诗中这一组意象，运用得十分委婉。

十八世纪中期以后，意象在浪漫主义诗歌中的运用似乎进入了另一种境界，立象以达意抒情的形象思维特征表现得更加突出。诗中意象不再仅仅是知性思维工具，而是把形象思维引入诗歌，成为一种重要的艺术思维形式。例如华兹华斯的"She Dwelt Among the Untrodden Ways"：

She dwelt among the untrodden ways

Beside the springs of Dove,

A Maid whom there were none to praise

And very few to love:

A violet by a mossy stone

Half hidden from the eye!

— Fair as a star, when only one

Is shining in the sky.

She lived unknown, and few could know

When Lucy ceased to be;

> But she is in her grave, and, oh,
> The difference to me!

诗中紫罗兰美丽明亮，犹如夜空中闪闪的明星。诗中间一节是一个名词性短语，其中没有任何解释性言语，而只用花朵和明星意象描绘出已逝女子的美丽。意象显然是这首诗的灵魂，也是打动读者的最主要的手段。如果没有中间一节所营造的意象，那么这整首诗的韵味将失之大半。

进入十九世纪，在阿尔弗雷德·丁尼生（Alfred Tennyson, 1809–1892）的诗里，我们经常会发现运用得十分纯熟而感人的意象。在下面一首诗中可以看到黑暗的屋子和零雨的拂晓两个意象，前者象征黑暗与绝望，后者透出凄凉与彷徨，它们给整首诗蒙上了浓重的感情色彩。

> Dark house, by which once more I stand
>   Here in the long unlovely street,
>   Doors where my heart was used to beat
> So quickly, waiting for a hand,
>
> A hand that can be clasp'd no more—
>   Behold me, for I cannot sleep,
>   And like a guilty thing I creep
> At earliest morning to the door.
>
> He is not here; but far away
>   The noise of life begins again,
>   And ghastly thro' the drizzling rain

On the bald street breaks the blank day.

丁尼生的"The Yew in the Churchyard"则通过千年老紫杉树意象,表达了诗人对于永恒和长寿及老树刚毅品格的仰慕和赞美之情,同时也流露了诗人心中难以名状的忧伤。

Old Yew, which graspest at the stones
  That name the under-lying dead,
  Thy fibers net the dreamless head,
Thy roots are wrapped about the bones.

The seasons bring the flower again,
  And bring the firstling to the flock;
  And in the dusk of thee, the clock
Beats out the little lives of men.

O not for thee the glow, the bloom,
  Who changest not in any gale,
  Nor branding summer suns avail
To touch thy thousand years of gloom:

And gazing on thee, sullen tree,
  Sick for thy stubborn hardihood,
  I seem to fail from out my blood
And grow incorporate into thee. [①]

---

① Robert Penn Warren. *Understanding Poetry*. Beijing: Foreign Language Teaching and Research Press, 2004: 108.

诗中的紫杉意象，让人不禁联想到《葬花吟》中黛玉以花自比，用凋零的落花所表达的血泪悲伤。

象征意象在现代派诗歌先驱艾米莉·狄金森（Emily Dickinson）笔下也曾多次使用。尽管她"坚持真实，对真实有一种不妥协的忠诚"，但是"她的诗……大多使用意象的语言"。[①] 狄金森所塑造的意象新颖深邃，充满现代派诗歌的象征意味。例如"Hope Is the Thing with Feathers"：

> "Hope" is the thing with feathers—
> That perches in the soul—
> And sings the tune without the words—
> And never stops—at all—
>
> And sweetest—in the Gale—is heard—
> And sore must be the storm—
> That could abash the little Bird
> That kept so many warm—
>
> I've heard it in the chillest land—
> And on the strangest sea—
> Yet, never, in Extremity.
> It asked a crumb—of me.

"希望"是一只羽毛丰满的小鸟，会飞翔，会唱无词的曲调。"希

[①] 江枫（译）：《狄金森诗选》，北京：外语教学与研究出版社，2012年，第 VI–XII 页。

望"意象的塑造是典型的由意寻象的创作手法。如果说它还不够含蓄,那么"A Fuzzy Fellow, Without Feet"则含蓄得让人难以捉摸其中的"fellow"究竟为谁:

> A fuzzy fellow, without feet,
>
> Yet doth exceeding run!
>
> Of velvet, is his countenance,
>
> And his complexion, dun!
>
> Sometime, he dwelleth in the grass!
>
> Sometime, upon a bough,
>
> From which he doth descend in plush
>
> Upon the passer-by!
>
> All this in summer.
>
> But when winds alarm the Forest Folk,
>
> He struts in sewing silk!
>
> Then, finer than a lady,
>
> Emerges in the spring!
>
> A feather on each shoulder!
>
> You'd scare recognize him!
>
> By men, yclept Caterpillar!
>
> By me! But who am I,
>
> To tell the pretty secret
>
> Of the butterfly!

从表面上看，这首诗写的是蝴蝶作为鳞翅目幼虫在一年四季中形态的变化，但作者的真意却并非那么简单。面容像天鹅绒，皮肤暗褐色，住草丛，攀高枝，引线穿丝，认不出往日形迹等形象若被作为单独意象组合到一起，其寓意则充满开放性，这种开放性本身充满了象征的魅力。

意象在诗歌实践中从自然走向自觉的标志，是美国意象主义诗歌及意象主义诗学的诞生。但实践中的理论自觉并不意味着意象艺术的提升。相反，许多批评家认为，美国的意象主义强调色彩、形状等视觉形象的独特性和审美意义，对意象的寓意内涵不够注重，所以比较肤浅，缺乏艺术上的厚重感和启示作用。在意象主义诗学中，意象多半追求形象的鲜明性和视觉效果，对其象征性则抱着抑制的态度，反对把意象塑造得像谜语一样晦涩难懂。比如希尔达·杜利特尔（Hilda Doolittle）的"Heat"：

> O wind, rend open the heat,
> Cut apart the heat,
> Rend it to tatters,
>
> Fruit cannot drop
> Through this thick air—
> Fruit cannot fall into heat
> That presses up and blunts
> The point of pears
> And rounds the grapes.
>
> Cut through the heat—

Plow through it,
Turning it on either side
Of your path.

作者在诗中着力塑造热的意象。热在这里充满质感，像一块石头，质地致密而坚硬，枝上掉落的果子穿不透它；热又像一把锉刀，能把梨的棱角锉平；还像一只手，能把葡萄拢圆。但诗人除了把热极力形象化之外，好像热不再有更深的含义。展卷之初，读者确实可以得到身临其境的感受，但若再往深处品味，则不免兴味索然。有些意象派诗歌意象在形象之外有寓意，意味悠长。比如詹姆斯·史蒂文斯（James Stevens）的"The Main-Deep"：

The long, rolling,
Steady-pouring,
Deep-trenched
Green billow:

The wide-topped,
Unbroken,
Green-glacid,
Slow-sliding

Cold-flushing,
On—on—on—
Chill-rushing
Hush-hushing
Hush-hushing ...

滚滚向前的巨浪是什么？大概最好的解释是，巨浪是无穷的生命力的象征。"Cold-flushing""chill-rushing"两个单个寒冷意象象征生命的艰辛；"Steady-pouring""slow-sliding"两个动作意象和"hush-hushing"一个声音意象，则象征生命的顽强不息。意象的象征性，使整个诗篇内涵富于质感。

通过以上对比不难看出，在两千多年的文学实践中，中西诗歌均有把意象当作诗歌创作艺术手法的传统，且都有比较长的历史。就意象观念而论，中西有共同之处，也有差别。共同之处在于，意象本质上都是诗人头脑中联想的物象，或是头脑中描绘的图画；意象主要是比喻和象征，用来抒情达意。其差别在于，从形成方式来看，西方诗歌中的意象，被塑造的多，采自物象的略少。换言之，多数诗的意象营造过程是由意寻象。一首诗往往致力于塑造一个意象，目的就是通过意象，化抽象为形象，使理与情相结合；而我国诗歌中的意象既有很多是采自物象，即立象以尽意，也有很多是通过联想经营得来，即由意寻象。从意与象的关系来看，西方诗歌中的意象一般比较直白，我国诗歌中的则比较委婉，亦即前者显，后者隐。当然，西方诗歌中的象征性意象，意义也并不易见，也惯于以曲折为上，常令人难以捉摸。从意象表达方式来看，西方诗歌总是喜欢把意象植入逻辑思维和语言。一首诗常常通过逻辑语言塑造一个意象，把理性意义形象化，或将其作为情感的喻体或象征。而我国诗歌则是用意象编织语言，就像摄影艺术中的"蒙太奇手法"，它本身就是理性和情感的呈现物，无须用逻辑语言做铺垫或阐释，甚至抵制"知性"语言参与。（叶维廉，1992：83-98）换言之，西方诗歌中意象常常是对意义和情感的归纳和总结，意与象之间有些许微妙的距离感。我国诗歌中意象则是意义和情感的显现和诉说，意与象难分彼此。诗歌这种情与景的零距离现象被王国维称为诗歌创作中"以物观物"的最高境界。(王国维,2003:10)西方诗歌的意象,尤其是意象派诗歌的意象,注重形状、色彩等视觉效果,即注重"象"本身的鲜明性,而我国诗歌的意象则更注重内意的广度和生动性,以及意的美感和力量。但是,二十世纪中叶以后,中西现代派诗歌意象的相似性大大增强,以至于难分彼此了。比如,德国现代派诗人波德莱尔《恶之花》中的意象和穆旦现代诗歌中的意象相比,大致就是如此。

随着意象理论的创生和不断发展,中西诗歌意象进入了文艺理论视野,并被文学界广泛讨论,其异同已被探讨得越来越清楚。

第二节　中西意象理论之比较

在实践上,尽管意象以《诗经》为开端,但中国古代并没有系统的文学意象理论。意象作为我国古典文学的理论范畴,其概念与实践相比,尚属晚出;我国的意象理论亦迟至今日方逐步得以完善。在我国古典文献中,意象最初属于哲学范畴,导源于《易经·系辞》中的"圣人立象以尽意",而作为一个文学理论概念,则至南朝刘勰《文心雕龙》,才初步完成由哲学范畴到文学概念,即所谓"神用象通,情变所孕"[①]的转变。屈光(2002)认为,作为审美表现成果的"意象",其概念内涵的发展过程大致可分为四

---

① 见刘勰《文心雕龙·神思》。

个阶段：萌生于汉代；发展于晋代；完备于六朝；盛行于唐宋。汉代时经学家们就已经对比、兴的意象功能有了一定认识。郑众曰："比者，比方于物"，"兴，托事于物"；孔颖达曰："比，见今之失，不敢斥言，取比类以言之。兴，见今之美，嫌于媚谀，取善事以喻劝之。"① 两者都"悟出了比兴是借助于客观外物以寄托主观情志的……与意象的内涵是同质"（屈光，2002）的道理。后经王逸②、陆机③等人进一步发展，至《文心雕龙》得以完备。屈光（2002）认为，《物色》篇和《比兴》篇都指出了意与象是相对应的概念。《物色》曰："是以献岁发春，悦豫之情畅；滔滔孟夏，郁陶之心凝；天高气清，阴沉之志远；霰雪无垠，矜肃之虑深。岁有其物，物有其容；情以物迁，辞以情发。"这里刘勰已明确指出情与物色的渊源关系。《比兴》亦曰：

> 观夫"兴"之托谕，婉而成章，称名也小，取类也大。《关雎》有别，故后妃方德；尸鸠贞一，故夫人象义。义取其贞，无从于夷禽；德贵其别，不嫌于鸷鸟：明而未融，故发注而后见也。且何谓为"比"？盖写物以附意，飏言以切事者也。故金锡以喻明德，珪璋以譬秀民，螟蛉以类教诲，蜩螗以写号呼，浣衣以拟心忧，席卷以方志固：凡斯切象，皆"比"义也。

---

① 孔颖达：《毛诗正义》，北京：北京大学出版社，1999 年，第 11 页。
② 王逸《离骚》序：《离骚》之文，依《诗》取兴，引类譬谕。故善鸟香草，以配忠贞；恶禽臭物，以比谗佞；灵修美人，以媲于君；宓妃佚女，以譬贤臣。
③ 陆机《文赋》："或本隐以之显，或求易而得难"，"若夫丰约之裁，俯仰之形，因宜适变，曲有微情"，"或言拙而喻巧，或理朴而辞轻"。屈光称其为"隐""曲""喻巧"说。

"'兴'之托谕……称名也小,取类也大"又明确了物以兴意,意寓于物,且意广于物的物–意关系。只是尚未使用意象的概念而已。

至盛唐,王昌龄《诗格·卷上》已经使用了相当成熟的意象概念:

> 诗有三思:一曰生思,二曰感思,三曰取思。生思一:久用精思,未契意象。力疲智竭,放安神思。心偶照境,率然而生。感思二:寻味前言,吟讽古制,感而生思。取思三:搜求于象,心入于境,神会于物,因心而得。

其中"未契意象"就是指意与象未能入契合之境。而"搜求于象,心入于境,神会于物,因心而得"则指诗人获得意象,进入意与象相契合之境。皎然、白居易对意象有进一步的论述。皎然"取象曰比,取义曰兴。义即象下之意。凡禽鱼、草木、人物、名数,万象之中义类同者,尽入比兴,《关雎》即其义也。如陶公以'孤云'比'贫士';鲍照以'直'比'朱丝',以'清'比'玉壶'"[①],初步阐明了意与象的内外关系。白居易《金针诗格》说:"诗有内外意。内意欲尽其理,理谓义理之理,颂美箴规之类是也。外意欲尽其象,象谓物象之象,日、月、山、河、虫、鱼、草、木之类是也。内外含蓄,方入诗格。"这进一步明确了"内意欲尽其理""外意欲尽其象"的内外关系。迨至晚唐,司空图《与李生论诗书》赋予意象以"韵外之致"和"味外之旨"的内涵,标志着意象概念在理论上的完善。屈光(2002:165)根据传统诗歌理论对意象概念

---

① 皎然:《诗式》,《历代诗话》(上册),(清)何文焕辑,北京:中华书局,1982年,第30页。

的内涵做了如下归纳：（1）象指一切具有物理形态的客观存在物，包括视觉不可见的物质和人自身的一切外在表现，如声音、风和人的情态行为等；意指诗人主观的一切意识活动，如感情、志向、认识、幻觉等；（2）意象的本质是寄托隐含，委婉不露，不直接言意而将意寄托隐含于象中，因而意象具有双重意义，即外意和内意，也称字面意义和隐意。不具有双重意义的词语、诗句或诗，不是意象；（3）意是主，象是宾；意是目的，象是手段；意是内容，象是载体；（4）象和意必须具有某种联系，才能构成意象；（5）意象是诗人独特的审美创造成果，同一个象，对于不同的作家和同一作家的不同时空，可以寄托不同的意。这是对意象内涵比较完整的概括。20世纪80年代以后，研究者们对意象的审美性质、种类、功能、形成过程等进行了研究，这使得意象理论又有了新的发展。

根据当代意象理论，意象的审美特征有三：（1）即有即无、即实即虚的朦胧美；（2）有限无限、无边无垠的超越美；（3）顺物之性、不设不施的自然美。（孟桂兰，2002）在此，意象已是一个比较成完善的文学概念，且审美性已经成为其根本属性。

屈光（2002：166-167）从两个角度对意象进行了分类。一，从诗人的构思过程，分为由意寻象和由象生意两类。（一）是由意寻象。诗人先有主观情感冲动或理性认识，然后搜寻相应的客观物象，实现寄托隐含，构成意象。这类意象的创造有明确的主观动机性。王昌龄所谓"搜求于象，心入于境，神会于物，因心而得"，即出于意识中的某种目的，而搜求的最终结果是得到了象。比如，李白《行路难》中"欲渡黄河冰塞川，将登太行雪满山"，先有理想壮志受阻的意，而后想象出"冰塞川""雪满山"之象，从而结合成意象。（二）是由象生意。诗人意识中的某一瞬间并没有某种情志浮现，由于象触动感官而兴发出某种情志，构成的意象就属于由象生意。《诗经》中有所寄托的"兴"，即属此类。正如孔颖达所言，"则兴者，起也，取譬引类，起发己心。诗文诸举草木鸟兽以见意者，皆兴辞也"。二，从存在形态看，意象可以分为单象意象、多象意象、组合意象和意象群等四种类型。这是从文本或鉴赏角度所做的分类。单象意象只是一个词或一个短语，或一句诗中的一部分，用以寄托一个完整的内意，内意不依赖于上下文中其他"象"。比如，元稹《离思》（其四）末两句"取次花丛懒回顾，半缘修道半缘君"中，"花丛"是个意象，内意是"美女群"。多象意象，即一个片断中任何一个词或短语都是象，但都不能单独体现内意，不能单独构成意象，这几个象组合以后才能构成一个意象，共同表达一个内意，彼此不能分割，所以称之为多象意象。如温庭筠《商山早行》颔联"鸡声茅店月，人迹板桥霜"中"鸡声""茅店""月""人迹""板桥""霜"等六个象组合后包含"道路辛苦，羁愁旅思"这个内意。组合意象，是几个单象意象相对独立，都有各自的内意，而又组合成一个整体意象，寄托一个整体内意，组合意象的内意由各单象意象的内意组合而成。绝大多数组合意象的词语中都有动词或形容词。如辛弃疾《摸鱼儿·更能消几番风雨》中"算只有，殷勤画檐蛛网，尽日惹飞絮"，是一个组合意象，内意是只有自己整日以恢复之事为怀。最后，意象群是指全诗或多数诗句中存在一个由许多意象组成的意象群，构成一个意象体系，可以称为意象诗歌，古代诗论称为比体诗。如曹植《吁嗟篇》以"转蓬"寄托流转不定的自怜之情。从诗歌文学史看，意象的运用从《诗经》至现代诗，走过了由萌发到成熟，由简单到复杂的过程，成为我国诗歌艺术中最重要的艺术要素。

与我国文学中的意象理论相比，西方意象概念的产生要晚得多。十八世纪浪漫主义诗人华兹华斯在其《抒情歌谣集》1815年版序言①中，论述了意象在诗歌中的艺术地位。这是意象概念在西方文学理论中首次被使用，尚不能算作是对文学意象概念的理论论述。华兹华斯在文中列举了公元前一世纪古罗马诗人维吉尔在诗中使用意象的例子，说明意象在西方诗歌中的使用也有悠久历史。但是，维吉尔诗中的意象与我国早期诗歌中的意象并不相同，其本质上不是以物象寓情志，内外结合，一显一隐，其所展现的往往只是诗人的一种想象力，并通过这种想象力给读者以美感。

　　西方意象概念的理论化及意象理论研究，要到二十世纪初庞德所倡导的"意象派"诗歌运动期间才得以真正开始，这就是创生于二十世纪初的"意象派"诗歌理论。"意象派"诗歌是在一战历史文化背景的冲击下，旨在改变英国维多利亚王朝颓靡诗风的意象主义诗歌运动。一战结束后，庞德首先起来反对自十八世纪以来浪漫主义自由体诗的语言风格。他认为，浪漫主义"自由体诗确实像它以前任何一种软弱无力的诗歌一样，变得冗长、噜苏。……就如我们的前辈们，甚至在没有任何理由的情况下也堆砌大量词汇，以填满格律，或完成一种'韵律-声音'的噪杂"②。1912年，庞德与希尔达·杜利特尔和理查德·奥尔丁顿（Richard Aldington）讨论制定意象派诗歌的原则，其中主要的三条是：(1) 直接处理无论是主观的还是客观的"事物"；(2) 绝对不使用无益

---

① 见伍蠡甫、胡经之（主编）：《西方文艺理论名著选编》（中卷），北京：北京大学出版社，2000年。

② 庞德：《回顾》，林骧华摘译，《西方古今文论选》，伍蠡甫主编，上海：复旦大学出版社，1984年，第421页。

于表现的词;(3)在韵律方面,用连续的音乐性语词写诗,而不用连续的节拍。^①直接使用意象来表达理性与情感是意象主义诗歌的首要诉求。《在地铁车站》(In a Station of the Metro)就是一个典型代表:

> The apparition of these faces in the crowd;
> Petals on a wet, black bough.

庞德在经过地铁车站时,在熙熙攘攘的人群中为一张张兴奋活泼的脸庞所深深感动。诗中湿漉漉的黑色树枝和花瓣,就是诗人在这样的情感波涛中,瞬间摄取的色泽鲜明的意象。

在语言形式上,意象派诗人主张要尽量排除主观评价和侧面烘托渲染,亦即不用游言余字和不能说明任何东西的形容词,力求用简洁、朴素、准确和浓缩的语言来表现鲜明的意象,表达温婉含蓄,这样的诗歌方为上乘之作。例如,威廉·卡勒斯·威廉姆斯(William Carlos Williams)写的"Red Wheelbarrow":

> So much depends
>
> upon
>
> a red wheel
>
> barrow
>
> glazed with rain
>
> water

---

① 庞德:《回顾》,林骧华摘译,《西方古今文论选》,伍蠡甫主编,上海:复旦大学出版社,1984年,第421页。

> beside the white
>
> chickens.

关于意象的概念，庞德认为，意象"是在一刹那时间中理智和情感的复合"①。"意象在任何情况下都不只是一个思想，它是一团，或一堆相交融的思想，具有活力。"② 这种情与理的复合体，需要形象来呈现，而且是一刹那间的呈现。庞德要求形象构建要精确。"形象所呈现的应该是准确的物质关系，可以用它来象征非物质关系。"③ 意象主义的另一个代表，托马斯·欧内斯特·休姆（Thomas Ernest Hulme）主张，诗歌应该追求意象，即通过形象，尤其是视觉形象，来表达诗人细微复杂的思想感情。休姆认为，有生命的意象是诗歌的灵魂；诗人的真诚程度，可以用其所用意象的数量来衡量。休姆也强调意象描绘的精确性，认为诗歌最重要的目的在于正确、精细和明确地进行描写，诗人须运用新鲜隐喻、幻想手法，重视意象的类比、暗示、感应等作用，在创作过程中必须找出那些对每一个类比加以补充，并产生奇迹感和产生同另一神秘世界相联系的感觉的东西。④

可见，意象主义所主张的意象，从性质上来看，也是一种物象；从形成方式来说，是经历由意寻象而形成的；其构成方式是一

---

① 庞德:《回顾》，林骧华摘译，《西方古今文论选》，伍蠡甫主编，上海：复旦大学出版社，1984年，第422页。
② 庞德:《严肃的艺术家》，《现代西方文论选》，伍蠡甫主编，上海：上海译文出版社，1983年，第251页。
③ 同上。
④ 休姆关于意象主义诗歌的主要论文被收入其《沉思录》和《沉思集》。

瞬间所呈现的精确的理性和情感的复合体；其功能则主要是充当情绪、情感和思想的象征。

就意象派诗歌的象征功能而言，有的学者将意象派看作象征主义的分支，因为意象派诗人大多有象征诗歌创作的经历。从发生学角度看，意象派诗歌固然受到了中国古诗①和日本俳句②的重大影响，但亨利·帕格森的直觉主义哲学、叶芝（William Butler Yeats）的象征主义诗歌，以及十九世纪欧洲象征主义诗歌，无疑是其另一个渊源。对于诗歌的象征性，庞德也十分重视。他认为，诗歌应该力避抽象，诉诸形象，方法就是运用自然事物进行适当的象征。（转引自朱立元，1997：23）然而，虽然意象派与十九世纪象征主义诗歌有某种渊源关系，但两者之间仍有着本质上的差异。象征主义诗歌常用意象，以意象为"客观对应物"，但仅把意象当作符号，注重联想、暗示、隐喻，是一种有待翻译的密码。象征主义主张，诗歌要让读者像猜谜一样去寻找意象背后的隐喻暗示和象征意义，即在表象与思想之间寻找某种神秘的关系。而意象主义则对象征主义的晦涩表达进行反拨，主张不用鲜明的形象去约束感情，不用说教和抽象的抒情、说理，而是让诗意在表象描述中一瞬间体现出来。意象派诗歌要求"从象征符号走向实在世界"，把重点放在诗的意象本身，即具象性上，让涌流的情感和思想在与外界物象的神遇中，一瞬间通过意象自然而然地表现出来。

综上所述，意象派的意象论与我国意象理论的异同已十分清

---

① 见韦勒克：《现代文学批评史》（第5卷），北京：中国人民大学出版社，1991年，第219–226页。

② Robert Penn Warren. *Understanding Poetry*. Beijing: Foreign Language Teaching and Research Press, 2004: 69.

楚。何清（2002：61-62）认为，意象派理论与我国意象说之间最具重合性的意义有三个方面：两者所谓的意象皆是指主体身心受到外物刺激，客观物象经与主体内心情感、理性相纠合而生成的一种意中之"象"，或意想之"象"；意象主义诗人以写出富有意象的诗歌为诗歌创作的最高境界；语言须简约凝练。但是，绝不可以把意象主义理论与中国传统美学中的意象说等同看待。两者相异之处亦有三个方面：第一，意象主义强调意象之"象"是形象在视觉想象上的投射，强调视觉性与色彩感。休姆指出，诗歌意象主要是一种记录轮廓分明的视觉形象的手段，并且这种诗像雕塑而不像音乐，它诉诸眼睛而不诉诸耳朵，它提供给读者形象与色彩的精美图画。这与中国传统诗学中的意象有了区别。前者更关注视觉上的感受，而中国之意象应是全身心的感受和体悟。第二，意象主义诗论中吸收了中国诗歌含蓄凝练的特色，同时又强调其意象的精确性，甚至提出一门艺术的检验标准是它的精确性。第三，意象主义同时要求使准确的意象成为情绪的对等物，而中国传统美学意象说提倡以意象进入玄远之境，从而沟通自然与人生。

如果说在英语文学理论界，华兹华斯首先提出和使用意象概念，意象派诗人发展了意象概念，并将意象理论深入到对意象功能的讨论中，那么，使意象理论进一步完善的则是英国当代文论家罗伯特·佩恩·沃伦（Robert Penn Warren）。沃伦在其《理解诗歌》（*Understanding Poetry*）一书中，认为诗歌意象的功能主要包括如下几种：营造气氛（aura），象征（symbol），隐喻（metaphor），使情（emotion）志（idea）交融。

关于意象营造气氛的功能，沃伦用丁尼生的"Mariana"做了论证：

With blackest moss the flower-pots
　　Were thickly crusted, one and all;
The rusted nails fell from the knots
　　That held the pear to the gable-wall.
The broken sheds looked sad and strange:
　　Unlifted was the clinking latch;
　　Weeded and worn the ancient thatch
Upon the lonely moated grange.
　　　　She only said, "my life is dreary,
　　　　　　He cometh not," she said;
　　　　She said, "I am aweary, aweary,
　　　　　　I would that I were dead!"
①
...

沃伦认为，丁尼生描绘这一旷野景象，其主要目的就是为弃妇的心境找到一种与之相对应的实物，从而为诗的后半部分的心理描写创造一种氛围。这种氛围具有象征意义。

　　意象的象征性有时很强烈。这使得意象的象征意义隐藏得很深，诗歌在整体上也变得十分晦涩难懂，甚至带上几分神秘的色彩。例如华莱士·史蒂文斯的《陶罐轶事》(Anecdote of the Jar)：

I placed a jar in Tennessee,
And round it was, upon a hill.

---

① Robert Penn Warren. *Understanding Poetry*. Foreign Language Teaching and Research Press, 2004: 197.

It made the slovenly wilderness
Surround that hill.

The wilderness rose up to it,
And sprawled around, no longer wild.
The jar was round upon the ground
And tall and of a port in air.

It took dominion everywhere.
The jar was gray and bare.
It did not give of bird or bush,
Like nothing else in Tennessee.①

这里的"jar"是人类，是文明，还是什么别的事物？其象征意义扑朔迷离。与此相类，威廉·布莱克《羔羊》中的"羔羊"和《老虎》中的"老虎"，也都是典型的象征性意象。

沃伦认为，意象最重要的功能就是隐喻。隐喻意象类似于象征意象，但又不同于象征意象。其根本区别在于，前者不能从字面上看出其意义，而后者可以。比如老虎意象，就可以从字面上看出其象征的是老虎的勇猛和威武。又如罗伯特·弗罗斯特（Robert Frost）的《荒地》（Desert Places）：

Snow falling and night falling fast oh fast
In a field I looked into going past,

---

① Robert Penn Warren. *Understanding Poetry*. Foreign Language Teaching and Research Press, 2004: 200.

And the ground almost covered smooth in snow,
But a few weeds and stubble showing last.
The woods around it have it—it is theirs.
All animals are smothered in their lairs.
I am too absent-spirited to count;
The loneliness includes me unawares.

And lonely as it is that loneliness
Will be more lonely ere it will be less—
A blanker whiteness of benighted snow
With no expression, nothing to express.

They cannot scare me with their empty spaces
Between stars—on stars where no human race is.
I have it in me so much nearer home
To scare myself with my own desert places.[①]

诗中的"benighted snow"可以从字面上理解为象征人们面无表情。"Desert places"则不同，在本诗中，它指的不是空间意义上的荒地，而是暗喻空虚的内心精神世界。

至此，我们可以把中西意象理论的异同做如下概括。首先，中西意象都是含有一定寓意的物象或是由感情运动而联想到的形象。其次，意象的功能在于比喻、象征或营造气氛，其最终作用在于审美。第三，意象的性质是审美性。第四，中西意象的使用方法不

---

① Robert Penn Warren. *Understanding Poetry*. Foreign Language Teaching and Research Press, 2004: 203-204.

同，前者重意，后者重象；前者立象以达意，后者则采象以发明。第五，意与象的关系不尽相同，前者象中有意，意象合一，后者则象为阐发的对象，象之意义一般由诗人直接阐发出来。第六，中国意象尚形象思维，西方意象赖知性思维；前者隐，后者露。

第三节　《诗经》意象功能及其分类

从我国当代意象理论的研究成果来看，意象在《诗经》中已经开始大量使用，是我国文学意象的滥觞。关于《诗经》中的意象，近年来已经成为诗经学研究的热点之一。据不完全统计，目前已有 87 篇论文对《诗经》中的意象进行了广泛而深入的讨论。王双（2009：36-39）认为，《诗经》意象研究主要集中在两个方面。其一，《诗经》文学的文化研究。众多研究者从图腾崇拜、生殖崇拜、神话、巫术、民情、风俗等跨学科视角进行研究。闻一多《说鱼》（1993）、赵霈林《兴的源起》（1987）、赵国华《生殖崇拜文化论》（1990）、李湘《诗经名物意象新探》（1989）等论著，对鱼、鸟等动物意象，莲、葛等植物意象，山、水、云、雨等自然意象等都做了深入的原型分析。其二，《诗经》文学意象的审美蕴含及功能研究。这项研究加深了《诗经》文学化研究。王长华（1987）将意象属性划分为装饰性、比喻性、排比性、夸张性等审美属性。郭建勋（1990）对《诗经》意象的审美价值和艺术功能进行了论述。孙伯涵（2001）就《诗经》意象的功能进行了分类研究。孙伯涵将其划分为三大类：（1）原始兴象；（2）比德意象；(3)审美意象。原始兴象发源于一定的原始宗教生活或民俗，是自然物象被赋予特定宗教观念之后而形成的一种意象。这类意象产生时间较早，是在神话思维状态下诞生的一种艺术，比如"关雎"等飞鸟意象，"束薪"等器物意象等；比德意象则是诗人将自己的伦理道德观念投射到自然物上，从而使自然物承载了人类道德情操和伦理道德内涵而形成的一种意象，如鹿马意象等；审美意象则是诗人完全摆脱了原始宗教和一般伦理道德观念，主要从审美心态出发而创造的一种意象，如《硕人》中的"瓠犀""螓蛾"，《蒹葭》中的"蒹葭""白露""伊人""凝霜"等。但从意象在诗篇中的具体使用情况看，这三种意象之间界限并不十分清楚，而是互相交叉。原始兴象中有比德和审美的成分，比德意象中有兴象和审美成分，审美意象也有兴象和比德的作用。因此，《诗经》意象总的特点是同时具有三个功能：作为原始兴象，它们当中有相当一部分与原始的宗教和民俗有着直接的渊源关系；作为比德意象，它们又是伦理道德言说的重要手段；作为审美意象，它们具有重要的审美功能。研究表明，日月、山水、飞鸟、雨雪、花树、器物等多种意象在《诗经》中就已经反复使用，大大增强了诗篇的审美趣味。这些意象为我国后代诗歌所继承和发展，形成了我国诗歌文学史上独特的意象传统。

　　原始兴象包含自然意象、动植物意象等多个种类。据现代诗经学研究，这些意象多与原始宗教、巫术、婚恋民俗等有关。闻一多在《说鱼》篇中从民俗学角度出发，旁征史书、古诗、现代民歌、谣谚等大量证据，得出《诗经》中的鱼"是匹偶的隐语，打鱼、钓鱼等行为是求偶的隐语……烹鱼或吃鱼喻合欢或结配"的结论。当代研究者们认为，山水云雨等自然景物，"是远古人类生殖意象在周代文化观念中的转换形态，它象征着当时人们对男女性爱和理想婚姻的热烈追求"（刘振中，1989）。例如，"山、隰"对举表示男女之爱、夫妇之情（李炳海，1990），"南山"意象多与男女情事相关，又与长寿多福有关（段学俭，1999）。比兴中的瓜果子实、束薪，也总与性爱、婚恋有关系。采摘意象常被用以表达男女之间的相思相恋，如《卷耳》《苯苢》《采葛》等，皆是如此。

比德意象多见于禽鸟意象。据蔡若莲（2007）研究，《诗经》中大部分禽鸟为良禽益鸟，例如，德比贤君的凤凰、节比君子的鹤等。诗人常通过益鸟比喻来进行道德教化，如以《振鹭》树立贤君典范，以《凯风》弘扬孝道观念，以《燕燕》《常棣》倡导兄友弟恭的精神，以《关雎》《葛覃》赞颂夫妇和睦之美等。诗中也有凶鸟恶兽，如食其子嗣的鸥、偷食黍和麦的硕鼠等，诗人常用它们来比喻恶人。总的来看，《诗经》通过禽鸟意象，建构了我国古代夫妇、父子、君臣、兄弟、朋友之间的伦理道德传统。

以上三类意象虽然都有审美意义，但审美意象包括更多种类。从文学意义上说，诗中的草、木、鸟、兽、虫、鱼，以及各种器物，都寄寓了诗人的喜怒哀乐，是抒情达意的重要手段。样样皆以起兴、比喻、象征等方式发挥着审美作用。在此不一一赘述。

值得注意的是，《诗经》中的意象体系，并不完全等同于唐诗宋词中的意象体系。唐诗宋词中的意象系统主要以审美意象为主，而与后代诗歌意象相比，《诗经》的意象多属草创，常导源于神话思维或民俗。在今天看来，《诗经》意象的喻意有时很难确定，对于同一意象，人们往往见仁见智，众说纷纭，给解读和翻译带来了很大困难。

第四节 《诗经》意象翻译——可能与不可能

从上文分析可知，中西意象艺术各自有着深远的历史渊源和文化内涵，在实践与理论上有许多共同点和不同点。这既给《诗经》意象翻译提供了重要基础，也在客观上设置了许多障碍。在此我们从接受美学关于文本与作品的理论出发，探讨《诗经》意象翻译的可能性问题。

根据 H. R. 姚斯和 W. 伊瑟尔提出的接受美学理论，文学文本和文学作品是两个性质不同的概念，它们之间的区别主要在以下三个方面：第一，文本是由作家创造的文学作品的自在状态，是被读者阅读之前的物质状态；文学作品"是一种交流形式"（伊瑟尔，1991：21），是与读者构成审美对象性关系的文本，它超越了孤立的自在状态，是融会了审美主体的情感、经验和艺术趣味的审美对象。第二，文本是以文字符号的形式储存着多种审美信息的物质性载体；作品则是在具有鉴赏力读者的积极阅读中，由作家和读者共同创造的审美价值的精神性载体；作品是为"创造性"的"接受者"而创作的。（姚斯，1987：23）第三，文本是一种物质性存在，独立于接受主体的审美经验之外，其结构形态也不会随时间而变化；作品则只存在于接受主体的审美观照和感受中，"是向未来的理解无限开放的意义显现过程或效果史"，受具体读者的思想情感和心理结构的支配，是一种相对的"历史性存在"（朱立元，1997：287）。由文本到作品的转变，是审美感知的结果。也就是说，作品是被审美主体感知、规定和创造的文本。

由此可见,《诗经》意象翻译实质上始终关系着两个核心问题,一个是原文本中的意象,一个是译文读者心目中的意象。意象翻译的实质不是从原文本到译文本在语言符号上的过渡,而是从原文作品到译文作品在精神上的沟通。原文作品和译文作品之间有无一致性,更具体一点讲,原文作品的意象能否在译文作品中得以再现,并为译入语读者所理解和接受,是判断意象能否翻译的基本标准。可以推断,由于语言文化及时代的原因,中西意象之间既有相当大的可译性,也有客观上的不可译性。从理论上推断,可以翻译的意象包括以下几类:(一)由意寻象而创造出的意象。这类意象在英语诗歌中居多,其象的含义一般在上下文中会得到阐发,或者说象与意均比较明显,经过翻译之后,仍然比较容易为读者所理解和感受。庞德在《地铁车站》中所创造的"花瓣"意象即如此。(二)寓意比较容易识别的意象。彭斯《一朵红红的玫瑰》中比喻美人的"玫瑰"意象,属于此类。(三)文化渊源不深,在理性上中西读者均比较容易理解,在情感上中西读者比较容易产生共鸣的比喻或象征性意象。例如,布莱克《老虎》中的"老虎"意象、李商隐《无题》中的"蜡炬"意象等。与此相反,以下四类意象则不可翻译,需在翻译时加注释:(一)我国诗歌中诗人经过由象寻意而创造出的寓意曲奥的意象和西方诗歌中寓意隐含较深的象征性意象。例如,陶渊明《饮酒》诗中的"南山"意象、"归鸟"意象,屈原《离骚》诗中的"兰"意象,史蒂文斯的《陶罐轶事》诗中的"jar"意象等。(二)我国古诗中具有原始宗教意味的原始意象。例如《诗经》中"鱼""束薪""山""隰""玉""琼琚"等意象。(三)文化渊源悠长而民族文化特色鲜明的意象。例如,我国诗歌中的

"月""梅""竹""菊"等传统意象,由于其传统悠久,寓意独特,在原诗中虽然容易为我国读者所理解,但在译文中,由于读者的跨文化背景,就不容易被正确理解。(四)取自典故的意象。如我国诗歌中的"嫦娥""青鸟""射雕"等意象,以及西方诗歌中取自圣经故事的意象等。

基于上文的推论,我们认为,从翻译须追求原文"作品"和译文"作品"一致的标准来衡量,《诗经》意象的可译性与不可译性各参其半。那么,《诗经》意象翻译状况究竟如何?在此我们试从翻译的方法和效果两个方面进行考察。

无论何种类型的翻译,都首先表现为解读,其次才是翻译,《诗经》翻译也不例外。因此,《诗经》意象解读上的困难必然会反映到翻译中来,成为意象翻译不可回避的问题。况且,翻译离解读还有不小的差距,即使意象已被正确解读,也不意味着会得到适当的翻译。虽然有些《诗经》意象可以翻译,且有很多意象在译诗中被成功地再创造,但是,翻译中的问题也比较多。从"作品"一致的观点来看,《诗经》意象翻译主要存在四个方面的问题。有些情况下,译文中意象被完全换易,造成原意象丧失。有些情况下,译文中有"意"无"象"或有"象"无"意",即"意""象"被人为分离,造成意象残缺。原文中"意""象"本为一体,若在译文中"意"或"象"任何一个元素被改变或者造成读者别样的理解,原来的意象实际上也不复存在。有些情况下,原文意象被彻底忽略不译,从而造成对原诗艺术整体的破坏。另一些情况下,译文中虽然保存了原文意象,却已经失去原意象含蓄委婉的特性,变为一种知性告白。下面我们就《诗经》意象翻译问题从五个方面分别论述。

一、"意""象"和谐

《诗经》中有不少诗篇意象十分鲜明,喻意也较为明确。对于此类意象,译者一般比较容易把握。比如,"桃之夭夭,灼灼其华"塑造了一棵阳春三月里的桃树意象,其叶蓁蓁,其华灼灼,诗人用以隐喻青春美貌的新娘。翻译时,这类意象从物象到喻意都比较容易保持,且两者不至于分离。再如,《摽有梅》中使用落梅意象刻画大龄女子自怜容貌日损、盼望出嫁的心情,形象鲜明,喻意也十分委婉。

> 摽有梅,其实七兮。
> 求我庶士,迨其吉兮。
>
> 摽有梅,其实三兮。
> 求我庶士,迨其今兮。
>
> 摽有梅,顷筐墍之。
> 求我庶士,迨其谓之。

各译本翻译效果如下(限于篇幅,只录第一章):

许译:The fruits from mume-tree fall,
　　　One-third of them away.
　　If you love me at all,
　　　Woo me a lucky day!

汪译:You see the plums drop from the tree,
　　　Lying on the way.

> If you want to marry me,
>
> > You'd better not delay.

理译: Dropping are the fruits from the plum-tree;

> There are [but] seven [tenths] of them left!
>
> For the gentlemen who seek me,
>
> This is the fortunate time!

詹译: Though shaken be the damson-tree

> > Left on it yet are seven, O.
> >
> > Ye gentlemen who care for me,
> >
> > Take chance while chance is given, O.

阿译: The plums are ripening quickly;

> > Nay, some are falling too;
> >
> > 'Tis surely time for suitors
> >
> > To come to me and woo.

韦译: Plop fall the plums; but there are still seven.

> Let those gentlemen that would court me
>
> Come while it is lucky!

庞译: Oh soldier, or captain,

> Seven plums on the high bough,
>
> plum time now,
>
> seven left here, "Ripe," I cry.

用作隐喻的意象，翻译时一般比较容易经营，因为喻体和喻旨都在诗中出现，译文读者比较容易在两者之间建立关联。如《野有蔓草》：

> 野有蔓草，零露漙兮。
> 有美一人，清扬婉兮。
> 邂逅相遇，适我愿兮。
>
> 野有蔓草，零露瀼瀼。
> 有美一人，婉如清扬。
> 邂逅相遇，与子偕臧。

韦利这样来译：

> Out in the bushlands a creeper grows,
> The falling dew lies thick upon it.
> There was a man so lovely,
> Clear brow well rounded.
> By chance I came across him,
> And he let me have my will.
>
> Out in the bushlands a creeper grows,
> The falling dew lies heavy on it.
> There was a man so lovely,
> Well rounded his clear brow.
> By chance I came upon him:
> "Oh, sir, to be with you is good."

仅就意象的创造来说，译文做得难能可贵。蔓草、露珠的样态在译诗中似触手可及，十分鲜活。《毛诗正义》曰："毛以为，郊外野中有蔓延之草，草之所以能延蔓者，由天有陨落之露，泫泫然露润之兮，以兴民所以得蕃息者，由君有恩泽之化养育之兮。"① 蔓草喻万民，零露喻君泽，两意象的寓意不难捕捉。有趣的是，译者将诗中的"一人"当成了男子。根据《诗小序》，"思遇时也。君之泽不下流，民穷于兵革，男女失时，思不期而会焉"，似是讲男子思邂逅女子，而韦利把原诗理解成女子思遇男子，则有违经学的合理解释。虽然原诗中的"一人"隐去了性别，可以有双解，但"a man""his"等字眼，则把性别确定为男性，若这不是因为译者疏于研读《毛诗传》以致犯错，而是有意为之，似不必如此标新立异。

詹宁斯没有如此经营，所得效果与经学之解颇为一致，而译诗中的意象营造与原诗颇相一致：

> Where creeping plants grew on the wild
>   And heavy dews declined,
> There was a fair one all alone,
>   Bright-eyed, good-looking, kind.
> Chance brought us to each other's side,
>   And all my wish was gratified.
>
> Where creeping plants grew on the wild,
>   And thick the dew-drops stood,
> There was the fair one all alone,

---

① 孔颖达：《毛诗正义》，北京：北京大学出版社，1999年，第321页。

　　　　Kind, as the looks were good.

　　　　Chance let us meet each other there,

　　　　Our mutual happiness to share. ①

译诗不仅完整保留了"蔓草""零露"两个原意象，使其喻美功能得以发挥，且成功隐去了"一人"的性别，保留了其多解性。

　　华兹生（Burton Watson）翻译的《青蝇》（原文见本书第二章61页）中，"青蝇"意象十分鲜明。

　　　　Buzz buzz, the blue flies,

　　　　lighting on the fence:

　　　　my joyous and gentle lord,

　　　　don't listen to slanderous words!

　　　　Buzz buzz, the blue flies,

　　　　lighting on the thorn:

　　　　slandering men know no limits,

　　　　they destroy every state around!

　　　　Buzz buzz, the blue flies,

　　　　they light on the hazel:

　　　　no end to slanderers' doings—

　　　　they set the two of us to quarreling! ②

---

　　① William Jennings. *The Shi King: The Old "Poetry Classic" of the Chinese*. London and New York: George Routledge and Sons, 1891: 110.

　　② Burton Watson. *The Columbia Book of Chinese Poetry*. New York: Columbia University, 1984: 37–38.

第五章 《诗经》意象翻译之可能与不可能

郑《笺》云："兴者，蝇之为虫，污白使黑，污黑使白，喻佞人变乱善恶也。言止于藩，欲外之，令远物也。"①译诗中意象生动，寓意也与郑说无异。

默克诺顿翻译的《小星》中的"little stars"的意象，其战战兢兢的姿态，读来颇令人恻隐：

> Trembled indeed
> > are the little stars.
> Now three, now five
> > are in the east.
> Hurry up, hurry up!
> > Tonight they go,
> Some early, some late,
> > to see the duke.
> Their lot
> > is not the same.
>
> Trembled indeed
> > are the little stars.
> There's Orion.
> > There's the Pleiades.
> Hurry up, hurry up!
> > Tonight they go,
> Catch their covers

---

① 孔颖达：《毛诗正义》，北京：北京大学出版社，1999年，第876页。

>   and clutch their sheets.
>   Their lot
>   does not
>   match hers. ①

有些意象，其喻意稍隐晦些，诗人立象以寓意，而不明言其意，但细细咀嚼，其意仍清晰。这类意象在翻译时也可以较完整地再现。例如，《蒹葭》中的"蒹葭""伊人""霜""湄""坻""沚"等意象及其喻意就能为译文读者所理解。

> 蒹葭苍苍，白露为霜。
> 所谓伊人，在水一方。
> 溯洄从之，道阻且长。
> 溯游从之，宛在水中央。
>
> 蒹葭凄凄，白露未晞。
> 所谓伊人，在水之湄。
> 溯洄从之，道阻且跻。
> 溯游从之，宛在水中坻。
>
> 蒹葭采采，白露未已。
> 所谓伊人，在水之涘。
> 溯洄从之，道阻且右。
> 溯游从之，宛在水中沚。

---

① William McNaughton. *The Book of Songs*. New York: Twayne Publishers, Inc., 1971: 59-60.

韦利这样来处理原文中的意象:

Thick grow the rush leaves;

Their white dew turns to frost.

He whom I love

Must be somewhere along this stream.

I went up the river to look for him,

But the way was difficult and long.

I went down the stream to look for him,

And there in mid-water

Sure enough, it's he!

Close grow the rush leaves,

Their white dew not yet dry.

He whom I love

Is at the water's side.

Upstream I sought him;

But the way was difficult and steep.

Downstream I sought him,

And away in mid-water

There on a ledge, that's he!

Very fresh are the rush leaves;

The white dew still falls.

He whom I love

Is at the water's edge.

Upstream I followed him;

But the way was hard and long.

Downstream I followed him,

And away in mid-water

There on the shoals is he! ①

译诗中使用了意象,但是仅限于"rush leaves""white dew""frost"和"mid-water"。译者把原诗中的"坻""沚"等意象改换,抑或是并没有认识到它们对追寻之"艰难"的强调作用。原诗中求贤而不得的意味在译诗中遭到削弱。

詹宁斯所用的意象与韦利稍有不同:

When reed and rush grew green, grew green,

  And dews to hoar-frost changed,

One whom they speak of as "that man"

  Somewhere the river ranged.

Upstream they went in quest of him,

  A long and toilsome way;

Downstream they went in quest of him;—

  In *mid*-stream there he lay!

When reed and rush grew tall, grew tall,

  And dews lay yet undried,

He whom they speak of as "that man"

---

① Arthur Waley. *The Book of Songs*. New York: Grove Press, 1996: 101−102.

>   Was by the riverside.
> Upstream they searched for him, along
>   The toilsome, deep defile;
> Downstream again—and there he lay,
>   Midway, upon the isle!
>
> When reed and rush were cut and gone,
>   And dews still lingered dank,
> He whom they speak of as "that man"
>   Was on the river's bank.
> Upstream they searched for him, along
>   The toilsome, right-hand road;
> Downstream,—and on the island there,
>   In *mid*-stream, he abode! ①

这首译诗整体上描写的是一个傲世脱俗的隐士形象，其中的意象有"rush grew green""dews changed to hoar-frost""downstream they went in quest of him""in mid-stream there he lay""in mid-stream, he abode"等，这些意象尽管与原诗意象不完全对应，但它们组合到一起，却从整体上创造了相似的情景，只不过译诗中"phantom"较原诗有稍过之嫌，求之而不得的贤士，不一定就是隐士。

理译中的意象与原文是完全一致的，其所发挥的作用和产生的效果亦与原诗十分相似；其不足在于诗行过于铺陈，语言意合度较

---

① William Jennings. *The Shi King: The Old "Poetry Classic" of the Chinese*. London and New York: George Routledge and Sons, 1891: 141.

低，诗行略显冗长，灵动性较弱。

> The reeds and rushes are deeply green,
> And the white dew is turned into hoarfrost.
> The man of whom I think
> Is somewhere about the water.
> I go up the stream in quest of him,
> But the way is difficult and long.
> I go down the stream in quest of him,
> And lo! he is right in the midst of the water.
>
> The reeds and rushes are luxuriant,
> And the white dew is not yet dry.
> The man of whom I think,
> Is on the margin of the water.
> I go up the stream in quest of him,
> But the way is difficult and steep.
> I go down the stream in quest of him,
> And lo! he is on the islet in the midst of the water.
>
> The reeds and rushes are abundant,
> And the white dew has not yet ceased.
> The man of whom I think,
> Is on the bank of the river.
> I go up the stream in quest of him,
> But the way is difficult and turns to the right.

> I go down the stream in quest of him,
> And lo! he is on the island in the midst of the water.①

关于《诗经》中的隐喻性意象，韦利认为，这种意象手法在中西传统诗歌中都有所使用。他举了一首英语民谣和波兰民谣为例。②英语民谣为：

> I lean'd my back against an oak;
> I thought it was a trusty tree.
> But first it bent and then it broke;
> My true love has forsaken me.

诗中的喻体和本体像两个事实一样被并列叙述出来，比喻词并不出现。波兰民谣也是如此：

> They have cut the little oak, they have hewn it;
> It is no longer green.
> They have taken away my lover,
> Have taken him to the wars.

因此，韦利主张在翻译过程中译者应该保持意象的隐喻性质，尽

---

① James Legge. *Chinese Classics with a Translation, Critical and Exegetical Notes, Prolegomena, and Copious Indexes*. London: Henry Frowde, Oxford University Press Warehouse, Amen Corner, E. C.（1939 年伦敦会香港影印所影印本）, Vol. IV-Part I: 195–197.

② Arthur waley. *The Book of Songs*. London: George Allen & Unwin LTD, 1937: 13.

量不把这些意象通过添加"as if""like"(好像)等字眼变成明喻。因为这样会使原诗的整体性丧失,亦即原诗通过隐喻意象而表现出的含而不露的委婉性质不能在译诗中反映出来。

这类意象之所以基本上能够在翻译时得以再现,最主要的原因是象和意之间的联系比较密切,且两者往往在同一语境中出现,读者比较容易捕捉整体意象;其次是因为这些意象是诗人取物寓意,藉物抒情,文化渊源不深,不像来自神话思维和民俗的意象那样隐晦曲折,对译文读者来说比较容易理解。与此相反,文化渊源较深远曲折的原始意象,在翻译中的景象就大不相同了。

二、存象失意

文化渊源较深远曲折的原始意象,从修辞上看也是一种隐喻,但其喻体不在诗中出现,若按上述方法将原始意象直接译出,则很难为目的语读者所理解。

《诗经》中的原始意象来自神话思维和周代各地的民俗,其文化渊源较为复杂。《诗经》中的鱼意象多隐喻性爱,瓜果多喻生子和性爱,这些皆为著例。原始意象在《诗经》意象中占相当大的比例,如南山意象、山隰对举意象、东门意象、玄鸟意象、鹿马意象、束薪意象、采摘意象、河水意象、鱼意象、瓜果意象,等等。这类意象,"象"和"意"之间的关系较其他意象更为松疏,若读者不能从民俗学的角度明察其来源,就很难懂得其喻意。例如《卫风·竹竿》:

籊籊竹竿,以钓于淇。

岂不尔思？远莫致之。

泉源在左，淇水在右。

女子有行，远兄弟父母。

淇水在右，泉源在左。

巧笑之瑳，佩玉之傩。

淇水滺滺，桧楫松舟。

驾言出游，以写我忧。

根据闻一多先生的"垂钓-性爱"说，这首诗所描写的不仅仅是《诗小序》中所言"卫女思归"，而是男女两情相悦。诗的开头两句，是典型而含蓄的性爱表达。这种基于民俗学观点的理解如今已为诗经学者所广泛接受。也只有这样理解，上下文才能贯通如一。否则，不仅开头两句作为起兴将失去落脚点，且后文的"巧笑之瑳，佩玉之傩"和"驾言出游，以写我忧"四句也将孤立无所由。这种幽远的婚俗内涵，即使译文再忠实，译语文化读者仅仅通过译诗语境本身也很难领悟到。如理雅各译文：

> With your long and tapering bamboo rods,
>
> You angle in the K'e.
>
> Do I not think of you?
>
> But I am far away, and cannot get to you.
>
> The Ts'euen-yuen is on the left,
>
> And the waters of the K'e are on the right.
>
> But when a young lady goes away, [and is married],
>
> She leaves her brothers and parents.

The waters of the K'e are on the right,

And the Ts'euen-yuen is on the left.

How shine the white teeth through the artful smiles!

How the girdle gems move to the measured steps!

The waters of the K'e flow smoothly;

There are the oars of cedar and the boats of pine.

Might I but go there in my carriage and ramble,

To dissipate my sorrow! ①

从语义上看,译文是十分忠实于传统经学的,但如此却很难令读者理解 "With your long and tapering bamboo rods, You angle in the K'e." 这两行诗讲垂钓究竟是何意?垂钓者究竟是谁?诗中主人公所思者究竟为谁?这些问题,都一并成为悬念。

詹宁斯在翻译中最为强调其中的文学特质,但就"垂钓"意象来说,其翻译却仍不算成功:

Rods of long and lithe bamboo,

　Used for angling in the K'i,

Go not back my thoughts to you,

　Now too far away to see?

---

① James Legge. *Chinese Classics with a Translation, Critical and Exegetical Notes, Prolegomena, and Copious Indexes*. London: Henry Frowde, Oxford University Press Warehouse, Amen Corner, E. C.(1939 年伦敦会香港影印所影印本), Vol. IV-Part I: 101-102.

> To the left the Fountain flow,
>> To the right that river K'i.
> Ah, when maids a-marrying go,
>> Parents, brothers, far must be.
>
> To the right that river K'i,
>> To the left those purpling Spring.
> Sweet bright smiles (I seem to see),
>> Tinkling gems on girdle strings.
>
> And the K'i's swift waters bear
>> Boats of pine with oars of yew.
> O to drive and wander there,
>> Then my frettings would be few!①

因为就诗的前半部分来看，竹竿加淇水是诗人儿时快乐生活的一部分，也是诗人婚后思念的对象，这在逻辑上是通畅的。但待到后文中"Sweet bright smiles (I seem to see), / Tinkling gems on girdle strings."出现之后，逻辑上的矛盾就达到了不可逾越的程度。读者不禁要问：是谁的灿烂笑容？是谁的环佩之声？这些与怀念淇水有何相干呢？

许渊冲以在译文中传达中国古代历史文化为要，但他也没能将"垂钓"意象的真意翻译出来：

---

① William Jennings. *The Shi King: The Old "Poetry Classic" of the Chinese*. London and New York: George Routledge and Sons, 1891: 86.

With long rod of bamboo,
I fish in River Qi.
Home, how I long for you,
Far-off a thousand li!

At left the Spring flows on;
At right the River clear.
To wed they saw me gone,
Leaving my parents dear.

The River clear at right,
At left the Spring flows on.
O my smiles beaming bright
And ringing gems are gone!

The long, long River flows
With boats of pine home-bound.
My boat along it goes.
O let my grief be drowned! ①

当然，理雅各、詹宁斯、许渊冲之所以在译文中遮掩了"垂钓"意象之"意"，主要原因在于其遵从了我国传统经学的阐释。若把这首诗的主题解作"卫女思归"，则译诗中的自相矛盾可以预见。

在《诗经》所有英美译者当中，韦利不仅有文学意识，而且是最有文化人类学意识的《诗经》译者。他在翻译这首诗时并没有遵

---

① 许渊冲（译）:《诗经》，北京：中国对外翻译出版公司，2009年，第62页。

从传统经学的阐释，而是采用了民俗学的视角进行解读，把该诗划入求爱诗一类：

> How it tapered, the bamboo rod
> With which you fished in the Qi!
> It is not that I do not love you,
> But it is so far I cannot come.
>
> The Well Spring is on the left;
> The Qi River is on the right.
> When a girl is married
> She is far from brothers, from father and mother.
>
> The Qi River is on the right,
> The Well Spring is on the left;
> But, oh, the grace of his loving smile!
> Oh, the quiver of his girdle stones!
>
> The Qi spreads its waves;
> Oars of juniper, boat of pine-wood.
> Come, yoke the horses, let us drive away,
> That I may be rid at last of my pain. ①

但是，即便如此，就英语读者来说，细细品味就会发现，这篇求爱诗整体上虽大致可通，在细节上却仍无法把对细长钓鱼竿的描绘与

---

① Arthur Waley. *The Book of Songs.* New York: Grove Press, 1996: 51-52.

后文的爱情关联起来,更无法理解"垂钓"形象的意义。

根据廖群(1995)的研究,《诗经》中束薪、采摘作为意象,象征古代的婚娶风俗和男女相思。例如《绸缪》:

绸缪束薪,三星在天。
今夕何夕,见此良人?
子兮子兮,如此良人何?

绸缪束刍,三星在隅。
今夕何夕,见此邂逅?
子兮子兮,如此邂逅何?

绸缪束楚,三星在户。
今夕何夕,见此粲者?
子兮子兮,如此粲者何?

关于本诗的首句,《毛诗传》曰:"兴也。……男女待礼而成,若薪刍待人事而后束也。三星在天,可以嫁娶矣。"① 廖群(1995)分析说,《诗经》中关于男女婚事常言及"薪",如《汉广》"翘翘错薪",《南山》"析薪如之何",《东山》"烝在栗薪",《车舝》"析其柞薪",《白华》"樵彼桑薪",等等。他引用段玉裁《说文解字注》"古以薪蒸为之烛"为证,认为婚礼因在黄昏后举行,需要燃薪照明,后来"束薪"遂成为婚姻礼俗之一,因此束薪所表达的是新婚之夜的夫妻情爱。那么,束薪的这层象征意义在译诗中能否得到

---

① 孔颖达:《毛诗正义》,北京:北京大学出版社,1999年,第388页。

第五章 《诗经》意象翻译之可能与不可能

再现？请看韦利的译文：

> Fast bundled is the firewood;
> The Three Stars have risen.
> Is it to-night or which night
> That I see my Good Man?
> Oh, masters, my masters,
> What will this Good Man be like?
>
> Fast bundled is the hay;
> The Three Stars are at the corner.
> Is it to-night or which night
> That shall see this meeting?
> Oh, masters, my masters,
> What will that meeting be like?
>
> Fast bundled is the wild-thorn;
> The Three Stars are at the door.
> Is it to-night or which night
> That I see that lovely one?
> Oh, masters, my masters,
> What will that lovely one be like? ①

不难看出，和《竹竿》中"垂钓"的寓意一样，译诗中"束薪"的象征意义也无法让英语读者理解。

---

① Arthur Waley. *The Book of Songs*. New York: Grove Press, 1996: 93–94.

以上诸例证明,如果在译文中把原始兴象这类含有原始宗教、巫术、古代民俗等象征意义的意象照例直接译出,客观上难免会在读者视野中造成"象"和"意"的分离。其结果是,虽然译诗中物象还在,但与之相应的寓意却不复存在。根据现代诗经学的研究,这类意象包括瓜果子实、束薪、束楚等植物意象,鹿马、鱼鸟等动物意象,山隰、河水等自然意象,采摘等动作意象,值得我们在翻译时引起重视。

实际上,意象翻译中存象失意问题的产生十分自然。从交际理论的观点来看,译文读者和诗人不处于同一个时代,也不属于同一种文化,他们之间在意象寓意问题上缺乏应有的共享信息,缺少彼此沟通的条件,因此读者无法仅通过上下文明白意象的含义。

所以,客观上我们不能把上述存象失意问题完全归咎于译者。忠实的翻译本来是传播原语文化最可靠的途径,但在这个问题上应该清楚这样一个事实:《诗经》中的原始兴象及比德意象与中华文化有着深远的渊源关系,因此它们本身富有民族性,既然它们不属于西方的意象系统,自然也就无法直接为西方读者所理解。翻译过程中欲避免"译文作品"有象无意的缺陷,从理论上讲,唯一有效的方法就是在译文后适当加注释。

三、意象的消解与浅化

如果翻译时只在语义层面翻译"象"而忽视"译文作品"中的"意"可能发生的变化,那么对于译文读者来说,"象"和"意"之间的关联就会断裂,这是意象翻译问题的主要表现形式之一。除此之外,还有一种情况值得我们注意,那就是原文意象常被翻译成

一组明喻,"意"被明示出来,由隐变为显。例如,阿连璧翻译的《椒聊》:

> 椒聊之实,蕃衍盈升。
> 彼其之子,硕大无朋。
> 椒聊且,远条且。
>
> 椒聊之实,蕃衍盈匊。
> 彼其之子,硕大且笃。
> 椒聊且,远条且。

> He shall be like the tree that groweth
> Fast by the river side,
> Which bringeth forth most pleasant fruit,
> In her due time and tide;
> Whose leaf shall never fade nor fall,
> But flourish and stand.
> Even so all things shall prosper well
> That this man takes in hand.①

首先,诗中"椒聊"是一个兴象,译文忽略了兴象的存在是错误的。《毛诗传》曰:"椒聊,椒也。"② 译者竟不追究椒聊究竟是什么

---

① C. F. R. Allen. *The Book of Chinese Poetry*. London: King Paul Trench, Trubner & Co., Ltd., 1891: 147.
② 孔颖达:《毛诗正义》,北京:北京大学出版社,1999年,第385页。

植物，就将其笼统地译作"tree"。诗人以"椒"做意象，本来是暗喻"沃之强盛，能修其政，知其繁衍盛大，子孙将有晋国焉"①。《毛诗正义》云："君子之人，见沃国之盛强，桓叔能修其政教，知其后世稍复藩衍盛大，子孙将并有晋国焉。昭公不知，故刺之。"② 译者对此不闻不顾，仅将喻体翻译成"He"，在"He"和"tree"之间形成一种明喻，但仅此而已。"He"究竟是谁？为什么做此比喻？其背后的历史意义是无法令译文读者明白的。从译文艺术效果来看，象和意分别以喻体和喻旨的形式被表现了出来，但这种传达方式却失之于把"象"的所指及寓意表面化，从而失去了原意象的含蓄性，失去了原诗暗喻以"刺"时的委婉笔法。所以，将意象翻译成明喻的方法实质上破坏了原意象的特性和审美价值。

尽管以上处理意象的方法不足取，但译文中毕竟还留了一丝原文意象的痕迹。意象翻译还有一种常见情况，即译者把意象彻底误读为一种环境描写，将其比喻或象征意义当成真实的信息加以传达，从而使意象变成了实实在在的故事背景。例如，阿连璧翻译的《杕杜》：

> 有杕之杜，其叶湑湑。
> 独行踽踽，岂无他人？不如我同父。
> 嗟行之人，胡不比焉？
> 人无兄弟，胡不佽焉？
>
> 有杕之杜，其叶菁菁。

---

① 见《国风·椒聊》小序。
② 孔颖达：《毛诗正义》，北京：北京大学出版社，1999年，第385页。

独行睘睘，岂无他人？不如我同姓。
嗟行之人，胡不比焉？
人无兄弟，胡不佽焉？

The pear-tree's leaves are thick and strong.
Beneath its shade I pass along
Unnoticed by the busy throng.

Ye travelers, to you I cry
For kindly aid and sympathy.
Unheeding still ye pass me by.

In vain. Your help I may not claim.
Strangers ye are, and not the same
As those who bear my father's name.①

这样一来，原来的意象实际上被完全消解了。原诗中"杕杜""湑湑"与"我"之间并没有现实中对象与背景的关系。《杕杜》本为"刺时也。君不能亲其宗族，骨肉离散，独居而无兄弟，将为沃所并尔"②，由于译者对"杕杜"意象的误读，在其引导之下，整个诗篇的内容都被改写了。加之译者将"独行"意象再次误读为一次真实的旅行过程，译文中竟出现了"travellers""strangers"的形象，从而把全诗对"骨肉离散"的比喻性的慨叹变成了对现实旅途中无

---

① C. F. R. Allen. *Book of Chinese Poetry*. London: King Paul Trench, Trubner & Co., Ltd., 1891: 149.
② 见《杕杜》小序。

人相助的感慨。这种对意象艺术手法的误读与改写,对译诗艺术性的破坏是致命的,其结果往往是不仅意象的真"意"没有译出,而且原诗的基本精神也都失之殆尽。

四、易"象"存"意"与易"象"易"意"

在许多情况下,译者往往谋求更换原来的物象,以为如此便可保持原诗意味。然而,物象一旦被更换,原意象的寓意就很难保持。换易"象"的情况有三种,一是将原物象换成另一完全不同的物象,二是将原物象换成似是而非的"原物象",三是用目的语文化中的类似物象代替原物象。例如詹宁斯翻译的《曹风·蜉蝣》:

> 蜉蝣之羽,衣裳楚楚。
> 心之忧矣,于我归处。
>
> 蜉蝣之翼,采采衣服。
> 心之忧矣,于我归息。
>
> 蜉蝣掘阅,麻衣如雪。
> 心之忧矣,于我归说。

> O the butterflies' wings!
> O the dresses so gay!
> 'Tis a trouble to me;
> To my home I'll away.
>
> O the butterflies' wings!

O the ways they are dressed!
'Tis but trouble to me;
I will homeward and rest.

See the chrysalids burst!
See the linen like snow!
'Tis but trouble to me;
To my home let me go. ①

　　《诗小序》曰："《蜉蝣》，刺奢也。昭公国小而迫，无法以自守，好奢而任小人，将无所依焉。"蜉蝣是一种体小的昆虫，生长于水泽地带，幼虫期较长，长成蜉蝣后，即不饮不食，一般都是朝生夕死。蜉蝣身体软弱，生一双透明漂亮的羽翼，在空中舞动时，姿态动人。诗人用蜉蝣讽刺朝中空尸其位的小人"徒整饰其衣裳，不知国之将胁迫，君臣死亡无日，如渠略然"②。蜉蝣的华丽外表与小人漂亮的装饰十分相似。蜉蝣朝生暮死，小人治国不知国之将亡，这两者极为相似。所以诗人用蜉蝣意象来比喻当道小人徒有华丽外表。

　　抑或在詹宁斯看来，蜉蝣外表不够华丽，所以在译诗中用"butterfly"（蝴蝶）取而代之，并自以为如此经营，译诗才能准确反映原诗意旨。③事实上，蝴蝶作为意象，与蜉蝣相比，其寓意少

---

① William Jennings. *The Shi King: The Old "Poetry Classic" of the Chinese.* London and New York: George Routledge and Sons, 1891: 156.
② 孔颖达：《毛诗正义》，北京：北京大学出版社，1999年，第470页。
③ William Jennings. *The Shi King: The Old "Poetry Classic" of the Chinese.* London and New York: George Routledge and Sons, 1891: 150.

317

了一层，即蝴蝶没有朝生暮死的特性。这样，"小人治国不知国之将亡"的寓意在译文中就丢失了。原诗"心之忧矣"用来哀叹两层意思，而到了译文当中，"'Tis but trouble to me"却只剩了哀叹朝廷卿士的衣着奢华、徒有外表这一层寓意，尤其是译诗最后一节，由于译者使用了"chrysalid"（蝶蛹）和"linen"（亚麻）两个词，已不能自圆其说。

汪榕培翻译的《卫风·硕人》与此十分类似，不同的是，汪译更改意象，所考虑的是意象的时代性对当代读者所造成的困难，但译诗意象确实留住了原文意象对庄姜美貌的赞美之意：

> 手如柔荑，
> 肤如凝脂。
> 领如蝤蛴，
> 齿如瓠犀。
> 螓首蛾眉，
> 巧笑倩兮，
> 美目盼兮。

> Her hands are small, her fingers slim;
> Her skin is smooth as cream.
> Her swan-like neck is long and slim;
> Her teeth like pearls so gleam.
> A broad forehead and arching brow
> Complement her dimpled cheeks
> And make her black eyes glow.

第五章 《诗经》意象翻译之可能与不可能

但若仔细品味就会发现,译诗除了"swan-like neck""pearl"等意象与所比喻的本体不够神似以外,译诗毕竟还少了些古风。

以上译例中译者更换意象都有明确目的,而有些情况下原意象之象被更换,却似乎是译者的无意之举。这主要是因为语言与所指物象古今有别的缘故。译者以为译文中的"象"是原"象",岂不知橘生淮北已成为枳。例如詹宁斯译《载驱》第一章:

> On flies her car, —with wicker blinds,
>   And leather mounts vermilion dyed.
> The way from Lu takes long to go;
>   Ts'i's daughter leaves at eventide. ①

文姜乘坐的车子变成"car"以后,不知道读者头脑中会浮现出怎样的意境。

有的时候,译者似乎是在偷梁换柱,物象在译文中还是原来的物象,但此物象已非彼物象,因为其作用已经发生了巨大变化。这种表面上相同的物象,本质上已经成为另一种物象。如韦利虽懂得《诗经》意象的作用,却如此翻译了《终风》的风、雷意象:

> Wild and windy was the day;
> You looked at me and laughed,
> But the jest was cruel, and the laughter mocking.

---

① William Jennings. *The Shi King: The Old "Poetry Classic" of the Chinese*. London and New York: George Routledge and Sons, 1891: 118.

My heart within is sore.

There was a great sandstorm that day;
Kindly you made as though to come,
Yet neither came nor went away.
Long, long my thoughts.

A great wind and darkness;
Day after day it is dark.
I lie awake, cannot sleep,
And gasp with longing.

Dreary, dreary the gloom;
The thunder growls.
I lie awake, cannot sleep,
And am destroyed with longing.①

根据《诗小序》，这篇诗本来是写"卫庄姜伤己也。遭州吁之暴，见侮慢不能正也"，韦利却将其改写成了婚恋诗。第一节中"终风"意象变成"粗野和多风的日子"，这是一个纯时间概念，在这样的日子里"你看着我哈哈大笑"，原因如何，则不得而知，因为下文似乎与这里的笑没有任何关系。第二节中"终风""霾"以喻时局动荡的意象变成了实在的"sandstorm"（风暴），也是一个纯天气概念，写的是在有风暴的天气里，情人不见了踪影。第三节中"阴天刮风"意象变成了"风"和不明原因的"黑暗"，这纯粹是一个

---

① Arthur Waley. *The Book of Songs*. New York: Grove Press, 1996: 27.

环境描写,在黑暗和风中,"我"无法入眠;第四节中"雷"意象,变成对打雷天气的描写,"我"因雷声而夜不成寐,为思念所煎熬。乍一看,译文中的物象如原文无异,但已非原意义上的物象,因为其已经完全不是比喻性的意象。

再看阿连璧《邶风·匏有苦叶》的译文:

> 匏有苦叶,济有深涉。
> 深则厉,浅则揭。
> 有弥济盈,有鷕雉鸣。
> 济盈不濡轨,雉鸣求其牡。
> 雝雝鸣雁,旭日始旦。
> 士如归妻,迨冰未泮。
> 招招舟子,人涉卬否。
> 人涉卬否,卬须我友。

"In the spring a young man's fancy lightly turns to thoughts of love."

  He speaks—

Now the winter's gone and over, and the waters which divide
Us true lovers, are now running with a high and swollen tide.
The gourds are still too heavy to support a swimmer's weight,
Yet I'll dare the angry river, and defy both death and fate.
If I find the crossing shallow I will doff my clothes and wade;
And to swim, if it be deeper, shall a lover be afraid?
I will say, to soothe my darling, if my danger makes her fret,

That the axle of my carriage at the ford was scarcely wet.
Did you hear the pheasant calling? It was for her mate she cried;
So my love would call her lover to cross over to her side.

She speaks—

Long before the ice was melted and the frost had passed away,
I received the appointed token at the earliest dawn of day
Now the ferryman is waiting, and he beckons with his hand
To his passengers to hasten. They may hasten, here I stand.
It is right for them to hurry, but I bide in patience here,
For I will not stir a footstep till I see my love appear.①

《诗小序》曰:"刺卫宣公也。公与夫人并为淫乱。"《毛诗传》曰:"以言室家之道,非得所适,贞女不行;非得礼义,昏姻不成。"②郑《笺》承毛说,称此诗为诗人坚持待礼仪而为婚。朱熹《诗集传》虽不赞同毛诗"刺宣公"的观点,但也认为其当是"刺淫乱之人"③。今人余冠英先生则说,此诗是写"一个秋天的早晨,红通通的太阳才升上地平线,照在济水上。一个女子正在岸边徘徊,她惦着住在河那边的未婚夫"④。写出了一个女子对情人来迎娶自己的强烈期盼。高亨《诗经今注》说,"这首诗写一个男子去看望已经订婚的女友"⑤。陈子展说它是"女求男之作,诗义自明,后儒大都不

---

① Clement F. R. Allen. *The Shih Ching*. London: Kegan Paul, Trench, Trubner & Co., Ltd., 1891: 48–49.
② 孔颖达:《毛诗正义》,北京:北京大学出版社,1999年,第144页。
③ 朱熹:《诗集传》,北京:中华书局,1958年,第20页。
④ 余冠英:《诗经选译》,北京:人民文学出版社,1982年,第33页。
⑤ 高亨:《诗经今注》,上海:上海古籍出版社,1980年,第46页。

晓。诗写此女一大侵早至济待涉，不厉不揭；已至旭旦有舟，亦不肯涉，留待其友人。并纪其顷间所见所闻，极为细致曲折"①。另有研究者则认为，这是一首写古代婚俗的诗。第一章以古代婚礼中最重要的饮酒仪式所用的工具"匏"和"济有深涉"为喻，表明自己对男女婚姻和家庭责任的深刻认识；以"济盈"和"雉鸣"为喻，传达强烈的求偶意愿；以"雝雝鸣雁，旭日始旦"比兴："旭日"比自己，"雁鸣"兴婚嫁。尽管本诗的诗旨有讽刺、爱情、婚俗等多种解释，但其与爱情有关是可以肯定的。译者虽然试图把这首诗翻译成爱情诗，却因变更原诗的"匏""济""雉鸣""雁鸣"等意象，把译诗变成了男子驱车渡水来迎接其心爱的女子，而女子耐心等待心上人到来的叙事诗。原诗的浪漫情调已荡然无存。

有的时候，译者似乎要在译诗中保持意象艺术手法，但苦于文化意象的不可通约性，不得不换易原诗意象。《麟之趾》的麟是《诗经》中颇具文化特色的动物意象，它是善良、仁厚、吉祥的象征。麟的这个象征意义来自民间对麟这一瑞兽的古老传说。由于麟这一神话传说的虚拟特征，翻译时无法在英语文化中找到相对应的替代物象。译者一旦试图用近似的动物去代替，就会把原诗的"意"和"象"全部破坏。

    麟之趾。振振公子，于嗟麟兮！
    麟之定。振振公姓，于嗟麟兮！
    麟之角。振振公族，于嗟麟兮！

---

① 陈子展：《诗经直解》，上海：复旦大学出版社，1983年，第102页。

请看韦利的译文：

> The unicorn's hoofs!
> The duke's sons throng.
> Alas for the unicorn!
>
> The unicorn's brow!
> The duke's kinsmen throng.
> Alas for the unicorn!
>
> The unicorn's horn!
> The duke's clansmen throng.
> Alas for the unicorn! [1]

许渊冲的译文也没能摆脱这一缺陷：

> The unicorn will use its hoofs to tread on none
> Just like our Prince's noble son.
> Ah! They are one.
>
> The unicorn will knock its head against none
> Just like our Prince's grandson.
> Ah! They are one.
>
> The unicorn will fight with its corn against none

---

[1] Arthur Waley. *The Book of Songs*. New York: Grove Press, 1996: 11–12.

Just like our Prince's great-grand-son.

Ah! They are one. ①

"unicorn"是现实世界中的独角龙。毋庸置疑，它在西方读者的心目中不可能产生麟的象征意义。这种翻译貌似流畅可读，但译文自身却已违背了自然界的规律：现实世界中的独角龙，作为一种野兽，怎能一定不害人！相信西方读者读了每章第一句译文之后，一定会深感迷惑不解。所以，这种翻译不仅自身无法成立，而且丢失了原文中的一切。"象"的这种改变不容易发现，但其对原诗艺术的伤害是巨大的。从文化传播的角度来看，它对西方读者也是一种误导。

上例中对"象"的换易似在不知不觉之中。然而，很多情况下，译者对"象"的变易却十分直接。韦利翻译的《敝笱》就颇令人深思：

In the wicker fish-trap by the bridge
Are fish, both bream and roach.
A lady of Qi goes to be married;
Her escort is like a trail of clouds.

In the wicker fish-trap by the bridge
Are fish, both bream and tench.
A lady of Qi goes to be married;
Her escort is thick as rain.

---

① 许渊冲（译）:《诗经》，北京：中国对外翻译出版公司，2009年，第11页。

> In the wicker fish-trap by the bridge
>
> The fish glide free.
>
> A lady of Qi goes to be married;
>
> Her escort is like a river.①

译文对原文意象的改易常常很微妙。原文的"敝笱"是"在梁"，意即破败的条编渔具被丢弃在渔坝上，而鱼在水中逍遥。诗人意在以此比喻"文姜"②，译文却仅言"条编渔具在桥边"，鱼都在渔具中，大概译者意欲用"鱼在渔具中"被逮住的意象比喻女子为丈夫所娶。这与下文齐女出嫁，众多车子相送是颇相一致的。但是，从诗篇细节来看，译者确实改变了原文的语义，如原文"梁"变成译文"桥"（bridge）等，从而改变了诗中的意象。单独来看，"笱"和"鱼"两物象仍然俱在，但是译文语境构成的意象组合却从本质上改变了原文的这两个意象。这种改变貌似在无意之间，但实际上译者意欲对诗篇做出新的文化阐释。这里所透露出的应是译者的文化人类学视野。

在翻译时对意象进行阐释，或者在译诗中随意添加意象，也可能造成对原诗意象艺术结构的重大破坏。例如许渊冲译的《东方之日》：

> 东方之日兮，
>
> 彼姝者子，

---

① Arthur Waley. *The Book of Songs*. New York: Grove Press, 1996: 81–82.

② 《诗小序》：敝笱，刺文姜也。齐人恶鲁桓公微弱，不能防闲文姜，使至淫乱，为二国危焉。

在我室兮。

在我室兮，

履我即兮。

东方之月兮，

彼姝者子，

在我闼兮。

在我闼兮，

履我发兮。

The eastern sun is red;

The maiden like a bloom

Follows me to my room.

The maiden in my room.

Follows me to the bed.

The eastern sun is bright;

The maiden I adore

Follows me out of door.

The maiden out of door

Leaves me and goes out of sight.

《诗小序》以为，此诗意在"刺衰"，乃"君臣失道，男女淫奔，不能以礼化也"。方玉润也认为此诗"刺荒淫也"[1]。两者道德判断虽如

---

[1] 方玉润：《诗经原始》，北京：中华书局，1986年，第231页。

此,但都承认诗的基本内容是关于男女情事。

　　许译应算是一首情爱诗。此处我们不论其他细节,只看每章开头的兴象。第一章原来只说"东方之日",而译文变成"东方之日红";第二章原文只说"东方之月",而译文变成"东方之月明"。这种意象阐释使得原意象的寓意趋于单一和定型,削弱了读者的审美想象空间。译者在第一章第二句"maiden"之后添加"bloom"(花朵),实乃画蛇添足。第二章第一句加"is bright",第二句加"I adore",使月意象与女子之间在美这一层喻意上失去了关联。因为明月可谓美,而"adore"的直接起因却并不一定是容貌美丽。

　　对《诗经》原意象改变程度最大的当数庞德。他用意象主义理论指导自己的《诗经》翻译实践,可谓纵横捭阖。一方面,庞德在译文中确实营造了一系列意象,但另一方面也阉割了许多原意象。这种情形从四始之首的《关雎》就开始了:

　　　　"Hid! Hid!" the fish-hawk saith,
　　　　　by isle in Ho the fish-hawk saith:
　　　　　　"Dark and clear,
　　　　　　Dark and clear,
　　　　So shall be the prince's fere."

　　　　Clear as the stream her modesty;
　　　　As neath dark boughs her secrecy,
　　　　　　reed against reed
　　　　　　tall on slight.
　　　　As the stream moves left and right,
　　　　　　dark and clear,

> dark and clear.
>
> To seek and not find
>
> as a dream in his mind,
>> think how her robe should be,
>>
>> distantly, to toss and turn,
>>
>> to toss and turn.
>
> High reed caught in *ts'ai* grass
>> so deep her secrecy;
>
> Lute sound in lute sound is caught,
>> touching, passing, left and right.
>
> Bang the gong of her delight.

诗中鱼鹰和河水两个意象得到夸张，而重要的采摘荇菜的意象却遭到阉割，取而代之的是芦苇和长袍等意象。其实，这样处理，不仅阉割了采摘荇菜的意象，也移除了意象所象征的婚恋之意。所以庞德译本总体上所造就的至多是一部英文"诗经"变体，其价值也只能在意象主义诗学框架内被认识和评价。再看庞德译的《芄兰》：

> 芄兰之支，童子佩觿。
> 虽则佩觿，能不我知。
> 容兮遂兮，垂带悸兮。
>
> 芄兰之叶，童子佩韘。
> 虽则佩韘，能不我甲。
> 容兮遂兮，垂带悸兮。

Feeble as a twig,

with a spike so big

in his belt, but know us he does not.

  Should we melt

at the flap of his sash ends?

Feeble as a gourd stalk (epidendrum)

to walk with an out-size ring

at his belt (fit for an archer's thumb

that might be an archer's,

as if ready for archery

which he is not)

we will not, I think, melt,

(complacency in its apogee)

at the flap of his sash ends.①

《诗小序》云:"《芄兰》,刺惠公也。骄而无礼,大夫刺之。"《毛诗传》曰:"惠公以幼童即位,自谓有才能而骄慢。于大臣但习威仪,不知为政以礼。"② 方玉润认为,此诗仅是"刺童子之好躐等而进,诸事骄慢无礼"③,并无惠公之谓。其间相一致的是该诗为讽刺诗。从诗篇本文来看则有可能有另外的解读。玉觿流行于商代,汉以后式微。历经数千年,玉觿不仅造型有所变化,而且作用也有了很大

---

① Ezra Pound. *Poems and Translations*. New York: The Library of America, 2003: 786-787.
② 孔颖达:《毛诗正义》,北京:北京大学出版社,1999年,第237页。
③ 方玉润:《诗经原始》,北京:中华书局,1986年,第183页。

延伸，从最初做解结工具发展成为具有象征意义的佩饰和传递男女爱情的信物。《毛诗传》也解释觿是"成人之佩"①。据《礼记·内则》载："子事父母，鸡初鸣，咸盥漱，栉，縰，笄，总，拂髦，冠，緌缨，端，韠，绅，搢笏。左右佩用，左佩纷帨、刀、砺、小觿、金燧，右佩玦、捍、管、遰、大觿、木燧。偪，屦著綦。"这表明男子如果佩觿，就标志着他已经是成年男子。因为芄兰的荚实和玉觿都是锥形，两者很相像，故诗中女主人公触景生情。女主人公与诗中童子可能是青梅竹马，当女子已到怀春之年，童子也已到佩带玉觿之时，童子却不解她的心结。

这样说来，这篇诗中的芄兰意象，其意在于比喻佩觿，而佩觿意象在于象征男女情爱。这样的理解是比较合乎情理的。庞德没有识得芄兰意象的这种象征作用，仅将"芄兰之支"简单翻译成"a feeble twig"（一根细弱的小树枝），加之佩觿又被改成"spike"（长钉），这一组合意象的"象"和"意"就一起变迁了。类似上述翻译现象，在所有《诗经》英译本中都相当普遍。

五、"意""象"皆失

从已有《诗经》诸译本的总体情况来看，理译本、詹译本、韦译本、许译本、汪译本等，都是较讲求行对句应的译本。庞译本比较重视意象构建，虽时而歪曲意象，却基本上没有置意象于不顾。如果说以上译本在实质上改变意象是较常见的现象，如在译文中只取意象的寓意而将原来的形象舍弃，却鲜有在译文中完全裁斥原文

---

① 孔颖达：《毛诗正义》，北京：北京大学出版社，1999年，第238页。

意象的做法。而英国译者中则唯有阿连璧和克拉默宾经常将原意象之"象"删掉不译。如阿连璧在翻译兴象时，往往采用删节的手法，因为这些兴象在他眼里是没有什么意义的。比如，阿连璧翻译的《关雎》就裁斥了整个首章中的意象，只剩下译者认为意思上符合逻辑的部分：

> They sent me to gather the cresses, which lie
> And sway on the stream, as it glances by,
> That a fitting welcome we might provide
> For our prince's modest and virtuous bride.
>
> I heard, as I gathered the cress, from the ait
> The mallard's endearing call to its mate;
> And I said, as I heard it, "Oh may this prove
> An omen of joy to our master's love!" ①

很明显，从语义和审美效果来看，译文仅反映了"关雎"兴象所寄寓的夫妇和合相亲的意旨，而几乎所有的意象艺术元素都没有得到反映。

克拉默宾翻译的《皇皇者华》与阿连璧翻译的《关雎》如出一辙：

> 皇皇者华，于彼原隰。
> 駪駪征夫，每怀靡及。

---

① Clement F. R. Allen. *The Shih Ching*. London: Kegan Paul, Trench, Trubner & Co., Ltd., 1891: 6.

第五章 《诗经》意象翻译之可能与不可能

我马维驹，六辔如濡。
载驰载驱，周爰咨诹。

我马维骐，六辔如丝。
载驰载驱，周爰咨谋。

我马维骆，六辔沃若。
载驰载驱，周爰咨度。

我马维骃，六辔既均。
载驰载驱，周爰咨询。

Galloping, galloping, gallant steed;
Six reins slackened and dull with sweat,
Galloping, galloping still we speed,
Seeking, counseling, onward set.

Galloping, galloping, piebald steed;
Six reins silken reins start and strain,
Galloping, galloping still we speed,
News—what news—from the King's domain.

Galloping, galloping, white and black;
Six reins glossy and flaked with foam,
Galloping, galloping, look not back!
On for the King—for the King we roam.

Galloping, galloping, dappled grey;

> Six reins true to the hand alone,
> Galloping, galloping, night and day,
> Seeking, questioning, galloping, gone! [1]

克拉默宾在译本前言中说，"我已经把这些诗，或者说尽力把这些诗翻译成诗"[2]。他认为，包括《诗经》在内的汉语古诗，长期以来学者们只翻译了字面，而丧失了诗的精神。他本人的翻译是负有文学责任的诗人对外国诗歌之美的公平翻译。然而，克拉默宾却没有做到真正传达原诗的内涵，也没能再现原诗整体的审美价值。他这种直陈意旨的方式和原诗中意象象征的方式相比，一显一隐，在艺术风格和文学效果上都有天壤之别。

阿连璧在翻译时常将某些意象完全舍弃，这种译法多运用在兴象翻译上。请看阿连璧译的《邶风·燕燕》：

> 燕燕于飞，差池其羽。
> 之子于归，远送于野，
> 瞻望弗及，泣涕如雨！
>
> 燕燕于飞，颉之颃之。
> 之子于归，远于将之。
> 瞻望弗及，伫立以泣！
>
> 燕燕于飞，下上其音。

---

[1] L. Cranmer-byng. *The Classics of Confucius—Book of Odes*. London: John Murray, Albemarle Street. 1908: 18.

[2] 同上，第 13 页。

之子于归，远送于南。
瞻望弗及，实劳我心！

仲氏任只，其心塞渊。
终温且惠，淑慎其身。
先君之思，以勖寡人。

She, who for many years has been my friend,
　　A gentle one and kind, and most sincere,
Departs for her own country, and an end
　　Has come to all I once considered dear.
Decorous was her person; though one love
　　We shared, no jealous doubt nor angry hate
Could e'er disturb her; nay she rather strove
　　My zeal and care for him to stimulate.
Far did I journey southwards, ere 'good byes'
　　Were uttered. Then she left me, and in vain
I gazed at her departing, for my eyes
　　Were blinded by the tears that fell like rain.
I watched the swallows in their flickering flight;
　　They too go southwards when the summer's o'er.
They will return when spring is warm and bright;
　　But my beloved friend comes back no more.[①]

[①] Clement F. R. Allen: *The Shih Ching*. London: Kegan Paul, Trench, Trubner & Co., Ltd., 1891: 41.

且不论译者在其他细节上所犯的许多失误，仅是因为忽视燕子上下翻飞的意象，译诗便变成清水一杯，索然无味。西方译者又能从该译文中读到什么呢？

《君子阳阳》原文中有"簧""房""翿""敖"四个意象，而阿连壁的译文却剔除了这四个意象，译诗从而变成了一串枯燥的独白：

> 君子阳阳，左执簧，
> 右招我由房。其乐只且！
> 君子陶陶，左执翿，
> 右招我由敖。其乐只且！

> The Good Man's Return
> My man comes home again.
> With music's sweetest strain
> I will welcome him. He beckons me to come to his embrace.
> In my gladness I will try
> To dance, to please his eyes.
> Oh, see the joy and rapture that are shining in his face! [①]

当然，裁斥原诗意象的翻译方式背后有其合理的理由，那就是，这样的译文较为符合西方诗歌的知性思维传统，便于西方读者在译诗

---

① Clement F. R. Allen: *The Shih Ching*. London: Kegan Paul, Trench, Trubner & Co., Ltd., 1891: 92.

中找到其早已习惯的意义逻辑。意义须符合逻辑是西方诗歌的审美基础，而没有意义逻辑的诗篇，对西方读者来说常是没有美感可言的。所以，这种翻译方式会更多地为强调西方诗学主导作用的西方译者所采用。而在他们的译文中，原诗兴象所包含的形象思维及其所依赖的高度的意合语言形式，则必然遭到抛弃。如此，原来的形式被抛弃的同时，一部分意义也不可避免地被抛弃了。

小　　结

意象是诗歌的血脉，也是诗歌翻译不可超越的元素。从诗歌美学角度来看，诗歌之美很大程度上来自意象之美。因为诗歌若没有了意象，便没有意境，没有意境，诗歌便失去了灵魂。因此，翻译诗歌，译者不能没有对意象的充分认识和关怀，不能不依靠对意象的精心经营。当然，从接受美学的理论来看，译者还应当有足够的跨文化意识，充分认识意象的文化属性，了解不同的文化有不同的意象传统。由于文化之间的差异，一种文化传统中的意象，有些可以为另一种文化的读者所共享，而更多的却因为有鲜明的民族特色而无法被共享。在翻译过程中，前者往往较容易在译文中被营造，而后者的经营则需要译者运用智慧和技巧来防止意象两方面的因素出现互不协调的现象。理论上，在翻译过程中遇到"意"和"象"不相协调的情况时，最有效的手段大概有三种：一种是采取加注释说明原意象的来龙去脉的方法，以帮助读者跨越文化障碍；一种是将原文化意象转化成本文化意象；最后一种是在译文中直接解释原意象所蕴含的某种或某些寓意。但是，第一种方法显然是比较奢侈的，因为短短一首诗的翻译，哪里容得下译文后再加上一长串烦琐的注释。即使有必要使用这种翻译手法，恐怕译者在具体做处理时也须十分节制。第二种手法是要将原意象转换成译入语读者能够心领神会的意象。这并不意味着一定要从译入语文化系统中寻求类似意象来取代原意象，而是要将"象"和"意"的组合做一种改变。然而，无论是替换还是改变原意象，接下来的问题是，原意象一旦改变了，译诗意境就必然与原诗有别。若仅从意象的寓意是否能够传达来看，意象总是能够翻译的，基本方法就是阐释。但是，问题在于诗歌意象一旦在翻译中被阐释，意象的内在张力将随之变松弛，其审美价值也随之降低，译诗也不再是蕴涵丰富的诗。纵观三者，竟无一能单独地彻底解决意象翻译问题。所以，意象的翻译，其最根本的原则还是从诗的整体意境出发，既注重个别意象的处理，又不斤斤计较于个别意象的得失，善于在诗的整个意象体系中进退腾挪，而始终不破坏诗的整体意境。只有把诗歌当作活的有机艺术整体来翻译，大概才是诗歌意象翻译之大道。也唯有如此，译诗方可最终臻于化境，并担当起中西文化交流之大任。

附　　录

附录一、《诗经》名物翻译对照表

说明：1. 限于篇幅，此表只包含《国风》中的名物。2. 以诗篇为单位统计。若同一名物在不同诗篇中出现，而译法不同，则皆列出。3. 从翻译的角度看，有些名物是两个或更多连在一起翻译的，所以作为一项列出。4. 意译者尽量照录。5. 未翻译者标"无"。6. 限于篇幅，此处只列四个译本的名物译名。

篇名	名物	译本与译名			
		James Legge	William Jennings	Arthur Waley	Ezra Pound
《关雎》	雎鸠	ospreys	waterfowl	osprey	fish-hawk
	洲	islet	islets	island	isle
	荇菜	duckweed	waterlilies	water mallow	reed
	琴瑟	lutes	lute and harp	zithern	lute
	钟鼓	bells and drums	bell and drum	gongs and drums	gong
《葛覃》	葛	dolichos	creepers	cloth-plant	vine
	黄鸟	yellow birds	golden orioles	oriole	oriole
	绨	fine cloth	lawn fine	cloth fine	fine cloth
	绤	lawn coarse	lawn coarse	cloth coarse	thick cloth
	私	private clothes	wardrobe	shift	无
	衣	robes	robes	dress	cloth

续表

篇名	名物	译本与译名			
		James Legge	William Jennings	Arthur Waley	Ezra Pound
《卷耳》	卷耳	mouse-ear	mouse-ears	cocklebur	curl-grass
	筐	basket	basket	basket	bucket
	行	highway	road	road	road
	马	horses	ponies	horse	horse
	金罍	gilded vase	golden goblet	bronze ewer	gilt cup
	兕觥	a cup from that rhinoceros' horn	horn-cup	horn cup	rhino horn
《樛木》	樛木	trees with curved drooping branches	trees bend low	a tree with drooping boughs	drooping tree
	葛藟	dolichos / creepers	creepers	cloth-creeper	wild vine
《螽斯》	螽	locusts	locusts	locust	locust
	桃	peach tree	peach-tree	peach-tree	omen tree
	兔罝	rabbit nets	rabbit-nets	rabbit net	rabbit nets
	干城	shield and wall	wall and shield	shield and rampart	wall
	中逵	where many ways meet	midway	where the paths meet	where the runs cross
《芣苢》	芣苢	plantains	plantain	the plantain	plantain
	乔木	trees without branches	stately poplars	upturning tree	tall trees
	薪	firewood	firewood	brushwood	kindling wood
	楚	thorns	thorn	wild-thorn	thorn
	马	horses	steeds	horse	horse
	蒌	southernwood	weed	mugwort	sandal trees
	驹	colts	two-year-olds	ponies	colt
《汝坟》	坟	banks	dykes	bank	levees
	条枚	branches and slender stems	twigs and boughs	faggot	boughs

续表

篇名	名物	译本与译名			
		James Legge	William Jennings	Arthur Waley	Ezra Pound
《汝坟》	条枚	branches and fresh twigs	shoots new-grown	bough	boughs
	鲂鱼	bream	bream	bream	square fish
《麟之趾》	麟	lin	lin	unicorn	Kylin
	趾	feet	hoof	hoof	foot
	定	forehead	brow	brow	无
	角	horn	horn	horn	无
《鹊巢》	鹊	magpie	magpie	magpie	jay
	鸠	dove	dove	cuckoo	dove
《采蘩》	蘩	white southernwood	herb	white aster	quince
	宫	temple	fane	ancestral hall	fane
	被	head-dress	head-gear	wig	wimple
《草虫》	草虫	grass-insects	crickets	cicada	hopper-grass
	阜螽	hoppers	hoppers	grasshopper	hopper-grass
	蕨	turtle-foot ferns	brackens	fern-shoot	turtle-fern
	薇	thorn-ferns	royal fern	bracken-shoot	jagged fern
《采蘋》	蘋	duckweed	water-wort	duckweed	reeds
	藻	pondweed	water-grass	water-grass	reeds
	筐	square baskets	basket round	round basket	baskets round
	筥	round baskets	basket square	square basket	baskets square
	锜	tripods	tripod	kettle	pots of earthen-ware
	釜	pans	cauldron	pan	pans of earthen-ware
	宗室	ancestral chamber	Hall	ancestral hall	shrine
	牖	window	light	window	light-hole
《甘棠》	棠	pear-tree	pear-tree	pear-tree	pear tree

341

续表

篇名	名物	译本与译名			
		James Legge	William Jennings	Arthur Waley	Ezra Pound
《行露》	露	dew	dew	dew	dew
	雀	sparrow	sparrow	sparrow	sparrow
	屋	house	dwelling	house	无
	狱	trial	forcing and compelling	suit	court
	鼠	rat	rats	rat	rat
	墉	wall	wall	wall	无
《羔羊》	羔	lamb	lamb	young lamb	lamb
	羊	sheep	sheep	young lamb	lamb
	皮	skins	skin	skin	skin
	紽	braiding	seams	strands	tassel
	緎	seam	sutures	strands	tassel
	总	joining	seams	strands	tassel
	素丝	white silk	white silk	white silk	white tassels
《摽有梅》	梅	plum-tree	damson-tree	plum	plum
	筐	basket	basket	basket	无
《野有死麕》	麕	antelope	gazelle	doe	deer
	白茅	white grass	reed-grass	white rushes	white grass
	朴樕	scrubby oaks	undergrowth	a clump of oaks	scrub elm
	鹿	deer	gazelle	deer	deer
	玉	gem	无	jade	jewel
	帨	handkerchief	kerchief	handkerchief	girdle-knot
	尨	dog	cur	dog	dog
《小星》	星	starlets	starlets	small stars	star
	衾	coverlets	quilt	coverlet	coverlets
	裯	sheets	coverlet	sheet	coverlets
《何彼秾矣》	唐棣	sparrow-plum	cherry	cherry	plum flowers
	桃	peach-tree	peach	peach	plum

342

续表

篇名	名物	译本与译名			
		James Legge	William Jennings	Arthur Waley	Ezra Pound
《何彼秾矣》	李	plum	plum	plum	plum
	华	flowers	blossoms	flowers	flower
	缗	lines	silken twine	fishing-line	fisherman's line
《驺虞》	葭	rushes	reeds	reed	rushes
	豝	wild boars	wild boars	swine	wild pig
	蓬	artemisia	grass	wormwood	rushes
	豵	wild boars	wild hogs	hog	boneen
《柏舟》	柏舟	boat of cypress wood	cedar boat	cypress boat	pine boat
	酒	wine	wine	wine	wine
	心	mind	heart	heart	heart
	鉴	mirror	mirror	mirror	mirror
	石	stone	stone	stone	Turning-stone
	席	mat	mat	mat	mat
	日	sun	sun	sun	sun
	月	moon	moon	moon	moon
	衣	dress	garments	dress	shirt
《绿衣》	衣	upper robe	robe	coat	robe
	裳	lower garment	skirt	skirt	skirt
	丝	silk	silk	thread	silk
	绨	linen, fine	lawn fine	broad-stitch	fine cloth
	绤	linen, coarse	lawn coarse	openwork	coarse cloth
《燕燕》	燕	swallows	swallows	swallow	swallows
	羽	wing	wings	wing	wing
	雨	rain	rain	rain	rain
《日月》	土	earth	earth	earth	earth

续表

篇名	名物	译本与译名			
		James Legge	William Jennings	Arthur Waley	Ezra Pound
《终风》	终风	wind	stormwind	windy	end wind
	霾	clouds of dust	dust	sandstorm	black solid cloud
	雷	thunder	thunder	thunder	thunder
《击鼓》	鼓	drums	drums	drum	drum
	兵	weapons	weapons	weapon	drill
	马	horses	steeds	horses	无
《凯风》	凯风	genial wind	gladdening breezes	gentle wind	soft wind
	棘	jujube tree	bush of thorn	thorn-bush	thorn-tree
	黄鸟	yellow birds	orioles	yellow oriole	yellow bird
《雄雉》	雄雉	male pheasant	male pheasant	cock-pheasant	pheasant-cock
《匏有苦叶》	匏	gourd	gourd	gourd	gourd
	雉	female pheasant	pheasant	pheasant	hen pheasant
	轨	axle	axle	axle	axle block
	雁	wild goose	wildgoose	wild-geese	wild goose
《谷风》	谷风	east wind	East winds	valley wind	wind of the East
	葑	mustard plant	some plants	greens	feng
	菲	earth melons	some plants	cabbage	fei
	下体	roots	roots	lower part	无
	畿	threshold	door	gateway	domain
	荼	sowthistle	lettuce	sow-thistle	thistle
	荠	shepherd's purse	cress	shepherd's-purse	shepherd's-purse
	梁	dam	fishing-dam	dam	dam
	笱	basket	wicker-nets	fish-trap	weir
	毒	poison	poison	poison	poison weed
《式微》	泥	mire	mud and mire	mud	mud

续表

篇名	名物	译本与译名			
		James Legge	William Jennings	Arthur Waley	Ezra Pound
《旄丘》	葛	dolichos	creepers	cloth-plant	vine
	狐裘	fox-furs	foxfurs	fox-fur	fox furs
	车	carriages	cars	wagon	transport
	褎	full robes	smile on	grand	embroidered collars
	充耳	ear stopped	deaf	ear-plug	cover your ears
《简兮》	庭	courtyard	ducal hall	yard	court
	虎	tiger	tiger	tiger	tiger
	辔	reins	reins	chariot rein	horse-reins
	组	ribbons	ribbons	ribbon	silk
	龠	flute	flute	flute	flute
	翟	pheasant's feather	pheasant's plumes	pheasant-plume	fan
	爵	cup	liquor	goblet	wine
	榛	hazel	hazels	hazel-tree	Hazel
	苓	liquorice	fungus	licorice	mallow
《泉水》	泉	spring	waters	fountain	spring
	脂	axle	oil	grease	vine
	辖	pin	axles	axle-cap	lynch-pin
	车	chariot	carriage	carriage	无
《北门》	北门	north gate	northern gate	northern gate	north gate
	雪	snow	snow	snow	snow
	狐	foxes	foxes	fox	fox
	乌	crows	crows	crow	crow
《静女》	城隅	corner of the wall	corner of the wall	corner of the Wall	angle in the wall
	彤管	red tube	vermilion pen	red flute	reed
	荑	white grass	shoot of couchgrass	rush-wool	*molu* grass

345

续表

篇名	名物	译本与译名			
		James Legge	William Jennings	Arthur Waley	Ezra Pound
《新台》	新台	New Tower	New Tower	new terrace	new tower
	蘧篨	vicious bloated mass	one deformed and old	toad	Ruckling relative
	河水	Waters of the Ho	Ho	waters of the river	Ho
	鱼网	fish net	net	fish net	fish-net
	鸿	goose	goose	wild goose	goose
	戚施	hunchback	hunchback	paddock	ruckling relative
《二子乘舟》	舟	boats	boat	boat	boat
《邶风·柏舟》	柏舟	boat of cypress wood	the boat of yew	cypress boat	pine boat
	河	Ho	Ho	river	Ho
	天	Heaven	Heaven	Heaven	Heaven
《墙有茨》	茨	tribulus	thorn-crop	star-thistle	vine
	冓	chamber	chambers	fence	harem
《君子偕老》	副	headdress	queenly head-dress	wig	hair-do
	笄	cross-pins	pins	pin	hair-do
	珈	jewels	jewelled	gem	jewelled
	象服	pictured robes	figured robe	blazoned gown	gown
	翟	pheasant-figured robe	festal robe	pheasant-wing	cloak
	鬒	false locks	false locks	false side-lock	无
	玉	jade	precious stones	jade	jade
	瑱	ear-plugs	ear-plugs	ear-plug	jade
	象	ivory	ivory	ivory	ivory
	揥	comb-pin	comb	girdle pendant	high comb
	绉絺	finest muslin of dolichos	crape and lawn	crepes and embroideries	erudite silk or plain flax

续表

篇名	名物	译本与译名			
		James Legge	William Jennings	Arthur Waley	Ezra Pound
《桑中》	唐	dodder	dodder	dodder	gold thread
	麦	wheat	wheat-ears	goosefoot	wheat crop
	葑	mustard plant	shallots	charlock	mustard
《鹑之奔奔》	鹑	quails	quails	quail	quails
	鹊	magpies	jay	magpie	pies
	定	Ting	Ting	Ding-star	the star of quiet
	宫	palace	Ts'u's palace walls	palace	Bramble hall
	室	mansion	Ts'u's palace halls	house	the wall
《定之方中》	榛栗	hazel and chesnut tree	hazel and chestnut-tree	hazels and chestnut-trees	chestnut and hazel tree
	椅桐梓漆	the e, the t'ung, the tsze, and the varnish-tree	dryandras, hardwoods, and the varnish-tree	catalpas, pawlownias, lacquer-trees	tung tree and varnish roots
	桑	mulberry tree	mulberry ground	mulberry orchards	orchard space
	桑田	mulberry trees and fields	mulberry lands	mulberry-fields	orchard and sown
	骍牝	tall horses and mares	mares	mare	tall horse
《蝃蝀》	蝃蝀	rainbow	rainbow	girdle	rainboe duplex
	隮	rainbow	rainbow	dawnlight	cloud-flush
《相鼠》	鼠	rat	rat	rat	rat
	皮	skin	hide and hair	skin	skin
	齿	teeth	tooth	teeth	teeth
	体	limbs	form—from tail to head	limb	feet

续表

篇名	名物	译本与译名			
		James Legge	William Jennings	Arthur Waley	Ezra Pound
《干旄》	干旄	ox-tails	oxtail-pennons	pole-banner	ox tails
	素丝	white silk bands	white silk	white band	plain silk bands
	良马	good horses	noble teams	fine horse	quadriga
	干旟	falcon-banners	falcon-banners	pole-banner	Falcon banners
	干旌	feathered streamers	feathered streamers	pole-banners	plumed flags
《载驰》	蝱	mother-of-pearl lilies	lily	toad-lilies	无
	麦	wheat	grain	caltrop	plains
《淇奥》	绿竹	green bamboos	green bamboos	kitesfoot	green bamboo
	充耳	ear-stoppers	stones	ear-plugs	jasper plugs
	琇	beautiful pebbles	gems	precious stone	jasper
	会弁	cap	bonnet	cap-gem	cap of state
	金	gold	gold	bronze	metal
	锡	tin	tin	White metal	metal
	圭	sceptre of jade	sceptre	scepter of jade	sceptre of jade
	璧	sceptre of jade	sceptre	disc of jade	sceptre of jade
《考槃》	槃	hut	cabin	gully	hut
	涧	stream	mountain stream	gully	vale
	阿	bend of the mound	mountain side	bank	brink
	陆	level height	hills	high ground	butte
《硕人》	锦	embroidered robe	robes embroidered	brocade	broidery
	褧衣	plain single garment	robes plain	unlined coat/ unlined skirt	profile
	荑	blades of the young white-grass	buds	rush-down	blade of grass

续表

篇名	名物	译本与译名			
		James Legge	William Jennings	Arthur Waley	Ezra Pound
《硕人》	凝脂	congealed ointment	unguent	lard	cream
	蝤蛴	tree-grub	tree-wrom's breed	tree-grub	glow-worm
	瓠犀	melon seeds	gourd' white seed	melon-seeds	melon seeds
	四牡	four horses	four male steeds	four steeds	four high stallions
	帧	ornaments	trappings	trapping	scarlet-tasselled bits
	翟茀	pheasant feather	plumes	pheasant-feather	pheasant tails in woven paravant
	罛	nets	nets	fish-net	nets
	鳣	sturgeonl arge	big sturgeons	sturgeon	sturgeon
	鲔	sturgeon small	small sturgeons	snout-fish	gamey trout
	葭	rushes	reeds	reed	无
	菼	sedges	sedges	sedge	无
《氓》	布	cloth	cloth	cloth	calico
	丝	silk	silk	thread	silk
	垝垣	ruinous wall	ruined walls	high wall	ruin'd wall
	卜	Tortoise shell	无	patterns	shells
	筮	reeds	straws	yarrow-stalks	staks
	车	carriage	waggon	cart	cart
	桑	mulberry tree	mulberry	mulberry-tree	mulberry-tree
	鸠	dove	dove	dove-dove	doves
	帷	curtains of my carriage	无	curtains of the carriage	carriage curtains
	桑葚	fruit	fruit	mulberry	mulberries
	帷裳	curtains	hood	curtains	carriage curtains
	隰	marsh	swampy fields	swamp	swamp

349

续表

篇名	名物	译本与译名			
		James Legge	William Jennings	Arthur Waley	Ezra Pound
《氓》	岸	banks	banks	banks	bank
	泮	shores	bounds	sides	edge
	总角	knot	maiden days	hair looped and ribboned	pig-tails
《竹竿》	竹竿	bamboo rods	bamboo	bamboo rod	slim poles
	佩玉	girdle gems	gems on girdle strings	girdle stones	stones at your belt
	桧楫	oars of cedar	oars of yew	oars of juniper	oars
	松舟	boats of pine	boats of pine	pine-wood	pine boat
《芄兰》	芄兰	sparrow-gourd	sparrow-gourd	vine-bean	gourd stalk
	支	branches	pod	branch	twig
	觿	spike	bodkin	knot-horn	spike
	韘	archer's thimble	archer's ring	archer's thimble	out-size ring
	垂带	ends of his girdle	ends of his girdle	gems	sash ends
《河广》	苇	reeds	rush	reed	reed
	刀	little boat	narrow boats	skiff	blade of a row-boat
《伯兮》	殳	halberd	spear and lance	lance	ten-cubit halbard
	飞蓬	flying[pappus of the]artemisia	flax-weed	tumbleweed	bush flying
	膏沐	anoint and wash it	anoint	grease	oil
	谖草	plant of forgetfulness	herb that memory kills	day-lily	forgetting-grass
《有狐》	狐	fox	fox	fox	fox
	梁	dam	weir	dam	bank
	裳	lower garment	trouserless	robe	skirt
	带	girdle	girdle	belt	belt
	服	clothes	garments	coat	clothes

续表

篇名	名物	译本与译名			
		James Legge	William Jennings	Arthur Waley	Ezra Pound
《木瓜》	木瓜	papaya	quinces	quince	quince
	琼琚	*keu*-gem	ruby	bright girdle-gem	beryl
	木桃	peach	peaches	tree-peach	peach
	琼瑶	*yaou*-gem	jasper	greenstone	gem
	木李	plum	plums	tree-plum	plum
	琼玖	*këw*-stone	dusky gem	bright jet-stone	ninth-stone
《黍离》	黍	millet	rice	wine-millet	black millet
	稷	sacrificial millet	millet	cooking-millet	black millet
	苗	blade	blade	sprout	sprout
	穗	ear	ear	in spike	panicled ear in the forming
	实	grain	grain	in grain	the heavy ears of the temple grain
《君子于役》	鸡	fowls	rooster	fowl	hen
	埘	holes in the wall	ledge	hole	wall-hole
	牛羊	goats and cows	goats and kine	sheep and cows	beasts
《君子阳阳》	簧	reed-organ	instrument	reed-organ	bamboo flute
	翿	screen of feathers	feathered fan	dancing plume	feather fan
《扬之水》	薪	firewood	faggots	firewood	fagot
	楚	thorns	thorns	thornwood	thorn-pack
	蒲	osiers	rushes	osier	osier
《中谷有蓷》	谷	valleys	vale	valley	vale
	蓷	mother-wort	motherwort	motherwort	dry grass
《兔爰》	兔	hare	hares	hare	rabbit
	雉	pheasant	pheasants	pheasant	pheasant
	罗	net	net	snare	无
	罦	snare	bait	trap	trap
	罿	trap	decoyed	net	无

续表

篇名	名物	译本与译名			
		James Legge	William Jennings	Arthur Waley	Ezra Pound
《葛藟》	葛藟	dolichos creepers	creepers	cloth-plant	vine
	浒	borders	beside the Ho	banks	along the Ho
	涘	banks	Ho's banks	margin of the river	edge
	漘	lips	Ho's steep bank	lips of the river	brink
	葛	dolichos	creepers	cloth-creeper	vine leaves
	萧	oxtail-southernwood	fragrant grass	southernwood	southernwoods
	艾	mugwort	mugwort	mugwort	tall grass
《大车》	大车	great carriage	grand carriage	great carriage	chariot
	毳衣	robes of rank	furred robes	coat	robes
	菼	young sedge	无	rush-wool	a green flare
	璊	carnation-gem	garnets	pink sprout	cornelian
	室	apartments	dwellings	house	house
	穴	grave	grave	grave	earthen cell
《丘中有麻》	麻	hemp	hemp	hemp	hemp
	麦	wheat	wheat	wheat	wheat
	李	plum trees	plum-trees	plump-trees	plum
	佩玖	*këw*-stones	girdle-trinkets	jet-stones for my girdle	girdle stone
《缁衣》	缁衣	black robes	jet-black robes	black coat	clothes
	馆	court	where lodgeth our prince	where you lodge	无
	粲	feast	feast	food	food
《将仲子》	里	hamlet	grounds	homestead	town
	树杞	willow trees	willow-trees	willows	willows
	墙	wall	garden wall	wall	wall

续表

篇名	名物	译本与译名			
		James Legge	William Jennings	Arthur Waley	Ezra Pound
《将仲子》	树桑	mulberry trees	mulberry-trees	mulberry-trees	mulberry boughs
	园	garden	garden plot	garden	garden
	树檀	sandal trees	sandal-trees	hard-wood	sandalwood tree
《叔于田》	田	hunting	meet	hunting-fields	hunting
	巷	streets	street/lanes	lane	lane
	酒	feasting	feasting	wine	drink
	野	country	plains	The wilds	wild field
	马	无	horsemen	horse	horse
《大叔于田》	田	hunting	plains	hunting-fields	field
	乘马	chariot and four	team	team of four	double team
	辔	reins	reins	rein	reins
	组	ribbons	ribbons	ribbons	silken stands
	骖	outside horses	off-steeds/the outer	helper	Outer stallions
	虎	tiger	tiger	tiger	tiger
	乘黄	four bay horses	bays	team of bays	wheel-bays
	服	two insides	inner pair	yoke-horse	stallions
	雁	two outsides	wild-geese	wild-geese	twin geese a-wing
	鸨	无	greys	无	stallions
	鬯	quiver	case	case	shoot
	弓	bow	bow	bow	bow
《清人》	驷介	chariot with its team in mail	mail-clad teams	armoured team	snorting horses
	矛	spears	spear and lance	spear	spears
	重英	ornaments	double plumes	pennon out-topping pennon	tassel
	重乔	hooks	hooks	hook topping hook	tassel

353

续表

篇名	名物	译本与译名			
		James Legge	William Jennings	Arthur Waley	Ezra Pound
《羔裘》	羔裘	lamb's fur	lamb's-fur	furs of lamb's wool	lamb-skin
	豹	leopard	panther	leopard	leopard
	英	ornaments	honour-badges	festoon	buttons
《遵大路》	大路	highway	highway	highroad	high road
	袪	cuff	sleeve	sleeve	sleeve
《女曰鸡鸣》	鸡	cock-crow	cocks	cock	cock
	凫	ducks	wild ducks	wild-duck	geese
	雁	geese	geese	wild-geese	geese
	琴瑟	lute	lutes	zithern	guitars and lutes
	杂佩	ornaments of my girdle	girdle-pendants	girdle-stones of many sorts	girdle stone
《有女同车》	舜华	flower of the ephemeral hedge-tree	hedge-rose	mallow-flower	hibiscus flower
	琼琚	*keu*-gems	gems	bright girdle-gem	gemmed belt
	舜英	ephemeral blossoms of the hedge-tree	hedge-rose	mallow blossom	hibiscus spray
	佩玉	gems	gems	girdle-stone	pendant
《山有扶苏》	扶苏	mulberry tree	myrtle-tree	nutgrass	noble ilex
	荷华	lotus flower	water-lily	lotus flower	marsh weed
	乔松	lofty pine	fir	tall pine	high pine
	游龙	spreading water-polygonum	dragon-vetch	prince's-feather	dragon flower
《萚兮》	萚	withered leaves	leaves	fallen leaves	withered
《褰裳》	裳	lower garments	skirts	loin	sark
《丰》	巷	lane	lane	lane	lane
	堂	hall	hall	hall	hall

续表

篇名	名物	译本与译名			
		James Legge	William Jennings	Arthur Waley	Ezra Pound
《丰》	锦	embroidered upper robe	mantle	brocade	hidden embroideries
	裳衣	a [plain] single garment	broidered robe	unlined coat	plain dress
	裳裳	a [plain] single garment	broidered skirt	unlined skirt	skirt of embroideries
《东门之墠》	茹藘	madder plant	madder-plant	madder	madder
	栗	chestnut trees	chestnuts	chestnut-tree	chestnut
	家室	houses	houses	houses	garden
《风雨》	鸡	cock	cock	cock	cock
	风	wind	wind	wind	wind
	雨	rain	rain	rain	rain
《子衿》	衿	blue collar	collar	blue collar	collar
	佩	girdle-gems	cincture	blue collar	sash
	城阙	look-out tower on the wall	watch-tower	wall-gate	gates of the towered wall
《扬之水》	束楚	bundle of thorns	a load of thorns	thorn-faggots that are well bound	a thorn fagot
	束薪	bundle of firewood	firewood faggots	firewood that is well tied	fagot bound
《出其东门》	东门	east gate	East-gate	Eastern Gate	great gate to the East
	缟衣	thin white silk	in white	white jacket	plain silk gown
	綦巾	grey coiffure	kerchief blue	grey scarf	gray scarf
	闉阇	tower on the covering wall	outer gate and tower	Gate Tower	the towers toward the East
	荼	flowering rushes	reeds in flower	rush-wool	flowers
	缟衣	thin white silk	in white	white jacket	red bonnet
	茹藘	madder-dyed coiffure	madder dyes	madder skirt	plain silk gown

355

续表

篇名	名物	译本与译名			
		James Legge	William Jennings	Arthur Waley	Ezra Pound
《野有蔓草》	蔓草	creeping grass	creeping plants	creeper	bind-grass
	零露	dew	heavy dews	falling dew	dew
《溱洧》	蕑	flowers of valerian	marsh-flowers	scented herbs	valerian
	勺药	small peonies	floral offering	peony	medicine
《苍蝇》	鸡	cock	cock	cock	cock
	苍蝇	blue flies	blue flies	green flies	blue fly
《还》	虫	insects	insects	gnat	fly
	肩	boars	boars	boar	wild pig
	牡	males	beasts	stag	boar
	狼	wolves	wolves	wolf	wolf
《著》	著	between the door and screen	gate	gate-screen	gate-screen
	充耳	ear-stoppers	tassels	ear-plugs	ear-plugs
	琼华	*hwa*-stones	coloured gems	bright flower	white silk tassels
	庭	open court	court	courtyard	court-yard
	琼莹	*yung*-stones	lustre	bright blossom	silken thread
	堂	hall	hall	hall	hall
	琼英	*ying*-gems	jewels	blossom bright	topaze
《东方之日》	室	chamber	abode	house/home	无
	闼	door	door	bower	door
《东方未明》	衣裳	clothes upside down	clothes	jacket and skirt	kilt coat
	裳衣	clothes upside down	garments	skirt and coat	coat kilt
	柳	willow	willows	willow	无
	樊圃	garden	garden hedge	fenced garden	garden fence
《南山》	雄狐	male fox	fox	male fox	fox
	葛屦	dolichos shoes	fibre-shoes	fibre shoe	vine-rope shoes

续表

篇名	名物	译本与译名			
		James Legge	William Jennings	Arthur Waley	Ezra Pound
《南山》	冠绥	string-ends of a cap	bonnet-strings	Cap ribbon	cap-strings
	麻	hemp	hemp	hemp	hemp
	薪	firewood	firewood	firewood	kindling
	斧	axe	axe	axe	axe
《甫田》	甫田	fields too large	broad field	too big a field	field
	莠	weeds	weeds	weeds	weeds
	总角	child with his two tufts of hair	twin tufts of hair	side-locks	tufted
	弁	cap	cap	tall cap of a man	grown man's cap
《卢令》	卢	hounds	hound	hound	hounds
	重环	double rings	leashed in pairs	double ring	double ring
	重鋂	triple rings	three and three	double hoop	triple ring
《敝笱》	笱	basket	fish-trap	fish-trap	wicker
	梁	dam	weir	bridge	weir
	鲂	bream	bream	bream	fish
	鳏	*kwan*	sturgeon	roach	fish
	鲔	tench	roach	tench	luce and perch
《载驱》	载驱	chariot	car	无	car
	簟茀	screen of bamboos	wicker blinds	Bamboo awning	woven leather
	鞹	vermilion-coloured leather	leather mounts	leatherwork	cinnabar
	骊	black horses	black coursers	black horse	quadrigas/ double teams
	垂辔	reins	long flowing reins	dangling rein	smooth-oiled reins
《猗嗟》	侯	target	disc	target	dot
	矢	arrows	shaft	arrow	arrow

续表

篇名	名物	译本与译名			
		James Legge	William Jennings	Arthur Waley	Ezra Pound
《葛屦》	葛屦	dolichos fibre	fibre-shoes	fibre shoe	fibre shoes
	裳	clothes		clothes	clothes
	象揥	ivory comb-pin	ivory pin	ivory pendant	ivory pin
《汾沮洳》	莫	sorrel	sorrel	sorrel	sorrel
	桑	mulberry leaves	mulberry	mulberry-leave	mulberry trees
	英	flower	floweret	jade	flowery
	芙	ox-lips	marsh-plants	water-plantain	ox-lip
	玉	gem	gem	jade	gem
《园有桃》	桃	peach trees	peach-trees	peach-tree	peach
	棘	jujube trees	date-trees	prickly jujube	blackberry
《伐檀》	檀	sandal trees	sandal-trees	hardwood	sandalwood
	廛	farms	farms	stack-yard	wu
	禾	produce/leaves/paddy	grain	corn	grain
	貆	badgers	badgers	badger	badger
	辐	wood for his spokes	spoke-wood	cart-spoke	spoke
	特	those three-year-olds	game	king-deer	boar
	轮	wood (for his wheels)	tire-wood	wheel	wheel rim
	囷	round binns	barns	bin	无
	鹑	quails	quails	quail	quail
《硕鼠》	硕鼠	large rats	monster rats	big rat	stone-head rats
	黍	millet	millets	millet	grain
	麦	wheat	crops of wheat	corn	wheat
	苗	springing grain	springing grain	rice-shoot	new shoots
《蟋蟀》	蟋蟀	cricket	crickets	cricket	cricket
	堂	hall	hall	hall	hall

续表

篇名	名物	译本与译名			
		James Legge	William Jennings	Arthur Waley	Ezra Pound
《山有枢》	役车	carts	cart	field-waggon	cart
	枢	thorny elms	thorny elms	thorn-elm	thorn-elm
	榆	white elms	white elm	white elm-tree	white elm
	衣裳	suits of robes	robes and gowns	long robe	clothes
	车马	carriages and horses	carriage and steeds	carriages and horses	carriage
	栲	k'aou	varnish-wood	cedrela	Kao tree
	杻	nëw	wood	privet	shrub
	廷内	courtyards and inner rooms	courts and halls	courtyard and house	courtly dancing place
	钟鼓	drums and bells	bells and drums	bells and drums	bells, drums
	漆	varnish trees	lacquer-tree	varnish-tree	terebinth
	栗	chestnuts	chestnut	chestnut	chestnut
	酒食	spirits and viands	meats and drinks	wine and meat	wine
	瑟	lute	lute	zithern	lute
《扬之水》	素衣	robe of white silk	white red-collared robe	white coat	silk robe
	白石	white rocks	white rocks	white rocks	sharp-edged rocks
	朱襮	vermilion collar	white red-collared robe	red lappet	red lapel
	朱绣	vermilion collar, and embroidered	white red-collared robe	red stitching	broidered axe
《椒聊》	椒聊	pepper plant	pepper-tree	pepper-plant	pepper tree
	实	clusters	fruit	seed	pod
《绸缪》	束薪	firewood	firewood bundles	firewood	faggots
	束刍	grass	bundles of grass	hay	grass
	束楚	thorns	bundles of thorns	wild-thorn	thorn
	三星	Three Stars	Three Stars	Three Stars	Three stars

359

续表

篇名	名物	译本与译名			
		James Legge	William Jennings	Arthur Waley	Ezra Pound
《杕杜》	杜	pear tree	pear-tree	pear-tree	pear tree
《羔裘》	羔裘	lamb's fur	lamb's-fur	lamb's wool and cuffs of leopard's fur	lamb-skin coat
	豹袪	leopard's cuffs	cuffs of pardskin	leaves	leopard cuff
	豹褎	leopard's cuffs	bordered with the pardskin	leaves	leopard trim
《鸨羽》	鸨	wild geese	gannets	bustard	buzzards
	苞栩	bushy oaks	oak-tree	oak clump	oak
	稷黍	sacrificial millet and millet	millet crops	cooking-millet and wine-millet	grain
	苞棘	bushy jujube trees	copse of thorn	thorn-bushes	thorns
	黍稷	millet and sacrificial millet	crops of corn	wine-millet and cooking-millet	grain
	苞桑	bushy mulberry trees	mulberry grove	mulberry clump	mulberries
	稻粱	rice and maize	rice and maize	rice and spiked millet	rice or spiked-grain
《无衣》	衣	robes	robes	bedclothes	robe
《有杕之杜》	杜	pear tree	pear-tree	pear-tree	pear tree
《葛生》	葛	dolichos	creeper	cloth-plant	creeper
	楚	thorn trees	shrubs	thorn bush	thorn
	蔹	convolvulus	convolvulus	bindweed	bracken wilds
	域	tombs	grave	borders of the field	grave
	棘	jujube trees	throns	bramble	thorn
	角枕	pillow of horn	pillow of horn	horn pillow	thorn
	锦衾	embroidered coverlet	coverlet	worked coverlet	silk shroud
	居	abode	abode	where he dwells	house
	室	chamber	dwelling	home	house

续表

篇名	名物	译本与译名			
		James Legge	William Jennings	Arthur Waley	Ezra Pound
《采苓》	苓	liquorice	mouse-ear fungus	licorice	ling
	苦	sowthistle	fue-leaf	sow-thistle	thistle
	葑	mustard plant	parsley	cabbage	mustard
	车	carriages	carriages	coach wheels	chariots
	白颠	white foreheads	white-crested steeds	white forehead	white-fronted horses
	漆	varnish trees	varnish-tree	lacquer-tree	terebinth
	栗	chestnuts	chestnut	chestnut-tree	chestnut
	鼓瑟	lutes	lutes	zithern	lutes
	桑	mulberry trees	mulberry-tree	mulberry-tree	mulberry
	杨	willows	willow	willow	willow
	簧	organs	organ's strains	reed-organ	drum-beat and shamisan
《驷驖》	驷驖	four iron-black horses	irongreys	team of grays	iron grays
	辔	reins	reins	rein	rein
	辰牡	male animals of the season	season's game	old stag	boars
	拔	arrows	shaft	无	bow
	北园	northern park	north park	northern park	North Park
	輶车	light carriages	light-built carts	light cart	double teams
	鸾	bells	bells	bells at bridle	bells
	镳	bits	bits	无	无
	猃	long-mouthed dogs	hounds	greyhound	long-nosed hounds
	歇骄	short-mouthed dogs	hounds	bloodhound	short-nosed hounds
《小戎》	小戎	short war carriage	curricle of war	small war-chariot	service car
	收	boards	无	shallow body	无

续表

篇名	名物	译本与译名			
		James Legge	William Jennings	Arthur Waley	Ezra Pound
《小戎》	鋈	ornamental bands of leather	bindings	band	band
	辀	End of the pole	pole	upturned chariot-pole	curving pole
	游环	slip rings	sliding rings	slip ring	side shields
	胁驱	side straps	shoulder-braces	flank-check	silver'd trace
	靷	traces	cross-bar	trace	silver'd trace
	鋈续	gilt rings	silvered fastenings	silvered case	silver'd trace
	文茵	mat of tige's skin	tiger-skin	patterned mat	bright mats
	毂	naves	naves far-projecting	long nave	bulging hub
	骐	piebalds	piebalds	piebald	dapple
	馵	horses with white left feet	piebalds	whitefoot	white-foot
	玉	jade	无	jade	jade
	板屋	plank house	log-huts	plank hut	service shack
	牡	horses	colts	steed	great dapple
	辔	reins	reins	rein	rein
	骝	bay with black mane	piebalds	the bay with black mane	black-maned
	駰	yellow with black mouth	dappled greys	brown horse with black mouth	the darker pair
	骊	black with black mouth	dappled greys	deep-black horse	the darker pair
	龙盾	dragon-figured shields	dragon shields	dragon shield	dragon shield
	鋈䡅	buckles for the inner reins	silver-clasped each inner rein	buckle strap	silver-ringed rein
	俴驷	mail-covered team	four mailed chargers	team lightly caparisoned	team
	厹矛	trident spears	trident spears	trident spear	trident-haft

续表

篇名	名物	译本与译名			
		James Legge	William Jennings	Arthur Waley	Ezra Pound
《小戎》	鋈錞	gilt ends	shaft-ends silvered	silvered butt	silver-based butt
	伐	shield	shields	shield many-coloured	shield
	苑	feather-figured	painted wings	coating of feathers	emboss'd
	虎韔	tiger-skin bow-case	case of tiger skin	tiger-skin	bow-case of tiger's
	镂膺	carved metal ornaments	steel-mounted	chiseled collar	graved lorica
	弓	bows	bows	bow	bow
	竹闭	bamboo frames	bamboo frames	bamboo-frame	laths
	绲縢	string	strings	rattan	bound
《蒹葭》	蒹葭	reeds and rushes	reed and rush	rush leaves	reed and rush
	白露	white dew	dews	white dew	white dew
	霜	hoarfrost	hoar-frost	frost	frost
	湄	margin of the water	riverside	water's side	bank
	湀	无	无	无	marge
	坻	islet	isle	ledge	isle
	沚	island	island	shoal	isle
《终南》	条	white firs	silver firs	peach-tree	white fir
	梅	plum trees	plum-trees	plum-tree	plum
	锦衣	embroidered robe	broider'd robe	damask coat	broidery
	狐裘	fox-fur	fox-furs	fox fur	fox fur
	渥丹	vermilion	so ruddy	cinnabar	ruddy of face
	纪	nooks	nook	boxthorn	hall
	堂	open glades	open glade	wild plum-tree	hall
	黻衣	embroidered robe	flowery robe	brocaded coat	blue-black robe

续表

篇名	名物	译本与译名			
		James Legge	William Jennings	Arthur Waley	Ezra Pound
《终南》	绣裳	lower garment	train	embroidered skirt	blue-black robe
	佩玉	gems	jewels	jades	pendant jade
《黄鸟》	黄鸟	yellow birds	yellow birds	oriole	yellow wings
	棘	jujube trees	thorny tree	thorn-bush	thorn
	穴	grave	grave	tomb-hole	grave
	桑	mulberry trees	mulberry-trees	mulberry-tree	mulberry
	楚	thorn trees	thicket	bramble	thorn
《晨风》	晨风	falcon	sparrow-hawk	falcon	falcon
	苞栎	bushy oaks	groves of oak	a clump of oaks	thick oak
	六驳	(six) elms	elm-trees, six of them	piebald-tree	six grafted pears
	棣	sparrow-plums	cherry-trees	plum-tree	plum trees
	樕	high, wild pear trees	wild pears	pear-tree	peach blossoms
《无衣》	衣	clothes	clothes	wrap	clothes
	袍	robes	plaid	rug	cloak
	戈矛	lance and spear	spears and pikes	axe and spear	spear, lance and all
	泽	under clothes	skirt	under-robe	underwear
	矛戟	spear and lance	halberd and lance	halberd	lances and halbards
	裳	lower garments	kirtle	skirt	spare kilt
	甲	buffcoat	armour	armor	mail-coat and axe
	兵	weapons	arms	arms	axe
《渭阳》	路车	carriage of state	ducal car	big chariot	car
	乘黄	four bay horses	bay team	a team of bays	four bays
	琼瑰	a precious jasper, and gems	rich gems	ghost-stone	jasper
	玉佩	girdle-pendant	belt	girdle-pendant of jade	girdle stone

续表

篇名	名物	译本与译名			
		James Legge	William Jennings	Arthur Waley	Ezra Pound
《权舆》	夏屋	house large and spacious	fine houses	big dish-stands	Hia's house
	簋	dishes of grain	platters	dish	great courses
《宛丘》	鼓	drum	drummers	drum	hand-drum
	鹭羽	egret's feather	egret-plumes	egret feather	egret's feather
	缶	earthen vessel	porcelain drums	earthen gong	earthen pot
	鹭翿	egret's feather	egret-fan	egret plume	egret fan
《东门之枌》	枌	white elms	elms	elm	white elm
	栩	oaks	oak-trees	oak	oak
	麻	hemp	hemp	hemp	hemp
	荍	flower of the thorny mallows	blushing rose	mallow	the sun's flower
	椒	pepper plant	pepper-spray	pepper-seed	pepper
《衡门》	衡门	door made of cross pieces of wood	door	town-gate	a patched door-flap
	鲂	bream	bream	bream	bream
	鲤	carp	carp	carp	fish
《东门之池》	池	moat	moat	pond	Moat
	麻	hemp	hemp	hemp	hemp
	纻	boehmeria	flax	cloth-grass	the thickest hemp
	菅	rope-rush	couch-grass	rush	mat-grass
《东门之杨》	杨	willows	willows	willow	willows
《墓门》	墓门	gate to the tombs	lych-gate	Tomb Gate	Campo Santo gate
	棘	jujube trees	thorn-trees	thorn-tree	thorn
	斧	axe	axe	axe	axe
	梅	plum trees	plum-trees	plum-tree	plum trees
	鸮	owls	screech-owls	owl	owl

续表

篇名	名物	译本与译名			
		James Legge	William Jennings	Arthur Waley	Ezra Pound
《防有鹊巢》	防	embankment	dyke	dyke	mound
	鹊巢	magpies' nest	magpie's nest	magpie's nest	magpies nest
	邛	the height	brae	bank	higher ground
	苕	pea	wild-pea	vetch	sweet grass
	鹝	medallion pant	ribbon-plants	rainbow plant	无
	中唐	middle path of the temple	temple-path	middle-path	temple path
	甓	tiles	tiles	patterned tile	tile
	鹝	medallion plant	ribbon-plants	rainbow plant	blossom
《株林》	乘马	team of horses	team of four	horses	team of horses
《泽陂》	蒲	rushes	rush	reed	lotus rank
	荷	lotus plants	lotus-flower	lotus	lotus rank
	蕳	valerian	king-cup	scented herb	valerian in sedge
	菡萏	lotus flowers	mallow	lotus-flowers	lotus rank
《羔裘》	羔裘	lamb's fur	lambskin	lamb's wool	lamb's wool
	狐裘	fox's fur	foxfur	fox-fur	fox fur
	膏	ointment	unguent	glossy	fat
《素冠》	素冠	white cap	bonnet white	plain cap	white cap
	素衣	white [lower] dress	plain white dress	plain coat	white robe
	素韠	white knee-covers	white apron	plain legging	white knee-pads
《隰有苌楚》	苌楚	carambola tree	Goats'-peach	goat's-peach	vitex
	华	flowers	bloom	flower	flower
《匪风》	车	chariot	wheels	cartwheel	chariot
	鱼	fish	fish	fish	fish
	釜鬵	boilers	pots	cauldrons	cauldron
《蜉蝣》	蜉蝣	ephemera	butterflies	mayfly	banner fly
	衣裳	robes	dresses	dress	trappings

366

续表

篇名	名物	译本与译名			
		James Legge	William Jennings	Arthur Waley	Ezra Pound
《蜉蝣》	衣服	robes	the ways they are dressed	clothes	dress
	麻衣	a robe of hemp	linen	hemp clothes	hemp of its panoply
《候人》	戈	lances	lance	halberd	lance
	祋	halberds	pike	spear	signal stave
	赤芾	red covers	scarlet greaves	red greaves	red pads
	鹈	pelican	pelicans	pelican	pelican
	翼	wings	wing	wings	wing
	梁	dam	dam	bridge	dam
	服	dress	garnishing	dress	furnishing
	咮	beak	bill	beak	beak
	荟	vegetation	rank growth	pent	无
	朝隮	vapours	mists	dawn mists	dawn half alight
《鸤鸠》	鸤鸠	turtle dove	dove	cuckoo	dove
	桑	mulberry tree	mulberry-tree	mulberry-tree	mulberry tree
	梅	plum tree	plum-trees	plum-tree	plum tree
	丝	girdle of silk	silken zone	silk	silk sash
	弁	cap	checkered bonnet	cap	deer-spot cap
	骐	deer-skin	checkered bonnet	mottled fawn	无
	棘	jujube tree	thorn-trees	thorn	jujube
	榛	hazel tree	hazel	hazel	hazel bough
《下泉》	稂	wolf's-tail grass	weed-beds	henbane	wolf-grass
	萧	southernwood	wormwood	southernwood	sandal root
	蓍	divining plants	milfoil	yarrow	milfoil
	黍	millet	grain	millet	millet
《七月》	火	the Fire Star	heat	the Fire	heat
	衣	clothes	garments/clothes	coat	winter wear

367

续表

篇名	名物	译本与译名			
		James Legge	William Jennings	Arthur Waley	Ezra Pound
《七月》	褐	garments	wraps	serge	wool and hair
	耜	ploughs	prepare ploughing	plough	plow
	田畯	surveyor of the fields	steward	field-hands	inspectors
	仓庚	oriole	oriole	oriole	oriole
	懿筐	deep baskets	dainty baskets	deep basket	basket-bearing
	桑	mulberry trees	mulberry-trees	mulberry-leaves	mulberry
	蘩	white southernwood	white wormwood	white aster	southernwood
	萑苇	sedges and reeds	rush and reed	rush	reed and sedge
	斧斨	axes and hatchets	axe and bill	chopper and bill	little axe and small hatchet
	女桑	young trees of their leaves	virgin trees	Tender leaves	leaves of mulberry
	鵙	shrike	shrike	shrike	shrike
	绩	spinning	spinning-wheel	thread	spin
	裳	lower robes	无	robe	无
	秀葽	small grass	grass	milkwort	grass seed
	蜩	cicada	cicadas	cicada	cicada
	萚	leaves	leaves	bough	dead leaves
	貉	badgers	brock	racoon	badger
	狐狸	foxes	fox and wild-cat	foxes and wild-cats	wild-cat
	裘	furs	furs	fur	coat
	豵	boars of one year	young boars	one-year-old boars	piglets
	豣	boars of three years	full-grown boars	three-year-old boars	full-size boars
	蟊	locust	hoppers	locust	green hopper

续表

篇名	名物	译本与译名			
		James Legge	William Jennings	Arthur Waley	Ezra Pound
《七月》	莎鸡	spinner	hoppers	grasshopper	sedge-cock
	宇	eaves	eaves	farm	eaves
	户	doors	door	door	lintel
	蟋蟀	cricket	crickets	cricket	cricket
	鼠	rats	rats	rat	rat
	向	windows that face the north	windows	window	north-lights
	户	doors	doors	door	wattle-slats
	室	无	indoors	house	home
	郁	sparrow-plums	plum	wild plum	red plum
	薁	grapes	grape	cherry	wild-vine
	葵	k'wei	pulse	mallow	sunflower
	菽	pulse	rape	bean	bean
	枣	dates	date-trees	date	date
	稻	rice	rice	rice	rice
	春酒	spirits for the spring	spring-drinks	spring wine	saki
	瓜	melons	melons	melon	melon
	壶	bottle-gourds	bottle-gourd	gourd	calabash
	苴	hemp-seed	seed from hemp	seeding hemp	hemp seed
	荼	sowthistle	lettuce	bitter herb	trash, thistles
	樗	firewood of Fetid tree	worthless wood	ailanthus	stinking tree
	场圃	vegetable gardens for their stacks	stacking-place	stack-yards	summer garden-yard
	禾稼	sheaves	grain	harvest	field-sheaves
	黍稷	millets	millets	millet for wine, millet for cooking	millet

续表

篇名	名物	译本与译名			
		James Legge	William Jennings	Arthur Waley	Ezra Pound
《七月》	禾	grain	rice	paddy	beans/wheat
	麻	hemp	hemp	hemp	hemp
	菽	pulse	pulse	beans	beans
	麦	wheat	wheat	wheat	wheat
	茅	grass	thatching	thatch-reeds	grass
	绹	ropes	ropes	rope	thatch/rope
	谷	无	grain	grains	grain
	羔	lamb	lamb	lamb	lamb
	韭	scallion	leeks	garlic	leek roots
	朋酒	two bottles of spirits	the pair of spirit-flasks	twin pitcher	twin-bottle feast
	羔羊	lambs and sheep	sheep and lambs	young lamb	sheep
	公堂	hall of our prince	Master's hall	lord's hall	ducal hall
	兕觥	rhinoceros horn	horncup	drinking-cup of buffalo-horn	horn
《鸱鸮》	鸱鸮	owl	hawk/robber-hawk	kite-owl	great horned owl
	室	nest	nest	house	house
	桑土	roots of the mulberry tree	mulberry bark	the bark of that mulberry-tree	mulberries
	牖户	window and door	lattice and door	window and door	door and lattice frame
	荼	rushes	stalk	rush flower	thistle
	羽	wings	wings	wings	wings
	尾	tail	tail	tail	tail
	室	house	nest	house	house
《东山》	裳衣	clothes	gear	coat and gown	army clothes
	枚	gags	gagging	无	gag
	蜀	caterpillars	caterpillars	silkworm	worms

370

续表

篇名	名物	译本与译名			
		James Legge	William Jennings	Arthur Waley	Ezra Pound
《东山》	桑	mulberry	mulberry	mulberry-bush	mulberry trees
	车	carriages	wagons	cart	car
	果臝	heavenly gourd	creeping gourds	bryony	gourds
	宇	eaves	eaves	eave	eaves
	伊威	sowbug	woodlice	sowbug	sowbug
	蠨蛸	spiders	spiders	spider	spider
	户	doors	doors	door	door
	町疃	paddocks	paddocks	paddock	field
	鹿	deer-fields	deer	deer	deer
	场	deer-fields	haunt	paddock	forest
	宵行	glow-worms	glowworms	watchman	glow-worms
	鹳	cranes	white cranes	stork	crane
	垤	ant-hills	ant-hills	ant-hill	ant-hill
	室	rooms	rooms	chamber	home
	穹窒	crevices	crack	house	walls
	瓜苦	bitter gourds	bitter-gourds	gourd	bitter gourds
	栗薪	branches of the chestnut trees	sticks from the chestnut-tree	firewood cut from the chestnut-tree	chestnut boughs
	仓庚	oriole	orioles	oriole	oriole
	马	horses	ponies	steed	dapple team
	缡	sashes	sashes	strings of her girdle	formal sash
《破斧》	斧	axes	axes	axe	axe
	斨	hatchets	bills	hatchet	hatchet
	錡	chisels	chisels	hoe	work-tools
	銶	clubs	picks	chisel	work-tools
《伐柯》	柯	axe-handle	axes' helves	axe-handle	haft
	笾豆	vessels	feast	dish	无
《九罭》	九罭	nine bags	net	minnow-net	nine meshes of the net

续表

篇名	名物	译本与译名			
		James Legge	William Jennings	Arthur Waley	Ezra Pound
《九罭》	鳟	rud	rudd	rudd	rudd
	鲂	bream	bream	bream	bream
	衮衣	grand-ducal robe	dragon-robe	blazoned coat	bright-broidered clothes
	绣裳	embroidered skirt	skirts that with broideries	broidered robe	bright-broidered clothes
	鸿	wild geese	wild-geese	wild-geese	wild-geese
《狼跋》	狼	wolf	wolf	wolf	wolf
	舄	slippers	slippers	red shoes	red shoes
	胡	dewlap	wame	dewlap	jowl

附录二、相关《诗经》诗篇的译文

一、《关雎》英译文：

1. 理雅各译文：

The Kwan-ts'eu

Kwan-kwan go the ospreys,
On the islet in the river.
The modest, retiring, virtuous, young lady: ——
For our prince a good mate she.

Here long, there short, is the duckweed,
To the left, to the right, borne about by the current.
The modest, retiring, virtuous, young lady: ——
Waking and sleeping, he sought her.

He sought her and found her not,
And waking and sleeping he thought about her.
Long he thought; oh! long and anxiously;
On his side, on his back, he turned, and back again.

Here long, there short, is the duckweed;
On the left, on the right, we gather it.
The modest, retiring, virtuous, young lady: ——

With lutes, small and large, let us give her friendly welcome.

Here long, there short, is the duckweed;
On the left, on the right, we cook and present it.
The modest, retiring, virtuous, young lady: —
With bells and drums let us show our delight in her.

2. 詹宁斯译文：

Song of Welcome to the Bride of King Wàn

Waterfowl their mates are calling,
   On the islets in the stream.
Chaste and modest maid! Fit partner
   For our lord (thyself we deem).

Waterlilies, long or short ones, —
   Seek them left and seek them right.
'Twas this chaste and modest maiden
   He hath sought for, morn and night.

Seeking for her, yet not finding,
   Night and morning he would yearn
Ah, so long, so long! —and restless
   On his couch would toss and turn.

Waterlilies, long or short ones, —
   Gather, right and left, their flowers.

Now the chaste and modest maiden
 Lute and harp shall hail as ours.

Long or short the waterlilies,
 Pluck them left and pluck them right.
To the chaste and modest maiden
 Bell and drum shall give delight.

3. 庞德译文：

I

"Hid! Hid!" the fish-hawk saith,
by isle in Ho the fish-hawk saith:
 "Dark and clear,
 Dark and clear,
So shall be the prince's fere."

Clear as the stream her modesty;
As neath dark boughs her secrecy,
 reed against reed
 tall on slight.
as the stream moves left and right,
 dark and clear,
 dark and clear.
To seek and not find
as a dream in his mind,

think how her robe should be,

distantly, to toss and turn,

to toss and turn.

High reed caught in *ts'ai* grass
so deep her secrecy;
Lute sound in lute sound is caught,
touching, passing, left and right.
Bang the gong of her delight.

4. 汪榕培译文：

The Cooing

The waterfowl would coo
　　Upon an islet in the brooks.
A lad would like to woo
　　A lass with pretty looks.

There grows the water grass
　　The folk are fond to pick;
There lives the pretty lass
　　For whom the lad is sick.

Ignored by the pretty lass,
　　The lad would truly yearn.
The day is hard to pass;
　　All night he'll toss and turn.

There grows the water grass

 The folk are fond to choose;

There lives the pretty lass

 Whom the lad pursues.

There grows the water grass

 The folk are fond to gain;

There lives the pretty lass

 The lad would entertain.

5. 许渊冲译文：

Cooing and Wooing

By riverside a pair
Of turtledoves are cooing;
There is a maiden fair
Whom a young man is wooing.

Water flows left and right
Of cresses here and there;
The youth yearns day and night
For the good maiden fair.

His yearning grows so strong,
He cannot fall asleep,
But tosses all night long,
So deep in love, so deep!

《诗经》翻译探微

  Now gather left and right

  Cress long or short and tender!

  O lute, play music light

  For the fiancée so slender!

  Feast friends at left and right

  On cresses cooked tender!

  O bells and drums, delight

  The bride so sweet and slender!

6. 高本汉译文：

Kuan ts'ü

—1. *Kwan-kwan* (cries) the ts'ü-kiu bird,

  on the islet of the river;

  the beautiful and good girl,

  she is a good mate for the lord.

—2. Of varying length is the hing water plant,

  to the left and the right we catch it;

  the beautiful and good girl,

  waking and sleeping he (sought her:) wished for her;

  he wished for her but did not get her,

  waking and sleeping he thought of her;

  longing, longing, he tossed and fidgeted.

—3. Of varying length is the hing water plant,

  to the left and the right we gather it;

　　　　the beautiful and good girl,

　　　　guitars and lutes (befriend her:) hail her as a friend.

一4. Of varying length is the hing water plant,

　　　　to the left and the right we cull it as a vegetable;

　　　　the beautiful and good girl,

　　　　bells and drums cheer her.

二、《木瓜》英译文：

1. 许渊冲译文：

　　Gifts

　　She throws a quince to me;

　　I give her a green jade

　　Not in return, you see,

　　But to show acquaintance made.

　　She throws a peach to me;

　　I give her a white jade

　　Not in return, you see,

　　But to show friendship made.

　　She throws a plum to me;

　　I give her jasper fair

　　Not in return, you see,

　　But to show love fore'er.

2. 汪榕培译文：

A quince

A quince thou givest to me;
I have a gem for thee.
Not as requital I give,
But token of eternal love.

A peach thou givest to me;
I have a jade for thee.
Not a s requital I give,
But token of eternal love.

A plum thou givest to me;
I have a jewel for thee.
Not a s requital I give,
But token of eternal love.

3. 韦利译文：

A Quince

She threw a quince to me;
In requital I gave a bright girdle-gem.
No, not just as requital;
But meaning I would love her for ever.

She threw a tree-peach to me;

As requital I gave her a bright greenstone.

No, not just as requital;

But meaning I would love her for ever.

She threw a tree-plum to me;

As requital I gave her a bright jet-stone.

No, not just as requital;

But meaning I would love her for ever.

4. 阿连璧译文:

Friendship

A quince, a peach, and a plum, were the gifts which to me you made,

And I gave you an emerald back, with a ruby and piece of jade.

Do I measure the value of gifts which pass between me and you?

No! Friendship is greater than gifts, when friends are faithful and true.

5. 庞德译文:

X

Gave me a quince, a beryl my cover,

not as a swap, but to last forever.

For a peach thrown me, let green gem prove:

Exchange is nothing, all time's to love.

For a plum thrown me

I made this rhyme

With a red "ninth-stone"

To last out all time.

三、《芄兰》英译文

1. 理雅各译文（韵文体）：

Hwan-lan

Feeble as branch of sparrow gourd, this youth,

Wears spike at girdle, as if he, forsooth,

Were quite a man; but though the spike he wears,

He knows not us at whom he proudly stares.

How easy and conceited is his mien!

How drop his girdle ends, full jaunty seen!

Like leaf of sparrow gourd, that coxcomb young,

With archer's thimble at his girdle hung!

He wears the thimble, but he's not the swell

To lord it over us who know him well.

How easy and conceited is his mien!

How drop his girdle ends, full jaunty seen!

2. 汪榕培译文：

The Wistaria

Wistaria forked and soft,

On the sash the boy wears oft.

On the sash the boy oft wears;

My worth escapes him unawares.

How he stalks! How he strides!

How his sash behind him glides!

Wisteria leafed and soft,

On the thumb the boy wears oft.

On the thumb the boy oft wears;

My thought escapes him unawares.

How he stalks! How he strides!

How his sash behind him glides!

3. 高本汉译文：

Huan lan

Oh, the branches of the Metaplexis!

The youth carries a knot-horn at his girdle;

but though he carries a knot-horn at his girdle,

can he fail to know me?

Oh, his ceremonial knife, oh his suei gem!

Oh, the (shaking=) movements of his down-hanging sash!

Oh, the leaves of the Metaplexis!

The youth carries an archer's thimble at his girdle;

but though he carries an archer's thimble at his girdle,

can he fail to be familiar with me?

Oh, his ceremonial knife, oh his suei gem!

Oh, the (shaking=) movements of his down-hanging sash!

4. 庞德译文：

Wolf

Feeble as a twig,

With a spike so big

In his belt, but know us he does not.

  Should we melt

At the flap of his sash ends?

Feeble as a gourd stalk (epidendrum)

To walk with an out-size ring

At his belt (fit for an archer's thumb

that might be an archer's,

as if ready for archery

which he is not)
we will not, I think, melt,
(complacency in its apogee)
at the flap of his sash ends.

附录三、《诗经》各篇叠词及其出现次数统计

1. 《周南·关雎》：关关雎鸠（1见）
2. 《周南·葛覃》：维叶萋萋（1见）、其鸣喈喈（1见）、维叶莫莫（1见）
3. 《周南·卷耳》：采采卷耳（1见）
4. 《周南·螽斯》：诜诜兮（1见）、振振兮（1见）、薨薨兮（1见）、绳绳兮（1见）、揖揖兮（1见）、蛰蛰兮（1见）
5. 《周南·桃夭》：桃之夭夭（3见）、其叶蓁蓁（1见）、灼灼其华（1见）
6. 《周南·兔罝》：肃肃兔罝（3见）、椓之丁丁（1见）、赳赳武夫（3见）
7. 《周南·芣苢》：采采芣苢（6见）
8. 《周南·汉广》：翘翘错薪（2见）
9. 《周南·麟之趾》：振振公子、振振公姓、振振公族（3见）
10. 《召南·采蘩》：被之僮僮（1见）、被之祁祁（1见）
11. 《召南·草虫》：喓喓草虫（1见）、趯趯阜螽（1见）、忧心忡忡（1见）、忧心惙惙（1见）
12. 《召南·殷其雷》：振振君子（3见）
13. 《召南·小星》：肃肃宵征（1见）
14. 《召南·野有死麕》：舒而脱脱兮（1见）
15. 《邶风·柏舟》：耿耿不寐（1见）、威仪棣棣（1见）、忧心悄悄（1见）
16. 《邶风·燕燕》：燕燕于飞（3见）
17. 《邶风·终风》：悠悠我思（1见）、噎噎其阴（1见）、虺虺其雷（1见）
18. 《邶风·凯风》：棘心夭夭（1见）
19. 《邶风·雄雉》：泄泄其羽（1见）、悠悠我思（1见）
20. 《邶风·匏有苦叶》：雍雍鸣雁（1见）、招招舟子（1见）

21. 《邶风·谷风》：习习谷风（1见）、行行迟迟（1见）、湜湜其沚（1见）
22. 《邶风·简兮》：硕人俣俣（1见）
23. 《邶风·泉水》：我心悠悠（1见）
24. 《邶风·北门》：忧心殷殷（1见）
25. 《邶风·新台》：河水弥弥（1见）、河水浼浼（1见）
26. 《邶风·二子乘舟》：泛泛其景、泛泛其逝（2见）
27. 《鄘风·君子偕老》：委委佗佗（1见）
28. 《鄘风·鹑之奔奔》：鹑之奔奔（2见）、鹊之疆疆（2见）
29. 《鄘风·干旄》：孑孑干旄、孑孑干旟、孑孑干旌（3见）
30. 《鄘风·载驰》：驱马悠悠（1见）、芃芃其麦（1见）
31. 《卫风·淇奥》：绿竹猗猗（1见）、绿竹青青（1见）
32. 《卫风·硕人》：硕人敖敖（1见）、朱帻镳镳（1见）、河水洋洋（1见）、北流活活（1见）、施罛濊濊（1见）、鳣鲔发发（1见）、葭菼揭揭（1见）、庶姜孽孽（1见）
33. 《卫风·氓》：氓之蚩蚩（1见）、泣涕涟涟（1见）、淇水汤汤（1见）、言笑晏晏（1见）、信誓旦旦（1见）
34. 《卫风·竹竿》：藋藋竹竿（1见）、淇水滺滺（1见）
35. 《卫风·伯兮》：杲杲出日（1见）
36. 《卫风·有狐》：有狐绥绥（3见）
37. 《王风·黍离》：彼黍离离（3见）、行迈靡靡（3见）、中心摇摇（1见）、悠悠苍天（3见）
38. 《王风·君子阳阳》：君子阳阳（1见）、君子陶陶（1见）
39. 《王风·兔爰》：有兔爰爰（3见）
40. 《王风·葛藟》：绵绵葛藟（3见）
41. 《王风·大车》：大车槛槛（1见）、大车啍啍（1见）
42. 《王风·丘中有麻》：将其来施（1见）
43. 《郑风·大叔于田》：乘乘马、乘乘黄、乘乘鸨（2见）
44. 《郑风·清人》：驷介旁旁（1见）、驷介麃麃（1见）、驷介陶陶（1见）
45. 《郑风·有女同车》：佩玉将将（1见）
46. 《郑风·风雨》：风雨凄凄（1见）、鸡鸣喈喈（1见）、风雨潇潇（1

见)、鸡鸣胶胶(1见)

47. 《郑风·子衿》:青青子衿(1见)、青青子佩(1见)、悠悠我心(1见)、悠悠我思(1见)

48. 《郑风·野有蔓草》:零露瀼瀼(1见)

49. 《郑风·溱洧》:方涣涣兮(1见)

50. 《齐风·鸡鸣》:虫飞薨薨(1见)

51. 《齐风·东方未明》:狂夫瞿瞿(1见)

52. 《齐风·南山》:南山崔崔(1见)、雄狐绥绥(1见)

53. 《齐风·甫田》:维莠骄骄(1见)、劳心忉忉(1见)、维莠桀桀(1见)、劳心怛怛(1见)

54. 《齐风·卢令》:卢令令(1见)

55. 《齐风·敝笱》:其鱼唯唯(1见)

56. 《齐风·载驱》:载驱薄薄(1见)、四骊济济(1见)、垂辔沵沵(1见)、汶水汤汤(1见)、行人彭彭(1见)、汶水滔滔(1见)、行人儦儦(1见)

57. 《魏风·葛屦》:掺掺女手(1见)、好人提提(1见)

58. 《魏风·十亩之间》:桑者闲闲兮(1见)、桑者泄泄兮(1见)

59. 《魏风·伐檀》:坎坎伐檀兮(1见)、坎坎伐辐兮(1见)、坎坎伐轮兮(1见)

60. 《唐风·蟋蟀》:良士瞿瞿(1见)、良士蹶蹶(1见)、良士休休(1见)

61. 《唐风·扬之水》:白石凿凿(1见)、白石皓皓(1见)、白石粼粼(1见)

62. 《唐风·杕杜》:其叶湑湑(1见)、独行踽踽(1见)、其叶菁菁(1见)、独行睘睘(1见)

63. 《唐风·羔裘》:自我人居居(1见)、自我人究究(1见)

64. 《唐风·鸨羽》:肃肃鸨羽(1见)、肃肃鸨翼(1见)、肃肃鸨行(1见)、悠悠苍天(1见)

65. 《秦风·车邻》:有车邻邻(1见)

66. 《秦风·小戎》:厌厌良人(1见)、秩秩德音(1见)

67. 《秦风·蒹葭》：蒹葭苍苍（1见）、蒹葭凄凄（1见）、蒹葭采采（1见）

68. 《秦风·终南》：佩玉将将（1见）

69. 《秦风·黄鸟》：交交黄鸟（3见）、惴惴其慄（3见）

70. 《秦风·晨风》：忧心钦钦（1见）

71. 《秦风·渭阳》：悠悠我思（1见）

72. 《秦风·权舆》：夏屋渠渠（1见）

73. 《陈风·衡门》：泌之洋洋（1见）

74. 《陈风·东门之杨》：其叶牂牂（1见）、明星煌煌（1见）、其叶肺肺（1见）、明星晢晢（1见）

75. 《陈风·防有鹊巢》：心焉忉忉（1见）、心焉惕惕（1见）

76. 《陈风·泽陂》：中心悁悁（1见）

77. 《桧风·羔裘》：劳心忉忉（1见）

78. 《桧风·素冠》：棘人栾栾兮（1见）、劳心慱慱兮（1见）

79. 《桧风·隰有苌楚》：夭之沃沃（3见）

80. 《曹风·蜉蝣》：衣裳楚楚（1见）、采采衣服（1见）

81. 《曹风·下泉》：芃芃黍苗（1见）

82. 《豳风·七月》：春日迟迟（1见）、采蘩祁祁（1见）、凿冰冲冲（1见）

83. 《豳风·鸱鸮》：予羽谯谯（1见）、予尾翛翛（1见）、予室翘翘（1见）、予维音哓哓（1见）

84. 《豳风·东山》：慆慆不归（4见）、蜎蜎者蠋（1见）

85. 《小雅·鹿鸣》：呦呦鹿鸣（3见）

86. 《小雅·四牡》：四牡骓骓（2见）、啴啴骆马（1见）、翩翩者鵻（2见）、载骤骎骎（1见）

87. 《小雅·皇皇者华》：皇皇者华（1见）、駪駪征夫（1见）

88. 《小雅·常棣》：鄂不韡韡（1见）

89. 《小雅·伐木》：伐木丁丁（1见）、鸟鸣嘤嘤（1见）、伐木许许（1见）、坎坎鼓我（1见）、蹲蹲舞我（1见）

90. 《小雅·采薇》：忧心烈烈（1见）、四牡业业（1见）、四牡骙骙（1

见)、四牡翼翼(1见)、杨柳依依(1见)、雨雪霏霏(1见)、行道迟迟(1见)

91.《小雅·出车》:胡不旆旆(1见)、忧心悄悄(1见)、出车彭彭(1见)、旂旐央央(1见)、赫赫南仲(3见)、喓喓草虫(1见)、趯趯阜螽(1见)、忧心忡忡(1见)、春日迟迟(1见)、卉木萋萋(1见)、仓庚喈喈(1见)、采蘩祁祁(1见)

92.《小雅·杕杜》:其叶萋萋(1见)、檀车啴啴(1见)、四马痯痯(1见)

93.《小雅·南有嘉鱼》:烝然罩罩(1见)、烝然汕汕(1见)、翩翩者鵻(1见)

94.《小雅·蓼萧》:零露瀼瀼(1见)、零露泥泥(1见)、零露浓浓(1见)、鞗革冲冲(1见)、和鸾雍雍(1见)

95.《小雅·湛露》:湛湛露斯(3见)、厌厌夜饮(2见)、其实离离(1见)

96.《小雅·菁菁者莪》:菁菁者莪(3见)、泛泛杨舟(1见)

97.《小雅·六月》:六月棲棲(1见)、四牡骙骙(1见)、白旆央央(1见)

98.《小雅·采芑》:四骐翼翼(1见)、旂旐央央(1见)、八鸾玱玱(1见)、伐鼓渊渊(1见)、振旅阗阗(1见)、戎车啴啴(1见)、啴啴焞焞(1见)

99.《小雅·车攻》:四牡庞庞(1见)、选徒嚣嚣(1见)、四牡奕奕(1见)、萧萧马鸣(1见)、悠悠旆旌(1见)

100.《小雅·吉日》:麀鹿麌麌(1见)、儦儦俟俟(1见)

101.《小雅·鸿雁》:肃肃其羽(1见)、哀鸣嗷嗷(1见)

102.《小雅·庭燎》:鸾声将将(1见)、庭燎晰晰(1见)、鸾声哕哕(1见)

103.《小雅·沔水》:其流汤汤(1见)

104.《小雅·白驹》:皎皎白驹(4见)

105.《小雅·斯干》:秩秩斯干(1见)、幽幽南山(1见)、约之阁阁(1见)、椓之橐橐(1见)、殖殖其庭(1见)、哙哙其正(1见)、哕哕其冥(1见)、其泣喤喤(1见)

106.《小雅·无羊》:其角濈濈(1见)、其耳湿湿(1见)、矜矜兢兢(1

见）、室家溱溱（1见）

107. 《小雅·节南山》：维石岩岩（1见）、赫赫师尹（2见）、琐琐姻亚（1见）、蹙蹙靡所骋（1见）

108. 《小雅·正月》：忧心京京（1见）、忧心愈愈（1见）、忧心惸惸（1见）、视天梦梦（1见）、执我仇仇（1见）、赫赫宗周（1见）、忧心惨惨（1见）、忧心慇慇（1见）、佌佌彼有屋（1见）、蔌蔌方有穀（1见）

109. 《小雅·十月之交》：烨烨震电（1见）、谮口嚣嚣（1见）、悠悠我里（1见）

110. 《小雅·雨无正》：浩浩昊天（1见）、惽惽日瘁（1见）

111. 《小雅·小旻》：潝潝訾訾（1见）、战战兢兢（1见）

112. 《小雅·小宛》：交交桑扈（1见）、温温恭人（1见）、惴惴小心（1见）、战战兢兢（1见）

113. 《小雅·小弁》：归飞提提（1见）、踧踧周道（1见）、鸣蜩嘒嘒（1见）、萑苇淠淠（1见）、维足伎伎（1见）

114. 《小雅·巧言》：悠悠昊天（1见）、奕奕寝庙（1见）、秩秩大猷（1见）、跃跃毚兔（1见）、蛇蛇硕言（1见）

115. 《小雅·巷伯》：缉缉翩翩（1见）、捷捷幡幡（1见）、骄人好好（1见）、劳人草草（1见）

116. 《小雅·谷风》：习习谷风（3见）

117. 《小雅·蓼莪》：蓼蓼者莪（2见）、哀哀父母（2见）、南山烈烈（1见）、飘风发发（1见）、南山律律（1见）、飘风弗弗（1见）

118. 《小雅·大东》：纠纠葛屦（1见）、佻佻公子（1见）、契契寤叹（1见）、粲粲衣服（1见）、鞘鞘佩璲（1见）

119. 《小雅·四月》：秋日凄凄（1见）、冬日烈烈（1见）、飘风发发（1见）、滔滔江汉（1见）

120. 《小雅·北山》：偕偕士子（1见）、四牡彭彭（1见）、王事傍傍（1见）、燕燕居息（1见）、惨惨劬劳（1见）、惨惨畏咎（1见）

121. 《小雅·无将大车》：维尘冥冥（1见）

122. 《小雅·小明》：明明上天（1见）、睠睠怀顾（1见）

123. 《小雅·鼓钟》：鼓钟将将（1见）、淮水汤汤（1见）、鼓钟喈喈（1见）、淮水湝湝（1见）、鼓钟钦钦（1见）

124. 《小雅·楚茨》：楚楚者茨（1见）、我黍与与（1见）、我稷翼翼（1见）、济济跄跄（1见）、执爨踖踖（1见）、君妇莫莫（1见）、子子孙孙（1见）

125. 《小雅·信南山》：畇畇原隰（1见）、雨雪雰雰（1见）、黍稷彧彧（1见）、疆埸翼翼（1见）、苾苾芬芬（1见）

126. 《小雅·甫田》：黍稷薿薿（1见）

127. 《小雅·大田》：有渰萋萋（1见）、兴雨祁祁（1见）

128. 《小雅·瞻彼洛矣》：维水泱泱（3见）

129. 《小雅·裳裳者华》：裳裳者华（3见）

130. 《小雅·桑扈》：交交桑扈（2见）

131. 《小雅·頍弁》：忧心弈弈（1见）、忧心怲怲（1见）

132. 《小雅·车舝》：四牡骓骓（1见）

133. 《小雅·青蝇》：营营青蝇（3见）

134. 《小雅·宾之初筵》：左右秩秩（1见）、举酬逸逸（1见）、温温其恭（1见）、威仪反反（1见）、威仪幡幡（1见）、屡舞僊僊（1见）、威仪抑抑（1见）、威仪怭怭（1见）、屡舞傞傞（1见）、屡舞傞傞（1见）

135. 《小雅·采菽》：其旂淠淠（1见）、鸾声嘒嘒（1见）、其叶蓬蓬（1见）、平平左右（1见）、汎汎杨舟（1见）

136. 《小雅·角弓》：骍骍角弓（1见）、绰绰有裕（1见）、雨雪瀌瀌（1见）、雨雪浮浮（1见）

137. 《小雅·都人士》：狐裘黄黄（1见）

138. 《小雅·黍苗》：芃芃黍苗（1见）、悠悠南行（1见）、肃肃谢功（1见）、烈烈征师（1见）

139. 《小雅·白华》：英英白云（1见）、念子懆懆（1见）、视我迈迈（1见）

140. 《小雅·瓠叶》：幡幡瓠叶（1见）

141. 《小雅·渐渐之石》：渐渐之石（2见）

142. 《小雅·苕之华》：其叶青青（1见）

143.《大雅·文王》：亹亹文王（1见）、厥犹翼翼（1见）、济济多士（1见）、穆穆文王（1见）

144.《大雅·大明》：明明在下（1见）、赫赫在上（1见）、小心翼翼（1见）、牧野洋洋（1见）、檀车煌煌（1见）、驷𫘤彭彭（1见）

145.《大雅·绵》：绵绵瓜瓞（1见）、周原膴膴（1见）、作庙翼翼（1见）、捄之陾陾（1见）、度之薨薨（1见）、筑之登登（1见）、削屡冯冯（1见）、应门将将（1见）、文王蹶厥生（1见）

146.《大雅·棫朴》：芃芃棫朴（1见）、济济辟王（2见）、奉璋峨峨（1见）、勉勉我王（1见）

147.《大雅·旱麓》：榛楛济济（1见）、莫莫葛藟（1见）

148.《大雅·思齐》：雝雝在宫（1见）、肃肃在庙（1见）

149.《大雅·皇矣》：临冲闲闲（1见）、崇墉言言（1见）、执讯连连（1见）、攸馘安安（1见）、临冲茀茀（1见）、崇墉仡仡（1见）

150.《大雅·灵台》：麀鹿濯濯（1见）、白鸟翯翯（1见）、鼍鼓逢逢（1见）

151.《大雅·生民》：茀苜𦯆𦯆（1见）、禾役穟穟（1见）、麻麦幪幪（1见）、瓜瓞唪唪（1见）、释之叟叟（1见）、烝之浮浮（1见）

152.《大雅·行苇》：维叶泥泥（1见）、戚戚兄弟（1见）

153.《大雅·凫鹥》：公尸来止熏熏（1见）、旨酒欣欣（1见）、燔炙芬芬（1见）

154.《大雅·假乐》：显显令德（1见）、穆穆皇皇（1见）、威仪抑抑（1见）、德音秩秩（1见）

155.《大雅·公刘》：于时处处（1见）、于时言言（1见）、于时语语（1见）、跄跄济济（1见）

156.《大雅·卷阿》：颙颙卬卬（1见）、翙翙其羽（2见）、蔼蔼王多吉士（1见）、奉奉萋萋（1见）、雝雝喈喈（1见）

157.《大雅·板》：上帝板板（1见）、靡圣管管（1见）、无然宪宪（1见）、无然泄泄（1见）、听我嚣嚣（1见）、无然谑谑（1见）、老夫灌灌（1见）、小子蹻蹻（1见）、多将熇熇（1见）

158.《大雅·荡》：荡荡上帝（1见）

159.《大雅·抑》：抑抑威仪（1见）、子孙绳绳（1见）、温温恭人（1

见)、视尔梦梦（1见）、我心惨惨（1见）、诲尔谆谆（1见）、听我藐藐（1见）

160.《大雅·桑柔》：四牡骙骙（1见）、忧心慇慇（1见）、牲牲其鹿（1见）

161.《大雅·云汉》：兢兢业业（1见）、赫赫炎炎（1见）、涤涤山川（1见）

162.《大雅·崧高》：亹亹申伯（1见）、既成藐藐（1见）、四牡蹻蹻（1见）、钩膺濯濯（1见）、申伯番番（1见）、徒御啴啴（1见）

163.《大雅·烝民》：小心翼翼（1见）、肃肃王命（1见）、四牡业业（1见）、征夫捷捷（1见）、四牡彭彭（1见）、八鸾锵锵（1见）、四牡骙骙（1见）、八鸾喈喈（1见）

164.《大雅·韩奕》：奕奕梁山（1见）、四牡奕奕（1见）、百两彭彭（1见）、八鸾锵锵（1见）、祈祈如云（1见）、川泽訏訏（1见）、鲂鱮甫甫（1见）、麀鹿噳噳（1见）

165.《大雅·江汉》：江汉浮浮（1见）、武夫滔滔（1见）、江汉汤汤（1见）、武夫洸洸（1见）、明明天子（1见）

166.《大雅·常武》：赫赫明明（1见）、赫赫业业（1见）、王旅啴啴（1见）、绵绵翼翼（1见）

167.《大雅·瞻卬》：藐藐昊天（1见）

168.《大雅·召旻》：溃溃回遹（1见）、皋皋訿訿（1见）、兢兢业业（1见）

169.《颂·清庙》：济济多士（1见）

170.《颂·执竞》：钟鼓喤喤（1见）、磬筦将将（1见）、降福穰穰（1见）、降福简简（1见）、威仪反反（1见）

171.《颂·臣工》：嗟嗟臣工（1见）、嗟嗟保介（1见）

172.《颂·有瞽》：喤喤厥声（1见）

173.《颂·雍》：有来雍雍（1见）、至止肃肃（1见）、天子穆穆（1见）

174.《颂·载见》：龙旂阳阳（1见）、和铃央央（1见）

175.《颂·有客》：有客宿宿（1见）、有客信信（1见）

176.《颂·闵予小子》：嬛嬛在疚（1见）

177.《颂·载芟》：其耕泽泽（1见）、驿驿其达（1见）、厌厌其苗（1见）、绵绵其麃（1见）、载获济济（1见）

178.《颂·良耜》：畟畟良耜（1见）、获之挃挃（1见）、积之栗栗（1见）

179.《颂·丝衣》：载弁俅俅（1见）
180.《颂·酌》：蹻蹻王之造（1见）
181.《颂·桓》：桓桓武王（1见）
182.《颂·駉》：駉駉牡马（4见）、以车彭彭（1见）、以车伾伾（1见）、以车绎绎（1见）、以车祛祛（1见）
183.《颂·有駜》：在公明明（1见）、振振鹭（2见）、鼓咽咽（2见）
184.《颂·泮水》：其旂茷茷（1见）、鸾声哕哕（1见）、其马蹻蹻（2见）、其音昭昭（1见）、穆穆鲁侯（1见）、明明鲁侯（1见）、矫矫虎臣（1见）、济济多士（1见）、桓桓于征（1见）、烝烝皇皇（1见）
185.《颂·閟宫》：实实枚枚（1见）、赫赫姜嫄（1见）、六辔耳耳（1见）、皇皇后帝（1见）、牺尊将将（1见）、万舞洋洋（1见）、烝徒增增（1见）、泰山岩岩（1见）、新庙奕奕（1见）
186.《颂·那》：奏鼓简简（1见）、鞉鼓渊渊（1见）、嘒嘒管声（1见）、穆穆厥声（1见）
187.《颂·烈祖》：嗟嗟烈祖（1见）、八鸾鸧鸧（1见）、丰年穰穰（1见）
188.《颂·玄鸟》：宅殷土芒（1见）、来假祈祈（1见）
189.《颂·长发》：洪水芒芒（1见）、相土烈烈（1见）、如火烈烈（1见）、昭假迟迟（1见）、敷政优优（1见）
190.《颂·殷武》：商邑翼翼（1见）、赫赫厥声（1见）、濯濯厥厥（1见）

附录四、相关意象所在的诗篇

还原作用

穆旦

污泥里的猪梦见生了翅膀,
从天降生的渴望着飞扬,
当他醒来时悲痛地呼喊。

胸里燃烧了却不能起床,
跳蚤,耗子,在他身上粘着:
你爱我吗?我爱你,他说。

八小时工作,挖成一颗空壳,
荡在尘网里,害怕把丝弄断,
蜘蛛嗅过了,知道没有用处。

他的安慰是求学时的朋友,
三月的花园怎么样盛开,
通信联起了一大片荒原。

那里看出了变形的枉然,
开始学习着在地上走步,
一切是无边的,无边的迟缓。

出发

穆旦

告诉我们和平又必需杀戮,
而那可厌的我们先得去欢喜。
知道了"人"不够,我们再学习
蹂躏它的方法,排成机械的阵式,
智力体力蠕动着像一群野兽,

告诉我们这是新的美。因为
我们吻过的已经失去了自由;
好的日子去了,可是接近未来,
给我们失望和希望,给我们死,
因为那死的制造必需摧毁。

给我们善感的心灵又要它歌唱
僵硬的声音。个人的哀喜
被大量制造又该被蔑视
被否定,被僵化,是人生的意义;
在你的计划里有毒害的一环,

就把我们囚进现在,呵上帝!
在犬牙的甬道中让我们反复
行进,让我们相信你句句的紊乱
是一个真理。而我们是皈依的,
你给我们丰富,和丰富的痛苦。

I wandered lonely as a cloud

By William Wordsworth

I wandered lonely as a cloud
That floats on high o'er vales and hills,
When all at once I saw a crowd,
A host, of golden daffodils;
Beside the lake, beneath the trees,
Fluttering and dancing in the breeze.

Continuous as the stars that shine
And twinkle on the milky way,
They stretched in never-ending line
Along the margin of a bay:
Ten thousand saw I at a glance,
Tossing their heads in sprightly dance.

The waves beside them danced, but they
Out-did the sparkling leaves in glee;
A poet could not be but gay,
In such a jocund company!
I gaze—and gaze—but little thought
What wealth the show to me had brought:

For oft, when on my couch I lie
In vacant or in pensive mood,
They flash upon that inward eye
Which is the bliss of solitude;

And then my heart with pleasure fills,
And dances with the daffodils.

Ode to a Nightingale

By John Keats

My heart aches, and a drowsy numbness pains
My sense, as though of hemlock I had drunk,
Or emptied some dull opiate to the drains
One minute past, and Lethe-wards had sunk:
'Tis not through envy of thy happy lot,
But being too happy in thine happiness,—
That thou, light-winged Dryad of the trees,
In some melodious plot
Of beechen green, and shadows numberless,
Singest of summer in full-throated ease.

O, for a draught of vintage! that hath been
Cool'd a long age in the deep-delved earth,
Tasting of Flora and the country green,
Dance, and Provencal song, and sunburnt mirth!
O for a beaker full of the warm South,
Full of the true, the blushful Hippocrene,
With beaded bubbles winking at the brim,
And purple-stained mouth;
That I might drink, and leave the world unseen,

And with thee fade away into the forest dim:

Fade far away, dissolve, and quite forget
What thou among the leaves hast never known,
The weariness, the fever, and the fret
Here, where men sit and hear each other groan;
Where palsy shakes a few, sad, last gray hairs,
Where youth grows pale, and spectre-thin, and dies;
Where but to think is to be full of sorrow
And leaden-eyed despairs,
Where Beauty cannot keep her lustrous eyes,
Or new Love pine at them beyond to-morrow.

Away! away! for I will fly to thee,
Not charioted by Bacchus and his pards,
But on the viewless wings of Poesy,
Though the dull brain perplexes and retards:
Already with thee! tender is the night,
And haply the Queen-Moon is on her throne,
Cluster'd around by all her starry Fays;
But here there is no light,
Save what from heaven is with the breezes blown
Through verdurous glooms and winding mossy ways.

I cannot see what flowers are at my feet,
Nor what soft incense hangs upon the boughs,
But, in embalmed darkness, guess each sweet

Wherewith the seasonable month endows

The grass, the thicket, and the fruit-tree wild;

White hawthorn, and the pastoral eglantine;

Fast fading violets cover'd up in leaves;

And mid-May's eldest child,

The coming musk-rose, full of dewy wine,

The murmurous haunt of flies on summer eves.

Darkling I listen; and, for many a time

I have been half in love with easeful Death,

Call'd him soft names in many a mused rhyme,

To take into the air my quiet breath;

Now more than ever seems it rich to die,

To cease upon the midnight with no pain,

While thou art pouring forth thy soul abroad

In such an ecstasy!

Still wouldst thou sing, and I have ears in vain—

To thy high requiem become a sod.

Thou wast not born for death, immortal Bird!

No hungry generations tread thee down;

The voice I hear this passing night was heard

In ancient days by emperor and clown:

Perhaps the self-same song that found a path

Through the sad heart of Ruth, when, sick for home,

She stood in tears amid the alien corn;

The same that oft-times hath

Charm'd magic casements, opening on the foam

Of perilous seas, in faery lands forlorn.

Forlorn! the very word is like a bell

To toil me back from thee to my sole self!

Adieu! the fancy cannot cheat so well

As she is fam'd to do, deceiving elf.

Adieu! adieu! thy plaintive anthem fades

Past the near meadows, over the still stream,

Up the hill-side; and now 'tis buried deep

In the next valley-glades:

Was it a vision, or a waking dream?

Fled is that music: —Do I wake or sleep?

Tiger

By William Blake

TIGER, tiger, burning bright

In the forests of the night,

What immortal hand or eye

Could frame thy fearful symmetry?

In what distant deeps or skies

Burnt the fire of thine eyes?

On what wings dare he aspire?

What the hand dare seize the fire?

And what shoulder and what art
Could twist the sinews of thy heart?
And when thy heart began to beat,
What dread hand and what dread feet?

What the hammer? what the chain?
In what furnace was thy brain?
What the anvil? What dread grasp
Dare its deadly terrors clasp?

When the stars threw down their spears,
And water'd heaven with their tears,
Did He smile His work to see?
Did He who made the lamb make thee?

Tiger, tiger, burning bright
In the forests of the night,
What immortal hand or eye
Dare frame thy fearful symmetry?

Red Red Rose

By Robert Burns

O my luve is like a red, red rose,
That's newly sprung in June;
O my luve is like the melodie,
That's sweetly played in tune.

As fair thou art, my bonie lass,

So deep in luve am I;

And I will luve thee still, my dear,

Till a' the seas gang dry.

Till a' the sea gang dry, my dear,

And the rock melt wi' the sun;

And I will luve thee still, my dear,

While the sands o' life shall run.

And fare thee weel, my only luve,

And fare thee weel awhile;

And I will come again, my luve,

Tho's it were ten thousand mile!

参考文献

1) 蔡若莲,"中国人伦关系的构建——《诗经》中禽鸟意象的探讨",《诗经研究丛刊》,2007年。
2) 程俊英(撰),《诗经译注》,上海:上海古籍出版社,2004年。
3) 段学俭,"《诗经》中'南山'意象的文化意蕴",《辽宁师范大学学报》(社会科学版),1999年第3期。
4) 厄尔·迈纳,《比较诗学》,王宇根、宋伟杰等译,北京:中央编译出版社,2004年。
5) 冯浩菲,《历代诗经论说述评》,北京:中华书局,2003年。
6) 高亨(注),《诗经今注》,上海:上海古籍出版社,1980年。
7) 郭建勋,"《诗经》中的意象浅说",《中国文学研究》,1990年第1期。
8) 郭沫若,《青铜器时代》,北京:科学出版社,1957年。
9) 韩高年,"《诗经》与先秦崇玉习俗",《西北民族研究》,2010年第3期。
10) 何清,"庞德的意象论与中国传统美学的意象说",《四川师范大学学报》(社会科学版),2002年第4期。
11) 何文焕,《历代诗话》,北京:中华书局,1981年。
12) 贺麟,"文化的体与用",《哲学与哲学史论文集》,北京:商务印书馆,1990年。
13) 洪湛侯,《诗经学史》,北京:中华书局,2002年。
14) 胡塞尔,《现象学的观念》,上海:上海译文出版社,1985年。
15) 皇甫谧:《帝王世纪·世本·逸周书·古本竹书纪年》,济南:齐鲁书社,2010年。
16) 李炳海,"情感与哲理默契的复合象征——《诗经》山、隰对举发微",《中州学刊》,1990年第5期。

17）李湘，《诗经名物意象新探》，台北：万卷楼图书有限公司，1989 年。
18）李玉良，《〈诗经〉英译研究》，济南：齐鲁书社，2007 年。
19）李玉良，"庞德《诗经》翻译中译古喻今的'现实'原则与意象主义诗学"，《外语教学》，2009 年第 3 期。
20）廖群，"《诗经》比兴中性意象的文化探源"，《文史哲》，1995 年第 3 期。
21）刘毓庆，《从经学到文学——明代〈诗经〉学史论》，北京：商务印书馆，2003 年。
22）刘毓庆，"关于《诗经·关雎》篇的雎鸠喻意问题"，《北京大学学报》（哲学社会科学版），2004 年第 2 期。
23）刘振中，"论《诗经》山水云雨的象征意义"，《东岳论丛》，1989 年第 6 期。
24）陆侃如、牟世金，《文心雕龙译注》，济南：齐鲁书社，1980 年。
25）吕华亮，"试论'自然名物'与《诗经》的灵动美"，《社会科学家》2008 年第 3 期。
26）马瑞辰，《毛诗传笺通释》，北京：中华书局，1989 年。
27）孟桂兰，"意象理论研究述评"，《山东社会科学》，2002 年第 1 期。
28）潘富俊，《诗经植物图鉴》，上海：上海书店出版社，2003 年。
29）钱锺书，《七缀集》，上海：上海古籍出版社，1985 年。
30）谯周：《古史考》，三亚：海南出版社，2003 年。
31）屈光，"中国古典诗歌意象论"，《中国社会科学》，2002 年第 3 期。
32）孙伯涵，"《诗经》意象论"，《烟台师范学院学报》，2001 年第 2 期。
33）孙作云，"诗经恋歌发微"，《文学遗产》，1957 年第 A05 期。
34）童庆炳，"《文心雕龙》'比显兴隐'说"，《陕西师范大学学报》（哲学社会科学版），2004 年第 6 期。
35）汪榕培，"传神达意译《诗经》"，《外语与外语教学》，1994 年第 4 期。
36）王长华，"《诗经》的意象及其审美经验"，《天津师大学报》，1987 年第 3 期。
37）王国维，《人间词话》，上海：上海古籍出版社，2003 年。
38）王宏印，《穆旦诗英译与解析》，石家庄：河北教育出版社，2004 年。

39）王力，《诗经韵读》，上海：上海古籍出版社：1980 年。
40）王双，"新时期《诗经》意象研究述评"，《河北大学学报》（哲学社会科学版），2009 年第 2 期。
41）闻一多，"说鱼"，《闻一多全集》，武汉：湖北人民出版社，1993 年。
42）闻一多，《神话与诗》，上海：上海人民出版社，2006 年。
43）吴乘权，《纲鉴易知录》，北京：中华书局，1960 年。
44）吴钊（编），《中国古代乐器》，北京：文物出版社，1983 年。
45）夏传才，《诗经语言艺术》，北京：语文出版社，1985 年。
46）许渊冲，"再谈意美、音美、形美"，《外语学刊》，1983 年第 4 期。
47）许志刚，《诗经论略》，沈阳：辽宁大学出版社，2000 年。
48）姚斯，"文学史作为向文学理论的挑战"，《接受美学与接受理论》，大连：辽宁人民出版社，1987 年。
49）叶维廉，《中国诗学》，北京：三联书店，1992 年。
50）伊瑟尔，《阅读行为》，长沙：湖南文艺出版社，1991 年。
51）英伽登，《对文学的艺术作品的认识》，陈燕谷、晓未译，中国文联出版社，1988 年。
52）余冠英，《诗经选》，北京：人民文学出版社，1982 年。
53）袁愈荌：《诗经艺探》，贵阳：贵州人民出版社，1998 年。
54）赵国华，《生殖崇拜文化论》，北京：中国社会科学出版社，1990 年。
55）赵霈林，《兴的源起》，北京：中国社会科学出版社，1987 年。
56）朱立元，《当代西方文艺理论》，上海：华东师范大学出版社，1997 年。
57）朱怡芳，"西周宗法结构下的玉石文化特征分析"，《南京艺术学院学报》（美术与设计版），2008 年第 1 期。